A SPIRITED CHALLENGE

Damien clenched his jaw. "So I am suspect, am I? Playing some woman's trick to frighten my brother's intended senseless, an accomplishment which, from the looks of it, would be no difficult task."

It was now Caroline's turn to seethe, and she glared at the handsome, angry face.

"I shall make you an offer, my clever lady," said Damien. "Go ahead and wait for your ghost. I will stay by your side the entire time, always under your watchful eye. I shall enjoy sticking close to you. I only hope that blasted ghost appears. If it does not I shall most likely be blamed for it."

"I feel sure the ghost, much like yourself, will be unable to resist a challenge," said Caroline archly.

Damien eyed her speculatively. "You think so, do you? Let me offer you a word of advice, Lady Caroline. Be careful. Even the most clever hunter can sometimes become the hunted."

ZEBRA'S HOLIDAY REGENCY ROMANCES CAPTURE THE MAGIC OF EVERY SEASON

THE VALENTINE'S DAY BALL   (3280, $3.95)
by Donna Bell

Tradition held that at the age of eighteen, all the Heartland ladies met the man they would marry at the Valentine's Day Ball. When she was that age, the crucial ball had been canceled when Miss Jane Lindsey's mother had died. Now Jane was on the shelf at twenty-four. Still, she was happy in her life and accepted the fact that romance had passed her by. So she was annoyed with herself when the scandalous—and dangerously handsome—Lord Devlin put a schoolgirl blush into her cheeks and made her believe that perhaps romance may *indeed* be a part of her life . . .

AN EASTER BOUQUET   (3330, $3.95)
by Therese Alderton

It was a preposterous and scandalous wager: In return for a prime piece of horse-flesh, the decadent Lord Vyse would pose as a virtuous Rector in a country village. His cohorts insisted he wouldn't last a week, yet he was actually looking forward to a quiet Easter in the country.

Miss Lily Sterling was puzzled by the new rector; he had a reluctance to discuss his past and looked at her the way no Rector should *ever* look at a female of his flock. She was determined to unmask this handsome "clergyman", and she would set herself up as his bait!

A CHRISTMAS AFFAIR   (3244, $3.95)
by Joan Overfield

Justin Stockman thought he was doing the Laurence family a favor by marrying the docile sister and helping the family reverse their financial straits. The first thing he would do after the marriage was to marry off his independent and infuriating sister-in-law Amanda.

Amanda was intent on setting the arrogant Justin straight on a few matters, and the cozy holiday backdrop—from the intimate dinners to the spectacular Frost Fair—would be the perfect opportunities to let him know what life would be like with her as a sister-in-law. She would give a Merry Christmas indeed!

A CHRISTMAS HOLIDAY   (3245, $3.95)

A charming collection of Christmas short stories by Zebra's best Regency Romance writers. *The Holly Brooch, The Christmas Bride, The Glastonbury Thorn, The Yule Log, A Mistletoe Christmas,* and *Sheer Sorcery* will give you the warmth of the Holiday Season all year long.

Available wherever paperbacks are sold, or order direct from the Publisher. Send cover price plus 50¢ per copy for mailing and handling to Zebra Books, Dept. 3545, 475 Park Avenue South, New York, N.Y. 10016. Residents of New York, New Jersey and Pennsylvania must include sales tax. DO NOT SEND CASH.

A Ghostly Charade

Sheila Rabe

ZEBRA BOOKS
KENSINGTON PUBLISHING CORP.

For Rose, With Love.

ZEBRA BOOKS

are published by

Kensington Publishing Corp.
475 Park Avenue South
New York, NY 10016

Copyright © 1991 by Sheila Rabe

First printing: October, 1991

Printed in the United States of America

1

"A ghost!" exclaimed Lady Caroline Templeton. She sighed in disgust and laid her sister's letter in her lap. She had planned on a cozy autumn at Wembly Manor—a chance to inspect the rooms in need of repair and to go over the final plans for remodeling with the architect.

Poor Harold. He was most likely turning in his grave this very moment. It had been his last wish that his beloved Caroline carry out his plans for restoring Wembly Manor, and she had made him a deathbed promise she would do so. That was two years ago and things were still no further along than they had been when she so blithely told her dying husband not to worry.

Well, how could she help it? The delays that kept coming up were not of her making. There had been so much estate business to take care of that first year. Then, last year had been Phoebe's come-out. And while a season only lasted a few months, readying a young lady for her debut was more rigorous than planning a military campaign and had required months of preparation.

Of course, Mama and Phoebe had both insisted

they couldn't do without Caroline's help in this all-important enterprise. "It is not at all like it was for your come-out three years before," Mama had said. "After all, your papa was alive then."

Caroline had wondered what this had to do with anything, as Papa had contributed no help other than the necessary funds for her come-out.

"I simply cannot bring Phoebe out all on my own," Lady Harborough had declared. "It is all so difficult for a woman alone."

A woman alone, Caroline had thought cynically. And what, pray, did her mama think she was? A widow after she had barely had a chance to be a bride! "Uncle Alistair . . ." Caroline had begun.

Her mama had held up a plump hand in protest. "Please do not throw up your Uncle Alistair to me. He has been most disagreeable to deal with since your papa's death, and I cannot face having to discuss financial matters with him by myself on top of everything else. Besides, I have not the strength to face the London whirl unassisted. I absolutely must have your help in launching Phoebe, dearest. Wembly Manor will simply have to wait."

And wait it had. Of course, Caroline had enjoyed her sister's come-out nearly as much as Phoebe, herself. Caroline had found to her delight that as a young and attractive widow she had had her fair share of swains and a fairer share of freedom than her closely guarded sister.

After seeing Phoebe safely engaged to Clarence Gerard Morrivile Grayson, earl of Alverstoke, Caroline had found herself refreshed and ready to begin carrying out her husband's last wishes. But it seemed she had barely begun when this latest demand on her time had presented itself.

". . . I know, Caro dear, that you had planned a comfortable autumn commencing the restoration work at Wembly. But if you do not come and lend me your support I shall go mad before I ever become Lady Alverstoke. Mama is in such a state of terror she is threatening to call everything off, for she says she will not have me murdered in my bed by a ghost and end up walking these halls myself. Of course, I do not want to end up a ghost, but neither do I want to be parted from Clarence. He says it is all a hum, but Mama has seen the ghost and so have I. Please come, even if it is only for a fortnight. Naturally, I would prefer you to stay through Christmas. In fact, I wish you might sell Wembly and come live with us, at least until we have gotten rid of this ghost. That is the awful thing about all of this. I have no idea how to get rid of a ghost. Clarence says one cannot drive a ghost from its rightful home. Perhaps we could move to Wembly and live with you. Do you think Clarence would mind very much?"

Caroline laughed out loud at this and shook her head. "Oh no," she murmured. "Why should the earl of Alverstoke wish to remain in what has been his family's home for generations?" Phoebe was a goose and she and Mama had less sense between them than a peahen.

"Please," the letter continued, "come and help us or my life will be ruined. And do stop and pick up a costume for our Allhallows Eve ball on your way."

"Oh bother," muttered Caroline. "I suppose I must go. If I can get away before Christmas I shall be much surprised."

That very day Caroline dashed off a hasty but encouraging reply to her sister and informed her lady's maid they would shortly be leaving for Grayson Hall.

Sibby had much to say about this. Not verbally. The tightly shut lips self-righteously insisted that as a mere servant it was not her place to remind her

7

mistress of her deathbed promise. But the disapproval mingled with long suffering was easily readable on her pretty face.

"I know what you are thinking," said Caroline. "Would you like to hear *why* we are going to visit my sister instead of staying here at Wembly?"

"There is no need to explain to me, my lady," Sibby said in tones which insisted otherwise. "After all, I am only a servant."

"Who has gotten much too uppity for her own good," said Caroline in mock sternness. "Come now, Sibby dearest. You do not think that I would go haring off for no reason, do you? I am well aware of the importance of finishing the project which lies before me." Though how I will stretch the money Harold left I cannot imagine, she thought. Sometimes she dearly wished the place had been entailed.

Sibby sniffed and Caroline continued. "I am as committed as ever to restoring Wembly to its former glory. But I am afraid my family once more is in immediate need of my help. Phoebe is being threatened by a most inhospitable ghost."

"A ghost!" squeaked Sibby.

"Yes, a ghost. And things have come to such a pass that her future is hanging very much in the balance. Do you not think Harold would quite understand my leaving Wembly yet again? Surely, if he could speak with me now he would urge me to go."

Sibby nodded her agreement but still did not look happy.

"What is wrong now?" Caroline demanded in mild irritation.

"Perhaps there will not be room for me at Grayson Hall," Sibby ventured.

"And what, pray, am I to do for a lady's maid if I leave you here?" inquired Caroline.

8

Sibby was thinking hard. "You could take Betsy," she offered.

"I thank you kindly," replied Caroline. "How very generous of you to offer me my upstairs maid in your place. Are you suddenly tiring of being in my service after all these years?"

Sibby tried to look nonchalant and failed, and Caroline laughed. "I wonder why you would turn up your nose at a chance to visit a fine old place such as Grayson Hall. You surely aren't afraid, are you?"

"I merely suggested Betsy as I thought the experience might be good for her," said Sibby.

"Yes, and you are getting on in years now, aren't you? I daresay soon you will be retiring, and I shall need a replacement. Best start grooming someone for the post immediately."

Sibby, who was only a few years older than her lady, looked properly insulted.

"You are afraid," taunted Caroline. "Admit it. The same Sibby who was brave enough to distract Lord Basebury the night he was foxed and tried to drag me into Mama's bedchamber is afraid of a bogus ghost!" she teased. "Fie on you!"

"I am not afraid of bogus ghosts," Sibby insisted. "'Tis the real ones that scare me."

"There is no such thing," insisted Caroline. "Come now, Sibby. Do you think I would lead you into danger? Where is your trust?"

"Well . . ." said Sibby. She could hardly tell her mistress that, in spite of her air of confidence, Sibby knew her employer's proclivities. Lady Caroline's supreme confidence in her ability to get over any hurdle made her attract trouble like a magnet. Instead, Sibby resorted to gloomy generalities. "I just do not like the sound of this," she said. "We'll all be murdered in our beds, we will."

"Oh stuff!" scoffed Caroline. "I have just told you there is no such thing as ghosts."

"Have you ever seen one?" asked Sibby.

"No," said Caroline firmly.

"Then, how can you be sure there is no such thing?"

"Because I have never seen one."

Sibby replied she'd never seen the king, but she still believed they had one.

Caroline laughed. "Oh, Sibby! You are a truly brilliant woman. Which is exactly why I want you with me," she continued, suddenly serious. "I do not believe for a moment that my sister is being plagued by ghosts, but I do suspect something peculiar is going on at Grayson Hall. And I intend to find out what it is. And while I am poking around abovestairs I hope you will do the same thing belowstairs. I want you to keep your eyes and ears open. We are both shrewd women, and between the two of us we should be able to discover who is so wickedly trying to scare Phoebe." A martial light came into Sibby's eyes, and Caroline knew she had won the little maid over. "We shall pack first thing tomorrow," she said. "I wish to leave as soon as possible. And tell Betsy to pack, too. What with the ball we may need extra help."

"Yes, my lady," said Sibby. She bustled out of the bedchamber in search of someone to bully into digging out her ladyship's trunks.

Caroline smiled at the reflection in her dressing-table mirror. The expression on the face smiling back at her seemed positively conspiratorial. As Caroline took in the thick auburn hair, the large brown eyes and delicate brows, the small nose and dainty, full lips, she couldn't help but be pleased with what she saw. Not only did her mirror assure her that she was indeed a striking woman, but a very capable one. She

10

turned her head from side to side, assuring herself that her strong chin represented not stubbornness, but determination. Yes, here indeed was a woman capable of getting to the bottom of things, and that was exactly what she would do.

A week later, as her carriage drove up the tree-lined drive, her confidence in her capability did not desert her. The butterflies she felt were not from fear but excitement. The carriage stopped and the steps were let down and Caroline alighted, a soldier prepared to do battle.

Sibby followed her out and exclaimed in wonder at the rambling, half-timbered structure before them. Grayson Hall stood like an elegant ghost from the past. Its skyline was riddled with Elizabethan chimneys and gables. "Ah," sighed Caroline in appreciation. "Now, aren't you glad you came?"

"We will spend most of our time just trying to find our way," complained Sibby.

Caroline gave her a look of disgust and headed for the door.

Before Smythe, the properly stuffy butler who answered the door could even take Caroline's cloak and gloves, her sister burst out from a nearby room and came running to her. Lady Phoebe was short and pleasingly rounded. She had soft, yellow hair which, combined with brown eyes as big as her sister's, made her face as hard to forget. The eyes now were filled with tears of joy and she threw herself into her sister's arms. "Oh, Caro!" she sobbed. "I am so glad you are come. Now everything will be all right for I know you will know exactly what to do."

It was fortunate Caroline had removed her bonnet, otherwise with such fervent praise it might have begun to fit much too snugly. If the butler saw anything ludicrous in Lady Phoebe's belief that the

11

new arrival's mere presence would be enough to scare away Grayson Hall's ghost he said nothing. He merely waited in detached silence for Caroline to free herself from her sister, which she did, after giving Phoebe a warm hug and sisterly kiss. "Now then," she said briskly. "Suppose I freshen up before tea. I have time, do I not?"

"Oh yes. How silly of me to keep you standing here in the hallway. Do come upstairs." Phoebe linked her arm through her sister's and, followed by Sibby, led her up a long, curving staircase. At the top of the stairs they turned down a long corridor and after passing many doors Phoebe led her sister into a room done in shades of blue, with soft carpet and rich velvet drapes at the window. In anticipation of her arrival a fire was roaring in the hearth, and the room was warm and cozy. "How do you like it?" Phoebe asked eagerly as two footmen deposited Caroline's trunks on the floor and departed. "You are right next to me and Mama is down the hall."

"Where is Mama now?" asked Caroline.

"Napping," said Phoebe. "This has all been too much for her. Her nerves are quite unsettled, and she hasn't been sleeping at all at night."

Caroline smiled at this. She knew her mother well. Lady Harborough, when upset, expended a great deal of energy wringing her plump hands and flopping into chairs, attempting to swoon. Her actions under stress always reminded her daughter of a frightened hen. And while Lady Harborough often claimed she could never sleep when she was distraught, her daughter was well aware that her mama, if allowed to recline undisturbed, could fall into sleep anywhere in a matter of minutes.

"It has been dreadful," sighed Phoebe. "And I must admit I was terribly frightened, especially when I saw it."

"Yes, you said in your letter you saw the ghost. But are you positive it was a ghost, love? Perhaps you just saw . . ." Caroline paused, searching for some plausible thing which her sister could have mistaken for an apparition.

"It was a ghost," Phoebe said firmly. "And you shall see it, too, I am sure. Then you'll know I am not merely seeing things."

"What did the ghost look like?"

"It was a woman. And she was all in white. Her hair was black and her eyes were all," Phoebe's voice began to wobble, "pale and staring. It was frightful."

Caroline tried to look convinced, but her skepticism showed.

"It *was* a ghost, Caro," Phoebe insisted. She turned to Sibby, who had been only nominally involved in unpacking. She had been peeking cautiously behind the wardrobe, and at the sound of her name she gave a guilty start. Caroline laughed. "You may well laugh," sniffed Sibby. "But it all seems mighty strange to me."

"And do not forget, I was not the only one to see it," said Phoebe. "Mama was with me and she saw it, too."

"And I am sure she will tell me all about it at tea," said Caroline.

Lady Harborough did indeed tell her daughter all about the ghost at tea. She did, of course, ask Caroline how her journey had been but barely waited for an answer before launching into her terrifying tale.

Caroline fixed an expression of interest on her face and surreptitiously surveyed the other occupants of the winter parlor over her teacup. Her mother was running on at length about her harrowing meeting with the ghost—how she had felt, how she felt Phoebe had felt, what they had done, Phoebe had swooned. Lady Harborough had made an applaudable effort, throwing herself onto a conveniently placed chair and moaning. None of the listeners seemed tired of the subject.

Jarvis Woolcock, Esq., Clarence's cousin and current houseguest, appeared to be genuinely concerned, although Caroline was sure she had, on one occasion, seen the corner of his mouth twitch. He was built on smaller lines than his cousin Clarence, but was by no means slight. His face though not striking was pleasing—a square chin and a finely chiseled nose set under dark brown eyes. His manner was equally pleasing and he appeared to be a genial man.

Lady Grayson had introduced Miss Isobelle Payne as a dear old friend of the family and nearly a daughter of the house. Miss Payne was a beautiful creature with dark curls and brown eyes and a perfect rosebud mouth. She had come over in her dogcart from Hallowstone, the neighboring estate, for tea. Caroline wondered how many times poor Miss Payne had been subjected to hearing this tale. She was either as hen witted as the other women present or too well-mannered to appear bored, for she, too, listened intently to both mother and daughter's retelling of their encounter with the ghost.

Lady Grayson, as plump as Caroline's mama and every bit as empty-headed, listened also, shaking her head and making clucking noises at all the appropriate moments. She patted a wispy gray curl and bemoaned the fact that the ghost was being so very troublesome. "I almost wish, Isobelle dearest, that you had not joked with Phoebe about the ghost, for it is plain she did not appreciate being made fun of."

Isobelle looked properly penitent. "I am truly sorry, Lady Grayson. But really, who would have thought that the thing would turn up now, after all these years?"

"Perhaps," said Caroline, "we are all refining too much upon this. After all, I have yet to hear of a ghost murdering anyone."

"Except," said Isobelle, "there was one occasion when Lady Ripley, believe it or not, was said to have been chased by a ghost and in trying to escape fell down a flight of stairs and broke her neck."

"Was she killed?" asked Phoebe breathlessly.

Isobele stared at Phoebe and Jarvis hid behind his teacup.

"Yes, love," said Caroline patiently. "People do not remain alive once they have broken their necks."

Phoebe's lips made a soundless "oh."

"But you have nothing to fear," said Caroline encouragingly. "Just be sure you do not run if you should happen to see this ghost again."

"That is simple enough for you to say, Caro," said Phoebe. "You have not seen it."

Caroline's lip curled in contempt. "I doubt I shall."

Isobelle looked as if she might say something but refrained.

At that moment the door opened to reveal a tall, barrel-chested man in his late twenties with a head that looked as if it had been taken from a Greek statue. It was Clarence Gerard Morrivile Grayson, fifth earl of Alverstoke (or was it the sixth? Caroline could never remember). The love of Phoebe's life looked exactly what he was, a kind man of easygoing temper and slow wit. "I say, is there anything left in the teapot?" he boomed.

Phoebe looked at him with admiring eyes and poured him a cup.

"Nothing like a spot of tea after a hard afternoon's work," he said. (It was generally suspected by several present that the only work Clarence enjoyed in his study was sleeping, but those skeptics remained politely quiet.)

"Clarence, only look who has finally come," said Phoebe.

For the first time Clarence noticed there was an extra body in the room. "Belle! Glad you came over." Isobelle smiled coyly and gave Clarence her hand.

"No." Phoebe indicated the chair to Clarence's back. Clarence swiveled his head in the direction indicated. "Caro!" he cried. He grabbed her hand with a gentle paw, planting a resounding kiss on it. "Now that her clever sister is here, my little Phoebe will rest easy. I hope you have brought along some clever idea for getting rid of that pesky ghost."

"We can but try," Caroline answered modestly.

Clarence said he hoped she would succeed as they were all depending on her, then flopped onto a nearby chair, helped himself to a piece of seed cake, and launched into a recitation of his day's activities.

As he did Isobelle turned to Caroline. "You have doubts that the ghost will show again?" she asked.

Caroline shrugged. "It is one thing for a ghost to scare a green girl and a . . . highly excitable woman. It is quite another to convince a doubter."

"You do not believe in ghosts, then?"

Caroline shook her head. "I have no belief in the existence of malevolent spirits. Only in malevolence."

A fine, black eyebrow shot up questioningly, but Miss Isobelle Payne said nothing. And after remaining another ten minutes she announced her need to be on her way and rose gracefully from her seat. Jarvis offered to escort her out, and she smiled on him and murmured her thanks. "Come pay me a morning call soon," she urged, giving Phoebe a hug. "I do so want a chance to become better acquainted with your

16

charming sister." Phoebe beamed on her and assured her they would call, and Miss Payne bid a final farewell to the company and glided out of the room with Jarvis in tow.

"Fine figure of a woman," said Clarence admiringly as the door shut behind them. Phoebe did not look pleased by his obvious admiration, and he cleared his throat nervously. "Of course, she doesn't have what you do," he said to her.

"And what is it I have?" asked Phoebe encouragingly.

Clarence was not a man of eloquence, and her question threw him. His brows knit and he stared at her, nonplussed. "Well, don't know exactly," he admitted. "But whatever it is, I like it."

This was enough for Phoebe, and she smiled and poured him another cup of tea.

Dinner that night was uneventful. In fact, Caroline decided, if it had not been for Mr. Woolcock the evening would have been decidedly boring. She had been placed in the honored position next to the new earl, and she was thankful Jarvis sat on her other side. He was witty and urbane, speaking knowledgeably on everything from art to architecture. Clarence, on the other hand, seemed to confine his interests to hunting ("Good weather for grouse," he informed Caroline) and food ("There's nothing like the way Cook does a leg of lamb. Don't know what she does, but whatever it is, she does it just right.").

After dinner the gentlemen settled into a rubber of piquet while the ladies gossiped and chatted about fashion and Phoebe's trousseau. Lady Harborough sighed happily as the tea tray was brought in. "I must say, Caroline, I feel much better now you are here. I feel sure if we all put our heads together we may come up with some way of appeasing this dreadful ghost.

17

You were always so clever, just like your papa. If only he were alive today he would know what to do," she finished.

"Maybe we will see the ghost tonight," said Phoebe. "Once she's seen it, I am sure Caro will think of some way to get rid of it."

"Dear, dear," fretted Lady Grayson. "I do so hate to drive it off. After all, this has been its home for such a very long time."

"Yes, but it cannot stay here," protested Phoebe. "What if we were to . . ." she blushed and lowered her voice, "have a family. Think how it would frighten the children."

"Oh dear, yes. You are absolutely right," Lady Grayson agreed.

Caroline decided she had had quite enough for one night. "I am feeling rather fatigued," she said. "Would you mind terribly if I said an early good-night?"

Phoebe looked suddenly nervous. "If you are going upstairs now, perhaps I will retire, also. I am quite finished," she said, setting down her full cup.

"Alright, love," said Caroline.

"Perhaps I shall go also," said her mama.

"Let me ring for some candles," said Lady Grayson placidly.

A few minutes later the two sisters and their mama began the trek up the staircase to the dark, haunted corridor. "Phoebe," protested Caroline, "you are squeezing me up against the wall and dripping wax on my gown. Must you walk so very close?"

"I am sorry," said Phoebe. "But Mama is crowding me terribly."

Lady Harborough excused herself by stoutly insisting they should all stick closely together.

Caroline realized it was useless to protest, and the

three women huddled their way up the stairs. They entered the deserted corridor. A branch of candles placed on a small table cast a feeble light at the darkness. "This is where we saw the ghost," Phoebe whispered, grabbing a tighter hold on her sister's arm.

Caroline looked down the dark hallway, half expecting, half hoping to see the horrible apparition, but it remained stubbornly hidden. "Well, it is obviously not going to show itself tonight," she said. "We had best turn in."

Phoebe and her mama left the regretful Caroline at her door, and she stood watching them scurry nervously down the hall. She sighed. "Ghost indeed," she muttered and went into her bedroom to find Sibby waiting. "I see the ghost has left you unharmed thus far," Caroline observed.

"Yes, but it's here," said Sibby, coming forward to help her mistress out of her gown. "I have been waiting to tell you. There is much talk about the ghost in the servants' hall. Rose, your sister's maid, even claims to have seen it. Oh, my lady, must we stay?" she burst out suddenly.

"Sibby! Not you, too. Please don't you become hysterical on me now. It is quite enough having to deal with Phoebe and Mama."

Sibby sniffed and continued to unbutton her mistress's gown.

Caroline sighed. She was a sensible and enlightened young woman who prided herself on being ahead of her time in many ways. Old beyond her years, her mama had lamented. Far too independent. "I have already told you there is no such thing as ghosts," she said to Sibby. "They are merely the product of superstition and too much marzipan before bed. Surely you do not think I would bring

19

you here if I thought there was any danger with which we could not deal.''

"Danger!" Sibby pounced on the word. "There *is* danger. You have just admitted as much. My lady, I have enjoyed being in your service these many years, and I pray that you will accept my regretful resignation.''

"Such a long speech," laughed Caroline, stepping out of her gown. "Have you spent all evening rehearsing it?"

Sibby's chin went up. "If my lady wishes to joke about my feelings—"

"Oh, Sibby," said Caroline, instantly repentant. "I am sorry. Fear is a very real thing and I should not joke about it. Do forgive me. I should not make light of this situation, either, for although I do not believe any of us are in danger from a ghost, I do believe there could be a different kind of danger here. Someone, for some reason, is trying to frighten my sister. And that person is succeeding admirably. I had hoped you would stay and help me, but if you are this terribly frightened then I shall, of course, send you back to Wembly Manor to wait for my return.''

Sibby looked relieved, then guilty. She hesitated and Caroline could read her face and see the mental battle raging. Finally, she said with determination, "I shall stay. After all, I can hardly leave you to face danger with your gowns in disarray.''

"Wonderful," said Caroline enthusiastically. "I am sure that between the two of us we shall be able to help Phoebe.''

Sibby helped her mistress into a very expensive and, naturally, since it was French, daring night-gown. A flimsy peignoir was slipped over this and Caroline's hair combed out. The nighttime ritual finished, Sibby was allowed to retire, and her mistress gathered a blanket around her and sat in a chair before the fire to think.

Now that she was alone, Caroline had to admit to herself that she was just a little disappointed that the infamous ghost had not made an appearance for her benefit. Again, the thought crossed her mind that her sister had merely imagined seeing something. The fact that the housemaid also had seen the thing was no proof of its existence as far as Caroline was concerned. She knew imagination could be infectious, and servants were notoriously superstitious. Well, it is certain the thing won't come visiting me here, she thought, and decided to take her travel-weary body to bed.

She went to the window, pulled aside the curtain, and looked out. It was a fitful night—clouds flew past a three-quarter moon, leaving it powerless to light the earth for more than a moment at a time. She could see some bushes below her window which looked as if they might be rhododendrons. The bare bushes hunched against the house like evil creatures with twisted limbs. Caroline shook her head in disgust at her temporary flight of fancy. She cracked the window open, shed her peignoir, and tossed it on a nearby chair. She climbed into her bed and snuggled under blankets which had already been warmed by hot bricks. A gentle rain had begun to pelter on the roof. Feeling warm and safe, Caroline allowed its lullaby to put her to sleep.

Sometime in the night, the lullaby was drowned by a howl of wind. A noise at the window brought Caroline awake with a start. The uneasy feeling that she was not alone settled over her. She peered cautiously over her blankets and caught sight of something white dancing by the window.

2

Caroline was not an hysterical female. She didn't shriek. But something between a gulp and a gasp escaped her lips, and she backed herself against the headboard, her heart thudding. The ghost made no move to hurt her. It remained crouched by the window. Perhaps it intended to come no closer, but Caroline wasn't inclined to sit inactive in her bed watching it. With trembling fingers, she lit her bedside candle and held it up.

With the light, the ghost was transformed back to what it had been all along—Caroline's peignoir, which was slung over the chair by the window, fluttering in the breeze. Caroline laughed shakily and shut the window, and the ghost lay still. "What a goose I am becoming," she sighed. "We must solve this puzzle quickly, or my nerves will soon be as overset as Mama and Phoebe's."

She returned to her bed determined not to let her silly fright upset her, but, in spite of the fact that the ghost had been laid to rest, Lady Caroline Templeton found her mind haunted by uneasiness for the rest of the night.

It seemed she had barely found sleep before an

insistent morning sun was wrenching it away from her. "Your sister has asked me twice now if you are awake yet," Sibby informed her from behind the wardrobe door.

Caroline yawned. "If it had not been for such a bright, sunny morning I should still be asleep. I had a perfectly dreadful night."

"I could have sworn I had drawn that curtain shut," said Sibby. "You didn't . . . see anything, did you?"

Caroline laughed. "No. And if I didn't know better I'd swear you were hoping I had. It would be just like you, Sibby, to want me to see some grisly apparition just so you could enjoy saying 'I told you so.'"

Sibby looked properly insulted and insisted she would do no such thing.

"Well, if I do not see it perhaps you will."

"And if it frightens me to death will you have 'Right Again' inscribed on my tombstone?" asked Sibby, her sarcasm cloaked in tones of the utmost respect.

"Most certainly," replied Caroline, flinging aside her nightgown.

A mere half-hour later Caroline made her way down to breakfast properly attired in a peach-colored morning gown, a shawl thrown round her shoulders to protect her from drafts.

Neither of the older women were at breakfast, Lady Grayson because she had already eaten and begun her morning's routine, Lady Harborough because she had not yet stirred from her bedchamber. The others were present and finishing up their breakfast when Caroline made her appearance.

"Finally you are awake!" exclaimed Phoebe. "Did you sleep well? Did you see the ghost?"

"You appear to have almost as much concern for

23

me as Sibby," said Caroline, picking up a plate from the sideboard and helping herself to some deviled kidneys.

"Well," prompted Phoebe. "*Did* you see anything?"

"Nothing but my robe," admitted Caroline, "which I promptly mistook for your ghost. And I must say I was disappointed when I discovered all I had encountered was a flight of fancy."

Phoebe sighed. "I wish you had seen it."

Jarvis smiled. "Do not look so disappointed, cousin-to-be. I will be very much surprised if the famous family ghost does not pay another call. She seems so fond of you." Phoebe gulped. "If I were a ghost I should certainly want to pay a call on your sister as well," Jarvis continued. "Who would not want to haunt such a beautiful woman?"

Caroline found herself blushing. "I thank you sir," she said and sat down.

"It is a devlish fine morning," Clarence informed her. "Thought you might care for a morning ride around the estate."

Caroline said she would indeed like that and within an hour she stood in the hall suitably dressed for an outing in a dashing black riding habit trimmed with gold piping and a riding hat with a curled ostrich plume and a tantalizing black veil perched jauntily on her auburn curls. Caroline, taller than her sister and built on slimmer lines, looked lithe and supple.

Next to Caroline, Phoebe didn't show to such advantage in riding costume, looking rather lumpy, and, in spite of the elegant cut and expensive cloth of her habit, rather dowdy. But Clarence saw nothing amiss in his true love's appearance and told her she looked smashing, bang up to the nines.

Jarvis's eyes and appreciative smile paid Caroline a silent compliment, and they went down the front steps and mounted their waiting horses.

Clarence's domain was large, and the two couples were out the entire morning without covering it all. Of course, the fact they took a leisurely ride, enjoying the fine early October weather, stopping several times to visit with tenants contributed to this as much as the enormity of the estate.

Caroline thoroughly enjoyed her ride. The ever-witty Jarvis once again kept her well entertained. It was from Jarvis she learned that Isobelle had once fancied herself the future Lady Grayson. "So you can hardly blame her for taking a perverse delight in teasing your sister with tales of an ancestral ghost," he said with a smile.

Caroline had bridled at this. "I most certainly can. Within minutes of meeting her anyone can see my sister is a silly little widgeon. Miss Payne should have known this would upset her."

Jarvis conceded this with a nod. "She should have, but I am sure none of us, least of all Belle, thought Phoebe would actually start seeing things. Belle can be naughty, but she is not malicious. She is a good-hearted creature, gentle as a lamb."

Gentle as a wolf in lamb's clothing, thought Caroline the following morning as they sat in Isobelle's sunlit drawing room. The chairs were newly upholstered. The carpet was thick and unworn. Tea was served on fine Sèvres china. Everything reeked of elegance. Miss Payne obviously lacked for nothing—except the new earl, and Caroline was sure it rankled. She listened as Isobelle reminisced about her cozy childhood with the Grayson brothers, Clarence and Damien. She tried not to let her smile appear cynical as Isobelle enthused about the rosy future ahead for

25

the new countess of Alverstoke, how delighted everyone in the neighborhood was with her, and how happy they all would be.

Caroline remembered a chance remark Lady Grayson had made at tea which gave credibility to what Jarvis had told her. "We did think for a while that Clarence would offer for Isobelle, but then he met dear little Phoebe and lost his heart. And I am sure we are all delighted to have her as a Grayson."

Were "we" all delighted? Caroline eyed Isobelle over her teacup and wondered. What did it feel like to be a dethroned reigning beauty? What did one do? Surely Isobelle would not abdicate without a fight. Mama was already making threatening noises about removing Phoebe from Grayson Hall if its resident ghost didn't find a new abode soon. Caroline suspected Isobelle would shed no tears if the engagement were called off.

"Of course," Isobelle was saying, "it is Papa's dearest wish that I marry Clarence and join our two estates, but this is hardly the Middle Ages. And I always thought of Clarence as a brother."

"Your papa must have been very upset when Clarence offered for Phoebe," suggested Caroline.

"Oh, he has taken it in his stride," replied Isobelle airily. "And he has had to admit, after meeting Phoebe, that she is much better suited for Clarence than I."

As Clarence was rather a dolt, Caroline knew this was no compliment. She smiled stiffly and replied that, yes, Clarence was a kindhearted fellow and deserved an equally kind bride.

Only a quick flush on Isobelle's face betrayed the fact that the subtle barb had hit a nerve. "Of course," she continued, "it was always Damien, the younger brother, with whom I was madly in love. He was so

26

handsome, so dashing, so strong, even as a child."
She shook her head and smiled. "And such a temper.
His mother claims she named him Damien because
he cried so angrily when he was first born. Like the
devil himself, Lady Grayson used to say."

"Where is he?" said Caroline.

Isobelle fished out a handkerchief and dabbed at
her eyes. "He went to India to make his fortune and
never returned."

"No one ever heard from him?" asked Caroline in
astonishment. "Why did he not write?"

"Oh, he corresponded sporadically at first. But
then the letters dwindled off. Only last autumn,
Jarvis came with a letter which he had received from
a friend in India telling of Damien's death and
begging Jarvis to break the news to the family. It was
quite awful, really. A terrible loss for everyone. The
family had barely recovered from the old earl's death.
Of course, Clarence was inconsolable for some time.
He dearly loved his brother. It is fortunate Lady
Grayson made him stir himself and attend a few
functions last season, for he met Phoebe, who has
been very good for him. Before meeting her he was
desolated. For a time Lady Grayson feared he would
go mad with grief."

"Poor Clarence," said Caroline.

Phoebe held out a hand to Isobelle. "And poor Isobelle. How hard it must have been for you."

"It was hard for us all," said Isobelle sadly. She
sighed. "Something in me died the day I heard the
news. I doubt now I shall ever marry."

After having observed Isobelle making sheep's eyes
at both Clarence and Jarvis, Caroline rather doubted
this statement. She was beginning to feel an intense
dislike for Isobelle.

Phoebe was much less perceptive than her older

sister. "Isn't she a dear?" she exclaimed as they rode home. Caroline merely smiled and Phoebe continued, "She has been so very kind to me since I came."

"I am sure it has been nice for you to have another female with whom to visit since you have been here," said Caroline diplomatically.

"Oh yes. We have all been very friendly. It has been a most wonderful visit. In fact, it would be perfect if not for that horrid ghost." She looked imploringly at her sister. "We simply must catch it and drive it away," she urged.

"We shall, love," Caroline assured her.

"But how? It has not even showed itself since you have come."

"Patience, love. I have only just arrived. I suspect now that I have thrown down the gauntlet by expressing my doubt of its very existence it shall soon make an appearance."

Phoebe's face took on a worried cast. "Do you think you should talk so very . . ." She paused, searching for a word.

"Scornfully?" suggested Caroline.

"Yes, scornfully about the ghost? Telling Isobelle at tea that you thought the ghost lacked the intelligence to match wits with you, was that wise? If you go around saying things like that to people, you are going to make it angry."

"I hope so," said Caroline. "I should be very much surprised if our ghost does not take up the challenge some time in the next few nights. In fact, I am so sure it will appear I intend to lay in wait for it, starting tonight."

Phoebe's eyes widened. "Tonight?" she squeaked.

"Yes, tonight."

Phoebe was silent a moment. "If you are going to

sit up and wait for the ghost, then I shall bear you company," she said with determination.

Caroline smiled fondly at her little sister. "You are a brave girl," she said. "But there is no need—"

Phoebe held up a restraining hand. "No. If you are going to be brave enough to face a ghost on my behalf, the least I can do is help you."

"All right love," said Caroline. She reached across the carriage and patted her sister's hand.

The sisters returned to find the men gone to take advantage of the uncommonly fine weather and try their luck as anglers in the nearby stream, and the two mothers comfortably ensconced in the winter parlor, embroidering on elegant but useless projects. Luncheon was soon served. It was a rather dull affair, as the men had taken a well-stocked hamper with them and were not expected back 'til late afternoon.

When the gentlemen did finally return, the peace of the house was effectively shattered. The women could hear the commotion clear back in the parlor and came out to see Jarvis and a very wet, bedraggled Clarence at the end of the hall. Clarence was announcing quite boistrously that he had almost drowned and owed his very life to his cousin Jarvis. "And young Joe, here."

He put a paw on a gangly, dripping youth hovering in a corner and pulled him close. "Take Joe back to the kitchen and have Cook give him something to eat and some dry clothes," he instructed the gaping Smythe. "Then we are going to," Clarence paused to hiccup, "reward him for his bravery. He helped save me from a," another hiccup, "watery grave."

Clarence suddenly spied the women coming down the stairs. He held an arm out to Phoebe, who was

29

running to him and grabbed her in a wet hug.

"Oh, Clarence," she cried. "What has happened to you?"

"Lost my balance. Must have had just a teensy bit too much to drink," Clarence explained. "Fell in. Of course, Jarvis handed me a tree branch and tried to pull me out, but I'm no featherweight. Good thing Joe was fishing farther downstream. If he hadn't come and helped I'd have drowned."

"But Clarence, can you not swim?" asked Phoebe, amazed. "I thought all men could swim."

Clarence blushed. "I can swim," he insisted. "But I'd like to see how good a swimmer any man is with his boots on."

And a bottle or two of claret in him, thought Caroline.

"Oh, Clarence," fussed Lady Grayson. "You will catch your death."

"You are shivering," Phoebe informed him.

"Nah," scoffed Clarence. "It ain't that cold out."

"It may not be that cold when you are dry and dressed warmly," said Lady Grayson, "but it is not the case when you are wet."

"He must be gotten to bed instantly," insisted Lady Harborough.

"Go upstairs immediately and ring for Albert to help you out of your wet clothes," ordered Lady Grayson. "I shall instruct Cook to brew you a hot posset. Oh dear, I do hope you may not catch an inflammation of the lungs," she said, hurrying down the hall. She stopped after a few steps. "Jarvis, dear, thank you so much for saving my poor boy. Thank God you and this young man were present." With that she bustled off, leaving the other ladies behind to watch the two tipsy sportsmen drip their way upstairs.

30

"Do not fret yourselves, ladies," Clarence called cheerfully. "It takes more than a little dunking to harm me."

Clarence reappeared at dinner, having spent the afternoon snoring in his room. But rather than looking refreshed, he looked very much like a man who was fast becoming ill. His head was splitting, he said.

And no wonder, thought Caroline unsympathetically. He had gotten properly foxed. She looked at his flushed face and wondered how a man who was obviously a poor swimmer could have been so foolish as to get drunk and place himself at the edge of a deep stream.

As the evening wore on, he did appear to be suffering from more than a hangover. His face had become increasingly flushed and, despite the roaring fire in the drawing room, he complained twice of being cold. Finally, he drew his chair up as close as possible to the hearth and sat hunched by the fire.

Phoebe sat in a nearby chair, looking sympathetic and asking him every few minutes how he felt. "I am fine," he would say, attempting to sound jovial.

"Well, you do not look at all fine," said his mama. "Perhaps you should retire."

Clarence sneezed and stubbornly refused, insisting there was nothing wrong with him.

"You really do not look in plump current, old fellow," said Jarvis. "Why do you not call it a night? I shall be happy to entertain the ladies in your absence."

Clarence sighed and looked longingly at the door.

"Yes, do," urged Phoebe. "You do not look at all well. Really."

Lady Harborough seconded this opinion and informed Clarence that it was such a simple thing as

31

a chill which sent her husband into a decline. "If he had only taken better care of himself when first he took chill I am sure he would be alive today," she finished.

Clarence obviously had no desire to have Lord Harborough's fate befall him, so he apologized to the company and took himself off.

Phoebe sighed. "I daresay we had best put off waiting up for the ghost until Clarence is feeling better."

"Whyever should we do that?" asked Caroline.

"You had intended to have him help us, had you not?"

"Frankly—" Caroline began.

"What's this?" asked Jarvis. "Had you two daring ladies planned to go ghost hunting alone?"

"Well," Caroline said.

"How very selfish," he said in injured tones, "to want to keep such an adventure to yourselves. I am hurt."

"You are roasting us," laughed Caroline.

"I am most certainly not roasting you. I am genuinely hurt," insisted Jarvis, pulling down the corners of his mouth.

"Caroline! What are you planning to do?" demanded her mother.

"I am going to catch and expose this fraudulent ghost, whomever it may be."

"Fraudulent," snorted Lady Harborough. "There was nothing fraudulent about the horrible thing your sister and I saw, I can assure you."

"Never tell me you do not believe in ghosts," chided Jarvis.

"Caroline, I forbid you to do anything dangerous," said Lady Harborough.

"But Mama," Caroline protested, "is that not why

32

you and Phoebe asked me to come here, to find and rid you of the ghost?"

"Well, yes," admitted Lady Harborough. "Your sister did want your help. But I am sure no one expected you to do anything as dangerous as this to get rid of it."

"I do not intend to do anything dangerous," replied Caroline. "We are merely going to lie in wait for the ghost tonight in the hope that it will make an appearance."

"And what will you do if it does?" demanded Lady Harborough.

Caroline laughed. "Catch it, of course," she said.

"Oh, you must not. You will be hurt," said her mama.

"I do feel your mama is right, my dear," put in Lady Grayson. "Not that I feel our ghost would harm you, but you are liable to take a chill if you remain in the corridor. There is quite a draft. Of course, you could wait here in the drawing room," she said with sudden inspiration. "But then," she went on realistically, "I doubt the ghost would appear to you. She seems to prefer corridors."

"Oh dear," moaned Lady Harborough, wringing her hands. "If you do not catch a chill you shall be caught by a ghost."

"The ladies will be perfectly safe," Jarvis assured her. "I will stay with them."

"I hope you will not fatigue yourselves staying up all night," said Lady Grayson. She shook her head. "I am quite sure our ghost is harmless, poor thing, and we are all making much ado about nothing."

Lady Harborough looked properly insulted. "I do not call it much ado about nothing since it is *my* daughter whom this horrid thing has been haunting," she said.

"Yes, but it has not hurt her," pointed out Lady Grayson.

"It might," insisted Lady Harborough.

"Well, if it is settled, then," said Jarvis, "we shall lie in wait for Grayson Hall's ghostie tonight. I think I shall go and fetch my sword stick."

"And I believe I shall retire early," said Lady Harborough. "My nerves simply cannot stand this sort of thing, and I would as soon be in my room. Phoebe, love, I wish you might go to your room also," she said in tones which showed her wish to be a command. "Let your sister and Mr. Woolcock handle this matter. Caroline's nerves are much steadier than yours. And she stands in no danger from the ghost."

"I am sure the ghost wishes our Phoebe no harm," repeated Lady Grayson.

"Nevertheless," Lady Harborough began.

"Oh, Mama, I shall be perfectly safe with Caroline and Cousin Jarvis. Please let me help."

Lady Harborough hesitated.

"Do not worry, dear lady. We shall take excellent care of her," said Jarvis gently, leading Lady Harborough to the door. "May I escort you to your room?" he offered.

"I suppose," said Lady Harborough distractedly.

"I think I shall retire also," said Lady Grayson.

Jarvis turned at the door. "When and where shall we meet?" he asked Caroline.

"Let us meet at the end of the corridor, by the stairs," said Caroline. She turned to Phoebe. "What time of night did you last see the ghost?"

Phoebe screwed up her face in concentration. "We had had a late night, for I remember we were playing at loo. Then Jarvis got tired and suggested we retire."

"And what time was that?" prompted Caroline,

34

trying to curb her impatience.

"I believe the ladies went upstairs close to eleven-thirty," said Jarvis. "I stayed behind for a quick brandy with Clarence. I had just finished my brandy when I heard your sister scream. So she must have seen the ghost right around eleven-thirty."

"Then let us meet at eleven," Caroline suggested.

"Very well," Jarvis agreed, and left with the two dowagers.

At a few minutes before eleven Caroline fetched her sister and, armed with cashmere shawls to fight off drafts, the two young ladies made their way to the end of the corridor. The branch of candles in the hallway cast an eerie light, and shadows danced on the walls. Unconsciously, the sisters moved closer together as they walked.

A figure stepped out of the shadow at the end of the hall and both women jumped, Phoebe stifling a startled shriek. "Cousin Jarvis," she moaned, putting a hand to her heart. "I am sorry. I thought for a moment . . ."

"No, it is I who should be sorry. Please forgive me for startling you ladies so. I was going to suggest we hide over there on the back stairs. We will have a better view of the corridor from there and still be able to remain undetected."

"That will leave the main stairway unattended," observed Caroline.

"If you ladies would like to wait on one stair together, I could wait on the one opposite," offered Jarvis.

"No!" cried Phoebe. "I mean, let us all wait together. I think it would be so much safer that way."

"Very well," agreed Caroline.

The three positioned themselves partway down the

stairs and began their vigil. After half an hour Phoebe shivered. "What time do you think it is?" she whispered.

"It must be close to midnight," Jarvis replied. "I imagine if our ghost is going to visit us it will do so before the next half-hour is past."

Time crept by, and Caroline moved closer to Jarvis. "Are you cold?" he whispered.

She shook her head.

"I am," hissed Phoebe, who sat on the stair below him. He removed his coat and draped it over her shoulders. "Caro, do think we should give up and go to bed?" she asked.

Caroline sighed. She had been so sure. . . . "Let us give the thing a few more minutes," she whispered. She shut her tired eyes and rubbed them.

Phoebe suddenly grabbed Jarvis's arm and let out a terrified shriek. "There it is," she cried, pointing down the corridor.

3

Caroline's eyes snapped open and she looked up to catch a glimpse of a figure in a diaphanous gown floating along the far end of the hallway. Phoebe promptly fainted and slumped against the wall. Caroline clambered to her feet and made an attempt to bound off in pursuit. She lurched forward one step and promptly fell on her face. A ripping sound told her why she had been unable to continue.

"Sorry," muttered Jarvis. Removing his foot from her gown, he bent to help her up.

"Never mind me," she said tersely. "After the ghost!"

"Certainly," Jarvis said obediently and rushed past her.

Caroline muttered something very unladylike, gathered her skirts, and followed after him, leaving the fainting Phoebe where she had fallen. Hot on Jarvis's heels, she dashed down the corridor, the thrill of the chase making her heedless of the danger of tripping in the semidarkness. They reached the end of the corridor and, having lost sight of their quarry, ran down the stairs.

The entrance hall was deserted. Jarvis scooped a

candelabrum from the table and held it high, peering around. "Not so much as a mouse to be seen," he said in disappointment.

"Drat!" muttered Caroline.

Her companion's mouth twitched, but he made no comment on her ill-mannered language.

"The bedrooms!" she exclaimed, and dashed past him back up the stairs. Jarvis caught up with her at the top of the stairs and followed her down the corridor they had just run through, holding the candelabrum for her as she opened doors and peeped into rooms. The unoccupied rooms still remained so. Both Caroline and Phoebe's bedchambers were peacefully quiet. Jarvis peered into Clarence's room, and the snores coming from the big canopied bed told them all was quiet there as well. Caroline hesitated at Jarvis's door, good manners conquering desire. "By all means," said Jarvis, nodding. "We should look in every room." Again, good manners controlled her actions, and Caroline only gave the room a cursory glance. But it appeared to be as discouragingly empty as the others had been. The next room they came to was Lady Harborough's, and Caroline conducted this inspection alone, opening the door quietly and poking her head in. Her mother was snoring blissfully, and her room, too, looked undisturbed.

They covered the length of the corridor with no success. "Perhaps it went through a wall," suggested Jarvis.

Caroline was about to make a cynical remark when her face took on a thoughtful expression. "Yes," she said slowly. "Perhaps it did."

"I was merely jesting," laughed Jarvis.

Caroline smiled archly at him. "But I am not," she said.

"What do you mean?"

Caroline merely shook her head. "It is merely a thought I have just had, and for now I will keep it that way." They had reached the end of the corridor, and a low moan drifted up to them from the stairs. "Oh, goodness, Phoebe!" Caroline exclaimed and rushed back down the stairs.

Jarvis, unhampered by skirts, was able to reach Phoebe first. He put an arm around her shoulder and scooped her up, her eyes fluttering open. A scream choked to a stop halfway up her throat. "Oh," she sobbed, and buried her face in his shoulder.

"Phoebe, love. Are you alright?" asked Caroline.

Phoebe was unable to answer her sister for she was much too busy crying. Caroline bit her lip and mentally scolded herself for allowing Phoebe along on this adventure. She turned a worried face to Jarvis, who smiled encouragingly and said, "She is fine. Just a little upset. But she is a very brave girl," he crooned, and at the comforting sound of his voice Phoebe began to calm down.

She gave one final sniff and stuttered, "Did you catch it?"

"Not this time, love." Phoebe let out a wail and Caroline felt like wailing, also, from frustration. "Do not worry, dearest. I promise you I will find a way to put an end to this."

"You cannot," cried Phoebe. "Do you not see? It hates me. It will never rest until it has driven me from this house."

"Phoebe, love. You must get ahold of yourself. Try to remain calm."

Phoebe looked at her sister as if she were mad. "Remain calm?" she asked, her voice rising hysterically. "I should like to see you remain calm if you were being chased by a ghost."

"Well it won't be chasing you any more tonight," said Caroline bracingly. "We have run it off." She rose. "Come, love. I think it is time we got you to bed."

Jarvis helped Phoebe to her feet and, keeping a supporting arm around her, helped her up the stairs, Caroline preceding them to her room. Jarvis turned to Phoebe at the door and smiled apologetically. "I am sorry we did not catch your ghost," he said.

Phoebe sighed. "You tried, and I am grateful to you for that."

Caroline got her sister into her room and rang for her maid, talking encouragingly until the girl came, then escaped to her own room and rang for Sibby. "I don't suppose you have seen or heard anything peculiar in the last hour, have you?" she asked when her maid arrived.

Sibby shook her head. "But I did learn one interesting thing this evening. Did you know the earl had a brother?"

Caroline nodded distractedly. "Yes. Miss Payne told us about him. He is dead. You did not see anyone lurking around belowstairs? None of the servants saw the ghost tonight?"

Sibby's fingers froze on the tenth button of her mistress's gown. "You have seen the ghost."

"I have seen the *bogus* ghost," Caroline replied.

"Bogus?"

"Yes, bogus. This ghost who is scaring Phoebe is no more a ghost than I. Unfortunately, Phoebe's scream warned the creature away and we were not fast enough to catch her. By the time we had finally finished tripping over each other and reached the corridor she had escaped."

"This rip in your gown—" began Sibby.

"Is why we did not catch the ghost," said Caroline

40

bitterly. "I want you to ask around tomorrow and see if any of the servants saw anyone on the back stairs tonight."

"I shall ask. But I am sure if anyone saw anything I would have heard before you rang for me."

"You are most likely right," sighed Caroline. "But it bears looking into."

Sibby nodded. "That it does."

Sibby had nothing to report the following morning. No one had seen anyone or anything peculiar.

"Oh, drat," muttered Caroline, running a hand through her tangled curls. "Ah, well. I really did not expect you to learn anything. Our ghost is far too clever to be caught so easily."

"I do not understand any of this," complained Sibby. "Why is this ghost after Lady Phoebe?"

"Because," said Caroline, stepping into her hip bath, "someone does not want Phoebe to become the future Lady Grayson. And that someone is trying to scare her off. I only wish I may put a stop to this before things get out of hand and Phoebe is seriously injured. After last night I can see how easily someone running in the dark could trip and fall and be seriously injured."

Caroline was already in her favorite pea green morning gown and just putting on matching slippers when a gentle tapping on her door announced a visitor. Sibby looked questioningly at her mistress. "Phoebe," said Caroline simply.

Sibby opened the door to see that their early visitor was indeed Caroline's sister. "Caro, I must speak with you," she said, hurrying into the room. Sibby shut the door and hovered close by as Phoebe plunged into speech. "I am not going to marry Clarence," she announced. "Mama was right all along. As soon as Clarence is feeling better, I am

41

going to tell him."

"Phoebe! I thought you wanted to marry Clarence," scolded Caroline.

"I do," Phoebe whimpered. "But I am afraid, Caro. What fun will being Lady Grayson be if I am accosted by ghosts in the corridor every night before I go to bed?"

"You might get used to it," suggested Caroline. Phoebe's lips began to tremble. "I was merely roasting you," said Caroline. "Please, love. Do not do anything rash. Promise me you will give me a little more time to help you with this problem before you say anything to Clarence."

Phoebe looked at her sister hopefully. "Do you really think you can get rid of the ghost?"

Caroline nodded. "Yes. But you must give me more than two days in which to do it." Phoebe bit her lip, her inner struggle evident. "You do love Clarence, don't you?" prompted her sister.

"You know I do."

"Then do not do something rash which you will regret the rest of your life." Caroline took her sister's arm and propelled her out the door. "Let us go have breakfast. I am quite famished this morning."

Clarence was not at breakfast, and his mother reported he had caught a nasty cold and was going to stay in bed.

"Should you not send for the doctor?" suggested Lady Harborough nervously. "I should hate to see the poor boy fall into a decline."

"I shall check on him this afternoon and see if he desires me to send for Dr. Stone. Clarence detests doctors, so unless he takes a turn for the worse I should hate to—"

"Oh, but he very well might take a turn for the worse," interrupted Lady Harborough, highly agitated. "My own dear husband—" she began.

"Ah, but Clarence has an exceptionally strong constitution," said Lady Grayson.

"Even so, a cold can so quickly deteriorate into a horrid sore throat or an inflammation of the lungs," insisted Lady Harborough.

The two ladies continued their discussion at some length, and after a few more minutes of politely listening to the two amateur physicians, Jarvis turned to Phoebe. "It would appear your beloved is incapacitated and will be unable to entertain you properly today. Would you care to have me drive you and your sister to Hallowstone House to visit Isobelle this morning?"

"Oh, yes. I should like that," said Phoebe. Her face suddenly clouded. "But Clarence," she began.

"Truly is as strong as an ox and would be very upset if he learned you had been moping around on his account," said Jarvis.

Phoebe smiled. She turned to her sister. "Would you care to come, Caro?"

Caroline saw an opportunity unfolding and politely declined.

An hour later Phoebe was climbing into the gig next to Jarvis and was borne off down the gravel drive to Hallowstone House. As soon as she had waved good-bye to Phoebe, Caroline cornered Lady Grayson in the winter parlor. Lady Harborough, claiming a poor night's sleep had gone back to her bedchamber to nap and read the novel she had hidden under the bed, and Lady Grayson was alone with *La Belle Assemblée*. "Am I disturbing you?" asked Caroline.

"Not at all," said her hostess kindly. She patted the sofa cushion invitingly. "Do sit down and bear me company."

Caroline smiled and sat next to her. "You have a charming home and I am enjoying my visit very much," she said. Lady Grayson beamed. "But," Caroline continued, "I would like to know a little more of this resident ghost everyone is so worried about." Lady Grayson's face fell, and it was obvious to Caroline the subject was one which her ladyship would just as soon avoid. "I am sure this is all becoming most distasteful to you," said Caroline, "yet I would be so very grateful if you could bring yourself to answer a few nosey questions."

Lady Grayson smiled. "Of course, my dear," she said. "After all, we are almost family now, and I am sure you would like to know about the legend of the ghost."

"Indeed I would," said Caroline. "Who is this sad specter?"

"It is the first Lady Grayson. And her story truly is a sad one. During Elizabeth's reign our family was strongly Catholic. This belief cost them dearly and the first earl's lands were confiscated. His son finally managed to get back in the good graces of the throne and eventually our lands were restored. However, that did not help that poor, unfortunate woman. There was a raid one night, you see . . ."

As Lady Grayson talked, images sprang to Caroline's mind of the counterreformation, a dangerous time during the reign of Elizabeth I when loyal Catholic priests attempted to keep their religion alive by secretly conducting mass for believers in the homes of wealthy landowners. To harbor a priest incurred crippling fines, confiscation, and possibly death. On the advice of her two chief ministers, Queen Elizabeth established a secret service to ferret out priests and papists. At prearranged times when it was believed a priest was in the house, a gang of pursuers would arrive without warning and bang on the door, hoping to catch the religious criminals in the act.

"Cecil's men were at the door," Lady Grayson was saying. "The poor woman's husband was already in prison. The priest was being hidden in a priest's hole somewhere in the house."

"I thought so," murmured Caroline.

"I beg your pardon?" said Lady Grayson, confused.

"Forgive me," said Caroline. "Please continue."

"Well, you can imagine how distraught the poor dear was. Cecil's men broke down the door and before they could take her, she threw herself right over the bannister. Of course, having killed herself, she could not be permitted a proper burial, which is why the poor thing walks to this day."

"How often have you seen the ghost in recent years?" asked Caroline.

"Oh my! I have not seen the ghost in years. A housemaid once thought she saw it several years back when the boys were children. But it turned out the boys had learned of the legend, and the ghost of Lady Grayson turned out only to be Damien under a Holland cover." Lady Grayson was silent for a moment, lost in reverie. "I did see the ghost when I first came to the Hall as a bride. She was standing by the window and seemed to wave at me in greeting. Naturally, in spite of the fact that she seemed quite friendly, I was most alarmed. I lit a candle, but with the light she vanished."

Caroline thought of her dancing peignoir and smiled politely.

"It is said to be good luck for a Grayson bride to see it," Lady Grayson continued. "I certainly was very happy all those years. My husband was a wonderful man. He had a bit of a temper, but he was a good man. And the boys were such a joy, such mischiefs." Lady Grayson shook her head fondly. "Ah, well. Time moves on. I have lost a husband and a son, but I have gained a lovely daughter. Two lovely daughters," she amended, taking Caroline's hand. "I am sure our Grayson Hall ghost is merely welcoming Phoebe into the family, for who could not like such a dear girl?"

Who indeed? thought Caroline. Someone who stood to gain something if the future countess of Alverstoke fled Grayson Hall and cancelled the engagement. This ghost surely had something more sinister in mind for Phoebe than a mere welcome.

Phoebe and Jarvis returned in time for luncheon, and rather than having been cheered by her visit to Isobelle, Phoebe seemed to have been depressed. She was silent during the meal and afterwards asked Caroline if she would like to take a turn in the rose garden. The fair skies were fast disappearing, and Caroline would have liked to stay indoors, but she agreed and went to fetch her cloak. It was made of strong merino wool, but the air was pregnant with rain and chillingly cold, and Caroline shivered in spite of her cloak. Anxious to get to the point and get back inside, she asked. "What has happened to upset you?"

"I want to go home. Now."

"You want to break your engagement to Clarence now?"

Phoebe nodded. "The ghost will not rest 'til it has driven me off."

"Who told you that?" Caroline demanded.

"It is true," insisted Phoebe, ignoring her sister's question. "It is obvious the ghost of Grayson Hall does not approve of me as a bride for Clarence."

"Isobelle has been talking to you, hasn't she?" asked Caroline angrily. "Stop and think, love. Why would she be encouraging you to leave?"

"She didn't encourage me," said Phoebe. "When I told her about last night, she was very upset and concerned for me."

"Did she suggest that the ghost probably does not like you?"

"Well, yes."

"And you told her you had thought of breaking off the engagement and leaving," guessed Caroline. Phoebe blushed guiltily. Caroline glowered at her. "Whose advice are you going to listen to? Who is going to have your best interests at heart, your own sister or one of Clarence's former loves?" Phoebe hung her head, and Caroline gathered her cloak around her and headed for the house. "You insisted I come here and help you," she snapped, "and that is what I am going to do. We will have no more talk of leaving."

The responsibility for making dinner the satisfying affair it should be fell to Caroline and Jarvis that evening. Phoebe was subdued and had little to say for herself. Clarence was, his mother reported, feeling better, but had decided to take dinner in his room. With Phoebe so quiet, his boisterous presence was missed. Neither Lady Grayson nor Lady Harborough had the wit required to make lively dinner conversation. But Jarvis more than made up for their deficiencies. "I must say I am sorry, Mr. Woolcock, that we did not meet at some of the functions I attended with my sister last season," said Caroline after he had joined the ladies in the drawing room.

"I was on the Continent," Jarvis explained. "If I had but known what a lovely family my cousin had met I would have hastened back sooner. Clarence is a selfish beast. He was already engaged to one sister and yet I do believe he hoped to keep the other's existence a secret as well. But we Woolcocks are hard to fool."

"I am sure you are," laughed Caroline. "But how are you at cards?"

"As I said, we Woolcocks are hard to fool. Would you care to try your luck?"

"Indeed I would, sir," replied Caroline. "Phoebe, love, would you care to play at cards?"

Phoebe said she would, and Lady Harborough was persuaded to make a fourth. Lady Grayson did not play cards, but good-naturedly encouraged her guests not to let that worry them. "It is such a delight for me to see young people enjoying themselves," she said. "And I know Lady Harborough loves to play. I shall ring for Amy and have her fetch my book from the winter parlor, and I shall be quite cozy sitting here by the fire, reading."

As the evening progressed Phoebe became jumpy. She was not much of a card player to begin with, but that night she paid even less attention to her hand than usual, and Caroline had to repeatedly call her attention back to the game. "I am sorry," she said at last. "I simply cannot concentrate."

Caroline laid down her cards with a sigh. "Perhaps we had best concede the game," she said. "Mama and Jarvis are beating us soundly."

Smythe was summoned and the tea tray was brought in, the card table abandoned in favor of that final spot of tea and some poppy seed cake. "Where was your mind wandering?" asked Caroline as the players rose from the card table.

"Oh, nowhere," said Phoebe evasively.

"You must not let this ghost business distress

48

you," whispered Caroline. "I promise you we will keep you safe."

Much good her promise had done, thought Caroline, watching her sister. The nervous glances at the door as if it were something she dreaded approaching and the tiny smiles all betrayed Phoebe's edginess. Well, who could blame her. She had been most effectively frightened, thought Caroline angrily.

The polishing off of the contents of the tea tray signaled an end to the evening, and the members of the house party made their way to their respective bedchambers. Once inside her room, however, Caroline did not ring for Sibby. Instead, she threw another log on the fire and sat down to wait. After an hour had passed, she judged it safe to venture out. She grabbed her parasol, which she had packed, thinking it might make a suitable weapon, and picked up her candle. She stuffed the parasol under her arm, opened her door, and peeked out into the corridor. As she had hoped, it was cloaked in darkness and deserted.

Shaking off the feeling of uneasiness that had settled on her, she crept down the hallway. Somewhere along this corridor there had to be a priest's hole, she told herself. No Catholic home would have been without one in Elizabethan times. And while the house had been remodeled since the reign of Elizabeth I when it had first been built, Caroline felt sure the old structure still contained a convenient hiding place for a sneaky ghost somewhere.

She stood for a few moments, looking around her. It was a long corridor. Where to begin? The ghost had vanished somewhere among the bedchambers, but where? Caroline decided to be systematic and thorough. She would begin at the end of the corridor near the main stairway and work her way to the other end.

Parasol still tucked under her arm, she tiptoed to the end of the hallway and began her examination, holding her candle close to the wall and peering intently, occasionally tapping lightly to see if she could detect a telltale hollow sound.

She was so intent on her task she never heard the creak of floorboards at the top of the stairs, nor did she see the tall, dark figure until he was practically upon her.

4

Caroline let out a screech and swung her parasol, catching the unsuspecting man alongside the head. His eyes crossed, and he staggered back a step, but he recovered quickly enough. A thunderous look settled on his face and, putting a hand to his head, he swore.

Caroline raised her parasol threateningly. "Who are you and why are you slinking around these halls in the middle of the night?" she demanded.

"As this is my home, madam, I suppose I might slink around these halls if I wish," growled the stranger. "Now. Perhaps you would be so good as to tell me who you are and what you are up to. And put that thing down," he commanded, pointing to the offending weapon.

Caroline's shriek and the subsequent angry voices had roused several sleepers. Phoebe's head poked out her door, and Lady Harborough could be heard nervously calling Caroline's name from her room. Jarvis had also left his bedroom and dashed out into the hall, splendid in a brocade dressing gown. He stopped short at the sight of the stranger. "My God. Damien!" he gasped.

"Surprised to see me, cousin?" asked the stranger.

His lips curled into a sneer which, in spite of her rapidly growing dislike for the man, aroused a faint fluttering in Caroline's breast. The man was handsome, there was no arguing that fact. He looked like an escaped character from Lord Byron's imagination—dark and brooding. His nose was straight, his chin square, his eyebrows thick and scowling, and his eyes were demonically dark. In short, Caroline decided he looked like a villain. Ill-tempered, too. Appropriate. What villain was not?

"We thought you were dead," Jarvis was saying.

"Thought or wished?"

Jarvis stiffened and Caroline looked frankly shocked.

"I came close to sticking my spoon in the wall," said Damien. "Some cutthroat nearly murdered me in a back street in Bombay. I am sure he thought I was as good as dead, else he would never have left me."

Caroline was caught up in the newcomer's tale in spite of herself. "How did you survive?" she asked.

The long-lost brother shrugged. "Some good Samaritan found me and conveyed me to a hospital. It took me close to six months to recover."

By this time Phoebe had thrown on a wrapper and ventured a step out into the corridor. Lady Grayson also had been aroused. She appeared stuffed into a wrapper, her hair in curlpapers. "My heavens! Whatever is going on?" she began. She took a few steps closer to the group gathered in the corridor and her eyes flew open. "Damien," she gasped and collapsed on the floor.

Phoebe's mouth dropped. "D-Damien?" she stuttered. "Clarence's brother?"

Damien knelt by his mother and began to chafe her hand. "Ring for a footman," he ordered, and Phoebe disappeared.

"I must say this was a most inconsiderate way to let your family know you were not dead," scolded Caroline, kneeling opposite Damien and picking up Lady Grayson's other plump hand.

"I had my reasons for not writing," said Damien shortly. "Just as I am sure you have your reasons for interfering in something which is none of your concern."

"As I am shortly to be part of this family I imagine all this must now be my concern," snapped Caroline.

"And who, pray, are you?" inquired the villain.

"I am Lady Caroline Templeton, and I shall soon be your sister-in-law," said Caroline. "If you were not going to write," she continued, "you might at least have come home sooner."

"You forget, Lady Caroline Templeton, that I was incapacitated for some time. I set out for home as soon as I was able. God knows I knew Clarence would have need of me."

"Oh?"

"To protect him from villains and fortune hunters."

"And what, pray, might that mean?" demanded Caroline, bristling.

"Why, nothing—if you are neither a fortune hunter nor a villainess," replied Damien with the faintest of smiles.

Lady Grayson began to revive, ending all conversation between Caroline and the newcomer. Two sturdy footmen were pressed into service, and she was removed from the floor to her bedroom. "I hope you will all excuse me," Damien said to the three houseguests. "I imagine my mother will wish to speak with me."

Caroline watched him walk away and wished she had taken full advantage of her earlier opportunity and hit him harder.

She liked him no more when she came down to breakfast the next morning to discover he had already managed to intimidate Phoebe into a nervous silence. Jarvis also appeared to be affected by the presence of the new arrival, for his look of carefree confidence had been replaced with a more somber expression. He smiled apologetically at Caroline as if to say, "Please forgive me for being related to this lout." Caroline took a deep breath and prepared to do battle.

"Lady Caroline," said Damien cordially as she took a seat next to him. "I understand it is not you who is engaged to my brother, but your lovely sister."

"It would appear you have been furthering your acquaintance with her during breakfast," observed Caroline coldly.

"I am sure I am very happy to meet Clarence's brother," Phoebe said politely. "Although I would never have taken you for Clarence's brother. You are so different . . ." Damien raised a questioning eyebrow and Phoebe blushed. "I mean," she rushed on, "you do not look at all alike. Well, perhaps you do a little, but you seem . . ." She floundered and fell silent.

Clarence, who had emerged from the sickroom, laughed. "Oh, we are not at all alike. Damien is much smarter."

Damien smiled at his brother. "Yes, but you are much more likeable, old fellow. And much more trusting. Clarence has always been more easy to take advantage of," Damien said nonchalantly to Caroline.

His meaning was hard to mistake. It was plain to see he wanted Caroline and her family to know that while Clarence might appear an easy mark, his brother was a different story. Damien Grayson was now on the scene to protect his brother's interests, and all who meant to harm or take advantage of the house of Grayson had best beware.

Well, this insolent fellow had best beware himself! The Harboroughs were not some family of cits or adventurers, and his brother was fortunate to be marrying one of them. And if the Honorable Damien Grayson thought to cause problems for Phoebe he would have Lady Caroline Templeton with whom to contend.

Lady Grayson beamed on her long lost son with misty eyes. "It is so good to have both my boys again."

Clarence smiled fondly at his younger brother. "What say you to a ride over the estate after breakfast? Old Annie would love to see you."

Damien nodded. "She will be glad to see the black sheep safely returned after all her dire predictions before I left."

"You must be sure to take her some currant jam," said Lady Grayson. "She loves it so."

Clarence turned to Phoebe. "Come with us. Old Annie took a shine to you when she met you."

"Perhaps she would rather just see you and your brother," suggested Phoebe timidly.

Clarence shook his head. "Don't be silly. Why wouldn't she want to see you, too?"

Phoebe couldn't answer this question so she tried another excuse. "You and your brother might like to have some time together alone. To catch up on all the years you missed."

"Did that last night," said Clarence. "After he talked to Mama."

"Maybe Phoebe would rather not come," suggested Damien.

55

Phoebe looked very much as if she would rather not come, but she finally gave up fighting her fate and agreed to accompany the brothers.

"Good," boomed Clarence, rising. "It is settled then. Put on your riding togs," he said to Phoebe, "and we'll all meet in the front hall in half an hour, eh?"

Lady Harborough fluttered into the room at that moment. "Damien, dear," said Lady Grayson, "you have not met Phoebe and Caroline's mama, Lady Harborough. This is my son, Damien. It turns out he was not dead after all. Is that not wonderful?"

Lady Harborough looked in amazement at the handsome young man, and a speculative look came over her face. "I am pleased to meet you," she said. "How long have you been back in England?"

"I am only just recently arrived," said Damien.

"Of course, how silly of me," said Lady Harborough. "You would naturally wish to see your family before becoming involved in the social whirl or . . . allowing yourself to be captivated by any cunning young miss," she finished slyly.

Caroline blushed at this obvious fishing. "We mustn't detain the gentlemen, Mama," she said. "They are about to go out."

Clarence turned to Jarvis. "Care to ride along?"

Jarvis shook his head. "I shall stay here and entertain Lady Caroline," he said.

"Perhaps Caroline would care to come with us," suggested Phoebe hopefully.

"Excellent idea," said Clarence. "Let us all go."

But Caroline had other plans. Phoebe would be safe enough from the villain with Clarence along, and Caroline wished to question Jarvis more on the family history. She declined the offer and sent Phoebe off to her fate. She smiled at Jarvis and said,

"I do believe, as it is such a fine morning I should enjoy a chance to puzzle out the secret of the maze. It was so cold when I was out with Phoebe yesterday we got no farther than the rose garden."

"I should be delighted to show you," said Jarvis.

Fifteen minutes later they were lost between high hedges, Jarvis laughing with each wrong turn his companion chose. "Do you want help?" he finally offered.

"No, no. Please do not assist me," Caroline suggested. "I wish to discover the secret for myself."

"You are a woman who delights in a challenge," observed Jarvis.

"I cannot deny it," said Caroline. "And this family into which my sister is marrying challenges me greatly, I must confess. This sudden resurrection of the younger brother is most surprising."

"The fact he returned at all is surprising in itself," said Jarvis.

Caroline looked at him questioningly.

"May I be frank?" he asked.

"Indeed, I wish you might," said Caroline.

"There has always been . . ." Jarvis paused, searching for the right word.

"Bad blood?" suggested Caroline.

"No, not precisely. Let us call it a strong competition, which has persisted between the brothers over the years. Damien always hated being the younger son. He was smarter than Clarence, and I think he resented the fact that the title and the lands would one day go to his older brother. He and the old earl were very much alike. Tempers often flared."

Caroline could well imagine the kind of scenes that would be enacted between father and son. She took a wrong turn, and Jarvis pointed in the opposite direction.

"Damien was always wilder than Clarence," he continued. "Of course, he always got the blame for any mischief, even when we were boys. I suppose each of his children was a disappointment to the old earl—Clarence, because he had not the head nor the heart which his brother had for the estate, and Damien because he must go his own way. He rejected his father's plans for him to enter the church."

"The church!" exclaimed Caroline in disbelief.

"The old earl was not always wise in his choices," admitted Jarvis. "Damien, with his temper, was no more suited to the church than a cat to water. He was mad for a military career, but his father would have none of that and refused to buy him a commission."

"How very odd," said Caroline.

"Sometimes my uncle was a little odd," Jarvis admitted. "Perhaps he thought the church would settle Damien. At any rate, Damien would have no part of it. He went to India to make his fortune." Jarvis sighed heavily. "Obviously, he has not succeeded. He is home again, and I cannot help but wonder if he doesn't still wish the title for himself."

Caroline's eyes widened. "Gracious!" she exclaimed. "How badly do you think he wants it?"

Jarvis hastened to assure Caroline that Damien surely didn't want it badly enough to do anything desperate. "If that is what you are thinking I am sure you are very mistaken."

Caroline suspected Jarvis only half-believed what he was saying, and she wondered aloud if Damien would be above stirring up trouble between Clarence and her sister.

"It is obvious he was not pleased to return home to find his brother engaged to be married. But that is to say nothing against your sister. I doubt Damien would be pleased to see his brother engaged to any-one."

The beast, thought Caroline. So he wants to protect his brother from fortune hunters, does he? More likely he wants to prevent his brother from marrying and producing an heir.

That afternoon at tea Caroline turned her eagle eye upon Damien Grayson. He did seem to be fond of his brother and very interested to hear how Clarence had been managing the estate since their father's death. Too interested, perhaps? "Why did you let the north field lie fallow?" Damien was asking.

"Rutherstone advised it," said Clarence.

"Well, if Rutherstone advised it . . ." Damien began. He took a thoughtful sip from his teacup. "The old fellow does have some rather antiquated ideas. I think you should do a little to acquaint yourself with modern farming methods. On the ship I met a fellow who . . ."

The two brothers continued to talk estate business until Phoebe yawned. "Oh, boys," scolded Lady Grayson, "do let us talk of something a little more lively than cows and potatoes. You are quite boring us to tears."

Damien smiled at his mother, and his face suddenly looked kinder, less villainous. "You are right, of course," he said. "Clarence and I can talk of cows and potatoes another time." He turned to Caroline. "I have been remiss. I have yet to ask you how you have been enjoying your stay at Grayson Hall."

"Frankly, sir, I am disappointed," replied Caroline. "I have yet to see up close this famous ghost which is said to walk your halls."

"We could oblige you by draping Clarence in a Holland cover," offered Damien. He turned to his brother. "Remember how we scared poor Miss Timson?"

Clarence guffawed. "You scared her proper," he said.

"No," corrected his brother. "If I remember correctly, I scared her quite improper."

The others laughed and Clarence continued. "By the time Jarvis was done we had all the servants shaking in their shoes."

Jarvis smiled reminiscently and Damien, also smiling, regarded him through narrowed eyes. "Jarvis was always an expert in trickery," he said.

Jarvis's smile chilled. Caroline could feel the sudden tension in the air and shivered. There were undercurrents running in this house which she did not understand—treacherous undercurrents which she had not noticed before Damien's arrival.

She pondered this at length as Sibby brushed out her auburn curls. "The younger brother has brought something into the house which I cannot like," she said.

Sibby shrugged. "The servants all like him. It is said he has a temper, but no one seems to think any the worse of him for it."

"Hmm," said Caroline. She dismissed Sibby and crawled into bed, where she lay unable to sleep, her thoughts pricking her uncomfortably and making her body unwilling to sleep. She was sure, she finally concluded, that she did not wish Clarence's younger brother dead as he had been presumed. But she did wish he was still far away in India, buying and selling spices, or whatever it was second sons and rogues did over there.

A sudden scream shattered her thoughts. Phoebe! Grabbing her wrapper, she raced from her room. She was the first to reach Phoebe's bedchamber. The door stood slightly ajar, an observation that made Caroline's heart thump uncomfortably. Who had been in her sister's room, and what would she find when she entered? Caroline fearlessly burst into the room, calling Phoebe's name. She stubbed her toe in the dark and tumbled to the floor, just out of reach of the black moaning mountain of covers on the bed.

Light spilled into the room as Damien charged in, Clarence on his heels. Naturally, as his attention was all for his beloved, Clarence had not seen Caroline struggling to her feet. Like a wave, he pushed his brother forward and over the kneeling form in front of them and charged to the bed, crying, "Phoebe, Phoebe! Speak to me!"

The room was again plunged into darkness as Damien's candle flew out of his hand and its flame was snuffed out. Damien scrambled off Caroline with muttered apologies and felt around for his fallen candle.

Clarence, meanwhile, was trying at once to comfort his love and discover what had happened, not an easy task, as she was still huddled under her blankets. He took the blanketed form in his arms, imploring it not to cry.

Damien had by now found and relit his candle, and Caroline took a step to the bed. "If you do not allow her out from under those blankets she will not only stop crying, she will stop breathing as well," she snapped. She dug among the covers for Phoebe's head. It finally emerged, damp and gasping for breath. "Phoebe, what has happened?" she demanded.

"I . . . saw it again," Phoebe cried. "The ghost. It was here in my room!"

Lady Harborough had reached the bedchamber by now and Jarvis also, the light from their candles further illuminating the room. Lady Harborough took one look at her daughter's dampened curls and wild look and flew into the room. She wrenched Phoebe from Clarence's arms and cradled her in her own plump ones. "Oh, my poor, poor baby," she crooned.

"I saw it again," Phoebe sobbed.

Surely whoever was playing ghost would not be so bold as to enter Phoebe's room. Caroline's eyes fell on Phoebe's white satin wrapper draped over a chair near the bed. She snatched it up. "There is your ghost," she said.

"I know the difference between a wrapper and a ghost," cried Phoebe scornfully. "Anyway, a wrapper cannot talk."

"The ghost talked to you!" exclaimed Caroline in disbelief. "What did it say?"

"It said, 'Le-e-a-ve,'" Phoebe answered in wobbly tones, and then burst into fresh tears.

"Oh!" cried Lady Harborough unhappily. "What new horror will befall us next if we remain?"

If Lady Grayson had been present, she would have been quick to defend her beloved ghost. Her son, who had yet to see the apparition and was thoroughly confused by the mysterious goings-on in his house, could think of nothing to say to reassure his future mama-in-law. He scratched his head.

His brother was no help. He leaned against the wall, arms folded, a smile on his face. Oh, he would like to see us gone, thought Caroline angrily.

"I am afraid,' said Lady Harborough with solemn dignity, "that I simply cannot allow Phoebe to remain in danger. I am afraid I shall have to refuse the great honor you have done my daughter. We shall consider this engagement at an end."

Caroline's mouth dropped open, and Phoebe now

threw herself into Clarence's arms and began crying even harder. "Mama!" declared Caroline. "Whatever are you thinking of?"

"A very sensible decision, Lady Harborough," said Damien, and Caroline glared at him. "One can hardly blame you for wishing to remove your daughter from such dangerous premises."

"Mama is distraught," said Caroline sternly. "I am sure by morning she will have reconsidered, for I know she would not wish to sacrifice her daughter's future happiness on a whim."

"A whim!" exclaimed Lady Harborough. "My dear Caroline, I would hardly call it a whim wishing to save my daughter from a future filled with visits by terrible apparitions. I am only doing this for her good."

Caroline pointed to her loudly sobbing sister. She was working herself into a state. "*That* can hardly be good for her. At any rate, I have no inclination to leave Grayson Hall until I have seen this ghost in close quarters!"

Damien chuckled. "A true lady of spirit. I daresay if our ghost has overheard Lady Caroline it will be too frightened to show its shadowy face now."

"It would appear it is not going to show again tonight," said Jarvis. "May I suggest we all retire and hope for a glimpse of it another night."

"I, for one, do not want to see it again at all," declared Lady Harborough. "And do not think for a moment, young man, that I shall change my mind," she said, shaking a fat finger at Clarence. "This is all your fault."

Clarence looked pardonably incensed. "I say, it ain't *me* who has been haunting Phoebe. I love the girl."

"Come on, old fellow," said Damien, leading his

brother from the room. "Everything will look better after a good night's sleep."

Caroline shut the door behind them. Phoebe's sobs had quieted, and she lay sniffing in her mama's arms. Lady Harborough looked defiantly at her eldest daughter. Caroline went to the bed and sat on the other side of her sister and patted her arm absentmindedly. "Mama," she began.

"Yes, my dear. I know exactly what you are going to say," said her mother briskly, "and I think you are quite right. It is high time we went back to bed and allowed your sister to get some rest." She kissed Phoebe, ordered her to sleep well, and made a dignified retreat from the room before Caroline could say a word about her hasty decision.

"Drat," muttered Caroline. "Mama has outgeneraled me."

Phoebe raised pitifully swollen eyes to her sister. "I really *did* see the ghost, Caro," she said.

"Yes," said Caroline slowly. "I believe you did see someone. Not a ghost, but someone. Somebody wants very badly to frighten you."

"But why?" asked Phoebe. "Why would someone want to frighten me?"

"So you will leave, of course."

"But who would want me gone?"

A good question, thought Caroline. The list appeared to be growing daily. Isobelle would certainly shed no tears if Phoebe jilted Clarence, unless they were tears of joy. And another face sprang to mind, a handsome, darkly mocking face. Caroline glared at it. "Do not worry, love. Whoever it is now has *me* with whom to deal."

5

Caroline's sleep had been fitful. The burden of her sister's future happiness weighed heavily on her, and she awoke feeling far from refreshed. She studied her face in the looking glass and frowned at the dark smudges under her eyes. "Lord, I look thirty," she said aloud. But if she looked thirty, she felt ninety. How was she ever going to get to the bottom of all this with Phoebe having the vapors and Mama threatening to call things off?

She came down to breakfast to find Phoebe looking tired and haggard, and Lady Harborough looking mulish. Clarence and Damien were nowhere to be found. Jarvis, the lone male, was trying to pour oil on troubled waters. Caroline took in Lady Grayson's distraught face and shot him a smile of gratitude.

"Your mama has been telling me the ghost appeared to Phoebe again," Lady Grayson informed her.

"Yes," said Caroline cautiously.

"I know it has been very upsetting to our poor dear girl—" Lady Grayson began.

"I can assure you," interrupted Lady Harborough,

"that it has been equally upsetting to all the members of her family. And I must tell you we are considering—"

"Looking into this matter more carefully," Caroline finished for her.

Caroline's mama looked perturbed at her daughter's high-handed intervention and began again. "What I am trying to say is—"

"That we are very concerned about the state of Phoebe's nerves," said Caroline, once again preventing her mama from making her deadly announcement.

"Phoebe and Clarence must—"

"Mama!" exclaimed Caroline and Phoebe in unison.

"Must," continued Lady Harborough ruthlessly, "not marry."

Lady Grayson looked as though she herself had seen the ghost. Her eyes bulged and her face paled. Her mouth dropped open, and she set down her teacup with a clatter. "Whatever can you mean?" she asked in trembling accents.

"Mama, please," protested Caroline.

"It is not safe for Phoebe to marry Clarence," continued Lady Harborough, ignoring her daughter. "We shall have to call off the wedding. And I feel we should leave Grayson Hall as soon as possible, before that horrid ghost murders my child."

"But surely if our ghost were going to murder her it would have done so by now," protested Lady Grayson. "This is simply too dreadful. Why, this would break my dear Clarence's heart. Oh, you cannot do such a thing. You simply cannot. And what of the Allhallows Eve ball?"

"You cannot have sent out the invitations yet," said Lady Harborough heartlessly.

"No, but you may well remember we spent an entire afternoon only last week writing them. All our neighbors know of it, as well as most all our friends. Many have not yet met Phoebe and plan to come for just that purpose. We shall look utter fools. And poor Clarence. What am I to tell him? Oh, it is utterly ridiculous. We certainly cannot call off the wedding. No one has ever discarded a Grayson."

"But, my dear, I can assure you we are not discarding Clarence," insisted Lady Harborough. "Such a dear boy. I am merely trying to save my daughter's life."

Caroline looked pleadingly across the table at Jarvis, who merely shrugged helplessly.

"I cannot understand why our ghost is being so inhospitable to Phoebe," said Lady Grayson. "She is such a sweet child and perfect for my Clarence. She is the first girl who ever completely captured his heart. He always used to say he was not much in the petticoat line. We were only able to get him to stir himself after we thought Damien was dead," she explained to Caroline. "He is a loyal son and, naturally, knew his duty. And even though we tried hard to find a suitable female, I must confess I began to despair of ever finding a girl who would make a proper wife for Clarence. He said so many of them were too clever by half, and they made him uncomfortable. Phoebe is so sweet and Clarence can talk to her so easily and, oh, it will simply break his heart if he cannot marry her," she ended miserably.

"And Phoebe wants to stay," put in Caroline. On seeing the doubtful look on Phoebe's face, she hurriedly added. "She loves Clarence. Don't you dearest?" Phoebe nodded mutely and Caroline continued, "Mama, let us not do something hasty which will ruin Phoebe's future happiness. After all, the ghost has not made any attempt to hurt her," she added, hoping her mother would forget the fact that the ghost had spoken to Phoebe.

Lady Grayson seconded this. "Oh, yes. Let us not be hasty. It would quite break Clarence's heart if Phoebe were to reject him."

A little more pleading, a little more reasoning and Lady Harborough relented. "Very well," she said. "But I must reserve the right to remove my daughter if I feel the danger she is in to be increasing."

"Very well," agreed Lady Grayson. "But let us have no more talk of broken engagements. You must promise me, my dear," she said, taking Lady Harborough's hand. "As mothers we must join forces to ensure our children's happiness."

Lady Harborough was stirred to tears by this inspiring speech. "Oh, yes," she said, and Caroline breathed a sigh of relief.

"I am glad the future of Clarence and his beloved is once more secure," Jarvis said to her as they enjoyed a brisk walk in the garden later that morning.

"It was kind of you to jump into the fray," said Caroline. "But I must say," she continued teasingly, "I had not expected you to retreat when the battle became intense and leave me alone."

"Ah, but you handled it beautifully," said Jarvis. "I do believe, fair lady, you would have made an admirable diplomat's wife." Caroline smiled at him and he said, "Let me amend that statement. You would make *any* man an admirable wife."

Caroline blushed and said lightly, "I did. Once."

Jarvis led her to a small stone bench. "Do I detect a note of finality in that statement?" he asked charmingly.

"I was very happy as a bride," said Caroline. "But I am not unhappy as I am." In fact, I like my freedom, she thought to herself.

As if reading her mind, Jarvis said, "I suspect you rather enjoy your freedom."

Once again, Caroline blushed. It seemed, somehow, disloyal to her husband's memory to admit she had become rather fond of her widowed state, and she felt much as if she had been caught in an indiscretion. She turned the subject. "How very depressing a rose garden is in the autumn," she sighed, looking at the skeletal bushes. "The bushes look so very dead one wonders how they will ever come to life again."

"Spring always returns," said Jarvis, lifting her hand to his lips. The gentle brush of his lips sent a feeling fluttering through Caroline which reminded her there were some benefits to marriage that widowhood could not provide. "Perhaps we should go in," she suggested. "Much as I enjoy the fresh air, I must admit it is beginning to turn too cold even for my tastes." They rose and headed back to the house. "I am surprised we have not had more rain," she said conversationally.

"Yes," said Jarvis, following her lead and dropping more intimate subjects. "Let us hope the rainy season holds off until after my cousin's ball."

"Yes," agreed Caroline. "Entertaining is so much easier when the roads are not sloppy, and the guests have had a comfortable drive and not had to deal with their carriage wheels being bogged down in the mud."

Jarvis nodded. "How many parties have you failed to attend after looking out your window and then looking again to your comfortable fire?"

Caroline laughed. "You know my mama and my sister. How many parties do you think I am likely to have missed for such a feeble reason? And you do not strike me as a recluse. How many have you missed?"

Jarvis had to admit, when pressed, there had been few parties he had failed to attend because of foul weather. "Although there have been times when the weather provided a plausible excuse."

"Fie on you," laughed Caroline. "How very plausible an excuse do you really consider the weather?" Jarvis hung his head and she laughed again. "I suspect, sir, you can count on one hand the number of parties you have missed on account of weather. Or anything else." He smiled conspiratorially at her. "Now, your cousin," she continued. "I could well imagine missing a party on any excuse at all, no matter how flimsy."

"I suppose you mean Damien," he said.

Caroline nodded. "He really is a most unpleasant man," she said, remembering the conversation they had on their first meeting.

Jarvis's smile appeared to hold a touch of bitterness. "He has never had a need to make himself pleasant. However, that is not to say he cannot. When it suits him to do so, Damien can be most pleasant."

Caroline did not appear convinced. "I suppose you would be in a position to know," she said. "But your cousin seems to me a modern-day Hesiod, determined to blame his troubles on the nearest available female."

Jarvis's eyebrow crept up, and the corner of his mouth twitched.

Caroline caught the indulgent look on his face and gave him a saucy smile. "Yes," she said. "Your suspicions are correct. My stockings are just the tiniest bit blue."

They came laughing into the house and stumbled onto Clarence and Damien, emerging from the study. "Hey ho," called Clarence. "You are both very merry."

Caroline's face was flushed from the cold. A whisp

70

of hair had blown across her cheek, and she brushed it back and smiled at her future brothers-in-law. Damien wore his usual mocking smile, and the appraising look with which he favored her made Caroline's cold face feel suddenly very warm. Insolent brute, she thought, but lightly said, "On an autumn day as lovely as this, one cannot help but feel merry."

"Was it the lovely autumn day which was making you so merry, then?" demanded Jarvis. "I must admit for me it was the company . . . Pandora," he added in a low voice.

Caroline blushed again. "Will you gentlemen please excuse me?" she said, and beat a hasty retreat to shed her cloak and bonnet before luncheon.

That afternoon, at Lady Grayson's invitation, Isobelle drove over and joined the family for tea. She was ushered into the drawing room, a vision in a dark blue gown, her hair caught up by a matching ribbon. She paused a moment to smile at everyone. Her eyes fell on Damien and widened for an instant before the lids fluttered over them and she fell to the floor, her gown billowing around her.

"Isobelle!" squeaked Lady Grayson.

"Hartshorn!" prescribed Lady Harborough, digging in her reticule.

All three men rushed to her side. Jarvis and Clarence collided with each other in the process, giving Damien an edge. Phoebe, who had been sitting nearest the door was already on one side of the fallen beauty, chafing her hand, and Damien knelt on the other, taking her in his arms.

"Put her on the sofa," commanded Lady Grayson.

Damien scooped Isobelle up. "I do wish people would stop fainting at the sight of me," he complained.

"I suppose I should have mentioned something about your return in my invitation," said Lady Grayson.

"I suppose you should have, dearest," agreed Damien, laying his burden on the sofa.

Before Damien could remove his arm from around her, Isobelle's eyes fluttered open. "Damien," she whispered, and Caroline thought how like a caress she made the word sound. "We thought you were dead."

"Poor Izzy," murmured Damien. "This must come as a shock."

"Really, Damien," snapped Isobelle. "We are not children anymore. I wish you would not call me by that ridiculous name."

Damien released his hold on her. "There was a time when you liked it," he said softly. He moved away from the sofa and picked up his teacup. "It would appear my death was reported a trifle prematurely," he said. "Wishful thinking, perhaps?"

"Damien!"

Damien looked at his mother. Even at her sternest it was impossible for Lady Grayson to look forbidding. He smiled fondly at her and continued. "I very nearly died, but as you can see I am now fully recovered."

And restored to the bosom of your family, thought Caroline cynically. And if they are fond of taking vipers to their collective bosom I am sure they are very happy.

But the odd thing was, she had to admit, his family did seem genuinely happy to have him back. Lady Grayson, an indescriminatingly doting mother had talked enthusiastically of her naughty second son's return. But then, Lady Grayson loved everyone, including inhospitable ghosts. And Clarence seemed as delighted as his mama to have Damien back. But Clarence was a dolt. Sweet and kind, yes. But definitely a dolt. Clarence, if faced with brigands or thieves would react with all necessary speed and alertness. But Caroline doubted his ability to detect more subtle dangers. He was simply too trusting. Beside herself and possibly Phoebe (whose fear would be instinctual rather than logical), Jarvis alone seemed aware of the possible threat Damien presented.

Caroline watched with interest as Isobelle sat up and received her teacup from Lady Grayson with a shaking hand. Obviously, Damien had an unnerving effect on her. Of course, Caroline admitted, suddenly seeing someone whom one had supposed to be dead was bound to have an unnerving effect on a person. Damien would have no need of a costume for the Allhallows Eve ball. He could come as himself and easily scare the wits out of half his guests.

Isobelle did not stay long. She made a valiant effort to regain her composure and failed in the end. She finally begged to be excused, feeling sure her papa must have need of her. The ladies kindly accepted this feeble excuse and, nodding their understanding, they sent her off with their blessings. "Let me see you safely on your way," Damien offered, following her out. Isobelle made no objection. What good would it have done her? thought Caroline. Damien was obviously a man who never let others' objections prevent him from doing what he pleased.

"Well, well," said Clarence after the two had left the room. "I do think Belle is glad to see Damien."

"Such a dear girl," murmured Lady Grayson.

"I wonder," said Lady Harborough, fishing again, "if there is another Grayson wedding in the future."

73

"Damien and Isobelle?" asked Lady Grayson in surprise.

"Damien don't care for Belle above half," scoffed Clarence.

"Well, he used to when you were all younger," said his mama.

"'Til she started chasing after me," said Clarence. "After that he said he wouldn't have her if she came begging."

"It would be nice to see both my sons happily married," said Lady Grayson.

"Damien won't have trouble finding a female to marry him," said Clarence.

"I don't know," said Jarvis doubtfully. "It is not always so easy for a second son."

Lady Harborough looked thoughtful at this comment.

Damien reentered the room and the subject was quickly and politely changed.

Caroline watched him as he helped himself to a tiny slice of buttered bread and lounged lazily in a chair next to his mama. No, she thought, taking in the well-muscled thighs and the frilled shirt which could not hide an equally well-muscled chest, if Damien could win a bride on looks alone he would have no trouble. Her eyes moved upwards to the face and met dark eyes looking back into hers. An insolent smile curved his lips, informing her he knew exactly what she was thinking. Again Caroline felt a betraying blush spread across her face and tried to look away as nonchalantly as possible. Unfortunately for the Honorable Damien Grayson, it took more than good looks to get a man a wife. It took fortune and manners. And he was obviously lacking in both.

Afternoon tea concluded and family and houseguests disbursed—the men to the shovelboard parlor to play billiards and the ladies to rest before dressing for dinner.

Caroline accompanied the women upstairs, but, after seeing the others safely tucked away in their rooms, snuck back in to the corridor to continue her search for a priest's hole. Afte the previous night she was more convinced than ever that her persistence would be rewarded.

She was still sounding walls when Jarvis came upon her an hour later. "Looking for ghosts?" he asked.

Caroline smiled at him and shook her head. "I do not believe in ghosts, but I do believe in clever women. I am looking for a priest's hole where a pretend ghost could conveniently hide after frightening my sister."

"You are a very clever woman yourself," said Jarvis, "to think of such a possibility. What makes you think our ghost is a woman?"

"Two reasons," replied Caroline. "Legend has determined that the ghost be a woman. And this seems a woman's trick. A woman would try to frighten away an adversary. I believe a man would be perhaps a little more direct. A man would merely challenge his enemy to a duel or arrange a fatal accident and be done with the problem."

"But what female of our acquaintance would wish to drive your sister away, and why?"

"I have met a woman who would have good reason to wish my sister gone," said Caroline.

Understanding dawned, and Jarvis shook his head in disbelief. "Oh, now you are not going to go picking on poor Isobelle simply because she has fancied herself in love with both my cousins at one time or another, are you? And even if Isobelle were your ghost how would she get into the house in the dead of night?"

"She could have an accomplice inside the house," Caroline suggested.

"There are no suspicious females in this house," Jarvis pointed out.

"Then perhaps she has found a man to help her—someone who would prefer a more direct method but who is not above helping an enterprising lady if it seems to favor his cause."

Jarvis paled. "And now I suppose you will be accusing me of helping her."

Caroline smiled at him. "I had no such intention."

"Who else, then, do you consider worthy of the honor of being Belle's accomplice?" he asked.

"Perhaps an old childhood sweetheart recently returned to England," said Caroline, gently tapping the wall.

"Whom she thought dead and fainted at the sight of?" Jarvis's tone was slightly mocking.

Caroline chewed her lip thoughtfully. "I wouldn't be surprised to learn that Isobelle feigned her surprise. Perhaps your cousin returned from India earlier than any of us knew."

"I suppose that is possible," said Jarvis, rubbing his chin. "But I find this all a little difficult to believe. Damien is not the sort of man to resort to trickery."

"I quite agree," said Caroline. "But I wonder if he couldn't be persuaded to make an exception if he thought it was in his brother's best interest. *Or* his own, if you take my meaning. And difficult as I find it to believe anyone involved in such a wild scheme, I find it more difficult to believe there is really a ghost trying to frighten my sister away from her future home." Caroline sighed. "There must be a hiding place somewhere but I am having no luck finding it. I am sure that since this house dates from Elizabethan times it contains several priest's holes. And the most likely one for our ghost to hide in must be somewhere along this corridor. If I do not make haste and find it soon, my poor Phoebe will be in Bedlam before I can prove to her that her enemy is merely human."

"And even if you find it," put in Jarvis, "you can have no way of knowing if anyone has been using it." Caroline looked so crestfallen at this new thought that Jarvis laughed and said, "But then, again, your ghost may have left behind some telltale sign of its humanity. Let me help you look. I seem to remember a priest's hole somewhere near this end of the corridor. Clarence and Damien found it when they were boys. Clarence has most likely forgotten it, but I am sure Damien would remember where it is. In fact, so should I now that I think of it. I remember Damien shutting me in it once."

They proceeded along the corridor and began to sound the walls. Caroline could feel her excitement riding high. She expected a door to fly open before her very eyes at any moment.

Naturally, it was very disappointing when after half an hour they had still found nothing. "I am sorry," said Jarvis. "Alas, I suspect it has been too many years. I felt so sure I could remember its location."

"Thank you for trying," said Caroline. "I suppose it is nearing time to dress for dinner," she said regretfully.

"A pity we keep country hours here," agreed Jarvis. They strolled by unspoken consent in the direction of Caroline's bedchamber. "You may console yourself with this thought," said Jarvis. "Your ghost will most likely give you a few nights' respite. I am sure she prefers not to become a familiar."

Caroline acknowledged the pun and said, "I am sure she realizes she increases her chances of capture with each new appearance. You are right. She will not wish to overplay her hand." Caroline laid her hand on the door handle and turned her most charming smile on her companion. "Thank you again for your help," she said.

He bowed. "It was my pleasure," he said.

She watched him go down the hall. He was a fine-looking man. Built on smaller lines than his cousins, yes, but handsome just the same. And charming. What are you thinking? Caroline scolded herself. You are by no means lonely. And even if you were would you want to sacrifice your freedom for companionship?

Of course, she admitted, there had been nothing in her marriage which could account for such a fierce desire to remain free. Her Harold had been an exceptional man. But he had left her in a position of independence, which allowed her to do as she pleased when she pleased. Could she remarry and still live as she did now? Perhaps, if she found a man of equally independent spirit. Was Jarvis Woolcock such a man?

Caroline left the question unanswered and went into her bedchamber where she found Sibby fussing over her gowns. "Would you care to wear the green satin tonight?" suggested Sibby, holding up the gown.

It was Caroline's favorite, high-waisted with a décolletage low enough to leave little to the imagination. The gown's dark green color showed off her creamy skin and auburn curls, and when she was wearing it men rushed to fetch punch for her and trampled each other in an effort to talk to her.

Just because a lady had no intention of remarrying was no reason she should deny herself an occasional flirtation. Was the handsome Jarvis Woolcock fond of green? She would like to see. "Yes, I shall wear it," she said. "And the emeralds."

Sibby laid out her dress and began to search for a shawl, and Caroline sat down at her dressing table to review the events of the afternoon. In turn, each person who had been present at tea stood before her mind's eye and was subjected to her scrutiny. First there was Mama. She certainly was not making her daughter's job easy. When she was not trying to find a husband for Caroline she was busy attempting to rid Phoebe of hers. How could Caroline keep her mother from haring off with Phoebe before she could solve this puzzle? And Phoebe was nearly as hard to manage as Mama. And Isobelle. What did she really think about Damien's sudden return from the grave. Had she known of it before his family? Had her faint been a little too theatrical?

Caroline peered into her looking glass and demanded an honest answer of herself. Was she picking on Isobelle merely because she was beautiful and had known Clarence before Phoebe had appeared on the scene? Was she a rival to Phoebe only in Caroline's imagination? Caroline discarded the thought instantly. No. Isobelle was a wicked creature. Of that much Caroline was certain, and she could not afford to be fair or generous, not when Phoebe's safety was at stake.

But if Isobelle was their ghost, how was she getting in and out of the house? There was still only one answer to this question that Caroline could see. Isobelle had to have an accomplice. And if that were so, Damien remained the obvious choice. Since he stood behind his brother in line for the title, he would certainly be in no hurry for Clarence to marry and produce an heir. What a pair of villains! Where was he hiding her? Caroline drummed her fingers on the table. "Drat!" she exclaimed, jumping up.

Sibby jumped, too. "What is it?" she asked.

Caroline began to pace. "Why can I not find anything?" she asked herself in irritation.

"But what do you need?" asked Sibby, confused. "I have laid out your gown. And here is a lovely shawl to match."

"I was not speaking of clothes," Caroline explained. "I was speaking of hiding places. Where is that ghost hiding when she is not chasing Phoebe?"

"It is a big house," ventured Sibby.

"Yes, it is. But I shouldn't need to search the entire house to find what I am looking for," said Caroline. "I must concentrate my efforts. If the hidey-hole is not in the corridor it must be . . ." She stopped and tapped her chin thoughtfully. "Aha!" she exclaimed, and grabbed a candle from her nightstand.

"But where are you going?" demanded Sibby, watching as her mistress lit the candle and headed for the door. "It is time to dress for dinner."

"I shall return in a few minutes," promised Caroline. "Wait," she said, turning and smiling at her maid. "Bear me company. I think I am about to make an exciting discovery."

Sibby looked anything but excited about the promised discovery, but obediently followed her mistress out into the hall.

Caroline knew exactly where she was heading and darted quietly down the hallway, entering the empty bedchamber nearest the main stairway. Sibby timidly followed her in and stood looking around, perplexed, while her mistress headed to the nearest wall and began tapping. "Come help me," she commanded.

Again, Sibby obeyed. "But what are we doing?" she said, tapping reluctantly.

"We are looking for a priest's hole, a secret cupboard where someone could conveniently hide after masquerading as a ghost. I don't know why I did not think to start here before. It stands to reason it would be much safer to hide in a room rather than right off the corridor. One would have a few more precious seconds to secrete one's self away. Whereas the corridor—if our villainess tripped or became flustered she would be risking discovery."

Caroline moved to the inner end of the room and began to tap on the wall. She moved along, tapping and listening. "What is this?" she said suddenly, then moved a foot to the right and tapped again. A smile began to grow on her face, and she moved and tapped again where she had previously stood. She stood for a moment, studying the wall. Wordlessly, she handed her candle to Sibby, who nervously shifted feet and reminded her mistress of the necessity of dressing for dinner.

Caroline laid both her hands against the top of the wall and pressed against it. The board yielded and swung outwards, revealing a slit through which an average-sized person could easily squeeze. Taking the candle from Sibby, Caroline held it up and peered in. "Would you look at that," breathed Sibby.

Before the ladies was a small cupboard, not more than five feet high, lined with oak paneling. Caroline lowered her candle and looked at the dusty floor. Small footprints formed a pattern in the dust and here and there a small path had been etched, a path which looked very much as if it could have been made by a lady's skirt.

"And what, pray, have you found?" asked a voice from the doorway.

6

Caroline and Sibby both jumped, letting out startled squeaks. "Oh, you scared us to death," said Caroline, pressing a hand against her pounding heart.

Jarvis strolled into the room, resplendent in dinner attire. "I did not mean to. I was on my way downstairs when I heard what I thought must be giant mice scratching around in this room. The door was open and I must confess, my curiosity got the better of me."

"I do apologize for not fetching you," said Caroline. "But after all your earlier help it hardly seemed kind to haul you off on what could have been yet another goose chase."

"Well, I am glad to see that this time your efforts have been rewarded." Jarvis peered over her shoulder into the small room. "A most uncomfortable place to spend very much time I should think," he said.

"Yes, indeed," agreed Caroline. "How anyone could remain here for long without suffering from a sneezing fit is more than I can fathom. And now that I think of it I suppose I had best not remain in this room any longer or I shall never have time to dress for dinner."

Jarvis moved out of her way and smiled down at her. "I should imagine we will not run out of dinner conversation tonight," he said.

Caroline was silent a moment.

"What is it?" asked Jarvis.

"Would you mind terribly not mentioning anything about our discovery just yet?" Jarvis looked perplexed. "I think I should like an opportunity to lay a trap for our ghost," explained Caroline. "This will be a useful secret."

"As you wish," he said and escorted her from the room.

Caroline wore her green dress to dinner and was gratified to see the look of appreciation, not only on Jarvis's face, but mirrored in the faces of his cousins as well. "You look absolutely stunning tonight," said Jarvis, leading her in to dinner.

Caroline flashed him a brilliant smile and thanked him. Looking one's best did give one such a feeling of confidence, she thought, slipping her napkin onto her lap.

After dinner the two older women settled down to gossip and snooze. Clarence suggested he and Jarvis continue a project which they had started before Caroline arrived—teaching Phoebe to play piquet. This agreed with Damien, who had already announced his intention to become better acquainted with his future sister-in-law and was now ruthlessly propelling Caroline from the room. "Do you play billiards?" he asked, ushering her into the shovel-board parlor.

Caroline looked around her. The room was also sometimes referred to as the green salon and she could see why. Dark green carpet covered the floor and matching green drapes hung at the windows. The room was definitely a male domain. Besides a billiard table it contained several comfortable leather chairs. There were few frills, and the room smelled faintly of tobacco. "Billiards is a man's game," Caroline said, accepting a cue stick. "What makes you think I would know how to play?"

"You do not strike me as a conventional female," said Damien. "I could well imagine you playing at billiards." He set up the balls and motioned to the table, inviting her to go first.

Caroline bent over her cue stick, eyed the balls carefully, and broke them, successfully sending one into a leather pouch at the far corner.

"Beginner's luck?" asked Damien teasingly.

Caroline merely smiled and took aim again. Another ball shot into a leather pocket. On her third try she missed her shot and with a nod, abandoned the field to her opponent.

"I would be willing to wager," he said slowly, walking round the table, "that you do not attend silver loo parties or paint watercolors. You have bluestocking tendencies, but think you have concealed them well enough that no one would guess." Caroline made no reply and he continued. "I would also be willing to wager you are a bruising rider and you are not the least afraid of . . . mice," he concluded. Caroline acknowledged his perspicacity with the faintest of nods, and he took his shot. Repositioning himself on another side of the table he took another. "So. Since we both know you to be a fearless and intelligent woman, tell me, what do you think of this ghost which has become so restless after all these years?"

What was the man up to? Was he trying to discover how much she suspected about his nefarious activities? "I think it is all very peculiar," said Caroline. "And a very handy tool for someone unscrupulous enough to frighten a poor, silly girl into doing what they want. But her sister is not so silly, nor so easily frightened," she concluded, her look a challenge.

Damien watched thoughtfully as Caroline took her turn, sinking ball after ball into various leather pockets around the table. He gave her a respectful nod as the last ball fell into its pocket.

"I believe I have beaten you," she said, her smile a challenge.

"For now," he said with an answering smile. "But I am sure we will have a chance to match our skills again soon. Then we shall see."

They returned to the others, and Caroline was pleased to see her sister looking relaxed and happy in spite of her scare the previous night and her upsetting morning. Phoebe would be very happy as the countess of Alverstoke, living here with Clarence and his mama, and Caroline intended to make sure that happened. As they went upstairs to bed, Caroline found herself hoping the ghost would put in an appearance so she could expose the villains, but it was a clever one, and as Jarvis had predicted, left them alone.

Next morning Caroline decided it would be wise to let her sister in on her discovery. She dressed quickly for church then went along before breakfast to Phoebe's room. As she approached the door she heard the muffled sound of wailing and, without pausing to knock, entered. She found her sister in tears, her lady's maid bending over scattered sparkling shards of glass. "It slipped," wailed Phoebe.

"Seven year's bad luck," bemoaned Rose.

"Oh, cannot Clarence and I move to Wembly Manor and live with you?" Phoebe begged her sister. "Now that Clarence's brother is home I am sure he would not mind living here and running things."

"Phoebe!" Caroline scolded. "You must try to get a firm grip on your nerves."

"I cannot," said Phoebe. "That horrid ghost has me so upset."

"There is no such thing as ghosts," Caroline said. "It is all superstition. We have even found the place where the imposter hid," she said, and proceeded to tell Phoebe of the previous day's find.

"An old cupboard," said Phoebe scornfully.

"A priest's hole," Caroline corrected her. "Do you not remember this house was built in Elizabethan times? I would be willing to wager there are hidey-holes all over the house. Someone who knew their location could easily lie in wait to pop out and scare you and then quickly escape and hide themselves before you had time to collect your wits."

Phoebe shuddered. "I do wish Clarence lived in a new house. New houses do not have ghosts."

"Neither does this one," snapped Caroline. "Phoebe, love, have you not been listening to a word I have said?"

"Of course I have. But I do not see how finding an old cupboard helps prove anything. If the ghost is a person running around hiding in cupboards, how, pray, did she get into the house in the first place when all the doors were locked. And how could she have gotten out and left the doors locked behind her?"

"I suspect our ghost has an accomplice," said Caroline. Phoebe's eyes widened, and her lower lip began to tremble. "Now, do not worry, dearest," Caroline said, patting her sister's shoulder. "I have a plan. I am going to trap your ghost and put an end to this nonsense once and for all."

"When?" demanded Phoebe. "Tonight?"

"No," replied Caroline. "Somehow it hardly seems proper to be chasing spirits whether real or imaginery on a Sunday. But tomorrow night will do quite nicely.''

"Oooh," shuddered Phoebe. "You do not need me there, do you? The last time I saw the thing I nearly died of fright."

"No, love. I shall do fine without you. Come now. Let us go down to breakfast. It will never do to make the family late for church."

In its early days, when the house of Grayson was strongly Catholic, the family had gone no farther to church than the chapel, which had been an integral part of the structure. Now, however, the family was Church of England. The chapel went unused and the family went in to Upper Swanley, theoretically to obtain religious instruction, but in reality to impress the community and remind one and all of their benevolent presence.

Seeing Damien in the family pew caused as much excitement as Caroline had supposed it would. Word had spread of his miraculous return from the grave, and the townsfolk had turned out en masse to catch a glimpse of him.

"I know they did not come to hear my sermon," commented the vicar at dinner that evening.

"That may be true for some," replied Damien. "But not for all. I know I came with just that purpose in mind."

The vicar's wife smiled at him. "It is good to have you back again."

Damien twirled the stem of his goblet between his fingers. "Once again the good people of Upper Swanley will have something to talk about."

"As they did when you left," said Jarvis.

Damien shot him an angry look, and the vicar kindly put in, "You add color to our days." He smiled and shook his head. "How you and your fine brother used to torment my poor curate when you were lads. I can still remember the time you glued the pages of his favorite book together.''

A blushing Damien cleared his throat nervously and attempted to silence the vicar by nodding in his mama's direction.

"Damien! What is this?'' demanded Lady Grayson. "What have you been up to now?''

"Nothing, mother,'' said her son meekly. "I have been as good as gold since I came home. Have I not, Clarence?''

Clarence nodded.

"Oh, pooh!'' scoffed Lady Grayson. "You always protected your brother, Clarence. Why should you behave any differently now?''

The others laughed and Caroline looked at the two brothers speculatively. Clarence looked at his younger brother with big, innocent, slightly stupid eyes. Yes, Clarence was a trusting soul. His face was open and easily read. There was, however, no plumbing the depths of his brother's dark eyes.

The evening passed quietly and harmlessly. Once again the Hall's legendary apparition chose to stay hidden, and Caroline wondered if her sister's enemy was merely waiting for the house to empty of some of its guests before showing again or was now planning some new and more deadly way to rid herself of her rival. Perhaps she would have to flush it out. "Mama, I would have a word with you,'' she said as the ladies made their way to their rooms.

"Very well, my dear,'' said Lady Harborough. "Come along to my room.''

Caroline waited 'til her mama's maid was finished with her ministrations and had been dismissed before introducing the subject on her mind. "Mama, I want you to move up the date for Phoebe's wedding.''

"Move it up!" exclaimed Lady Harborough, pressing a hand to her breast. "My dear child, you must be jesting. Why, we cannot possibly have your sister ready to be married before April. We have not even finished ordering her bridal clothes. And think of the weather. It is positively dismal in the winter. And most undependable before April. I remember only last year we had a snow flurry in the middle of March."

"I realize it might be a little inconvenient to move up Phoebe's wedding date," admitted Caroline.

"A little inconvenient! Child, have you so soon forgotten your own wedding? Do you not remember what is involved?"

"I have not forgotten, Mama," said Caroline placatingly. "But I feel Phoebe would be ever so much safer. Once she is married she will have Clarence to protect her, and she will not have to worry about this ghost business any more."

Lady Harborough considered this.

"Only think," said Caroline, pushing her advantage home. "With Phoebe safely married you could quit worrying about her and return to London. I am sure Lord Winthrop misses you," she finished innocently.

Again Lady Harborough looked thoughtful. "When did you think we should have the wedding?" she asked.

"A Christmas wedding is always nice," ventured Caroline.

"Christmas!" Lady Harborough was in a panic all over again.

"Just think, Mama. Phoebe can have her wedding dress trimmed with fur and carry a muff trimmed with a sprig of holly. Will not that be charming? And we could have the wedding right here at Grayson

Hall. Just family and a few close friends. Then in the spring we could have a ball to celebrate properly. And Phoebe would be safe. I am sure it would be a relief to Lady Grayson if you were to suggest moving up the date. Everyone would be happy."

A little more fast talking and Caroline had her mama convinced not only that idea was an excellent one, but that it had been her own. We shall kill two birds with one stone, thought Caroline as she went to her room. Phoebe shall become Lady Grayson sooner than originally planned (something for which Clarence will be glad), and I shall flush out the enemy who is trying to destroy my sister's happiness.

"This will bring out our ghost," she told Sibby with a smile. "And when next she walks I shall catch her. And her accomplice."

"A very clever idea," said Sibby. "But why not tell your mother your suspicions?"

Caroline looked at her maid in astonishment. "Sibby. You should not even have to ask such a question. You know Mama. If I told her my suspicions, everyone at Grayson Hall down to the lowest servant would know within a day and the entire neighborhood within a week." Caroline shook her head. "No. It is best if Mama remains ignorant of my suspicions. I took enough of a chance telling Phoebe."

The next morning Lady Harborough put forward the suggestion which she now considered completely her own. Caroline was on hand, holding her breath as her mama spoke, but there had been no cause for worry. Lady Grayson agreed with alacrity. "What an excellent idea," she said. "A Christmas wedding does sound most delightful."

Phoebe shed tears of joy, whispering to her sister that once they were wed she would make sure they remained safely at the Grayson townhouse in London until the ghost had been exorcised.

I hope it will not come to that, thought Caroline.

The weather was still holding fine, and Clarence soon appeared in the doorway to offer the sisters an invitation for a morning ride. "I should love some exercise," said Caroline.

Phoebe was not the horsewoman her sister was, but she agreed to leave the cozy winter parlor and venture out in the crisp autumn air.

Before whisking the ladies away, Clarence was informed of the change in plans regarding his nuptials and greeted the news enthusiastically, scooping Phoebe up and swinging her around.

"Clarence," scolded his mama. "Please try for some decorum. Whatever will Lady Harborough think?" Caroline suspected what Lady Harborough thought was really of little concern to Clarence, but he did as he was bid and sedately escorted the sisters from the room.

An hour later, five elegantly dressed riders trotted through a copse of silver birch trees, Phoebe accompanied by the two Grayson brothers and Caroline and Jarvis following behind.

"Clarence tells me the date for his wedding has been moved up," said Jarvis.

Caroline nodded.

"I wonder. Is that a wise thing to do considering the fact that this ghost which so dislikes your sister has not yet been caught?"

"I intend to catch the ghost very soon," replied Caroline. "In fact, I am going to lie in wait for it, starting tonight. If our ghost is going to be rid of my sister before she marries Clarence at Christmas, she will need to begin haunting Phoebe in earnest. Won't she?"

Jarvis studied Caroline's face. She returned his look with one of unblushing innocence. "I do believe this ghost has a worthy adversary in you, Lady Caroline," he said.

"It has," Caroline answered lightly. She watched Damien turn his horse and canter toward them and her eyes narrowed. "And I *shall* catch it," she added as he joined them. He turned his horse and walked beside them. "In fact," she continued, eyeing him, "if the ghost were to appear tonight I could catch it."

He cocked an eyebrow. "I should like to see that," he said.

"You shall. Although if you are present, perhaps our ghost will not show," replied Caroline boldly. "Or will be unable to."

Damien's eyes narrowed and an angry flush stole across his face. "And what might that mean?"

"Why, what should it mean?" asked Caroline. "You do not appear to me to be a man who is afraid of ghosts. Mayhap they are afraid of you."

Damien eyed her suspiciously.

"I wonder," Caroline continued provocatively, "are you not just the tiniest bit afraid I shall catch your ghost?"

"*My* ghost! What the devil do you mean by that?"

"Ah, ah. Temper, temper," cautioned Jarvis, and Damien scowled at him.

Caroline had not meant for this conversation to go so far, but now, goaded by Damien, she pushed it further yet. "I mean that it was not until shortly before you returned home from India that this . . . ghost appeared. What a very odd coincidence, to be sure. If I remember correctly, before this rash of appearances the last time she walked she turned out to be . . ." Caroline peeked coquettishly up at him from under the veil of her riding hat. "You. Was it not? Running the halls in a Holland cover."

Damien's jaw began to work. "So I am suspect, am I? Playing some woman's trick to frighten my brother's intended senseless, an accomplishment which, from the looks of it, would be no difficult task."

It was now Caroline's turn to seethe, and she glared at the handsome, angry face.

"I shall make you an offer, my clever lady," said Damien. "Go ahead and wait for your ghost. I will stay by your side the entire time, always under your watchful eye."

"Tonight?" asked Caroline, taking up the gauntlet.

"Tonight," agreed Damien.

"Very well," said Caroline. "You will remain where I can see you at all times, starting when we return to the Hall."

Damien bowed. "You will, of course, forgive me if I do not invite you to bear me company while I am dressing for dinner. I do not think my mother would understand."

Caroline flushed at this statement and tossed her head angrily. "I fear you have been away too long, sir."

Damien turned his gaze to his brother and Phoebe, riding some twenty feet ahead of them. "Perhaps I have," he said softly. "Nevertheless," he continued, returning his attention to Caroline, "we do wave the British flag in India. Granted, we are only second sons and adventurers, but we are somewhat civilized. And we do not fling wild accusations at people we barely know."

"Oh? You do not?" came the haughty reply.

Jarvis cleared his throat. "Perhaps I had best go chaperone the lovers."

"An excellent idea," agreed Damien. "One can only wonder why you did not think of it sooner."

Jarvis' expression was one of a sorely tried saint. "If he should show signs of becoming violent you have only to call," he told Caroline and cantered ahead of them.

Damien glowered after him. "Curst tulip," he muttered. He turned to Caroline and his expression softened. "I do apologize for that remark about your sister," he said penitently. "I have a nasty temper and a harsh tongue."

"Did you say there was only one attempt on your life when you were in India?" Caroline asked sweetly.

Damien threw back his head and laughed. "You are a fire-eater," he said. "I shall enjoy sticking close to you tonight. I only hope that blasted ghost shows up. If it does not I shall most likely be blamed for it."

"I feel sure the ghost, much like yourself, will be unable to resist a challenge," said Caroline.

Damien eyed her speculatively. "You think so, do you? You are a very clever woman, Lady Caroline," he said, suddenly serious. "Let me offer you a word of advice. Be careful. Even the most clever hunter can sometimes become the hunted."

Caroline was about to ask him to explain himself when Jarvis returned to their side. "I do believe I am not wanted up there," he said.

"You are not wanted here, either," said Damien.

Jarvis ignored this comment and directed his next words to Caroline. "So my cousin joins the ghost hunt tonight, does he?"

"It would appear my presence is very much expected," said Damien. "Either in evening dress or Holland cover."

Caroline and Phoebe returned from their ride to find an invitation from Isobelle waiting for them. "Do come spend the afternoon with me or I shall die of boredom," read Phoebe.

Here was the opportunity for which Caroline had been hoping. "One ghost in the neighborhood is quite enough. We had best go," she said.

Isobelle acted delighted to see the sisters, greeting them warmly. She was looking enviably beautiful that afternoon in a pale pink muslin gown, a cashmere shawl artfully draped around her shoulders. Caroline looked at the beautiful picture she presented and wondered why Clarence hadn't offered for her. Was Isobelle one of those women whom Clarence had described as being too clever by half? Or maybe she had been overconfident, so much so that she failed to act swiftly enough. Watching Isobelle, Caroline suspected the latter. Sure of her prize, Isobelle had not bothered to secure it, and some other woman had stolen it from right under her nose.

"I am so glad you have come," said Isobelle. "Papa is abed with the gout, and I was feeling very solitary." She settled her guests in her elegant drawing room and fed them tea and cakes, serving up some amusing bits of local gossip as well.

"Oh, Isobelle," giggled Phoebe. "I am so going to enjoy being your neighbor."

Isobelle smiled as she poured the last of the tea into Caroline's cup. "I am looking forward to that," she said. "And, really, it will not be long now. April will be here before you know it. Then you shall be married and by the end of summer you will be back and settled into Grayson Hall as its new mistress."

"Phoebe will most likely be mistress of Grayson Hall before then," said Caroline. "The wedding has been pushed forward."

Isobelle was silent a moment but recovered quickly. "Why, how marvelous! When does the happy event take place?"

"Christmas," replied Phoebe.

"My, that is soon," said Isobelle. "So much to plan. Will you be ready?"

"I certainly hope so," said Phoebe. "But even if all my bride clothes are not made I shall still marry Clarence. Then we can go live in London where the ghost can never find us."

"But you cannot live in London forever," protested Isobelle. "You must return to Grayson Hall some time."

"Not," said Phoebe firmly, "until the ghost is gone."

"Don't be such a goose," said Caroline. "Once you are married you will have Clarence by your side to protect you."

"Well, let us see what the future holds," suggested Isobelle gaily. "Are you finished with your tea?" Her companions nodded. "Then turn your teacups over onto your saucers," she commanded, "and we shall read your tea leaves."

"Oh, marvelous!" declared Phoebe. "Isobelle, when did you learn to read tea leaves?"

"A few years ago. We had gypsies camped in the woods. Papa forbid me to go anywhere near them, so naturally I stole away to their camp as often as I could." She lifted her cup from her saucer and studied the leaves. "Oh," she breathed. "The leaves are surely wrong. Look." She pointed to a line of brown specks. "If this is to be believed I shall one day have a nursery bulging with children. One, two, three . . . eight of them. Oh, my! And here is my life line. See how short it is. No wonder, with all those children!"

The three women laughed, and Isobelle motioned for Caroline to hand over her teacup. Caroline obeyed, and Isobelle removed the cup and studied the saucer. "My, my," she said. "The leaves show marriage in the not-too-distant future. And, oh goodness." She smiled at Caroline. "It would appear your nursery will be nearly as full as mine."

Phoebe giggled. "Do me," she urged, lifting up her cup and holding out her saucer.

Isobelle smiled and took it. As she studied it, however, her smile faded.

"What is it?" asked Phoebe. "What is wrong?"

"Nothing. Nothing is wrong," said Isobelle lightly. "Your future is much the same as ours. It is a silly game, anyway, meant to entertain gypsies and children." She put the saucer down.

"No. Something is wrong," said Phoebe. "My tea leaves were not the same as yours. I could tell by your face."

"It is nothing," said Isobelle. "And besides, you probably jiggled the saucer when you handed it to me. Naturally, that would change things."

"Tell me what they said," Phoebe insisted.

Isobelle bit her lip and looked at Phoebe.

"Well?" prompted Phoebe.

"They foretold a fatal accident," she said finally.

Phoebe blanched and gripped the arms of her chair for support.

Caroline looked at Isobelle's face, a study in concern, and wished she could arrange a fatal accident for her. "It is as Isobelle said," she told her sister comfortingly. "Just a game."

"Yes, of course," murmured Phoebe. She bit her lip and her eyes were very bright.

"Oh, dear," said Isobelle. "Please do not let this upset you. Have another seed cake."

Phoebe stared at the plate of cakes and shook her head.

"Would you like to go home, love?" asked Caroline gently, and Phoebe nodded.

"I am so sorry. It was stupid of me," Isobelle began.

"Please do not fret yourself over this. It was one of those things," said Caroline politely. "We really should be going, anyway." I have accomplished what I set out to do, she thought.

"I shall have your carriage brought round," said Isobelle, reaching for the bellpull.

Isobelle was still apologizing when the butler came to announce the sisters' carriage was ready. Caroline turned to their hostess. "Thank you for a . . ." What? She could hardly thank Isobelle for a delightful afternoon. "Thank you for everything," she said. "I am sure we will be seeing you soon." Very soon, she thought. Perhaps tonight?

In spite of Caroline's efforts to set her sister's mind at ease, Phoebe remained convinced her days were numbered. She was somber and quiet at dinner and extremely edgy afterwards. The sisters had been playing cards with Damien and Clarence, Jarvis lounging nearby and advising Phoebe on how to play her hand. In spite of his help, she made Clarence a terrible partner. Three times he had to call her attention to the game. She finally laid down her cards and invited Jarvis to take her place. "I simply cannot concentrate tonight," she apologized, rising. A muffled jangling outside the door made her jump and grab for Clarence. "What was that?" she whispered.

Damien threw a casual glance to the ormolu clock on the mantel. "Judging by the time, I would guess it to be Smythe with the tea tray."

"Oh," Phoebe said and sank into a chair.

Caroline set her jaw. Wait 'til I get my hands on that horrid Isobelle, she thought. She so wants to be a ghost I may just help her become one.

The party broke up early, with Clarence offering to see Phoebe safely to her room.

Jarvis turned to his aunt. "May I escort you and Lady Harborough to bed, Aunt?"

With the idea of bed placed in her head, Lady Grayson decided she was, indeed, tired, and both she and Lady Harborough laid aside their teacups and rose.

Caroline had kept Damien under her watchful eye the entire evening, and she had no intention of leaving him unattended now. As he showed no inclination to leave the room, she remained in her seat, an action of which her mama obviously disapproved. "Caro, love. Are you coming to bed?"

"In a little bit," said Caroline.

"But dearest, we are all going to bed now," said her mother.

"I am not in the least bit sleepy," said Caroline. "You go ahead. I shall be up presently."

Her mother looked at her meaningfully.

Caroline merely laughed. She went to her mother, gave her a gentle kiss and an equally gentle push in the direction of the door. "I am no longer a green girl, Mama. And besides, Damien and I are very near to becoming brother and sister."

"I promise I shall be every inch the gentleman," said Damien soberly.

"Well, of course you will," said his mother complacently.

Lady Harborough shook her head, a guilty blush on her face. "Oh, I certainly did not mean, that is, I would never—"

"Good night, dearest," said Caroline, escorting her mother out the door. She returned to her seat and did her best to ignore Damien's teasing smile. He sat regarding her while she pretended to enjoy her tea, the smile continuing to play on his lips. Finally she could stand it no more. She set her cup down with a clink. "Oh, go on and say it, do. We shall both feel so much the better."

Damien looked surprised. "Say what?" he asked.

Caroline gave him a reproachful look. "You are dying to observe that surely my mama has enough to do looking after her unmarried daughter without hovering over her eldest, who has no need of the same careful guarding," she informed him.

"Do you need guarding?" asked Damien in lively tones. He leaned forward in his chair and looked at her eagerly.

Caroline laughed in spite of herself. "Odious man," she said, and thought, it is a pity you are such a villain.

"I must say that color becomes you," he said. "Nearly as well as that green gown you wore last night. Perhaps you do need someone to stand guard over you."

Jarvis returned and the smile left Damien's face. "And here comes just the person to do so. Have you seen the ladies safely upstairs?" he asked coldly.

Jarvis nodded, his face equally devoid of warmth. He turned to Caroline and his smile returned. "And you are ready to begin our watch?"

Caroline looked at the clock. "I doubt the ghost will show until the house is quiet. We may as well wait her where it is warm a while longer."

Damien sent Smythe off to bed, and they sat in the drawing room, making idle conversation. That is, Caroline and Jarvis made conversation. Damien contributed little, his cousin's arrival seeming to have pushed him into a sullen silence.

Caroline was about to suggest they put out the candles and leave the room when the door opened and Clarence entered. No one had invited Clarence to take part in the ghost watch. Caroline had no knowledge of the others' motives, but for herself she had seen no need to have an extra person along. It would be just one more body to run into or trip over in the heat of the moment. And if anybody was going to get in the way, Caroline was sure it would be Clarence. She smiled at him and wished he would go away.

"What is everyone doing?" he asked.

"Waiting," said Damien.

"Waiting for what?" asked Clarence.

Damien raised his hands and wriggled his fingers menacingly. "For the ghost of Grayson Hall to walk," he replied in a shivering voice.

"Hey ho, what sport!" exclaimed Clarence, rubbing his hands together in anticipation. "Phoebe said Caro was going to try and catch the ghost. I shall wait with you."

Caroline looked at Jarvis, who merely shrugged helplessly. "It may be a long wait," she said discouragingly. "And for all we know the ghost may not even appear tonight."

Clarence shrugged. "Don't feel tired, anyway," he said.

The others were silent. Caroline forced a smile for Clarence and looked at Damien. He was smiling hugely, enjoying the whole thing. He thinks to throw a rub in my way, she thought. But he shan't.

Another half-hour and the ghost hunters deemed it safe to venture upstairs. "You are the leader of this hunt," Damien said to Caroline. "Where would you like us to lie in wait?"

"We should have someone guarding the back stairs to prevent our ghost fleeing in that direction," said Caroline. She turned to Jarvis. "Perhaps you would not mind standing guard over the back stairs."

"You command and I obey," he said with a bow. He turned and ran lightly down the corridor and disappeared partway down the stairs.

What to do with Clarence and Damien? Caroline had no intention of letting Damien out of her sight. For a moment she considered sending Clarence off to stand watch with Jarvis. But if she had to fetch Jarvis for any reason she would be leaving Damien alone, giving him the perfect opportunity to do all manner of mischief. She could easily envision them cornering the ghost in the priest's hole she had discovered, then Damien hiding her in some other place while Caroline went to summon the others. Clarence would make a good messenger. Best keep him with them. "I think the three of us might safely hide together at this end of the corridor," she said.

"Very well," said Damien, and he and Clarence fell in step behind Caroline and followed her into the murky darkness of a deserted bedchamber across from the one where she had found the priest's hole. They left the door partially open, crouched behind it, and peered out.

"This is some sport, eh?" whispered Clarence loudly. He elbowed his brother. "Reminds me of when we were boys. Remember creeping out of bed to hunt for the ghost when we thought everyone was asleep?"

Damien chuckled and whispered back, "You caught it that time. I got back to bed before Father discovered me."

"Left me to face the music," added Clarence. "Dashed unheroic."

"Heroism has never been my strong suit," replied Damien.

"Ssh," hissed Caroline. "You two will scare away our ghost if you do not be quiet."

"Do you think so?" asked Damien.

Caroline was about to make a retort, but Clarence let out a shout and pointed down the corridor, and all conversation was at an end. The three sprang forward, Clarence managing to knock both Caroline and Damien over. "Beg pardon," he muttered. He yanked Caroline to her feet and deserted her, dashing off down the hallway ahead of his brother.

A thud and an "oomph" told her Clarence had encountered yet another obstacle, and she slowed her pace. Damien brushed by her, his candle held high. Even in its weak light it was plain to see the hallway was already deserted. But Caroline didn't care about the corridor. She only cared about the room where she had discovered the priest's hole. "This way," she said.

Damien followed her into the room and the candle's feeble light brought dancing shadows to the walls. Caroline's words seemed to echo in the empty room. "We have her now," she said.

Clarence soon stumbled in after them. "I lost her," he said.

"On the contrary," said Caroline. "We have her. You may fetch your cousin, Clarence," she said over her shoulder.

"By Jove, that is smashing!" declared Clarence. He looked around. "But where is it?"

Caroline smiled triumphantly. "You shall see. But first, please fetch your cousin."

Clarence loped off down the corridor in search of Jarvis, and Caroline folded her arms and gave Damien a smug look.

"So you think you have trapped the ghost," he said with a cynical smile.

"Shall we see?" she asked. And without waiting for a reply, she pushed against the panel and opened the priest's hole with a flourish. "There!" she exclaimed as the door slid open.

"Is what?"

Caroline poked her head into the empty cupboard and her jaw dropped. "It is empty," she said.

"An accurate observation," observed her companion.

Thudding feet announced the approach of Clarence and Jarvis, and Caroline steeled herself for humiliation. Clarence was the first on the scene. "Hey ho, what is this?" he said in awed tones. "Did you know about this, Dam?"

"But where is our ghost?" asked Jarvis.

"Laughing comfortably in some other hidey-hole, most likely," said Damien. "We all know of at least two other places in the house."

104

"You all knew there was more than one hiding place?" asked Caroline.

"We used to play in them when we were boys," said Clarence. "But the only one I remember is the one in the nursery."

"I remember that one, too," said Jarvis. "I shall go check there."

"By all means, do that," said Damien agreeably.

Caroline was unaware of his departure. Pardonably perturbed, she turned on Damien. "You allowed me to believe we would catch the bogus ghost when you knew all along there was more than one hiding place where it could vanish," she said accusingly.

Damien gave an eloquent shrug. "My dear Lady Caroline. You led me to believe you were in full control and that you had prepared for any possible twist of circumstance. How was I to know you had not prepared for this eventuality? Surely a woman with your great intellectual powers must know that any proper Elizabethan home would most likely have more than one priest's hole."

Of course she had known that, but she did not think to find more than one on the same floor. Her palm itched to slap the arrogant face smiling down at her. With great restraint she kept her hand by her side and settled instead for fixing her tormentor with an icy look before flouncing out of the room. Her dramatic exit turned to farce as, sweeping down the corridor, she tripped over a tiny spot where the carpet had gotten bunched and crashed noisily into a small table. She knew immediately who let out the ungentlemanly chuckle that came from the bedchamber and wished a similar fate on him.

A light appeared at the end of the corridor—Jarvis returning from his search. "Did you find anything?" she asked.

Jarvis shook his head. "I am afraid not. I suspect our ghost is already back snug in its bed by now." Caroline sighed. "I am sorry," he said. "Perhaps we shall have better luck next time."

"Perhaps," said Caroline noncommitally. Next time, she thought, I shall be sure to stalk the villainess alone. I will surely do better on my own than I have done with all this so-called help.

"Let me light you to your room," Jarvis offered.

"Thank you," said Caroline. She thanked him again at her door for his help.

"Do not despair. If your ghost is human as you think, I am sure you will catch it," he said with a smile.

"Do not tell me you believe in ghosts," said Caroline.

Jarvis caught her hand and lifted it to his lips. "I believe you are a formidable adversary for any creature, whether spirit or flesh and blood. Good night," he whispered, and turned and made his way down the corridor.

Caroline entered her room feeling positively light-hearted in spite of her failure. Sibby had been waiting for her and came forward eagerly at the sight of her mistress. "Did you find it?" she asked.

Caroline's spirits plummeted and she scowled. "No," she said. "Our ghost and its accomplice outwitted me." She sighed. "It is my own fault. In issuing a challenge I put them on their guard. That was really very stupid of me. He is probably at this moment letting her out the—Oh my! He may be at that!" Caroline exclaimed.

"Sibby, be a love and creep down the back stairs to the servants' quarters. Have a look in at the kitchen and see if anyone is coming or going by that door. I shall try the front door. Here." She handed her maid a candle. "Take this. You will probably need a light more than I. Once I am to the stairs I shall be able to see the door below from the light of the candles in the entrance hall."

Sibby looked anything but excited by her mistress's orders, but she followed her out the door, her candle shaking slightly in her hand. The two women slipped down the corridor in opposite directions, Caroline feeling her way cautiously as Sibby and the little pool of light surrounding her moved slowly away. She reached the first landing on the stairs without mishap. Peering down below to the entrance hall she saw Damien walking from the door and mounting the stairs. A startled gasp escaped her, and he looked up. She ducked back out of sight and began to make her way back up the stairs with as much haste as she dared. She could hear a light footfall on the stairs and knew her enemy was in hot pursuit. Lifting her skirts, she ran the rest of the way up the stairs and upon reaching the corridor ran to what her panicked mind thought was a deserted room and grabbed the door handle.

She had just opened the door when Damien's voice accosted her. "Visiting my brother at this hour?" he inquired. "How very strange. I thought it was your sister to whom he was engaged."

Caroline blushed and stepped away from the door. A mixture of feelings clamored in her mind for attention: embarrassment over having been caught in a stupid blunder, fear of the enemy, anger. Most of all, anger. How dare he try to turn the tables on her. *She* was not the villain! "And what were *you* doing just now?" she demanded.

"I was checking the front door to see if it was locked."

"You were not, by any chance, seeing someone out?"

A sigh of exasperation escaped Damien. "I was

checking to see if I could detect any signs of someone else having recently done so," he said. "Here." He took her arm and escorted her firmly down the hallway. "Let me see you safely to your room."

The last thing Caroline wanted was to be seen safely to her room, especially by Damien, but rather than create a scene that would bring everyone running she went with him. "Thank you," she said frostily over her shoulder and let herself in, shutting the door in his face. She tore off her shawl, rolled it in a ball, and threw it fiercely onto a chair. "Beast! Odious wretch! Horrid, vile—" The door opened and Caroline gave a guilty start. "Oh, it is you."

Sibby looked at her mistress as if to say, "And who else should it be at this hour?"

"Did you find anything?" asked Caroline.

Sibby shook her head. "Nothing."

Caroline sighed. "Oh, I suppose I did not think you would. Come get me out of this gown, and let us see if we can get some sleep." Sibby obediently started unbuttoning the tiny buttons at the back of her mistresses's gown and Caroline began to think out loud. "He got word to her."

"Who got word to who?" asked Sibby.

"Damien," replied Caroline. "He and Isobelle are in this together, I am sure of it."

"Not Mr. Grayson," said Sibby, disbelieving.

"Can you think of anyone else with as much reason to be involved in such a havey-cavey business?" asked Caroline, effectively silencing Sibby. "They were prepared for me," she continued. "She has used that cupboard before, but she did not use it tonight. Why? Perhaps she does not use the same hiding place twice. But where did she go? How did she escape? Obviously, she knew ahead of time we would be watching for her. They must have arranged for her to hide in a more unlikely place. The nursery?" Caroline answered her own question with a shake of the head. "No. Surely Jarvis would have caught her, for she did not have that great a head start on us. Where then? It could have been anywhere. Damien himself said there were several priest's holes in the house. And while we were searching one, she could have been sneaking out of another and down to the door."

"I don't know about all that," said Sibby. "But if I were a man and I was going to hide a lady, I would hide her in my room. In the wardrobe."

Caroline cocked her head thoughtfully. "In your room, you say?"

Sibby shrugged. "That is what I would do," she said simply.

Caroline considered this suggestion and finally rejected it with a shake of the head. "That is too simple," she said. "And too chancy."

"I don't see how as it is so chancy," said Sibby, defending her theory. "You would not have demanded to search the gentleman's bedchamber."

Caroline remembered her reluctance to enter Jarvis's room on the last ghost chase. "You are right about that," she admitted. She chewed her fingertip. "Wherever he hid her, it had to be prearranged. How did he get word to her? Who is their messenger? Were any servants dispatched to Hallowstone House today?"

Sibby bit her lip, trying to remember. "John was sent to take a dinner invitation to Sir John for next week, and Rose sent a note with him. She said it was for the groom there. Claims he can read," Sibby said in disbelief. "Anyway, he is the only one I know of who went to Hallowstone House."

"Hmph," said Caroline, stepping out of her gown.

"We are facing two very clever adversaries, Sibby."
Sibby helped her out of her chemise and brought her
nightgown to her. "We shall have to tread carefully
if we are to catch them. And quietly. I shall not make
the same mistake of tipping my hand again. And we
are going to have to work quickly, too. Mama has
announced her intention to move the wedding
forward, and our ghost knows her days are numbered.
She is bound to get more desperate as time goes by.
And she is bound to slip up sooner or later. When she
does I shall get her."

against her and held her close to her
..........to her. "We shall have to continue ... fully
..........to catch them, and quietly, I shall but make

8

Caroline did not have to tell Phoebe she had failed yet again to catch the ghost. It was evident at breakfast that Clarence had been regaling the ladies with his version of the previous night's adventure. "Caro had found the hiding place earlier," he was saying. "Dashed pity it was empty by the time we got to it. Caro!" he called cheerfully, spying his future sister-in-law. "I was just telling 'em about last night. Good sport, eh? Too bad the ghost disappeared before we could catch it."

"Ghosts have a way of doing that," said Lady Grayson.

"Caro, love," scolded Lady Harborough. "I wish you might not go haring around after ghosts at night like some kind of hoyden. Tearing up and down stairs, prying into bedchambers."

"But, Mama," protested Caroline, "there was no one staying in that bedchamber. And besides, how else do you expect me to catch the ghost?"

"Well, there must be some more ladylike way to go about it," said Lady Harborough vaguely. Later, as they left the room, she told her eldest daughter, "This must come to a stop soon. One daughter being

111

pursued by ghosts, another chasing them. I vow I shall go mad."

Caroline patted her mother's arm reassuringly. "Do not worry, dearest. Everything will be all right."

The clear skies of early morning had become clouded, and a gentle drizzle precluded any form of outdoor exercise. The men opted for billiards, and the ladies settled into the winter parlor with their stitchery. Caroline stitched, smiled, and wondered where the priest's hole in the nursery was located.

Half an hour of inactivity was all she could stand. She laid aside her stitchery and announced her desire to explore the nursery and schoolroom. "If you have no objections, Lady Grayson."

Lady Grayson could not understand why Caroline was interested in the old nursery, but she had no objection.

"Would you care to accompany me?" Caroline asked her sister. "You might enjoy seeing the rooms where your husband-to-be spent his childhood days."

Phoebe knew from Clarence's earlier account that the nursery had possibly been part of the ghost's stalking grounds, and she shook her head vigorously. "Mother Grayson showed them to me when we first came," she said.

Hen-hearted. The girl was positively hen-hearted, thought Caroline, disappointed.

Her disappointment in her sister must have showed, for Phoebe said, "If Clarence appears and would like to take me there we shall join you later."

"Let me ring for Betsy," said Lady Grayson. "She can conduct you there."

The servants had obviously also heard about the great ghost hunt of the night before. Betsy conducted

112

Caroline as far as the nursery wing, then scuttled away quickly.

Caroline sighed, feeling deserted. For a moment she found herself wishing she had asked Jarvis to conduct her on a tour and show her the location of the secret cupboard. But that was only for a moment. She remembered her resolve of the night before. The more things she did alone, the less chance of her enemies finding out what she was up to and stealing the advantage of surprise from her. Anyway, it would be a challenge to see if she could find this hiding place on her own.

She walked down the corridor and opened the first door she found. She entered a dim, dusty room and looked around. Old furniture swathed in Holland covers was scattered about what was obviously once a playroom. An old rocking horse stood in the corner. Caroline crossed the room, opened another door, and found herself looking at what must have served as the schoolroom. She smiled at the three small battered desks and chairs and crossed the room for a closer look. Damien and Clarence had each carved their names in one. Clarence's name was misspelled. In one corner of his desk Damien had carved, "I am not a bad boy."

Caroline smiled, imagining what Damien must have been like as a child—mischievous, temperamental, misunderstood. Is he still misunderstood? she wondered.

She looked up at the sound of footsteps to see Damien himself entering the room. In the midst of child-sized furniture he looked like a giant. Caroline's heart beat faster in spite of the fact that she certainly was not afraid of the likes of Damien Grayson. Nevertheless, she asked, "Where are Jarvis and

Clarence? I thought you gentlemen were playing billiards."

"Clarence has gone in search of his intended and, as the rain has let up, Jarvis has ridden out to court the fair Isobelle."

"Does he court her?"

"If he is not he should. The Payne fortune is no small plum. And God knows someone must pluck it."

"So why do you not do so? It seems easily within your grasp."

"My dear Lady Caroline, what a shocking, insensitive thing to say," said Damien in mock horror.

"Yes, wasn't it? I should hate you to think yourself the only person capable of shocking and amazing others," Caroline retorted.

Damien smiled and rocked back on his heels. "You are a fascinating woman," he said. "It is a pity you were gently born. You should have made a marvelous courtesan."

Now it was Caroline's turn to smile. "I have heard it said that courtesans are fascinating. But I suspect they are required to be much less outspoken and more compliant than I should ever wish to be."

"The same may be said of wives," suggested Damien.

"Is it not fortunate, then, that I am no longer one?" Caroline answered flippantly, then blushed at the insensitivity of remark. A fine thing for a widow to say! "You odious man! See what a horrid thing you have provoked me into saying."

"I am sorry," replied Damien, looking quite the contrary.

"We both know you are not," snapped Caroline, "so pray, do not add lying to your list of noticeable vices."

"No. I am sorry. Truly."

Caroline studied his face, suddenly serious. He looked sincere. "Well, I suppose I must believe you since you look so very sincere," she said grudgingly.

"I am sincere. And I am also sincere in saying that I feel it would be an extreme waste if you were to remain a widow indefinitely."

Caroline felt herself blushing. The wretch was certainly charming when he chose to be. But she hadn't forgotten his insinuating remark about her fortune-hunting family or his insulting remarks about her sister. Nor could she afford to lose sight of the fact that he was the one person most likely to be assisting Isobelle in her efforts to be rid of Phoebe. If he thought he could throw Caroline Templeton off balance simply by tossing a compliment or two her way he was very much mistaken.

"You are much too young to be putting yourself on the shelf," Damien continued.

"Frankly, sir, I find it most comfortable on the shelf and have no intention of hopping off." Caroline moved to the third desk in the room and examined it. "I hate Damien," she read aloud. "Have you always had such a talent for making friends?"

Damien smiled and joined her, reading over her shoulder. "A memento of the year he spent under our roof. Alas, poor Jarvis and I have never been the best of friends. He was a hypocritical, sniveling little boy. I must say he has changed little with the years." Before a bridling Caroline could deliver a reproof Damien changed the subject. "If you wish to see the nursery's hidey-hole I should be happy to show you."

"You would?" asked Caroline suspiciously.

"It is really no great secret I am revealing. Clarence and Jarvis both know of this secret cupboard. Even Isobelle, if I remember correctly. She used to run

115

tame over here as a child. Mama took a fancy to her, indulged her terribly." He walked over to the chimney. "There is a false chimney here and the priest's hole is in that."

Caroline's mouth dropped as Damien leaned inside the hearth and moved a stone slab to reveal a small hole and disappeared inside. She approached the fireplace and peered into the hearth. "Come inside," said Damien. "There is room."

Caroline bent over and entered the cupboard and looked around her. It was hardly spacious, but she supposed two men of average size could hide in the cell for some time. The room was bare now, but she imagined at one time there might have been a chair in there, possibly a small table. "Amazing," she murmured.

"Nicholas Owen was a clever man," said Damien, "beloved by Elizabethan Catholics. God alone knows how many hiding places he built in how many houses in his lifetime."

"Mmm," said Caroline absently, studying the floor.

"What are you looking for?" asked Damien. He took a step forward, and Caroline was suddenly conscious of how small the room was, and how very close she was standing to a man she knew little and trusted less. As if reading her mind Damien smiled wickedly and said, "It is rather close in here, is it not? But let us, for the moment, ignore that delightful circumstance and talk about what was so absorbing your attention before I distracted you."

Caroline inched away from him as much as the confined space they were in would allow. "I was looking to see if I could detect any signs of recent use," she said coldly. "Such as footprints in the dust." She bent over. "Other than yours, I see nothing."

"Those I freshly made when I came in here," he said defensively. "I could certainly not have made them last night for I was, if you remember, under your watchful eye the entire evening. A lovely place to be, I might add," he concluded with an irritating smile.

Caroline cast him a look which clearly said she was neither impressed nor amused.

"Hello there!" called a deep voice from the end of the room. "I say, are you here, Caro?"

Caroline ducked and climbed back out of the cupboard and emerged from the hearth. Her sister gave a startled yelp and grabbed Clarence's arm. "Oh, Caro. It is you," she breathed. "You gave me such a fright just now. Whatever were you doing in the fireplace?"

Damien emerged on her heels and Phoebe's mouth dropped. "Hello, old fellow," he said jovially. "Phoebe."

"I say! The old nursery priest's hole. You know, I had forgotten where it was," said Clarence, striding on long legs to where his brother stood. He peered into the hearth, then squeezed through the opening. "It seemed bigger when we were boys," he called out. Phoebe had followed him timidly across the room. She bent over and peered in. "Come on in Phoebe," he said.

She shook her head nervously.

"It is perfectly safe. There is no one in here but me." But Phoebe had no desire to enter the priest's hole, so Clarence squeezed back out.

"You have forgotten about this secret cupboard," said Damien. "Have you also forgotten the time you

117

shut me in here and then could not remember how to get me out?''

"How did you escape?" asked Phoebe breathlessly.

"I was saved because Isobelle had been a party to this particular escapade, and she, fortunately, remembered which slab to move."

Clarence laughed. "Now you mention it, I do remember that. What a lark."

"For you," said Damien.

Clarence looked at his brother uncomprehendingly.

"Jarvis told Father it was I who shut you in the cupboard. And it was I who had to report to the library."

"Oh." Clarence was momentarily silent. "I had . . ."

"Forgotten," Damien finished in unison with him.

Caroline sighed. "I suppose we may as well return downstairs. There is nothing more to be learned here. Our ghost obviously did not use this hiding place." She shook out her skirts and sneezed.

The ladies preceded the men out of the room. Phoebe turned a despairing face to her sister. "It really is a ghost," she said in a small voice. "That is why it keeps getting away. That's why you cannot find it anywhere in these cupboards."

"It is not a ghost," said Caroline in an undervoice. She took her sister's hand. "You must be brave a little longer," she whispered. "We shall come about yet. I have every intention of catching the wicked person who is doing this to you. So do not worry."

That afternoon at tea the subject of the cupboard and the ghost hunt was discussed at great length. Lady Harborough made no mention of removing her daughter from the premises, but the expression on her face plainly told what she thought of the situation, and Caroline began to squirm.

"I do wish this would stop," said Lady Grayson, wringing her handkerchief. "We have not had such worries since Clarence was set upon by footpads."

"The Grayson brothers appear to inspire violence," said Damien, helping himself to a cucumber sandwich. "When did this happen?"

"It was only a few months ago, in London," said Lady Grayson. "After we learned you were dead. I mean after we thought you were dead," she corrected herself. "They wounded him terribly."

"Not before I took down two of 'em with my swordstick," put in Clarence. "The dogs."

"I felt sure he would miss the entire season," said Lady Grayson. "But fortunately he recovered in time to meet our dear Phoebe," she concluded, beaming on Phoebe.

"Phoebe is indeed a dear girl," said Lady Harborough. "So why any ghost should take a disliking to her is more than I can understand. And, in spite of what may have been said earlier I am beginning to feel—"

"That you made the right decision in remaining?" put in Caroline quickly. "I couldn't agree with you more, Mama. For how should it look to the world if word were to get out that a Harborough broke their word. No one would believe our story of ghosts. Everyone would be sure that Clarence had thrown Phoebe over. We should be the laughingstock of the ton. No, Mama, I firmly believe you have made a very wise decision in staying to fight this out. And I am sure Clarence and Phoebe will thank you for this one day, also, when they are happily married."

Lady Harborough had tried to get in a word during this speech and had, indeed, opened and shut her mouth so many times she looked like a plump

119

fish. By the time her daughter was finished her lady-ship was completely nonplussed. "Well, er, yes, of course," she said doubtfully and took a restorative sip of tea.

Damien acknowledged Caroline's clever tactics with a knowing smile. She ignored him, and he turned once again to his brother. "How many men beset you?" he asked casually.

"Don't remember," said Clarence. "Most likely not more than three or four."

Damien gave his brother a quizzical look. "You are rather difficult to get rid of, aren't you?"

Difficult to get rid of? Caroline fell silent and began some serious cogitating. Footpads were common enough in London, so who would suspect a scheming brother if some fell upon Clarence and killed him. She stole a glance at Damien's dark profile. Who had sent the message of his death from India? Could Damien himself have done so? Certainly no one would accuse him of trying to murder his brother if they presumed him dead. How long had he been in England, anyway? There was something very peculiar about all this, and, in spite of her warm shawl, Caroline shivered. Someone was playing a deep game here. Someone with a lot at stake. Isobelle might merely wish to scare away a future bride, but her accomplice had something much more evil in mind.

That evening after dinner she found it more difficult than ever to be civil to Damien. Fortunately, the company was absorbed in singing madrigals and as Caroline's attention was taken by the pianoforte she was able to escape the necessity of making polite conversation with him much of the evening.

The next morning, Isobelle rode over to see how Phoebe was and to offer her condolences to Caroline.

As Phoebe had gone into Upper Swanley with the two mamas in search of some apple green ribbon, a paper of pins, and any diversion which might present itself, Isobelle was unable to do the former. Caroline suspected she had come to do neither anyway, but to gloat. "Jarvis told me the ghost eluded you again," she said. "How very frustrating. It must be a very clever apparition."

Caroline caught the sly innuendo—and you must not be as clever as you thought since you cannot catch it. She smiled at Isobelle and said, "She thinks she is very clever, to be sure. And I must agree with her. Our ghost is clever. But not so clever as she thinks."

Isobelle shook her head. "I marvel at your bravery," she said.

Caroline laughed. "Marvel not so much at my bravery, but at this poor ghost's foolishness. Its conceit will be its undoing."

Isobelle's eyes widened then narrowed. "You are indeed a brave woman. But I wonder if you are not being a bit reckless. After all, there are some things which we should not mock and with which we should not tamper."

"Such as," Caroline paused for effect, "another's happiness?"

Isobelle had the grace to blush. "Of course," she murmured. "But I was speaking of the supernatural."

Caroline merely smiled, and the two women fell into a politely strained silence. "Well," said Isobelle finally. "I had best be returning home. I am sure Papa will be missing me."

"If you feel you must go I shall not be so selfish as to try and detain you," said Caroline politely, reaching for the bellpull.

The ladies had just risen when a bloodcurdling scream caused them both to jump and shriek themselves. "What was that?" gasped Isobelle.

"It came from upstairs," said Caroline. She ran from the room and, picking up her skirt, took the stairs at a most unladylike two at a time, Isobelle following close behind her.

Caroline burst into the corridor where the bedchambers were only to collide with an equally fast-moving body coming from the opposite direction. The two people bounced off each other and fell backwards, landing on the floor. Caroline strugled to her elbows to see a still-hysterical Betsy. "I am so sorry, my lady," she sobbed, clambering to her feet. She grabbed Caroline's arm and began yanking desperately, trying to speed Caroline to her feet.

"Betsy, stop this!" demanded Caroline, pulling her arm away.

Similar words echoed down the hall. "Betsy, stop!" A breathless little blue-eyed maid came running into sight.

"The ghost," Betsy panted. "I saw it!"

"Where?" demanded Caroline and Isobelle in unison.

The second maid came to a panting halt in front of the other three women. She bobbed a curtsey to Isobelle and Caroline. "Ghost?" she said, and looked nervously over her shoulder.

"You did not see it?" asked Betsy in amazement. "How could you miss it when it was right there in the room with you? Oh, Sarah, thank God it did not get you." She turned pleading eyes to Caroline. "Please, my lady. Can we leave before it comes after us?"

"Wait," commanded Caroline. "You saw no ghost?" she asked Sarah.

Sarah shook her head, puzzled. "I do not know what Betsy saw. I was just shaking out the bed linen."

122

"You were shaking out . . . ?" Caroline smiled and shook her head. "Come with me," she said, and led the maids back in the direction from which they had come. "Which room were you in?" she asked Sarah.

Sarah pointed to Lady Grayson's bedchamber. Caroline entered the room and picked up the dropped sheet. "Here is your ghost," she said to Betsy, holding it up.

Betsy's mouth fell open. "But how . . . ?" she began.

Caroline shook the sheet vigorously, and it came to life, flapping and dipping. "At a casual glance this would look very much like a ghost," she said.

Betsy blushed and shuffled her feet.

"Never mind," said Caroline kindly. "Anyone could have made the same mistake."

"It would appear the entire household is being upset by this ghost," Isobelle observed as the two ladies made their way back downstairs.

Caroline shrugged nonchalantly. "Servants are so impressionable," she said.

Isobelle said nothing. She didn't need to. The smug smile which had settled on her lips spoke volumes to Caroline.

Caroline would love to have pulled every hair out of that conceited, treacherous head, but being a lady she had to content herself with a more subtle attack. "Only servants would be silly enough to be terrified by pranks and nursery tales. The mind behind all this is not a great one. And I am not in the least worried about catching this person quite soon."

Two red spots on Isobelle's cheeks were the only sign that Caroline's shaft had hit its mark. "Do be careful," she cautioned. "And do not forget the old proverb which says pride goeth before a fall. You could be dealing with something not of this world.

And very dangerous. In fact, I wonder you are willing to gamble your sister's safety.''

You are hoping I will decide not to, thought Caroline angrily. Wicked creature! She smiled at Isobelle. "I am sorry you must rush off. Phoebe will be sorry to have missed you." And I wish I had been equally fortunate, she thought.

"I hear we missed seeing our fair neighbor," said Jarvis later that day as he came upon Caroline pacing in the courtyard.

"Yes, you did. Now aren't you sorry you gentlemen went out shooting?" Caroline teased. "You missed seeing the fairest in the land."

"One of the fairest," said Jarvis.

Caroline laughed. "Oh, well said."

"And to what did we owe the honor of this visit?"

"She came to offer her condolences to me."

Jarvis cocked an inquiring eyebrow. Caroline merely smiled at him. "Oh," he said, a slow smile growing on his face. "Our fair neighbor came to gloat. I should not have told her."

"She pretends beautifully," said Caroline. "She was the very picture of sympathy, but I know full well she finds this all very amusing. Oh, enough talk of ghosts," she said quickly. "I am sure you are becoming heartily sick of the subject. Tell me how you gentlemen fared. Did you shoot many grouse?"

"Enough to make a tasty dish to put before you ladies tonight," said Jarvis.

They turned by unspoken consent and headed into the house, meeting Damien in the hallway. "I hear we had a visitor," he said. "A shame you missed her, Jarvis. I am certain she was sorry to have missed you."

"I was going to suggest the same thing to you, dear cousin," said Jarvis coldly. "I am sure you and Miss

124

Payne would have much to talk about."

"Perhaps. But I suspect *you* and Isobelle might have even more," replied Damien.

An angry flush crept up Jarvis's neck, and Caroline began to feel very uncomfortable. She half-expected to see the two men break into fisticuffs at any moment. "I hope you gentlemen will excuse me," she said and made good her escape, scuttling off to the winter parlor in hopes of finding some peace.

What dangerous undercurrents flowed in this house! Just for a moment Caroline wondered if she could really help Phoebe when she herself was beginning to feel the strong undertow. Perhaps Mama had been right after all. Perhaps they should take Phoebe and leave while they were all still in one piece. Stop this, she scolded herself. If you cannot outsmart the likes of Isobelle Payne you are a very poor creature, indeed. And as for the two fighting cocks, let them fight. Perhaps it will keep them occupied and out of my way, she reasoned. One of them I would especially like out of my way until I have solved this puzzle. Then, after I have proved him as deeply involved as I suspect he is . . . then there will be time for fighting in earnest.

9

The next few days went by without incident. Showing an unexpected wisdom, the ghost decided to remain invisible, and time passed pleasantly enough. Damien and Jarvis continued to observe an uneasy truce and, except for an occasional sneer or barbed comment, behaved civilly to each other. Isobelle, thankfully, had left the family alone. Caroline was sure Jarvis was still unconvinced that Isobelle's heart was as black as Caroline painted it. Twice he had offered to escort the sisters to see her, but Caroline had begged to be excused, once because of a feigned headache, and now, this morning, her promise to help Lady Grayson arrange flowers for the evening's dinner party made a handy excuse. Phoebe, too, Caroline explained, would be needed. There was, after all, no sense encouraging Phoebe to be thick as thieves with the creature. "But do give her our best and tell her we look forward to seeing her tonight," said Caroline diplomatically.

He gave Caroline what looked uncomfortably like a knowing smile, and she blushed. "I suppose that does sound very insincere considering my suspicions, but then sincerity and politeness do not always go hand in hand, do they?"

Jarvis laughed. "Sincerity and politeness rarely go hand in hand. I shall deliver your message."

Caroline smiled and bid him farewell and turned back to her flowers and vases.

That evening she greeted Isobelle politely (insincerely, but politely).

Isobelle's papa, Sir John Payne, had felt well enough to accompany his daughter. He was a short slight man with outdated clothes and a mane of white hair which he powdered and tied elegantly with a velvet ribbon. Always a connoisseur of feminine pulchritude, he greeted the older ladies in a courtly fashion and looked at the younger ones appreciatively and bowed over their hands. It wasn't hard for Caroline to combine sincerity with politeness when she told Sir John it was good to finally meet him. He was a charming old rogue. And it was plain to see he doted on the beautiful daughter born to him late in life.

His wife had finally given up her efforts to present her husband with a son and died after giving birth to the one baby who lived. Sir John had, naturally, done as any other man in his position would have and spoiled his daughter shamelessly.

Watching her, it was obvious to Caroline that he had raised Isobelle to believe that nothing was too good for her. And, when it came right down to it, why should she not think this? For years she had enjoyed the reputation of being the neighborhood beauty. Her family had wealth and property, and Lady Grayson had made the girl her protégée. Small wonder she grew up thinking it only right she should go from the daughter of a knight to a countess. In spite of what Lady Grayson might say or imply in a moment of sentimentality, Caroline seriously doubted she had ever considered Isobelle as a possible wife for either of her sons. To occasionally see the Paynes here in the country, removed from the fashionable salons of London suited Lady Grayson fine. To take the motherless girl under her wing was one thing, but to raise her and her family to the same social standing as the Graysons would be quite another.

The vicar and his wife had also been invited for this occasion, and they arrived shortly after Isobelle and her papa. "Frightfully cold night," said the vicar after the proper greetings had been exchanged.

"I do hope we are not in for an early winter," said Lady Grayson. "I would hate to have it turn so wintry cold by Allhallows Eve."

"I am sure a little cold will not keep any of your guests away from the wonderful evening you have in store for them," said Isobelle.

"Oh, yes, your ball," said the vicar's wife in slightly disapproving tones. It was obvious what she thought of encouraging people's superstitions by giving a ball in honor of what had become a strictly pagan holiday.

Lady Grayson, for all her flightiness, had not spent twenty-six years as a countess for nothing. She gave the vicar's wife a look which effectively reminded her of her position and silenced her.

Caroline pressed her lips together in an effort not to smile. She wondered if the vicar's wife's disapproval of the upcoming ball would have been so strong if she had received an invitation. But then, only the cream of the surrounding families had been so privileged. Isobelle and her papa had been invited out of benevolence. But, kind as she was, Lady Grayson's benevolence did not extend to uppity vicar's wives who had no proper notion of their station nor understanding of what was owed their betters.

Much as she shared Lady Grayson's dislike of the vicar's wife, Caroline quite liked the vicar and was delighted when she found herself seated next to him at dinner. Having Damien on her other side was not what she would have wished, but she bore it with good grace and talked to him no more than courtesy demanded.

That did not, however, prevent him from making several attempts to engage her in conversation or from attempting to eavesdrop on her conversations with the vicar. And she was finding it very difficult to learn what she wanted to know without being forced to share the information with Damien.

"As you know," the vicar was saying. "I have a passion for that period, the history as well as the architecture."

"I suppose you would know about such things as priest's holes and other hiding places," Caroline said casually.

"I suppose I should," he said spiritedly. "For, of course, history, religion and art all intersected so wonderfully at that time. It was, of course, a sad time. But necessary. Very necessary. The dissenters had to be gotten rid of for the church to stay healthy."

Caroline was not so sure of this, but she held her tongue, knowing that any comment would certainly sidetrack her dinner companion.

"Naturally, a great deal of imagination had to be poured into the designing of these hiding places," he continued.

"How many priest's holes do you think an Elizabethan house usually had?" asked Caroline.

"Oh, several," said the vicar cheerfully. "And some

houses even had a secret passage."

"A secret passage?" Caroline put down her spoon. Her soup sat cooling, ignored.

"Oh, yes. Now, I am not saying all houses had such a thing. But a few did."

"Do you think this house might possibly have such a thing?" Caroline asked.

"As strongly Catholic as the house of Grayson once was, that is a very strong possibility."

A smile grew on Caroline's face. A secret passage, eh? Very interesting, indeed. Her gaze traveled around the table. Lady Grayson and Caroline's mama were deep in a fashion debate with the squire's wife and, from the look on that good lady's face, it would appear she was losing. At the other end of the table Sir John and Clarence were carrying on a noisy discussion on the merits of various kinds of hunting guns. Jarvis appeared to be equally absorbed with the subject. Isobelle, sitting between her father and Clarence looked completely bored and was toying with the food on her plate. Caroline's smile widened. Just as she was congratulating herself that no one had been paying the least attention to her conversation with the vicar her wandering gaze caught Damien's eyes. He smiled at her, and she knew with a sudden, sinking feeling that he had overheard every word. Of course, if there was such a thing in Grayson Hall as a secret passage Damien probably already knew of it. But Caroline did not particularly want him to know her suspicions. She had no desire to tip her hand. She had made that mistake already. And once was enough.

"I had the opportunity to visit Grosmont Abbey," the vicar was saying. "It had a most interesting vault of conveyance. At one stairhead within the stone wall there was a post about the size of a man's body. It looked for all the world to be a supporting beam, but the thing was hinged and swung to and fro. It covered a hole which a man could easily descend then lock fast from beneath with ironwork. The vicar shook his head appreciatively. "Very clever, indeed."

"In what other forms do these secret passageways come?" asked Damien, inserting himself into the conversation.

Caroline fought to hide her feelings of extreme irritation. As if he didn't know! There was a secret passage somewhere in this place, and he and his ghostly accomplice had obviously been making good use of it.

"Oh, there are many places where one could put a secret passageway," said the vicar. "Garderobe shafts and drainage tunnels. One establishment very similar to your Grayson Hall had a secret room situated over the kitchen on the ground floor. A room was entered through a sliding panel ingeniously constructed in some wainscoting. From this a narrow shaft led down to the ground. At its base an underground passage led off under the moat."

Caroline had a sudden premonition she would be finding herself in need of sustenance later that night.

"And, of course, Irnham Hall in Lincolnshire," continued the vicar, "had a tunnel five feet high which could be entered from a flagstone in the hearth of the main hall and which led out under the wall of a yard and finished in a small chamber adjacent to a beech tree about fifty yards away."

"Indeed," said Caroline, pretending mere polite interest. She then turned the subject, hoping to convince Damien she had no thought of applying the vicar's discourse to the architecture of Grayson Hall.

The evening dragged after dinner. Caroline found it difficult to pretend any interest in the ladies' conversation as they waited for the gentlemen to join them in the drawing room. She enjoyed herself no more once the gentlemen were present, in spite of the fact that Jarvis was especially attentive.

So was Sir John, and if Caroline had not been so on edge and preoccupied, she would have found the evening vastly amusing. Jarvis had seated himself next to her, but left his seat for a moment to assist Lady Grayson in a search for her spectacles. Sir John, who had been seated next to Lady Harborough, took advantage of his abdication and slipped into his chair.

The look on Jarvis's face when he tried to return to his seat and found it occupied by the old libertine was comical, but Caroline was not amused by any of this. She felt she would scream from frustration as she made polite conversation and waited for the tea tray to be brought in which would signal the beginning of the end of the evening.

It did finally arrive at ten o'clock. The guests dutifully drank their tea and ate their cakes, then went away, and the family breathed a sigh of relief.

"The vicar is a dear, kind man," said Lady Grayson. "But I must admit I find his wife to be . . ." She paused, searching for the right word.

"Tiring," supplied Damien.

His mother blushed at her son's frankness. "Well, yes. I hate to have to say it, but too large a dose of that woman's presence does tire me."

"The woman really is quite forward," agreed Lady Harborough. "Can you imagine her telling me she saw a patterned shawl exactly like mine in one of the local shops?"

Lady Grayson's bosom heaved in a sigh. "One does have a social responsibility to the neighborhood," she said.

"My dear," put in Lady Harborough. "Social responsibility is one thing. Torture is quite another."

Damien laughed heartily at this. "I quite agree with Lady Harborough. I have suffered enough torture for tonight. I think I shall retire."

"What? So early?" complained Clarence. "I was about to propose a game of billiards."

"Not tonight," said Damien. "The company of fools fatigues me. I shall take to my bed." And with that he bid the company goodnight and sauntered out of the room.

Phoebe was yawning over her teacup, and her mama bustled her out of the room as well.

"Is everyone going to bed?" demanded Clarence.

"C'mon, coz. I will go a game or two with you," said Jarvis amiably.

Drat, thought Caroline as she followed Phoebe and her mother from the drawing room. I wonder how long I shall have to wait now before everyone is asleep.

"I must say," said her mama as the three women made their way to their bedchambers, "it would appear that Mr. Woolcock has formed a *tendre* for you, Caro dear."

"And so has Sir John," giggled Phoebe.

"Hmph," said Lady Harborough. "Rather rising above himself, I should say.

So was Mr. Woolcock, when it came right down to it, thought Caroline.

"And really," said her mama. "Chasing after a girl young enough to be his granddaughter. I must say I have never approved of selling young girls to older men for the mere price of a title or fortune."

Caroline laughed. "Now, Mama dear, was it not his very title which made my husband so attractive to you?"

"Harold was merely fifteen years older than you," said her mama, "not forty. I hope you will do nothing to encourage Sir John in his foolishness, especially when you have a much more eligible man interested in you."

"Mama, I hope you are not thinking of doing any matchmaking," said Caroline.

"I?" said her mother innocently. "I was merely pointing out to you that which you might not have noticed. Mr. Woolcock seems interested in you. And I must say, I find his manners more pleasing than those of his cousin, Damien."

"Mama. Neither of them have a title at all," Caroline pointed out. "I just think you want me to discourage Sir John so you can have him for yourself," she teased.

"Caroline!" exclaimed her mother. "I am shocked."

Phoebe giggled, and Caroline put an arm around her mother. "Mama, you know I am only roasting you."

If Caroline had hoped to distract her mother she failed. "I wonder how much a year Mr. Woolcock—" she began.

"Mama," interrupted Caroline. "Please let us talk no more of Mr. Woolcock or Sir John or Damien Grayson. Now, I want you to promise me you will not discuss my matrimonial prospects with Lady Grayson. Not a word, Mama. Promise me."

Lady Harborough looked disinclined to cooperate.

"There is no need to pry into Mr. Woolcock's background or the current state of his finances. I am in no hurry to become a bride after having so recently become a widow."

"Recently! I should hardly call an event which took place two years ago recent," said Lady Harborough. "At your age you should be thinking of remarrying."

"Oh, Mama. I have no need to remarry. Harold left we well enough provided for. I have a roof over my head."

"A leaky roof," put in Lady Harborough.

"A roof, nevertheless. And once I am done with the improvements—"

"You shall not have a shilling to your name. I must say I think Harold's arrangements all a trifle strange. All this work to restore his ancestral home when he has no heir to enjoy it."

"I shall enjoy it," said Caroline.

"Eccentric," muttered her mama. "Positively eccentric."

They had reached her mother's bedchamber, a perfect excuse for Caroline to bring their conversation to an end. "Now Mama, promise me you will not say *anything* to Lady Grayson. Please. No hints about Cupid's arrow, no subtle questions about Mr. Woolcock's finances."

"Oh, very well," said Lady Harborough petulantly. "I shall not bring up the subject."

"Thank you, love," Caroline murmured, kissing her mother a fond goodnight.

Phoebe also dutifully kissed the plump cheek, and the two sisters left their mother at her door and made their way down the corridor. "I suppose she will find some way to wriggle out of the promise," Caroline sighed.

Phoebe made no reply. She was nervously looking down the corridor.

Caroline smiled and patted her sister's arm. "Let me walk with you to your room," she said.

No ghost appeared to impede their progress, nor was there anything terrifying lurking in Phoebe's

135

room. Caroline left her to the ministrations of her maid and returned to her own room.

She found Sibby waiting and ready to help her undress. "And why, I wonder, are you here before I have even rung for you. Such devotion," said Caroline. She studied her maid, who began to blush. "Aha!" Caroline gloated. "There is more than devotion that brings you to my room. And who, pray, might you be hiding from? Smythe? Or is it the underbutler?" Sibby's blush deepened and Caroline chuckled. "Never mind. You may safely hide here. I shall not give you away. But for the moment I do not need your services. Go ahead and go to sleep yourself as I shall be staying up late tonight."

The thought of her mistress having to struggle to undress herself unassisted was a shocking one, and Sibby looked properly horrified. "I shall wait up," she said. "I am not at all sleepy."

Caroline smiled. "You will be long before I am ready for bed," she said. "Come now, Sibby. You are a servant, not a slave. Allow me my occasional kind gesture."

Sibby looked properly chastised. "I cannot imagine what you will be doing that you will be . . ." It appeared Sibby could imagine what her mistress would be doing at such a late hour. Sibby stopped in mid-sentence and looked at Caroline with wide, disapproving eyes.

"Sibby, I am sure there is a secret passageway somewhere leading out of the house," said Caroline in an excited rush. "And I intend to find it."

"Tonight?" asked Sibby doubtfully.

"Yes, tonight. The vicar gave me a very informative lecture on Tudor architecture. It shouldn't take me long to find the thing, for I have some good ideas as to where it might be hidden."

136

"Do you think I should go with you?" ventured Sibby.

"My faithful bodyguard. My, how brave you have become since I dragged you off to sound walls."

"I have not become brave at all," said Sibby. "But you might need help."

"No. I shall be fine. Anyway, if I am caught prowling around the kitchen I can claim sudden hunger. But how would I explain you?"

"I went to fetch you something to eat but was too slow, so you came yourself," suggested Sibby.

Caroline laughed. "What a clever creature you are, to be sure. But no. I must refuse your help, for I may have to search more than just the kitchen, and I would have a hard time explaining why I am wandering the house with my maid in tow."

"Very well," Sibby said reluctantly, then added with the firmness with which only a long-trusted servant could speak, "But I shall wait up for you."

"Very well," said Caroline. "Best take yourself off and nap now, then."

Sibby obeyed, vanishing into the dressing room to lay on the cot.

Caroline picked up a book from her bedside table and curled up in a chair to wait for the gentlemen to retire for the night. Finally at twelve o'clock she peeped out her door into darkness and judged it safe to proceed.

Candle in hand, she tiptoed downstairs to the back of the house where the kitchen and buttery were located. The kitchen was deserted and quiet. Eerily quiet. Caroline swallowed. Don't be such a ninny, she scolded herself. But in spite of her resolve, her hand shook as she moved along the wall, causing shadows to jump mockingly after her. As time went on, and she became absorbed in her search, however,

137

her nerves began to steady.

After careful examination of the walls, she concluded that she would not find what she sought in the kitchen. She headed for the great hall, remembering yet another of the vicar's examples. A room which was once a central part of English social life had seemed, at first thought, to Caroline a strange place to have a secret passageway. But the more she thought of it, the more she appreciated its cleverness. If the family was holding mass in secret, they would hardly be entertaining in the great hall. The room would be deserted. And a deserted room was much easier to enter than one in an area where there was much traffic, such as a bedchamber.

The door of the great hall stood slightly ajar, and Caroline could see a shaft of light coming from the room. Obviously, it was not deserted now. Caroline suddenly felt goosebumps on her arms which had nothing to do with the cold. With her free hand she pulled her shawl more tightly about her and crept toward the door. She peered in.

The room was dimly lit by a branch of candles, but the only people in the room were those painted on the frieze on the wall. And Caroline quickly discovered why. With a wildly thumping heart, she approached the hearth. The flagstone had been moved, leaving a dark cavity. Who had preceded her into that dark passageway? Caroline bit her lip. She knew she had to enter that Stygian darkness and follow the passage wherever it led. But perhaps she didn't need to do it tonight.

Curiosity and good sense fought a heated battle inside her mind, and curiosity won. Yes, someone had already entered the passageway, but Caroline's extreme self-confidence advised her to risk an encounter with the enemy. She grabbed the fire poker and ducked inside the dark hole.

She followed stone steps down into a drafty, dark tunnel. Her candle flame flickered, but Caroline was able to shield it from assaulting drafts, and it continued its feeble effort to light her way for a good twenty steps. It would have probably seen her to the end of the tunnel had she not stumbled and grabbed the wall to steady herself. With an evil puff, a passing draft extinguished the flame. "Oh, drat," she muttered. Well, there was nothing for it but to turn back. She had no idea how far the tunnel ran and no desire to walk the rest of it in pitch darkness.

She had begun to inch her way back when she caught sight of a pinpoint of light farther down the tunnel, growing larger. What to do? She knew she could not beat her approaching enemy out of the passage. He had the advantage of light and could move more quickly than she who would be forced to inch her way along in the dark. If she tried to run she would surely fall and hurt herself. Retreat was impossible. She had no choice but to stay and fight. She gripped the fire poker tightly.

Before the approaching light got much closer, it was suddenly snuffed out. Caroline heard a muttered oath, then the shuffling sounds of booted feet feeling their way along the passage. She raised her poker, forcing herself to breathe as shallowly and quietly as possible.

When the footsteps were almost upon her, she swung the poker and had the satisfaction of hearing a grunt of pain. The curse that followed, however, told her she had missed the enemy's head. Caroline did not stop to rationally consider what she should do next. She turned and fled.

Rather than vanquishing her enemy, she had irritated him, and he set out in hot pursuit. The chase was a short one. Her unseen assailant grabbed her gown and pulled. There was the sound of ripping fabric and a terrified squeal, and before she knew it the brute had an arm about her waist. Another had found her upraised arm in the darkness and shook the poker loose from her hand. It fell to the ground with a metallic clatter. "Do not tell me," said her opponent. "Let me guess. Lady Caroline, I presume?"

"You! I suspected as much. What are you doing here?"

"The same thing as you," said Damien. "I was looking for, and found, the secret passageway."

"I suppose you wish me to believe you have just now found it," said Caroline.

"If you prefer you may think I was oiling the hinges on the door to keep it in good working order," said Damien tartly. He moaned and rubbed his shoulder. "I do wish you would stop hitting me with things. What was that you brought down on me, a poker?"

"I am sorry," said Caroline stiffly. "I hope you are not too badly wounded."

"I shall live," he said.

"Where does this lead?" she asked.

"Out under the garden. It stops at the edge of the copse. The entrance is hidden by a large boulder and a clump of gorse bushes. If you promise not to hit me with anything I shall be happy to conduct you on a tour."

"Thank you," said Caroline politely.

"But first we shall have to return to the great hall and relight our candles."

They returned to the great hall and Damien relit their candles and led Caroline back into the passageway. They edged their way along and within a matter of minutes were emerging at the end. Caroline looked back at the house. The lawns stretched out before them. She could see the maze, its green hedges black in the moonlight. The house rose above it like a dark giant. How quickly someone could make their escape from the house. It would be a simple thing to leave a horse tied in the woods, then mount and ride leisurely home while pandemonium reigned supreme at Grayson Hall.

"Interesting, is it not?" said Damien casually.

Perhaps diabolical would be a better word, thought Caroline. "It is interesting," she said. "It is also cold. I think I have seen enough."

Damien nodded and ushered her back into the tunnel. "It is rather dark and eerie in here," he suggested.

Caroline had been thinking the same thing herself. Was he trying to scare her?

"I wondered," Damien continued, "how anyone could bring themselves to traverse such a dark, unpleasant path. But after encountering you here tonight, I can see that even a member of the fair sex could master the terrors of traveling underground if she were determined enough."

And if she had enough at stake, thought Caroline. Surely a female with her heart set on marrying an earl could screw up enough courage to use this secret passageway. And a man who hoped to be the future earl would be delighted to conduct her safely out, or to distract her pursuers while she made good her escape. On the night of their vigil Damien had most likely hidden Isobelle in his bedchamber until the commotion had died down, then escorted her safely from the house. And that was where he had come from when

Caroline had spied him. He had not been checking the front door at all. He had been returning from the secret passageway.

They emerged from the hearth and stood once more in the great hall. The big deserted room suddenly looked menacing, and Caroline wanted nothing more than to be safely away from this dangerous man. "If you will excuse me I think I shall retire," she said.

Damien bowed. "I thank you for the pleasure of your company," he said.

Caroline inclined her head regally, turned, and sailed from the room with as much dignity as her fear would allow, her torn gown offering a tantalizing view of feminine underclothing.

Damien watched her go, a smile playing at the corners of his mouth. "Ah, Lady Caroline," he murmured, pouring himself a brandy. "You are a very remarkable woman. Clever, fearless, inquisitive. I can only hope you do not get in my way."

the night door at all. He had been returning from the
stiff passeng...

They emerged from the hearth and stood once
again in the sitting...

10

Caroline was in no mood to talk with anyone, not
even Sibby. She managed to undress alone, letting
Sibby sleep. She gasped when she saw the large tear
in her gown. "The beast," she growled and hurled it
onto a nearby chair. "He might have told me."

She climbed into bed but was too keyed up to sleep.
Too many thoughts kept tumbling about in her
mind. How was she ever going to catch these villains? They always seemed to be one step ahead of
her. Caroline tossed under her covers and sighed. If it
was Isobelle alone with whom she had to contend
Caroline had no doubt she could bring this dangerous farce to an end. But she was pitted against two
minds working together against her. What chance
did she have of helping Phoebe?

Caroline threw off her covers and began to pace the
floor. What to do? What to do? After twenty minutes
of pacing she had no answer, and cold and exhaus-
tion drove her back to bed.

Sleep finally came to her some time in the predawn
hours and left her again much too early. She struggled up onto her elbows and looked at the figure
silently tiptoeing past the foot of her bed. With a

moan she fell back and covered her eyes with her arm. "Oh, Sibby. Go away, do," she said. Sibby started to obey. "No, wait," Caroline commanded. "What time is it?"

"Ten," said Sibby.

"Mmm. We are hardly keeping town hours. I had best get up. I suppose everyone has already breakfasted." Sibby said nothing, and for the first time Caroline noticed the expression on her maid's face. "Oh. I see. I am in disfavor this morning."

Sibby still said nothing.

"Sibby. Where is your gratitude? I do you a kindness and let you sleep and this is my reward, a stony silence, a sour face?"

"It is my job to help you," said Sibby.

A slow smile spread across Caroline's face. "I see. That is why you are upset. Not only did I exclude you from last night's adventure, but I was also rude enough not to wake you and report everything that happened."

Sibby feigned shock. "My lady! As if your activities should be any of my concern." She picked up Caroline's gown, and her eyes grew wide at the sight of the large tear in the back. She stuck her hand through it and looked questioningly at Caroline.

"He ripped my gown," she said.

Now Sibby truly looked shocked. "Who ripped your gown?" she demanded in horrified accents.

"Damien," sighed Caroline. "I encountered him in the secret passageway."

Sibby fell onto a footstool. "He ripped your gown in the secret passageway?" she said weakly.

Caroline proceeded to tell Sibby of her previous night's adventures. "At least now we know how our ghost has been able to escape undetected from the house," Caroline concluded.

144

Sibby shook her head. "What a nasty thing to do," she said. "Sneaking around, scaring people half out of their wits."

"Yes, it is a very nasty thing to do," agreed Caroline. "And if I could just catch our ghost in the act, I could put an end to this." She sighed. "But I am beginning to wonder if that is ever going to happen. She has the advantage over me, I fear. There must be hidey-holes all over this place. And her accomplice knows them all."

"Never fear," said Sibby encouragingly. "Everything will turn out all right."

"You think so?"

Sibby nodded. "I am sure you will get to the bottom of things."

Caroline rubbed her forehead. "I wish I could be sure of that."

"I wish I could be sure his Lordship's brother is the villain you make him out to be," said Sibby.

"Can you think of anyone better suited to be the villain?" asked Caroline.

"No," admitted Sibby. "From what you have told me of him I cannot say that I can. Not unless one of the servants has been paid well to do a nasty job."

Caroline shook her head doubtfully.

Sibby gave a sympathetic sigh. "'Tis almost enough to make one wish Lady Phoebe had accepted Lord Daltry," said Sibby.

"Almost," agreed Caroline despondently.

The mere thought of breakfast was too much for Caroline that morning. She sent Sibby to fetch her some hot chocolate, which she sipped while Sibby did her hair. Then, in no mood for company, she bundled into her bonnet, cloak, and muff and headed outside to lose herself in the maze.

She had finally found her way to the heart of it

145

when the crunch of gravel told her she was about to be deprived of her solitude. "I thought perhaps I might find you here," said Jarvis.

Caroline smiled at him. "Good morning," she said.

He looked at the dark circles under her eyes and said, "I have no need to ask you how you slept last night. I can see the answer to that question on your face."

"I must admit I fared poorly," said Caroline with a sigh.

"What troubles you?" he asked gently.

"This family troubles me. I begin to think I might have made a mistake in discouraging Mama from breaking Phoebe's engagement."

"And why is that?"

Caroline shrugged. "Phoebe has always had a happy home. I am not sure this is the kind of happy family into which she should marry."

Jarvis said nothing. He sat looking sympathetic while Caroline paced and continued to argue with herself, weighing the pros and cons of whether Phoebe should stick it out or leave. "Clarence will be upset," he said finally. "But you and your mama must do what you feel is best for Phoebe. It has been a week since our ghost has walked. Perhaps she will leave your sister alone now. But then again, it all becomes rather a dangerous gamble, does it not?"

Caroline nodded. "Yes, it does. Now that the ghost knows I have been in her bag of tricks we may not see her again. But it is not only ghosts that trouble this house. And I do believe Phoebe could be in more danger than she was before. Not to mention the grave danger in which Clarence most assuredly must lie."

"What do you mean?" asked Jarvis. "Oh, surely you are not still thinking evil thoughts of our dear

146

Damien. He is rather a nasty fellow, but I doubt he has any plans to assist fate in tossing the title his way, no matter how greatly he may covet it."

Caroline shivered, not merely from the cold. "Let us go in before we turn to ice," she said. "No wonder our ghost walks in the house. It is much warmer there. I fear I shall soon have to follow her example and take my exercise within doors, for I swear it becomes colder every day."

They turned and began to make their way out of the maze, Jarvis following Caroline. At some point she took a wrong turn, and they found their way blocked. Caroline smiled at her companion. "Perhaps you should have led the way out. It would appear I have not mastered this as completely as I thought."

"I perceive you are walking more than one maze right now," said Jarvis. "And if you stay, you yourself could end up in danger. Please do not keep any secrets. Do not attempt to battle your adversary alone. Not when there are those nearby who would willingly risk any danger for you."

Caroline blushed and thanked him. "You are very kind," she murmured. "And I shall remember your offer."

"Come now," he said. "Let us see if you can get us out of this labyrinth."

Caroline tried again to find her way out of the maze. And soon they were laughing as they passed the same bench and statue of Puck for the third time. "I am sure he is taking great delight in all this," said Jarvis.

"So are you, it would appear," said Caroline. "It is wicked of you not to help me."

"I would if I thought you could not find your way," Jarvis replied. "But you are doing fine," he

147

said encouragingly. "Do not give up."

Caroline finally found her way out, and they emerged, still laughing, to see Damien approaching across the lawn, a sight which sobered them both quickly. "I'll wager he has come to spy on us," said Caroline.

"You both appear to have been having a most pleasant morning," commented Damien as he turned and fell in step with them.

"We were," replied Jarvis in chilly tones.

Damien refused to be offended. He smiled at Caroline. "I thought as it is such a fine morning you might enjoy a ride," he said.

Caroline would have enjoyed a ride, but she was not sure she would enjoy a ride with Damien. She hesitated, and Jarvis offered to come along.

"My dear Jarvis, are you the lady's protector that you feel you must go everywhere with her?" He turned to Caroline. "Or is the fearless Lady Caroline afraid of riding out alone with me?"

Caroline's back straightened. "Certainly not," she snapped. "I should be delighted to ride out with you, sir."

The expression on her face belied this statement, but Damien beamed cheerfully at her. "Good," he said. "How long will it take you to get ready?"

Before an hour had passed Caroline was in her riding habit and trotting down the drive on what Damien had informed her was the most feisty filly in the stables. "You do not strike me as the kind of woman who would beg for a safe mount."

Caroline's jaw set in determination as her horse danced along, straining at the tight rein. "How very considerate of you," she said sarcastically.

Damien smiled at her, and Caroline wished she was not so fully occupied with controlling her horse.

She dearly would have loved to slap the smile from that impudent face. The horrid man. What was he up to? Was this a ploy to demonstrate his own superiority? Did he hope to humiliate her? He should have to do better than this if that was his aim. Caroline had never run with the horsey set, but she had a good seat and a strong will. She tightened her grip on the reins and flashed Damien the Lady Caroline special—a blinding smile.

They reached open country. "Shall we give them their heads?" suggested Damien.

For answer, Caroline loosened the reins and spurred her horse. The filly shot forward and began thudding across the pastures. Caroline leaned forward and let her body catch the rhythm of the horse's movement, exulting in the fact that she was ahead of her arrogant companion.

They raced on through open fields and finally into a copse of trees, barely lessening their pace, jumping over fallen logs, swerving or ducking to avoid low-hanging branches. The woods thickened, and just as Caroline deemed it time to slow her pace, she rounded a bend and came suddenly upon a fallen tree sitting much higher off the ground than any obstacle had a right to sit. The horse jumped and cleared it. So did Caroline. Unfortunately, she and her horse did not clear it together.

Caroline hit the ground with an unladylike "oomph," and the animal trotted callously off. Whimpering, she struggled to her hands and knees, then sat with a plop in the underbrush and ran a shaking hand through her tumbled curls. Her hat. Where was her hat? "Clear over there," she moaned. Still shaking, she got back on hands and knees and leaned over into the underbrush, reaching for it.

Just then she heard the thunder of hooves. Damien

jumped from his horse and ran to her. "Caroline," he cried, pulling her into his arms. "Are you all right?"

A properly bred female would have taken full advantage of such a situation, feigning mortal injury, thereby either snaring her man or, as in Caroline's case, properly punishing him for mounting her with such a challenging horse. Caroline was too irritated to behave like a properly bred female. "I am fine," she snarled, pulling away from him with more vehemence than was necessary. She lost her balance and fell backwards into the bracken.

Of course, a properly bred gentleman would never laugh in such a situation. Unfortunately, Damien failed to act like a properly bred gentleman. He began to snicker.

"Oh, laugh," snapped Caroline. "I am glad you find it all so amusing."

He did. He put his hands on his hips, threw back his head, and did as she had suggested.

The ridiculousness of the whole situation hit Caroline and she, too, began to laugh.

Damien offered her his hand, and she took it and allowed him to help her up. "I am sorry," he said. "I seem to have run the gamut of emotions here. You frightened me to death. I suppose I was laughing as much in relief as anything."

Caroline smiled at him. "It would have served you right if I had broken my neck," she scolded. Perhaps that was what he had hoped would happen, she thought suddenly, and the smile fell from her face.

"I assure you it was not my intention to take you out riding and break your neck," he said, as if reading her mind.

Caroline was not so sure. She bravely ignored the sudden nervous thumping inside her chest and began to dust her skirts. "I look a fright," she said.

150

"On the contrary," said Damien. "You look utterly ravishing. It is always a treat to see a woman with her hair flowing."

Caroline blushed and pulled at her loosened curls, trying to put them back in place.

Damien bent and retrieved her hat, which she set back on her hair as best she could. "I'll fetch your horse," he said.

He returned and helped her remount, and they rode the rest of the way to Isobelle's without incident. In her disheveled state Caroline had hoped Damien would suggest they return. But he did not mention it, and pride kept her from asking to go back. She did hint, however.

Damien chose to be obtuse. "It is not far to Hallowstone House from here, and I think a few minutes with Isobelle's maid and a restorative cup of tea would be of benefit to you," he said comfortingly. "Did anyone tell you Hallowstone House is built on the site of an old abbey?" he asked conversationally, spurring his horse forward.

"How fascinating," said Caroline irritably, following him.

"Heavens!" exclaimed Isobelle upon hearing about Caroline's fall. "How fortunate you had Damien with you."

A number of replies came to Caroline's mind, all unladylike as well as ungracious. She merely smiled and allowed herself to be led off and set to rights. She returned to Isobelle's elegant drawing room to find the tea things set out and a cheery fire burning in the hearth, and, in spite of her intense dislike for Isobelle, a feeling of warmth stole over her at the sight of such creature comforts. This feeling was followed immediately by a sinking sensation as she perceived that Sir John had joined them. He struggled from his chair and came and took her hand, gallantly conducting her to the sofa and asking her how she felt.

"I am fine," she assured him, but he continued to fuss over her. "Truly," she said. "What was hurt most was my pride." Out of the corner of her eye she could see Damien lounging in a chair. His boots were still gleaming, his clothes were clean, and he was smiling hugely. Caroline smiled kindly at her host. The smile she turned on her future brother-in-law was anything but kind.

He coughed and hid his mirth behind his teacup.

After half an hour's worth of small talk Damien suggested they leave. "Oh, so soon?" said Sir John. "You have only just come. I was hoping for a little more time to talk to your beautiful houseguest."

"I shall bring her again," Damien promised. "Do you feel recovered enough to start back?" he asked Caroline.

"Certainly," said Caroline, rising.

They bid Isobelle and her father farewell and rode home. A very short visit, thought Caroline, as they trotted down the drive. Of course, it had probably not taken long for Damien and Isobelle to congratulate each other on their success and agree on the next step in their plan. But why bring her along? She couldn't help marveling at the effrontery of a man who would take his enemy with him on a visit to his accomplice. He was obviously enjoying this dangerous game, pretending concern for her one moment, flaunting his partner in crime in front of her the next. She looked thoughtfully at Damien. What new plans had he and Isobelle concocted before she and Sir John had joined them? She supposed she would find out soon enough.

They were less than halfway home when a lone

figure on horseback cantered into view. Damien swore under his breath.

Caroline was frankly pleased and more than a little relieved. Being in Damien's company was anything but relaxing, and she always left him with her mind in a tangle.

Damien scowled as Jarvis rode up to them and reined in his horse. "I suppose you are going to tell us this is pure coincidence. You were just out for a ride and happened onto us."

"If you like I should be happy to tell you that," said Jarvis, smiling at Caroline. "How have you fared on Persephone, here?" he asked her.

Persephone, the mythical female who was dragged off by Hades, king of the dead to be his wife. Damien, Persephone. This family had a penchant for strange names. "We have come to an understanding," she said.

"I am glad to see you are still in one piece," said Jarvis.

"I would not have let any harm come to her," Damien said. "Persephone is temperamental, but she's not vicious."

Jarvis said nothing, but the expression on his face told Caroline what he thought of this assessment of Persephone's character. Unconsciously, she tightened her hold on the reins.

They arrived back at Grayson Hall without incident. No mention was made of the secret passageway, either during the ride or when the company sat down to eat their midday meal. Caroline looked at Damien speculatively. What would his next move be in this dangerous game they were playing? Would the haunting of Grayson Hall come to an end? And if so, what dangerous new prank would take its place?

That evening after dinner the two mamas begged

to hear some music from the younger generation. Caroline was fond of music as was Phoebe. And Clarence was a ham. The younger generation was happy to oblige.

Jarvis was quick to pull up a chair next to Caroline as she sat down at the pianoforte, offering to turn pages for her. Flattered by his attention, Caroline smiled sweetly and thanked him.

But Jarvis was not as assiduous in his page turning as he had been on previous occasions. Twice Clarence had to order him to turn the page so they could get on with the song. Jarvis shook his head. "I do not know why I am so stupid tonight. I am suddenly rather sleepy."

"Too much port," said Clarence knowledgeably.

"I had no more than you," protested Jarvis.

Clarence shrugged and looked mystified.

Jarvis sat blinking for another ten minutes, trying to stay awake. But soon his chin dropped to his chest, and he began to snore loudly.

Damien shook his head and reached for the bell-pull. "Poor old fellow. He must have drunk more than he realized." Two footmen were sent for and Jarvis was conveyed, still snoring, off to his bedchamber.

The singing continued a little longer, then Clarence proposed a game of cards.

"Perhaps you and Phoebe would not mind playing alone," said Damien. He turned to Caroline. "Now that my rival is eliminated, would you care to match skills at the billiard table again?"

Caroline was not anxious to spend more time alone with Damien. But she politely agreed and accompanied him to the shovelboard parlor turned billiard room. "What did you mean by your comment a few moments ago?" Caroline asked as he

154

shut the door behind them.

"What comment?"

"Oh, let us not fence. That statement about eliminating your rival may have been merely a figure of speech, but I tell you plainly, sir, it sounded positively sinister."

Damien smiled broadly. "What a cold-hearted villain you think me, dear lady. I did not poison him, if that is what you are thinking. After this morning I came to the conclusion that if I were to have any time with you apart from my charming cousin, I would have to resort to desperate measures."

Caroline cocked an enquiring eyebrow.

"I slipped something in his wine," said Damien. Caroline's eyes grew wide, and he gave her his most charming smile. "Do not fret. He will be fine in the morning."

"Where did you learn such a trick?" she demanded.

"In India. It is really very useful knowledge."

"I can imagine," said Caroline sarcastically.

"But hardly acceptable in polite circles?"

"Hardly," said Caroline in disapproving tones. "Surely you do not find it necessary to resort to the methods you used in an uncivilized country here."

"Civilization has many benefits," said Damien. "But there are times when it is safer to act like a barbarian."

"I am sure you will be very safe, then," said Caroline. A vision of the snoring Jarvis came unbidden to her mind, and her lips stretched in an unconscious grin. Damien had been watching her closely and he, too, grinned. She giggled. He chuckled. They both began to laugh. She suddenly remembered with whom she was laughing and recovered her dignity. "What an odious man you are," she said.

155

"I am not odious all the time."

"I have yet to see you when you are not being odious."

"I was not odious this morning," said Damien, handing her a cue stick.

Caroline made no reply. She was still trying to understand the purpose of the morning's outing. Honestly, she could not decide whether or not Damien Grayson wished to court her or kill her. Why was she here with this man? She should have pleaded a headache and retired to the safety of her bedroom. She leaned over the table and took her shot.

Silence reigned for a few moments as both she and Damien concentrated on their game. Finally Damien sighed as he sized up the table. "You have left me nothing," he complained.

"There is a shot," said Caroline, pointing to a ball.

"I should have to be a contortionist to get it," said Damien.

"A player of skill could make that shot," taunted Caroline.

Damien made a face. He planted one knee on the edge of the table and leaned forward. Powerful thigh muscles bulged beneath the cloth of his breeches. He leaned forward farther, straining to make his shot. The cloth of his breeches was strained as well, but, unlike Damien, was unequal to the stress. There was a gentle ripping sound, and he slowly straightened up, a blush growing under his dark skin. "I fear that under the circumstances I will have to forfeit the game," he said solemnly.

Caroline tried to maintain a straight face, but human nature triumphed over breeding, and she was unable to stifle a giggle. Once escaped, that giggle loosed others, and soon she was laughing uncontrollably.

Damien gave her a charmingly embarrassed smile.

"Oh, I am sorry," said Caroline finally, wiping her eyes. "How extremely rude of me."

"I began to think only Jarvis had the gift of being able to make you laugh," he said. "And if I must play the fool to hear that sound I shall take the part gladly."

"I suppose we may call it an even score now," said Caroline, remembering her embarrassing morning. "For it has not been so very long since you laughed at me."

"I am rightly served," he said. He smiled a crooked smile and bowed. "You will forgive me my rather odd departure," he said, backing toward the door.

Caroline nodded and smiled politely at him. The smile still played on her face even after the door had shut. But she soon came to her senses. "Fool," she scolded herself. "Whatever are you thinking of?" This was exactly what the wretch wanted. He was being kind to her, trying to win her over and allay her suspicions, trying to lull her into a mental stupor. Once she abandoned her watchful attitude he would strike again. And who knew what he would do? She quickly wiped the smile from her face and joined the others in the drawing room, determined to have no more cozy tête-à-têtes with the enemy.

Clarence greeted her on her return with the kind of casual warmth one reserved for family. No one could accuse Clarence of being brilliant, but he was a dear, sweet fellow, and surely he and Phoebe deserved to be happy. Caroline set her jaw in determination. She simply could not retreat and leave the field to the enemy. There would be no more thought of leaving. And there would also be no more fraternizing with the enemy.

11

If Jarvis suspected he had been deliberately sent to the land of Nod the previous night, he made no mention of it, although Caroline noticed his greeting to Damien at breakfast was frostier than usual. "How did you sleep last night, dear boy?" Lady Grayson asked him innocently.

Jarvis gave her a charming smile. "Quite well, I thank you. I shall have to be more careful what I drink from now on, however." He looked at Damien when he said this, but Damien took no notice as he was fully occupied spooning marmalade onto his plate.

"Dam tells me there is a cockfight in Upper Swanley tonight," Clarence announced. "What say we take it in?"

"Excellent idea," said Jarvis. "I am sure the ladies would forgive our absence for one evening."

Lady Grayson wrinkled her nose in disgust. "Such a barbaric entertainment."

"Men are all barbarians at heart, Mama," said Damien. "You should know that having lived with three of them."

"I was always glad I had daughters," said Lady Harborough smugly.

Damien cocked an eyebrow. "How unfortunate that you will be soon acquiring a son."

"Oh well, yes, of course," said Lady Harborough.

"And I am sure there is no one else she would rather have for a son than Clarence," said Caroline, coming to her mama's rescue and smiling at Clarence, who blushed and cleared his throat nervously.

"Yes, yes," agreed Lady Harborough, looking relieved.

"But if you all leave us who will be here to protect us from the ghost?" ventured Phoebe.

"We will be back before the witching hour," Damien promised.

The fact that she did not drop a subject which Damien obviously considered closed showed how much it weighed on Phoebe's mind. "But what if the ghost should not wait?" she said in a small voice.

"No self-respecting ghost ever walks before midnight," said Damien confidently.

"He's right, don't you know," put in Clarence. "Ain't done."

"Will you be back by midnight?" Phoebe asked her intended.

Clarence scratched his head. "Well," he said.

"We shall try," said Damien diplomatically.

Which means they won't be, thought Caroline.

"I think it is beastly," said Lady Grayson later that morning as the ladies sat sewing in the winter parlor. "Making sport out of watching two poor roosters peck and claw each other to death."

"Yes, it is cruel," agreed Lady Harborough.

Lady Grayson sighed. "It is terribly rude of the

159

boys to run off and leave us."

"Well, we shall enjoy a quiet evening by ourselves," said Lady Harborough comfortingly.

"If the ghost does not appear," said Phoebe in despondent tones.

"Oh, I am sure your sister has quite frightened it away," said Lady Harborough complacently. "It has not troubled us for some time now." She smiled at her eldest daughter. "You were quite right about our not calling off the engagement and leaving. It would have been a pity to spoil the children's happiness. Especially since everything has blown over."

Caroline saw no sense in ruining the morning by telling her mama that the ghost was still alive and well and that nothing had blown over, that most likely the worst of the stormy battle still lay ahead. She smiled weakly.

Her smile weakened further when, a few minutes later, Isobelle was ushered into the room. Lady Grayson beamed fondly on her. "Did you ride over, dear?"

"I took the dogcart," replied Isobelle. "It is a fine morning. I did see some clouds in the distance. We may be in for a storm later on."

"I hope we do not have a thunderstorm," said Phoebe. "Horrible things always happen during a thunderstorm."

"Stuff," said Caroline scornfully.

"I do wish the men were going to be home," Phoebe continued fretfully.

"They are all going to be gone?" asked Isobelle innocently.

Oh no, thought Caroline.

"Yes," replied Lady Grayson. "They are deserting us to go into town tonight and watch a cockfight." She shuddered. "Disgusting."

Isobelle looked properly sympathetic, then properly grateful when her ladyship invited her to stay for luncheon.

"And after luncheon perhaps an excursion into town might be a good idea," Lady Grayson continued. "I am nearly out of gold thread, and I should like to finish this altar cloth by the end of the week."

Lady Harborough begged to be excused, sure she would be feeling fatigued after lunch and ready for a nap, but the three younger women agreed, two of them with alacrity.

"Of course," said Lady Grayson, "if it rains before afternoon I am not so sure I shall want to go. I find it quite unpleasant to go from shop to shop in the rain." Phoebe's face fell. "But then, I see no reason why you girls should not all go. I am sure Caroline would not mind acting as chaperone for you and Isobelle."

"If it rains I should as soon not go," said Isobelle. "I detest being cold and damp. In fact, I left orders with Smythe to keep me informed. If it looks the least like rain I shall have to be on my way."

"Nonsense," said Lady Grayson. "We shall, as always, send you home in the carriage."

The sky became gray but, other than casting gloom over the countryside, the clouds showed no intention of raining, and after luncheon the ladies went to fetch bonnets and gloves. Caroline was just tying on her bonnet when Phoebe came to her room, visibly upset.

"What is it, love?" asked Caroline.

"My yellow gloves," Phoebe lamented. "I have lost one."

"Your tan chevrette ones will do as well. I am sure your yellow glove will turn up," said Caroline.

"No, you do not understand," cried Phoebe. "I have looked everywhere and it is gone. Do you not

161

know what that means?"

Understanding dawned. "That is mere superstition," Caroline said sternly. "You are not going to have bad luck simply because you cannot find your glove. Put the other one back in your drawer and let us be going. I shall help you search for the missing one when we return."

Phoebe did as she was bid but she still looked worried as the ladies went out to the carriage. "Is something bothering you, my dear?" asked Lady Grayson as the carriage rolled down the drive.

"I have lost a glove," said Phoebe in desolate tones.

Lady Grayson gasped. "Oh, dear," she said.

"But we shall find it as soon as we get back," said Caroline.

"Let us hope so," said Lady Grayson.

Phoebe continued to look worried for the rest of their ride into Upper Swanley. Once in town, however, she forgot her worries and enjoyed browsing in the shops, chatting animatedly. Until they passed a glovers. "Look at those lovely lavender gloves!" exclaimed Isobelle. Phoebe's face fell. "Oh, I am sorry," said Isobelle. "I am sure you will find your glove."

"But if I don't . . ." Phoebe's voice trailed off.

"Yes," agreed Isobelle sympathetically. "That would be most awful."

Phoebe sighed. "So many awful things have happened since I have come here. That horrid ghost has frightened me near to death. I broke my mirror. And now I have lost my glove. Caroline is so brave. But I am not. If much more happens I vow I shall go mad."

Isobelle patted her arm comfortingly. "You poor thing," she murmured. "Who could blame you if you were to have second thoughts about marrying Clarence."

Phoebe said nothing, but her lower lip trembled. Caroline came out of the shop next door and Isobelle said, "Look. Here comes your sister. Try to look cheerful, dear. There is no sense in upsetting her for she will only scold you."

On returning home both Lady Grayson and Phoebe urged Isobelle to stay for tea. Caroline was not sorry when she declined. The clouds were darkening ominously, and she claimed she was anxious to be going. "I had best get home to see how Papa does," she said.

"Such a dear girl," said Lady Grayson after she had gone. "So devoted to her papa. Such a kind heart."

Such a bag of moonshine, thought Caroline cynically.

The gentlemen joined them for tea, and Phoebe told Clarence her awful news. "Lost a glove, eh?" he said. "That is serious."

"I am sure we will find it stuffed in a corner of your drawer," said Caroline consolingly.

"Are you going to help me look for it?"

"Yes, I will help you look for it," Caroline promised, and then turned the subject, hoping to direct her sister's thoughts in a more pleasant direction.

Damien, however, seemed determined to keep poor Phoebe in a state of worry. "Interesting," he said. "I had quite forgotten that old superstition. How many years' bad luck will you have if you do not find your glove? Is it the same amount of misfortune as you suffer when you break a mirror?"

Phoebe's face went white. "Oh dear, I do not know. She did not tell me."

"Who did not tell you?" Caroline demanded. Phoebe looked at her sister blankly. "Someone told you all this, but you did not learn it from us, for it has

163

never been a particular suspicion of Mama's or mine."

"That is quite true," said Lady Harborough. "I was forever losing gloves and never thought a thing about it. Why, the year your Papa died I lost three pair."

Phoebe's eyes grew round at this, and her lower lip began to tremble.

"If you are finished with your tea, why don't we go look for it now?" Caroline suggested, setting down her cup.

"Oh, yes," said Phoebe. "We must find it as soon as possible."

The sisters excused themselves and hurried upstairs to Phoebe's bedchamber. "Who told you about this superstition?" Caroline asked again as they hurried down the corridor.

"I don't know," said Phoebe distractedly. "I think it was Rose."

"Your new maid!" exclaimed Caroline. She said nothing more until they had entered the bedchamber, then asked casually as they began their search, "Who recommended Rose to you, love?"

"Isobelle did," said Phoebe. "She had served in Isobelle's house as a parlormaid and was anxious to become a lady's maid. And I must say, she has served me very well," Phoebe finished.

I'll wager she has, thought Caroline.

A thorough search was made, not only of the drawer where Phoebe kept her gloves, but of the entire room. The bottom of the wardrobe was checked, every reticule emptied. Phoebe even looked beneath her bed, but the missing glove remained stubbornly hidden.

Caroline could see her sister was becoming increasingly distraught as the fruitless search continued.

With sudden inspiration she snatched the bereaved yellow glove and slipped it in the pocket of her gown. "Oh, my," she said, rummaging through Phoebe's drawer. "Now where has that other glove gone?"

"What?" squeaked Phoebe. She backed out from under the bed and ran across the room to stand next to her sister. Frantically, she pawed through the gloves and handkerchiefs. "It was here only a moment ago."

"Do you mean to tell me you have now lost the other glove as well?" asked Caroline in mock astonishment.

In answer Phoebe began to cry.

"But this is marvelous, wonderful!" Caroline hugged her sister, who had stopped crying and was looking at her in amazement.

"Whatever do you mean?" demanded Phoebe. "Now I have lost both gloves and I shall have twice as much bad luck," said Phoebe.

"Oh no," said Caroline. "That is not how it works at all. When you lose one glove it is bad luck. But if you lose its mate as well that completely cancels all the bad luck the loss of the first one has brought you."

"Do you mean I shall not have bad luck after all?" asked Phoebe hopefully.

"That is right. How very fortunate that you have managed to lose the other glove as well," said Caroline.

"Oh, yes," agreed Phoebe, all smiles.

Caroline left her sister and went to her room to do some serious thinking. On arriving there she found Sibby waiting for her. "Well, now," said Caroline. "You are looking very much like the cat who swallowed the canary. What have you discovered?"

"Something I thought you would want to see,"

said Sibby. "Especially after all the fuss this morning about the missing glove." She held out her hand and there, dangling between two fingers, was a dirty yellow glove.

"Well now," said Caroline. "What's this?" She took the matching glove from her pocket and she and Sibby exchanged knowing glances.

"I went for a walk this afternoon and saw a corner of this poking out of the ground by one of the rose bushes in the garden. Someone must have been in a hurry to be rid of it. They did not bury it with much care."

"This is most interesting," said Caroline thoughtfully. "You will never guess who recommended Phoebe's maid. It was none other than our dear Miss Payne. Oh, it all begins to fall together now. How very handy to plant such an accomplice in the house. When the fair Isobelle is not around to frighten Phoebe she can depend on Rose to keep her properly stirred up. I wonder what other services Rose has performed for our friendly neighbor."

"Maybe it was Rose who has been letting Miss Payne in and out of the house and not Mr. Grayson," suggested Sibby.

Caroline chewed her lip thoughtfully. Rose had been present when Caroline shared her discovery of the priest's hole with Phoebe and had heard Caroline announce her plan for trapping the ghost. Could it have been Rose who warned Isobelle to beware of a trap? Had she, Caroline, been following the wrong trail? Was this strictly a conspiracy of women? Was Clarence's encounter with footpads merely a coincidence? Were all the evil and nasty things she had attributed to Damien mere imagination? "I don't know," she said thoughtfully. "One thing we can be sure of. Rose is in this up to her ears."

"Lady Phoebe should have brought her own maid with her," said Sibby. "It is always best to bring your own maid along when you are visiting."

"Whether she wants to come or not," said Caroline, giving her maid a mischievous look.

"I am sure it pleases you to make fun of me," said Sibby in injured tones.

"Oh, Sibby," laughed Caroline. "You are so funny. Phoebe could hardly expect her maid to be of any service to her with the grippe." Suddenly serious, she said, "You have been very helpful to me in all this. I am grateful for your help and most glad you came."

Sibby smiled, placated. "So what will you do now?" she asked.

"I shall dress for dinner," said Caroline lightly.

She entered the drawing room in time to hear Jarvis inquiring of Phoebe whether or not she had found her missing glove.

"No," said Phoebe. "But I have lost the other one now, which is nearly as good as finding the missing glove."

"Oh? And how is that?" asked Jarvis politely.

"Did you not know? If you lose one glove it is bad luck. But when you lose its mate, that cancels all the bad luck you would have had." Phoebe caught sight of her sister. "I was just telling Jarvis what you told me," she said.

"How very interesting," said Jarvis. "This is something I never heard before."

"I am surprised," said Caroline lightly. "It is a very old belief."

Dinner was announced and the family filed into the dining room. "A very old belief?" Jarvis whispered to Caroline. "How old?"

"Oh, at least one day," she answered, smiling at

167

him from under her lashes.

The family took their places around the table, and Caroline found herself sitting next to Damien. He smiled admiringly at her. "You are looking especially enchanting tonight," he said. "That cream color becomes you. So does a simple décolletage. For some women frills at the bodice are a necessity, but on you they would be a most unwelcome distraction."

In spite of her recent discovery, Caroline found it hard to dismiss Damien as having no part in these doings, and she told herself his admiration was unwanted. And to prove it, she ignored the faint fluttering feelings trying to take flight somewhere deep inside her. She ignored him as much as possible during their meal, but Damien Grayson was not an easy man to ignore, especially when he was bent on being charming. Caroline found this as irritating as everything else about the man. "I wonder, sir, how much longer you will be staying at Grayson Hall," she finally said rudely.

Damien's eyebrows rose in surprise. "Why, as long as it pleases me to stay," he replied. "I have no pressing engagements elsewhere. And I have been away from home a long time. I am enjoying being once again in the bosom of my family. Would you have me end my visit so soon, just when we are getting to know each other?"

That was exactly what she would have had. "I suppose there is only one answer you would wish to that question," said Caroline.

Damien smiled—a full-lipped smile that betrayed shiny, white teeth and made him look rather like a wolf. "That is true," he admitted. "Although I know what answer you would like to give, future sister. But you could not really be so cruel as to wish me gone and deprive me of the thrill of watching you catch our famous ghost. Now, would you?"

Caroline knew he was baiting her, and in that moment she knew he was not innocent. Rose may have a hand in this, she thought, but she is not the brain behind it all. An angry flush stole up her neck, but she smiled at her dinner companion. "Does not your cockfight begin soon?" she asked sweetly.

Dinner ended and the gentlemen left for Upper Swanley in search of sport and strictly male company.

Partway through the evening the clouds which had been gathering burst, bringing a steady, unrelenting rain. "To think the poor boys are out in this," said Lady Grayson, looking out the window into the darkness. Silver droplets made frantic tapping noises on the window pane. A sudden bolt of lightning brought a branch outside the window eerily to life, and Phoebe jumped.

"I am sure they are still at the cockfight or safely in the private parlor of the Boar's Head, enjoying a roaring fire," said Lady Harborough unconcernedly. "At any rate, dampness and mud do not seem to bother gentlemen."

Of course not, thought Caroline. They have no skirts to drag in the mud and hamper them, and they can wear sturdy boots to keep their feet warm. She had to admit, however, that even if she had access to breeches and sturdy boots, she wouldn't want to be out in this. Ah well, the weather would most likely keep the fair Isobelle from sneaking out to play ghost. She appeared to hate being out in the rain as much as any female.

The storm continued to rage, and the ladies lingered over their teacups. Phoebe's eyes kept straying to the drawing-room door, obviously hoping

Clarence would return home from the cockfight in time to escort her upstairs. Caroline knew it was a forlorn hope. There was no sense prolonging the inevitable. "Shall we retire?" she suggested.

"I should like one more cup of tea," said Phoebe timidly.

"You have already had three," pointed out Caroline. "One more and you will not sleep at all tonight."

"I probably won't sleep at all anyway," said Phoebe.

"Come, love," coaxed Caroline. "I am sure the men will be home soon."

"Then can we not wait for them?" begged Phoebe.

"Your sister is right," said Lady Harborough firmly. "We may as well go to our nice, warm beds. And as for the boys, I am sure they will not be home for some time yet. There is no sense waiting up for them."

The ladies managed to mount the stairs and get down the corridor unmolested by the ghost. "The storm appears to be letting up," Lady Harborough observed. "Perhaps we shall get a good night's sleep after all."

Caroline went to her room, but instead of ringing for Sibby to help her undress, she settled in a comfortable chair by the fire, put her feet up on the stool, and drew a blanket over her legs. After the storm they'd just had she was sure the chances of Isobelle's appearing were slim. But one never knew what discomfort a desperate woman was willing to endure for the sake of the man (and the title) she wanted.

Sibby put in an appearance, wondering aloud why, when everyone else had rung for their maid, she'd been left waiting unwanted in the servants' quarters. Caroline attempted to send her off to bed,

170

but Sibby stubbornly refused, insisting that if there was going to be trouble she wanted to be on hand to help.

Caroline capitulated, knowing it was useless to argue. "Very well, then. As you are determined to be loyal rather than sensible, you had best take a chair by the fire. We could wait all night and see nothing, so we may as well be comfortable."

The two women settled by the fire, Sibby dosing off first and Caroline, in spite of her determination to stay awake, nodding off soon after.

Caroline did not know she had fallen asleep until a noise dragged her up from the dark depths.

Across from her, Sibby jumped. "What was that?" she gasped.

A scream coming from the corridor answered her question.

"Goodness!" exclaimed Caroline, jumping up. "That sounds like—" Her door burst open and Caroline's mouth dropped at the sight of the figure in white standing in the doorway.

12

"Mama!" gasped Caroline. "Whatever are *you*
doing up? And what has happened?"

"Of all the silly questions," snapped Lady Harborough. "After all that tea what do you think I am
doing? Oh," she moaned, clutching at her heart,
"how can you waste time talking about ordinary
things when your only mother is about to expire."

"Have you seen the ghost?" asked Caroline.

"Yes. Just now in the corridor."

Caroline didn't wait to hear any more. She dashed
past her mama and out the door.

"Caroline! I think I'm about to faint! Where are
you going?" demanded Lady Harborough.

"To catch the ghost," Caroline called over her
shoulder. She heard a dramatic moan followed by a
thump, but ruthlessly pressed on. She would deal
with their tormentor first, then return to pick Mama
up from the floor.

Caroline ran down the corridor, her skirts held
high, and flew down the stairs. As she rounded the
corner onto the first landing, she collided with a tall,
muscular body. The body emitted a startled "oomph,"
but remained upright. Caroline was not so lucky.

The impact sent her sprawling.

Two more bodies entered her field of vision, and the three men stood for a moment, staring stupidly at her. It was Damien who spoke first. Offering her his hand and pulling her up, he asked, "Are you all right?"

"Yes, no thanks to you," she snapped ungraciously. "Excuse me, please," she said and ran down the stairs.

"Where are you going?" called Damien, setting off in pursuit.

"I am chasing the ghost," she called.

"Phoebe!" exclaimed Clarence, and headed off in the opposite direction.

Jarvis let Clarence go upstairs alone. He turned and followed Damien and Caroline downstairs at a more leisurely pace. It wasn't difficult to find them. He merely followed his ears to the great hall, where he discovered the combatants standing nose to nose, both very red in the face. "What do you mean by that?" Damien was demanding.

"I mean, of course, it is no use now. You have delayed me just enough to allow your precious ghost to escape. Oh, how convenient this all was! We have not seen the ghost for days. And now she suddenly reappears the same night that the men are from home. I call that a very strange coincidence."

"So do I," said Damien.

"So do I," said Jarvis, entering the room.

Damien's eyes narrowed to slits at the sight of his cousin.

"And how were you going to continue your chase from this room?" asked Jarvis lightly. "Climb out the window or break through the wall?"

"Neither," replied Caroline. "There is a secret passageway." Still glowering at Damien, she pushed the stone in the hearth. Jarvis came close and peered into the dark cavity. He wrinkled his nose. "Ugh! What a smell. Where does it lead?"

"Out past the garden and to the copse," answered Damien absently, regarding Caroline. "And you were going to chase our ghost down that dark passage alone?"

"If I had not been detained I might have caught her before she even got inside," said Caroline, still in a nasty temper. With that remark she stalked from the room, leaving the two men staring after her.

Jarvis ventured a smile at Damien and shrugged. "My father said they are all a little crazy. Perhaps he was right."

Damien was not amused. He returned no answer, but also stalked from the room, leaving Jarvis to shut the door to the passageway.

The next morning Caroline received the imperious summons she had been expecting. Lady Harborough was still in bed when her daughter was ushered into her room. Every bit the queen, she sat propped up on pillows, crowned with a nightcap, her hair still in curl papers and her hot chocolate in her hand. She eyed her daughter with disfavor. "How are you feeling this morning?" asked Caroline meekly.

"My daughter, who left me fainting on the floor, a helpless victim for any apparition which might happen to float by, finally has the goodness to ask me how I am?"

Caroline bit her lip. Mama was going to be difficult this morning. She made an effort to sound contrite. "I am so sorry, Mama. I was trying to protect you."

"Hmph," snorted Lady Harborough. "Much protection you were, out haring around the house while

174

I lay on the floor gasping. People running everywhere. Pandemonium. I tell you, child, I shall not spend another day in this house. I do not care whether this ghost is real or pretend. And I do not care to stay here any longer trying to find out."

"But Mama," Caroline began.

Lady Harborough held up a hand. "I will speak no more about it. We are leaving and that is final. You may stay and chase shadows if you like, but I am taking your sister back home with me. I am sure next season she will meet another man equally as nice as Clarence."

"Mama!"

"That is an end of it. My trunk is being brought up now. We will leave this afternoon."

"But Mama. The ball is less than a fortnight away."

"We could all be dead in a fortnight," snapped Lady Harborough.

"We already have our costumes," continued Caroline, ignoring this remark. "Uncle Alistair would not be happy if he learned you had gone to such expense buying costumes and then never used them."

"Uncle Alistair need never know," said Lady Harborough.

"Someone might tell him," said Caroline.

"Caroline! You would not do such a thing," exclaimed her mother, shocked.

"I did not say *I* would," said Caroline. "I merely said someone might. And, of course, someone might also tell him you broke Phoebe's engagement to a title and fortune because you thought you saw a ghost."

"I *did* see a ghost," insisted Lady Harborough hotly. She looked suspiciously at her daughter.

"This sounds like blackmail to me," said her mother.

"Perish the thought," said Caroline, looking properly horrified. "But you know Uncle Alistair is bound to find out. Most likely, if you end things this way he will be very displeased. He will say you scotched a perfect match for the sake of mere feminine hysterics."

"I certainly did not!" interrupted Lady Harborough.

Caroline continued, ignoring the interruption. "He will, most likely, refuse to pay for another London season for Phoebe, for he will say it is wasteful extravagance to finance another season of husband hunting when Phoebe had a perfectly good man and discarded him. No doubt he will cut back on your allowance."

Lady Harborough chewed her lip thoughtfully, and Caroline pressed on. "Of course, if we stayed until after the ball, we could then tell Uncle Alistair that at least the money we spent on costumes was not wasted. And we may have caught the ghost by then. However, it is your decision, dearest. I must say *I* should hate to face Uncle Alistair with the news of a broken engagement," Caroline finished ruthlessly.

"Yes, yes. You are quite right," agreed Lady Harborough. "We shall postpone leaving until after the ball and hope that this terrible situation will have straightened itself out by then."

"That is an excellent idea," murmured Caroline, biting back a smile. Dear Uncle Alistair. No mere ghost could compete with him when it came to striking terror in her mother's heart.

Caroline left her mama and went down to breakfast. Damien was not present, nor were Phoebe or Clarence, but Jarvis and Lady Grayson were both at table and enjoying a comfortable coze. "Here is our

176

brave lady now," said Jarvis, rising. "I must say if I doubted it before, last night would have convinced me that you are truly an amazing woman."

"Nonsense," laughed Caroline. "If I was truly amazing I would have caught the thing." She turned to Lady Grayson. "How did you sleep?"

"Fine, I must admit," said Lady Grayson. "I am only sorry my guests did not sleep as well."

"I feel refreshed, nonetheless," said Caroline, helping herself to some eggs. "And where is everyone else? Surely not sleeping."

"Oh, no," said Lady Grayson. "Clarence has gone out shooting and Damien, well, I have no idea where Damien is," she confessed. "Perhaps he is in the library or the shovelboard parlor, playing at billiards."

"Or perhaps he is still sleeping," said Jarvis, rising. "If you ladies will excuse me, I think I shall see if I can find our elusive cousin."

If Jarvis found Damien before luncheon Caroline never heard, and by the time the family had gathered to eat a much more pressing subject was at hand. "Well," boomed Clarence as everyone took their seats at the table. "I'll wager I had a much more exciting morning than any of the rest of you. Some curst poacher took a shot at me again."

Lady Grayson dropped her spoon. "Oh, mercy!" she exclaimed.

"Must've mistaken me for a grouse," said Clarence.

"More like a deer," said his brother. "You are hardly the right size for a grouse. In fact, you are much too big for a deer as well."

Clarence laughed good-naturedly at this. "I guess I am at that," he said.

"You had best be paying a visit to our tenants tomorrow and see if you can discover who our Robin

177

Hood is before someone puts a bullet in you," advised Damien.

Phoebe smiled at Clarence. "I am glad the poacher did not hit you," she said.

"Almost did. He put a hole right through my hat."

Phoebe shuddered. "Oh, how dreadful," she said.

"That is a little too close for comfort," agreed Jarvis.

"You must be careful," scolded Lady Grayson.

"Else we shall have a new head of the family yet again," said Jarvis.

"And I imagine you do not fancy me in that role," said Damien. He slung an arm over the back of his chair and regarded his cousin with an unpleasant smile.

"You would make a terrible host," replied Jarvis calmly, taking a sip from his wine.

After luncheon, Jarvis asked Caroline if she fancied a walk.

"If you mean somewhere other than out of doors," said Caroline, looking out the window at the afternoon drizzle, "I should be glad of some exercise." And I should be glad of a chance to ask you if you ever found your elusive cousin, thought Caroline.

"I think I should enjoy a bit of exercise, myself," said Damien. "You two don't mind if I join you, do you?"

Caroline would liked to have replied that she minded very much, and she suspected Jarvis felt much the same. But one could hardly be rude to one's cousin in front of his mother. Unfortunately.

Caroline and Jarvis both smiled politely, and the three made their way to the long gallery. The gallery was rather a gloomy place. In spite of an oriel window at each end, it seemed to lack light and cheer.

178

The frowning, sober faces of Graysons past looked down on their three visitors as if they considered them intruders. "Has my cousin given you the history of our illustrious family?" asked Damien.

Caroline shook her head, and he pointed to the nearest painting. A swarthy-looking man glared out across the hallway. The resemblance to Damien was striking. "The first Lord Grayson, himself," said Damien. "Quite friendly with the throne. Until it was discovered he had chosen the wrong religion." Damien moved along to the next portrait. "This is our famous ghost," he said, pointing to the picture of a woman in her twenties with small lips, a pinched nose, and large, vacant-looking eyes. "Painted before she became an apparition, of course. She hardly looks like the kind of woman who would be able to scare anyone, whether dead or alive."

Caroline studied the painting and thought she saw much of Clarence in that face. Not in the nose or mouth, but in the coloring and the eyes. After seeing this lady, she thought she knew who must be held responsible for Clarence's less-than-sharp wits.

As if reading her mind, Damien said, "Yes, there is a resemblence between our restless relative and my brother. I have heard, though not terribly intelligent, this Lady Grayson was famous for her kindness and beloved by all."

"Very like your brother," said Caroline kindly.

"There is none kinder," agreed Damien. "Or, at times, stupider. Come, we have an excellent portrait of Edward, the Grayson who won back our title and lands by some invaluable service to the Queen and disservice to his fellow man."

He walked down the gallery, leaving Caroline to gape after him. Heaven only knew her mama and sister were hen-witted, but she would never be so disloyal as to announce that fact to another living creature. What a beast this man was, to be sure.

Damien managed to keep Caroline and Jarvis company for the better part of the afternoon. Caroline finally had enough of both the long gallery and her future brother-in-law's company and excused herself, pleading a need to rest.

She escaped to her room and, on lying on her bed, realized that she was indeed tired. She shut her eyes, simply to rest them and, before she knew it, opened them to discover Sibby shaking her gently, asking if she was going to tea. "Tea? It surely cannot be so late in the day," said Caroline groggily.

"Oh, but it is," said Sibby. "You were having such a nice nap I hated to disturb you."

"I am glad you did," said Caroline. "Else I should never have slept tonight. In fact, I wonder even now if I shall be able to do so after sleeping so soundly these past two hours."

As it turned out, Caroline had no cause to worry. The evening passed quietly enough. Damien behaved himself and said nothing to bait her. She was able to lie down on her bed, close her eyes, and get a good night's sleep, unassailed by ghosts, either in the corridor or in her dreams.

The next morning dawned crisp and cloudless, and when Jarvis offered her a morning ride she was delighted to accept. Damien and Clarence were making the rounds to the estate tenants in search of the mysterious poacher, so she knew they would be free of Damien's unwanted company. Perhaps now, thought Caroline, she would have a chance to talk to Jarvis about the things weighing so heavily on her mind. And talk she did. As soon as Grayson Hall was out of sight she shared her suspicions.

"I must admit Damien has much to profit from by

breaking his brother's engagement. Even more by killing him, but—"

"You still do not believe him capable of such a thing, do you?" Jarvis started to reply, but Caroline gave him no time, rushing on. "Do you remember when his mother talked about footpads, how his ears pricked up? Now, I wonder why. Perhaps he had hired those footpads himself. It is possible. After all, we have no knowledge of how long he has been back in England. I can still remember him telling his brother how hard he was to get rid of. I tell you frankly, I am becoming more worried with each passing day. If this wedding is not called off for lack of a bride it surely will be for lack of a groom."

"Really, you are beginning to alarm me," said Jarvis.

"I hope so, for I believe this situation has gone well past being a malicious prank. Only look at this latest incident. I would be willing to wager this poacher will never be caught. Where was your cousin yesterday morning. Did you ever find him?"

"No," answered Jarvis in tones of dawning horror.

"I beg you to keep a careful watch over your cousin," said Caroline, "for I feel sure his brother will try to harm him again."

"This is all so difficult to believe," Jarvis said. "I find it hard to imagine Belle would be a party to murder."

"I doubt she is," said Caroline. "Damien has, no doubt, gone along with her pranks and told her nothing of his own plans. In fact, I should be very much surprised to learn he had not encouraged her in her folly, for it cannot hurt him to be rid of our family. And these ghostly appearances distract everyone from the near-fatal accidents his brother keeps having—dangerous encounters with footpads,

181

poachers, and heaven knows what else that Clarence has never thought to tell anyone about."

"You may well be right," admitted Jarvis. "I shall try my best to keep an eye on Clarence. But my best may not be good enough. I cannot, unfortunately, watch my cousin all the time."

Caroline nodded. "Yes, I know. But I am hoping we will be able to catch this bogus ghost before long. If I can do that I shall be able to prove my suspicion that there is a connection between its sudden restlessness and the reappearance of Clarence's long-lost brother. Then, perhaps, Clarence will send his brother back where he came, and he and Phoebe will have a chance for happiness."

"You show a good deal of concern for your sister's happiness," said Jarvis. "I wonder, do you ever think of your own?"

Caroline smiled at him. "Of course, I do," she said simply. "But for the moment, my happiness can wait."

Jarvis looked as if he might say more on the subject of Caroline's happiness, and she waited with a fluttering heart, but instead he turned the subject and, slightly disappointed, she followed his lead.

At tea that afternoon Clarence had no news for his family regarding the poacher. "Perhaps you had best not go out shooting anymore," suggested Lady Grayson.

"Stay out of my own woods?" snorted her son indignantly.

"My dear boy, we really cannot have you being shot before your wedding," said his mother sternly.

"A fine brave fellow I should look hiding in my house all the time," said Clarence scornfully.

"Damien, please talk some sense into your brother," commanded Lady Grayson, but Damien merely shook his head and smiled.

The next morning Clarence asserted his independence, announcing his intention to go riding. Alone.

"Must you?" asked Phoebe tearfully.

"I need some fresh air," said Clarence stubbornly. He smiled at Phoebe. "When I come back I shall drive you into Upper Swanley, and you can do some shopping. How does that sound?"

"There is an excellent idea," said his mother. "Why not do that instead of going out riding?" Her words fell on deaf ears. "Damien! Do something."

"I intend to, dearest," said her son, rising. "I am going to the library to read."

Lady Grayson set down her teacup with a loud clink and glared at her son.

Jarvis, too, excused himself and rose from the table, offering to accompany Clarence to the stables.

"If you think you are going to play nursemaid," Clarence began.

"Not at all, old fellow," said Jarvis. "I had planned on paying a morning call on the Payne family."

"Oh, well then, that is a different matter," said Clarence.

Caroline did not like this turn of events. Excusing herself, she hurried to her room, rang for Sibby, and took out her riding habit. "Going riding?" asked Sibby cheerfully when she entered the room. "Here, what's this? Is something wrong?"

"Something could be. Hurry, Sibby."

In a matter of minutes Caroline was dressed and hurrying to the stables. "I need a fast mount. And hurry!" she told the groom.

The man tipped his hat and hurried to do her bidding. He returned, leading her old nemesis, Persephone. Caroline eyed the beast. "You had better be on your best behavior today," she told the horse. "I have no time for foolishness.'' The filly nickered and tossed its head. ''All right, then,'' said Caroline. ''Remember your promise and you shall have a lump of sugar when we return.'' She mounted Persephone, and the horse began to dance, anxious to be gone. ''Which way did his lordship ride out?'' she asked the groom.

''That way, my lady. Toward the stream.''

The words were barely out of his mouth before Caroline was on her way, going down the graveled drive at a gallop. She headed out the gates and down the narrow lane full speed, rushing by pastures and fields, only slowing down when a lone rider came into view. He turned, and at the sight of her his face showed a mixture of surprise and guilt. ''Going to pay a morning call on the Payne family?'' she asked. ''If so, you are headed in quite the wrong direction.''

''So I am,'' he agreed.

''Oh, come. Admit it. You were as worried about Clarence as I.''

''I doubt that,'' he replied.

Caroline ignored this remark. ''Have you seen him?'' she asked.

Jarvis shook his head. ''Not yet.'' He turned his horse off the road and into the pasture. ''Let us try going this way. There is a nice hedge or two off to the east, and Clarence is very fond of jumping.''

Half a mile brought a tempting little hedge in sight. ''Care for a bit of sport?'' asked Jarvis.

For answer Caroline let Persephone have her head and Jarvis followed. They sailed over the hedge one after the other. Their last landing, however, was less than perfect as a strangled yelp and a suddenly moving figure startled their horses. Persephone whinied and reared, sliding Caroline off her back and sidling away. Jarvis managed to keep his seat, but with great difficulty.

"Damn! You scared the wits right out of me," croaked Clarence.

Caroline moaned and struggled to her feet, rubbing her sore posterior. "Clarence! Whatever are you doing sitting under that hedge? And where is your horse."

"Ran off. Damien went to fetch him."

"Damien! But I thought he was in the library," said Jarvis.

"Came following after me like some curst nursemaid. Dashed ridiculous, I call it. A fellow can't even go for a ride without somebody following along behind."

"Were you thrown?" asked Caroline.

"Not taking the jump," said Clarence. "Why, I've taken that hedge a thousand times. So has Brutus. We took the hedge easily. But after we came down he went crazy. Bucked me off before I even knew what had happened."

At that moment, an empty-handed Damien returned and dismounted. Clarence scowled. "What are you two doing here, by the way?" he asked suspiciously. He turned to Jarvis. "I thought you were going to see Belle."

"So did I," said Jarvis innocently. "But I ran into Lady Caroline and changed my mind."

"Caro. You don't think I need watching, do you?" asked Clarence, his pride obviously hurt.

"Of course not," said Caroline reassuringly. "Under normal circumstances I know you to be well able to take care of yourself. But," she continued, looking accusingly at Damien, "I am beginning to think someone near to you means to harm you and—"

"Someone near to me," interrupted Clarence.

"Nonsense!" He clapped his brother and cousin on the back. "I would trust anyone in my family with my life. It is that nag I don't trust anymore."

"Loyal steed that he is, your horse is probably half-way back to the stable by now," said Damien. He fetched Persephone and handed his brother the reins. "I think she's up to your weight. I should take you up with me, but together we would kill off old Windy. Besides, if I am to be crammed onto a horse with another person I had much rather it be with someone soft and lovely than a big clunk such as you." He offered Caroline his hand.

The thought of a cozy ride back to the Hall with Damien Grayson did not appeal to Caroline in the least, but rather than appear churlish, she accepted his hand up and swung herself into the saddle. He mounted in back of her and slipped an arm around her waist and cantered off ahead of the others. "You really are a most delicious morsel," he murmured.

Caroline ignored this comment. She also tried to ignore the fact that, in spite of the cold, her riding habit was suddenly feeling very warm.

"It is really too bad you have taken up such an intense prejudice against me," he continued.

"I never said I disliked you," said Caroline stiffly.

"And I have never said the sun rises in the morning," countered Damien.

"Look!" cried Caroline. "There is Clarence's horse."

A large roan was grazing peacefully in the pasture. Damien trotted up to it, dismounted, and took the beast's reins. Caroline jumped down and came up next to him. "What do you suppose made the animal behave as he did?" she asked.

Damien shook his head. "A sudden fright, perhaps." He looked thoughtfully at the saddle and

Caroline, jumping ahead of him, ran her hand underneath it. "Ouch!" she cried.

Damien lifted the saddle and produced a good-sized prickly burr. Caroline glared at him as he stood staring at it.

Clarence and Jarvis rode up and dismounted. "Well, old fellow," Clarence said to his horse. "We found you at last, have we?"

"That is not all we found," said Caroline.

Damien held out his hand. "Here is the cause of the beast's sudden ill humor. You are no featherweight, you know. It must have hurt like the devil when you came down after that jump."

Clarence scratched his head. "Now, how the devil did that get there?" he wondered.

Damien shrugged. "Who knows? I suggest you have a word with Jem. It wouldn't hurt to make sure the stableboys were made to work a little harder. Perhaps they would have less time for pranks."

"Surely no one in your service would be so insolent as to play such a prank as this," said Caroline.

"No one in my service would," said Damien.

"How else would it get there?" asked Clarence. "Anyway, you know how it is with boys. They don't think. We played our share of those kind of jokes ourselves, eh Dam?" He elbowed his brother. "Didn't you do the exact same thing to old Jarvis once?"

Damien and Jarvis both blushed at this. "I think I am ready for luncheon," said Damien, remounting.

The others followed suit, and they cantered back to the house.

A close call, thought Caroline, watching Clarence. She heartily wished someone had placed a burr under his brother's saddle.

13

If not for the fact that Clarence's mama happened to meet him on the stairs, the rest of his family might not have found out about his accident. "Clarence!" she exclaimed. "You are positively filthy. Whatever have you been doing?"

"Nothing, Mother," said Clarence, attempting to brush by her. "Just riding."

"Merely riding does not get you covered with mud from head to toe," said Lady Grayson. "What happened?"

"Nothing. I took a spill, that is all."

His mother pursed her lips and shook her head. "I knew you should have stayed home," she said.

If Clarence had hoped his mother was through with the subject, however, it was a vain one. As soon as the family was seated at table she began again. "It was very reckless and inconsiderate of you to go out," she told him. "You could have been badly injured and lain for hours like that."

"I was hardly alone," said Clarence. "Had a whole curst army of nursemaids tagging after me."

"After getting shot at only yesterday," began Lady Grayson.

"But I did not get shot at," protested her son.

"Nevertheless, *something* happened," said Lady Grayson. "That is why I told you not to go out. I knew something would happen." She turned to Lady Harborough for support. "Did I not say as much to him?"

"Yes, Evangeline. You did. But then, children can be so willful when they are grown," she concluded, and looked accusingly at Caroline.

Caroline deemed it best to change the subject. "My, I am hungry. These stewed pears certainly look delicious. I don't think even Carlton House can boast a cook as excellent as yours," she said to Lady Grayson.

Lady Grayson beamed at Caroline and followed where she had been led, talking at some length about the merits of her cook.

The rest of the meal passed smoothly, and afterwards Clarence and Phoebe excused themselves and set off for Upper Swanley. "The sun is out," Damien announced. "And I believe it has warmed up considerably. He turned to Caroline. "Would you honor me by accompanying me on a walk?"

Caroline hesitated.

"I should fancy a stroll, myself," said Jarvis.

"I am sure you should," said Damien, taking Caroline's hand and putting it through his arm. "May I suggest a stroll along the stream, close to the edge."

"I should be delighted to accompany you, sir," said Caroline sarcastically as Damien led her from the room.

"I am sure you are anything but," he said, heading for the stairs, "but please join me, anyway." He looked pleadingly at her. "Please?"

"Very well," said Caroline. "I shall fetch my cloak and be right back."

"Thank you," he murmured.

She ran upstairs with a fluttering heart, telling herself that, while it might be similar to what she felt the first time Harold took her driving, this peculiar feeling she was experiencing was nothing more than nerves. She joined Damien a few minutes later, and he led her out the back of the house and through the garden. "Have you learned the secret of the maze yet?" he asked.

"I think so," she replied.

"Let us see, then. Lead on."

Caroline accepted the challenge and began to make her way to the heart of the maze.

"Very good. I am impressed," Damien said after she had successfully negotiated two turns. "You are a very clever woman. I wonder how many men have ever bothered to tell you that."

"Few enough," she admitted. "Cleverness is not something most men look for in a woman."

"That is their mistake," said Damien. "Did your husband look for cleverness?"

"Yes, I believe he valued my intelligence," Caroline said. "This is a most interesting conversation we are having. Where is it leading?"

"Only to my conclusion that you are not yet using your full intellectual powers here at Grayson Hall," replied Damien.

"And, pray, what might that mean?" asked Caroline, bridling.

Damien chuckled. "How many gentlemen of your acquaintance have told you that you have a nasty temper?" he asked.

"None!"

"And why is that, I wonder."

"Most likely it is because few of the men of my acquaintance are so provoking," snapped Caroline.

"Have you ever noticed that sorrel in the stables?" asked Damien suddenly.

"I wonder," countered Caroline, "have any of the women of your acquaintance commented on this habit you have of jumping from subject to subject so precipitously?"

"Well, have you?" asked Damien, ignoring her comment.

Caroline had indeed noticed the fine-looking animal. "She is lovely. I have wondered why she is never brought out and ridden."

"That is because, sweet as she looks, she has a nasty temper."

"Why keep her, then?" asked Caroline.

"Clarence thinks he will break her. I have my doubts. At any rate, she makes a good object lesson."

"Oh?"

"No," said Damien, taking her arm. "Do not turn that way. You will never get to the heart of the maze."

The gentle pressure on her arm stirred a variety of feelings in Caroline. Some she still refused to acknowledge, as they were hardly proper feelings to have toward a villain such as Damien Grayson. The other feeling rising in her was easily identifiable. It was one of panic. Whyever was she out here alone with this dangerous man?

Damien still held her arm, oblivious to the effect he was having on her. "That sorrel appears harmless enough. But she is actually dangerous. Wouldn't you agree that people can also be equally deceptive?"

Caroline's throat felt dry and she swallowed. "I suppose that is true," she said.

They had reached the heart of the maze. "Very good. I congratulate you," Damien said, and drew her to the little stone bench.

Caroline was hardly the innocent her younger

sister was, yet she found herself feeling increasingly more uneasy. Her legs buckled, and she sat down rather gracelessly.

Damien smiled. "Are you nervous about something?" he asked, sitting down next to her.

"Nervous?" she stammered. Pretending to adjust her skirt, she moved a little, trying to put some distance between them. "Why should I be nervous?"

Damien inched closer. "I do not know. You are not afraid to chase ghosts. Surely you are not afraid of a mere flesh-and-blood man."

"Certainly not," said Caroline, sliding as close to the edge of the bench as she could. Damien smiled and leaned toward her. She leaned to the side and lost her balance. With an unladylike yelp she toppled off the bench.

Damien chuckled and held out his hand to her, which Caroline chose to ignore. "Are you hurt?" he asked.

"And what would you do if I said I was?" she asked, brushing off her skirt.

"I could tend your wounds," he offered.

Caroline's eyes narrowed.

Damien chuckled and bid her sit down. "Honestly," he said, "do you think I am insane enough to ravish you right here in the maze on a chill autumn afternoon? Or are you afraid I am about to strangle you?"

Both thoughts had crossed Caroline's mind. And it angered her that he made them both sound ridiculous. "Odious man!" she declared.

Before she could move, Damien's arm had encircled her waist and drawn her to him. "Your expectations of me are high indeed. I should hate to disappoint you," he murmured, and kissed her gently on the lips.

She should have slapped him. She meant to slap

192

him. She would have slapped him. She assured herself of that later when she had time to relive the whole irritating scene. But the sound of approaching footsteps and a loud hello stopped her.

Damien released her. "We're here," he called. Then, looking down at Caroline said, "Don't worry, dear lady. I will give you another opportunity to slap me some time in the future."

"I shall look forward to that," said Caroline.

Damien frowned at the sight of his cousin. "Jarvis," he muttered. "Why did you not go see Isobelle? Surely she is pining away from neglect."

"I am sure she is," replied Jarvis. "You should have called on her today."

Damien made a face.

"Is it not rather cold to be sitting?" asked Jarvis.

"Indeed it is," said Caroline, rising. "I think I should like to go inside now."

Jarvis offered her his arm, and they headed back to the Hall, Damien following behind.

Caroline found it hard to concentrate the rest of the afternoon. "Caroline! You have not been attending to a single word I have said," scolded her mama.

"I am sorry, Mama," said Caroline humbly. After that she made a concentrated effort to appear attentive. She was glad when the time to dress for dinner came and she could escape to her room.

Before ringing for Sibby, she sat down to think. There was no sense pretending any longer. She put a name to her feelings regarding Damien. Attraction? Yes, traitorous creature that she was, she was undeniably attracted to him. But love? No. It couldn't be love. She surely would not be foolish enough to fall in love with a murderer. Would she? She sincerely hoped not, for that would make it so much harder to expose him. And expose him she must. Expose him she would, no matter how much he made her heart flutter. But I had best do it soon before my heart betrays me completely and I shrink from the task, she thought. She would have to do something to bring things to a head, and as she rang for Sibby an idea occurred to her.

Sibby entered the room to find her mistress writing busily at the escritoire. "I have a job for you," she called over her shoulder. "There. This should do it," she said. She reread her handiwork. *Come again tomorrow night. No one will be expecting you.* "I think that might pass for a man's hand," she said, looking at the bold scrawl. She handed the note to Sibby. "Have the footman deliver this to Miss Payne. If she asks him who it is from, he is to say it is from her friend at the Hall."

Having accomplished this, Caroline was able to go down to dinner, confident that a very irritating period of her life would soon be at an end. Sibby had tried a new hairstyle, piling all her curls high on her head, accentuating her long neck. A low-cut gown showed off tantalizing soft shoulders and most of a delicately full bosom, decorated by emeralds. Caroline smiled as she descended the stairs, sure she would mesmerize one gentleman of the house party and hoping to taunt another.

She succeeded. Both Jarvis and Damien smiled appreciatively when she entered the room. "I wonder if, in all its years such beauty has ever graced this hall," said Jarvis gallantly, taking her hand and touching it with his lips.

"I am sure it has," said Damien, who remained in front of the fireplace. Caroline frowned. "But not in a long time," he added. He smiled and gave her a look which set her traitorous heart jumping.

She smiled at Jarvis, ignoring her other admirer.

"That was prettily said, sir," she told him.

"And heartily meant," he replied.

Damien said nothing. Only a skeptically raised eyebrow showed that he had been paying attention to any of the conversation.

"You are also looking lovely tonight," he said to Phoebe. "Did you enjoy your afternoon in town?"

Phoebe smiled and replied that she did, and Caroline looked at her, amazed. When had her sister become so comfortable with Damien Grayson? When he had first come to the Hall he had frightened her to death. Funny, thought Caroline. He no longer upsets Phoebe, but he has a most unsettling effect on me.

Dinner passed pleasantly enough, and when the gentlemen rejoined the ladies in the drawing room, Clarence said heartily, "Well. What shall we do tonight to entertain ourselves. Anyone care to sing?"

Assuming that everyone cared to do exactly that, he strode over to the pianoforte and began to paw through the music cabinet which sat next to it.

"Do see if you can find "Greensleeves," said Phoebe. "For we did that one quite well the other night."

Clarence obliged and, with Caroline accompanying them at the piano, the amateur performers gathered and began to sing, Caroline trying her best to keep up. They finished their first song and the mamas clapped and declared them all very accomplished—praise with which everyone was prepared to agree.

Caroline looked up amid the general laughter and chatter and caught Damien watching her. He smiled at her, and she blushed and lowered her eyes. It was fortunate she was bringing this farce to an end soon, she thought, and determined to pay Isobelle a visit the next morning to ensure that all went as planned.

It wasn't hard to talk Phoebe into paying a call. "Oh, yes!" she exclaimed. "We have not seen Isobelle in days. What an excellent idea."

Lady Grayson agreed and, as it was a cold, rather drizzly morning, sent the sisters off in the carriage.

Isobelle was delighted to see them. "I had thought of visiting you," she said, "but it was such a damp, gray morning, I found I could not bring myself to go out."

"Well, we have come to you," said Phoebe cheerily. "So now you need not go out at all."

The three ladies settled in around the fire and chatted of neighborhood doings. The butler came in bearing a silver salver laden with goodies, and, while Isobelle poured tea, Caroline took the conversational reins and began to steer. "I hope we do not have damp, drizzly weather for the ball," she said. "It is so horrid to have to go out in nasty weather."

"At least you will have no fear of losing any of your guests in the snow," said Isobelle, handing a cup to Phoebe.

"Yes, they will all be there to meet the future Lady Grayson," said Caroline, smiling at her blushing sister.

Isobelle hesitated only a few seconds before pouring Caroline's tea. "Milk?" she asked.

"Yes, please," smiled Caroline. "Only think, love," she continued, "once the ball is past it will be only a short time until your wedding. And I do believe even the infamous Grayson ghost will not object when that day comes. She seems to have finally accepted you, my dear, for we have not seen much of her lately."

"Of course, Mama saw her," Phoebe said.

"Mama *says* she saw her," said Caroline. "But you

196

know how Mama is sometimes. Her nerves," she explained to Isobelle.

"I hope," said Isobelle, picking up her cup, "that everything is as you say. I must admit, if I were in our dear Phoebe's shoes I should be terribly nervous."

"Oh, Phoebe is not afraid of the ghost anymore," answered her sister airily. "Are you, love?"

"I suppose not," said Phoebe doubtfully.

Caroline smiled at her sister. "I know you will be very happy as Lady Grayson. I am sure Clarence will be a most generous husband. Think of all the pretty new clothes you shall have. And, of course, there are the Grayson rubies. I am sure you will look lovely in those. And, of course, you will be very busy entertaining and going to balls, for everyone will wish to entertain the new earl and countess—"

Isobelle sat her cup down with an angry clink, and Caroline looked at her in surprise. Isobelle pulled her lips into a smile. "I am sure we will all look forward to entertaining the new Lady Grayson," she said politely.

Sure her shaft had effectively gone home, Caroline turned the subject. The sisters stayed another half-hour, then headed home. "Really, Caro," said Phoebe as their carriage drove sedately down the tree-lined drive. "I wish you had not gone on so. I was quite embarrassed. And I am sure Isobelle was, too. I believe she and Clarence were good friends before he met me, and I sometimes wonder if she wouldn't have liked to marry him herself. If that is so it must be hard for her, sometimes, to think of me as Clarence's wife. He is such a dear man," Phoebe concluded fondly.

And our sweet Isobelle thinks he has such a dear title and lovely fortune, thought Caroline darkly. She patted her sister's hand. "I know you will be happy, love," she said. "Just hold onto that knowledge and don't let anything, not even a ghost, take your future from you."

After lunch Damien announced his intention of going for a ride, and Clarence took Jarvis off to play billiards. Caroline, who had hoped to speak with him and enlist his help, sighed inwardly. She would have to find a time to speak with him later.

She finally met him on the stairs en route to his room. "If you could spare me a moment, I should like a word with you," she said.

"Most certainly," he agreed. By unspoken agreement, they entered the long gallery, stopping beneath the portrait of the most famous of the ladies Grayson. "Poor woman," said Jarvis. "What a pity she did not know when she died how very busy she would be in the afterlife. I almost think if she had she would have been more careful to live to a ripe, old age and would have died quietly and properly in her bed." He looked at Caroline and cocked his head to the side. "I assume it is this lady who has sparked your desire to be with me and not my considerable charm."

"Oh, I am sure your charm plays a part in my desire to be with you," Caroline assured him.

"Does it?" he asked, raising her hand to his lips.

Caroline smiled at him and some little demon in the back of her mind pointed out that being alone with Jarvis was not half so exciting as being alone with Damien. Not half as dangerous, either, Caroline thought, effectively silencing it.

"What clever plot are you now concocting? Behold me all ears," said Jarvis gallantly.

"I should like to enlist your help," she said.

He bowed. "Your servant."

"As you have so cleverly guessed, I have been concocting something," said Caroline. "I plan to trap our ghost tonight. But I will need help to do so. I feel sure she will make her escape using the secret passage, and I was hoping you would be willing to stand guard over it. When she makes her appearance in Phoebe's room I intend to chase her. If I do not catch her you will be there, in the great hall, waiting to cut off her escape."

"A very good plan, indeed," admitted Jarvis. "And if she should try to make her entrance using the secret passage I will be there to meet her."

"That would be so much the better," said Caroline. "But she has more than one accomplice in this house, and I would be very much surprised if she does not make her entrance by the servant's door." Caroline chewed her lip thoughtfully. "In fact, I will wager one of her accomplices was making plans with her this afternoon.

"Where did Damien go on his ride? He never did say. Perhaps he paid a call on Miss Payne."

"Perhaps," agreed Jarvis.

"Just think," Caroline exclaimed. "If we catch Isobelle tonight she will have to tell us who her accomplice is."

"Let us hope, then, that we shall be successful," said Jarvis.

Dinner passed pleasantly enough, and the family amused themselves afterward with conundrums, a pastime which appealed strongly to Caroline, for it gave her a chance to sharpen her wits and ready herself for the night ahead.

The evening came to an end, and Caroline prepared for battle. She did not bother to undress after going to her bedchamber. Instead, she sat by her fire, waiting for the household to settle down. After she was sure everyone had retired, she slipped out of her room and went downstairs to the great hall.

A single candelabrum lit the room. Jarvis stood by the French doors, looking out into the darkness. He turned and smiled at her. "Do you care for the addition of a door and balcony?" he asked. "This was not part of the original house."

"I wondered about that," said Caroline.

"I find it rather jarring," he continued. "If this house were mine, I think I should return this room to its former state."

Caroline shivered. "It is a pity you cannot have a fire," she said. "I hope you may not freeze to death in here."

"We could lay a fire," teased Jarvis.

Caroline clapped her hands. "Oh, that would be delightful. If we could be sure our apparition would not be making her entrance through the hearth, I should love to so effectively cut off her escape. But I certainly do not want to do anything to discourage her entrance."

"This is cozy," said a voice from the door. "Do I interrupt anything?"

Caroline muttered something very unladylike under her breath, and Jarvis smiled. "No. We were just leaving," he said to his cousin.

"What a pity," said Damien, holding up a decanter and two goblets. "I plan to stay for some time. I thought, perhaps, you might care to keep me company."

Caroline and Jarvis exchanged glances, and Caroline glowered at Damien.

He shrugged and sauntered into the room. He handed Jarvis a glass and filled it with claret, then filled his. "To a successful night," he said, raising his glass.

"And what, pray, might you mean by that?" demanded Caroline.

Damien looked at her in surprise. "Why, only that I hope we may be successful in catching our famous ghost. That is why you came skulking down here, is it not?" He smiled at her.

She looked at Jarvis as if to say, "Now what shall we do?"

Jarvis took a deep sip from his glass. "We shall be fine," he said to Caroline. "If you will excuse me for one brief moment, I think I shall fetch my sword-stick."

"An excellent idea," said Caroline, regarding Damien coldly.

Jarvis left them, and she and Damien stood looking at each other, she with a frown on her face, he with an insolent smile. "You were eavesdropping," she said accusingly.

He shrugged. "People who do not wish to be overheard should not leave doors open for any passerby to stop and listen."

Caroline turned her back on him, looking out the French doors into the darkness. She had an uneasy feeling that things were not going to go as planned. Jarvis returned, and she left the gentlemen to stand watch and went to her sister's bedchamber, tapped on the door, and called Phoebe's name softly.

"Who is it?" called a small voice.

"It is I, Caro. Let me in."

The door opened and Phoebe peered out. "Caro! Whatever are you doing here?"

"I have come to bear you company for awhile," whispered Caroline, entering and closing the door behind her.

"I do not understand," said Phoebe.

"I am sure our ghost will make an appearance tonight. And I mean to catch her."

Phoebe's face drained of color, and she took an instinctive step back toward the bed. "Do you think she will come in here?"

"You are the one she wishes to be rid of. It is you whom she will visit," said Caroline. "But never fear, for I shall be right here with you, and I will make sure nothing happens to you." Phoebe did not look properly heartened by this speech. In fact, she still looked very much afraid.

"Everything will be all right," insisted her sister. "Really." She led Phoebe back to bed and tucked her in. "Go back to sleep. I shall be sitting in this chair here, and if the ghost should appear I shan't even wake you."

Phoebe moaned. "I vow I shall never be able to sleep a wink now."

"Try," said Caroline. She kissed her sister on the forehead and curled up in a chair to await the specter's appearance.

Midnight came and went and still the ghost did not show. Caroline yawned. The perverse creature. Always she came before midnight. Perhaps she had been warned away. Caroline's eyelids drooped. Finally, too weighted to stay open, they fell. "I will just rest my eyes," she told herself. "Just rest . . ."

A low moan startled Caroline awake. Disoriented, she sat up and blinked, her eyes still heavy. There it was again. "Caro," said a shaky voice. "Caro!" Why would the ghost be calling her? "Caro!"

"Wha—"

"It was just here . . . in the doorway," stammered Phoebe from under her blankets.

"What?" Caroline jumped from her seat and threw her blanket aside. She dashed to the door and looked out into the corridor. At the end of it she caught sight of a fleeing figure in white. "I have you now," she cried, running after it. The creature had a head start on her, but Caroline knew she would not escape this time, not with Jarvis in the great hall to cut off her escape. She gained the stairs in time to see her quarry. She lost sight of her once, the curve of the staircase blocking the ghost from view, but saw her again at the foot of the steps. The woman never paused for so much as a second, flying in the direction of the great hall. You are cornered thought Caroline smugly, and she flew down the stairs, anxious to enjoy her triumph.

As she approached the great hall the same feeling of doom she had felt earlier settled over her. There was no sound of voices coming from the huge room. Surely the sound of crying should have echoed out to her. Voices raised in argument. Something. Her steps slowed as she approached the room. Almost reluctantly, she stepped over the threshold and felt anything but triumph as she beheld the scene before her.

There was no sign of the female in white, and the door to the secret passageway was closed. Damien was unconscious, sprawled in a chair, and there, practically at her feet, lay Jarvis, surrounded by a pool of blood.

14

But Caroline clung to his arm anyway, and together they made their way back upstairs. "I am sorry you were hurt," she said again. "I certainly

A snore coming from the chair across the room told her Damien was unhurt. She knelt next to Jarvis, relieved to discover the liquid on the floor was not blood, but claret. "Oh, thank God," she breathed. "Jarvis!" she cried, shaking him by the shoulder. "Oh dear, whatever shall I do?" she asked no one in particular. She rolled him over onto his back and gently patted his cheek. Her efforts were rewarded, and he moaned and moved his head. "Oh, I am so glad you are all right," she said. "What on earth happened?"

Jarvis tried to sit up and fell back with a moan. "Damien drank himself into unconsciousness. Or at least pretended to," he said. He rubbed the back of his head and winced.

"And you, what happened to you?"

"I thought I heard someone approaching. I came to the doorway to look, and someone came up behind me and hit me on the head." He looked at the broken glass. "That was a nice decanter. I am glad it was not lead crystal, else I should be dead."

"Oh, dear," said Caroline. "I am truly sorry."

Jarvis rolled over onto one elbow. "It is merely a

204

slight bump on the head," he said. "I shall be fine."
He attempted to get up, and Caroline grabbed an
arm, rising with him. "Where is our ghost?" he
asked.

"Gone," said Caroline. "Once again we have been
outmaneuvered." She looked contemptuously at the
inert figure in the chair, then returned her attention
to her wounded helper. "Here. Let me help you
upstairs."

"I am fine. Truly," he protested.

But Caroline clung to his arm anyway, and
together they made their way back upstairs. "I am
sorry you were hurt," she said again. "I certainly
never dreamed things would misfire so."

"It is not your fault. You are up against a clever
mind. Two if you count our dear Belle."

Caroline sighed. Things looked black indeed. She
left Jarvis and returned to her own bedroom. She
removed her slippers and fell on her bed exhausted
and discouraged.

She awoke the next morning feeling far from
refreshed. Her sleep had been troubled and restless,
and the morning's light did little to dispel the black
gloom which had settled over her. What would she
tell Phoebe this morning? And then there was Mama.
She was bound to hear of last night's adventure, and
Caroline felt totally unequal to the task of talking her
mother out of leaving for what she felt sure must
be the hundredth time. She rang for Sibby, sat down
on her bed, and stared gloomily into space.

"Heavens!" gasped Sibby when she arrived and
saw her mistress's disheveled condition. "You slept
in your clothes," she said accusingly.

"I am afraid I did," admitted Caroline. "A bath
would do much to restore me. And please add extra
salts."

An hour later, bathed and perfumed, Caroline stepped into a plain morning gown of dove gray. Sibby dressed her hair simply, pulling up the curls with a matching gray ribbon. Gray, thought Caroline. The color matches my mood. With reluctant steps she headed down the corridor.

She had just reached the threshold of the dining room when a crying Phoebe ran past her. "Phoebe, wait!" Clarence's voice boomed from the dining room. A moment later Caroline was nearly trampled by Clarence.

"Clarence! Whatever is going on?" she demanded.

"Don't know," said Clarence. "All I said was I thought it was curst unsporting of everyone to be up and chasing the ghost without me, and she started to cry. Said I didn't care about her feelings at all." Clarence stood looking at Caroline as if waiting for her to explain her sister's behavior.

Caroline patted him consolingly on the arm. "She is tired. And her nerves are overset. This has all been very trying for her." Clarence sighed, and Caroline suspected it had all been rather tiring for him, too. Poor fellow. "Would you like me to speak with her?"

He nodded gratefully.

"Very well," said Caroline. "I shall go see if I can calm her down." She turned to leave, then stopped. "Clarence. Is my mother up yet?"

Clarence shook his head. "Haven't seen her."

"And your mama?"

"Already come and gone."

"Thank goodness," sighed Caroline. "I think, perhaps, there is no need to tell our mothers that Phoebe is upset."

"Oh, yes. Course not," agreed Clarence, looking relieved.

He turned back into the dining room, and

Caroline hurried after her sister. She found her face down on her bed, sobbing. Thank God she had not gone to Mama, thought Caroline. "Now," she said gently, coming to sit next to her sister. "What is this all about?"

"He . . . he . . . he does not care at all that that horrid ghost has frightened me half to death," she sobbed. "You never came back last night either," she continued accusingly. "I was so scared. Nobody cares," she wailed.

"I am sorry I did not return," said Caroline. "But I knew it would not reappear and that you would be safe. But let us not talk of me. Let us talk of Clarence. Do you honestly think if Clarence thought you were in any danger he would ever be talking of sport? It is because he feels well able to protect you that he spoke thusly this morning."

Phoebe sniffed.

"Phoebe, love. You must be brave," said Caroline. "If you allow yourself to become upset Mama will be upset and talk of leaving. And we really must stay, for I believe Clarence himself is in danger, more so than you."

Phoebe sat up. "What do you mean?"

"I think someone would like to be rid of Clarence," said Caroline. "He has had too many dangerous accidents. Shot at by poachers, a fall from his horse which could have, at the least, caused great bodily harm. Did he tell you what caused that fall?"

"He fell taking a fence."

"He fell after he took the fence. Someone put a prickly burr under his horse's saddle, and the beast became crazed when the spines were driven deeply into its flesh." Phoebe's eyes widened. "We must stay and pretend nothing is wrong until we discover who is behind all of this. I am sure, somehow, the appearances of the ghost and Clarence's near-fatal accidents all fit together. And Clarence will not be safe until we solve this puzzle."

"Oh my," said Phoebe in a wobbly voice.

"There is no need to tell Clarence any of this," said Caroline. "For we do not want to worry him." Or have him try to help and then get under foot, she thought. "Now," she said briskly. "Can you try and act as if nothing has happened?"

Phoebe nodded, a look of determination on her face.

"Very well," said Caroline. "Dry your eyes and let us go down to breakfast. And whatever you do, do not let Mama know that anything is amiss. She need never know."

"All right, Caro," said Phoebe. She dug out a handkerchief, blew her nose and dried her eyes, and the two women returned to breakfast.

The breakfast table was rather sparsely populated this morning. Only Jarvis and Clarence were present. Clarence was making a hearty meal, his plate piled high with eggs, thick slices of ham, and freshly baked bread. Next to that sat a bowl which had been already drained of its porridge. "Well, here is Caro," he announced. "And Phoebe. Are you feeling more the thing?"

Phoebe nodded and sat down, looking disinterestedly at her plate.

Caroline helped herself to a small serving of eggs and sausages from the sideboard and sat down next to Jarvis. "How is your head?" she asked in a low voice.

"I shall live," he replied.

"And what has become of your brother?" she asked Clarence. "Surely he should be up and stirring by now." And I hope he has a tremendous headache, she thought.

"Haven't seen him," said Clarence. "He is still sleeping, most likely."

"Well, then," said Caroline in a brisk, cheerful voice. "And what do you gentlemen plan to do with yourselves today?"

"I am going to see if I can get a brace of partridge," said Clarence. He turned to Phoebe. "Should you fancy partridge for dinner?"

"Partridge is always to be fancied for dinner when one can have it," said a voice from the door. Damien sauntered in, looking neat and freshly scrubbed. He hardly looked to her like a man suffering from the aftereffects of a night's overindulgence, and Caroline found herself more convinced than ever that Damien had pretended that drunken sleep. Someone had snuck up behind Jarvis and struck him on the head, and it could not have been Isobelle.

"Morning, Dam," said Clarence cheerfully. "Do you fancy a little sport this morning?"

Caroline shot Jarvis a nervous look and, taking her cue, he said, "I daresay I should be up for a morning's shooting."

"You may both go with my blessing," said Damien. "I had quite enough sport last night."

"So I hear," said Clarence. "I call it dashed shabby of you to let me go off to bed while the rest of you stayed up adventuring."

"Is that what you call it?" asked Damien, looking intently across the table at his cousin. "I can think of another name for it."

If Damien had thought to get a rise out of Jarvis with this mysterious comment, he failed. Jarvis dabbed at his mouth with his napkin and suggested

209

to Clarence that they be off.

"Don't go shooting in the woods," begged Phoebe, suddenly coming to life.

Clarence looked at her, astonished. "But where else do you expect me to go shooting?"

"If you keep doing this the poachers are bound to get you," she said.

"I will be perfectly safe. After all, I shall have Jarvis with me."

"Oh, I had forgotten," said Phoebe, relieved.

"And what shall you do while I am gone?" asked Clarence.

"Wait for you to come back," she said simply.

He smiled. "We shall play some piquet this afternoon. How does that suit you?"

Phoebe replied that it suited her fine, and the two men left in search of sturdy boots, guns, and dogs.

Damien showed no inclination to follow them. He remained at the table, pouring himself another cup of tea. "A most interesting night, last night," he said to Caroline.

"Yes, it was," Caroline agreed. "How would we have fared without your help, I wonder?"

"No better, I assure you," he said.

"I am not so sure," she said coldly.

The undercurrents in the room made Phoebe stir nervously in her seat. "What will you do while your brother and cousin are out getting our dinner?" she asked Damien, changing the subject.

Damien had been glaring at Caroline. Reluctantly, he took his gaze from her. "I intend to spend the morning snoozing in the library," he said. "If you ladies will excuse me." He rose and stalked from the room.

"Oh, dear," fretted Phoebe. "Why is he so angry?"

"It is nothing you said, love," said Caroline consolingly. "He is just in a bad temper."

"He seems to be in a bad temper very often," observed Phoebe.

"Yes," agreed Caroline. "I wonder his brother dotes on him so."

"Yet he can be very kind," said Phoebe, springing unexpectedly to Damien's defense. "Clarence says he has always had a temper, but that he really is a very good sort."

Caroline couldn't help but smile at this. She strongly suspected that there was not a single one of his fellow creatures whom Clarence did not consider a good sort of fellow. And Phoebe was the same. Both saw the world through innocent and trusting eyes. Clarence, especially, walked blindly past danger after danger, while those around him scrambled to keep him safe. How long could they keep scrambling? Caroline felt a sudden desire to read. "Excuse me," she said. "I think I shall fetch a book from the library."

She did not expect to see Damien laid out on the library sofa when she entered the room. She blushed guiltily when he bid her enter. "I thought I would entertain myself with a book this morning," she said, excusing her presence.

"Somehow, I thought you might feel a sudden urge to read," said Damien.

"It is as good a time as any to do so," said Caroline defensively.

"And as good a time as any to check and see if I was really where I said I would be," added Damien. "Now that you see I am here and not out stalking my brother with a gun you may breathe easier."

Caroline ignored this comment and went to the bookshelf to choose a book. Damien rose leisurely from the couch and came up behind her. "Do you think you are seeing things as they truly are?" he asked softly. She did not answer him nor look around, but pulled a random book from the shelf. "Do not forget that the loveliest beast in Eden was also the most dangerous," he said.

"I am sure I do not know what you are talking about," said Caroline coldly. "I imagine you would like to continue your nap undisturbed so I shall leave you now," she concluded, brushing past her tormentor and hurrying from the room.

Drat the man, she thought as she mounted the stairs and headed for her room. How did he manage to affect her so? Why did her encounters with him leave her feeling so . . . what? What was a suitable word for the way that odious, irritating villain made her feel? Nervous? No. That could hardly describe it. Upset? Not really. Unsettled, unbalanced? Those words were probably more accurate. Being with Damien was much like having a loose saddle girth. One had a feeling of constantly slipping, as if one were about to be unseated any moment. And Caroline did not like it one bit. Well, she would not let him throw her. She entered her room and rang for Sibby. There was something she should have dealt with long ago. This was as good a time as any to work with another piece of the puzzle. Perhaps this would be the key piece, the piece which caused all the others to fall into place, and which would give her the proof she needed to rid Grayson Hall of its menace. "I wish to speak with Phoebe's maid," she told Sibby. "Fetch her to me, if you please."

"It's about time," muttered Sibby gleefully, and disappeared.

Rose did not look pleased to see Lady Caroline. She followed Sibby into the room, blinked, and licked her lips nervously. "You wanted to see me, my lady?" she squeaked.

"Yes, I did," said Caroline. "I want to know who is helping your mistress to frighten my sister."

Rose's eyes widened, and she took a step backwards. "I don't understand," she stammered. "My mistress is your sister, Lady Phoebe."

"I do not think so," said Caroline sternly. "Come now," she snapped. "Let us not play games, for I am in no mood for it."

At this Rose began to cry. "She said she would pay me well. And that nobody would be hurt. It was just a prank," Rose blubbered, fishing in her apron for a handkerchief.

"Just a prank to scare my sister senseless with all your talk of bad luck? Just a prank to hide her glove and upset her? Just a prank to let your mistress into the house at night to run these halls and terrorize us all?"

"No, no! I never let nobody in," wailed Rose. "I swear it."

"Do not lie to me," said Caroline.

"I wouldn't lie to you, my lady," said Rose earnestly. "That's a real ghost as is walking these halls. Everybody knows that."

"You have been sending notes to Hallowstone Hall," Caroline accused. Rose turned red at this. "They were for Miss Payne, weren't they?" insisted Caroline.

The red in Rose's face darkened. "They were to . . . I have a . . ." Rose hesitated, obviously not wanting to go on, but Caroline waited mercilessly for her to continue. "I have a sweetheart at Hallowstone. I sent him a note. Just one. Betsy helped me write it."

"Who else is helping your mistress?" Caroline

demanded, pursuing another line of questioning.

Rose looked at her blankly.

"Come now, girl. I already know someone else in this house is aiding your mistress in this evil scheme of hers. You have but to name him, and you will be handsomely rewarded."

Rose looked desperately at Caroline, unable to speak.

"Come now, out with it! If you do not tell me I shall see to it you are turned off without references."

Rose broke into fresh tears. "I don't know," she sobbed. "I don't know."

Caroline looked at the crying girl in disgust. "Send her away," she told Sibby. "She knows nothing."

Rose hesitated. "Will I be turned off without references?" she asked in a small voice.

"It is no less than you deserve, you wicked girl," said Caroline. "But if you have told the truth, then you have nothing to fear. But woe to you should I discover you have lied to me," she added in sepulchral tones. "And if your former mistress asks you to perform any new service you will report to me immediately. Is that understood?"

Rose bobbed a curtsey. "Yes, my lady," she whispered and fled the room.

"Do you think she was telling the truth?" asked Sibby, shutting the door.

Caroline sighed. "Most likely. If she was lying she is a most accomplished actress."

"What will you do now?" asked Sibby.

Caroline held up her book. "I shall read until luncheon."

The midday meal was a quiet affair, the company being composed of just the ladies. Clarence and Jarvis were still out shooting, and Damien had mysteriously disappeared, no one quite seemed to know where.

"I do not know how those boys can bear to be out in the cold so long," said Lady Harborough.

"It is not raining," Lady Grayson pointed out.

"True," agreed Lady Harborough. "It is not raining. But it is so very cold."

"Yes, it is cold. But at least it is not raining," said Lady Grayson.

Caroline took a bite of her cutlet and heartily wished at least one of the men were present. Even Damien's odious presence was preferable to this. She mentally ticked off the number of days until the ball. Six days remaining. Five if she did not count this day. She fervently hoped by then things would have been taken care of and she could return home. She had had enough female company to last her for some time. But what of the male company? Will you not miss that? prompted something deep within her. She took a meditative sip of tea. She would miss Jarvis. If he were to offer for her would she accept him?

"Caroline!" Her mama's voice interrupted her reverie.

"I am sorry, Mama. I was not attenting."

"I know very well you were not attenting," said her mother. "This is the third time I have had to speak your name."

"I am sorry, Mama," said Caroline humbly. "What were you saying?"

"I was telling Lady Grayson about when you caught that terrible cold the time you went driving. It was on just such a cold day as this. And I remember when you came home you had to be put to bed directly."

"Yes. But Mama, I was already not feeling quite

215

the thing when we set out," said Caroline.

"Nonetheless, I think it was the cold that brought it on," said her mother. "It is not good to stay out in the cold for any length of time, I am sure."

"Oh, I quite agree," said Lady Grayson. "But it is not so bad if it is not raining."

"Yes, I suppose you are right," said Lady Harborough graciously. "However, I had a cousin," she began.

Caroline excused herself and made good her escape. She went to the winter parlor, which afforded a view of the garden and the woods beyond, and looked out the window. Where was Damien? Was he out in those woods, too, now? If he was, he was not hunting partridge. I do wish they would come back, she thought, picking up her stitchery.

The other ladies joined her shortly, and the afternoon crawled by as they sat stitching. It was getting close to tea time when Caroline looked out the window and saw Clarence and Jarvis walking across the lawn. She breathed a sigh of relief. Clarence was still in one piece. But he did not appear to be happy, in spite of the dead birds he carried. His stride was not the relaxed one of a man who had spent a satisfying day trudging in the woods. Instead, it was the quick, determined gait of an angry man.

Twenty minutes later, Clarence's voice could be heard outside the winter parlor. "I'll not have it," he was saying.

"It looks as if the boys have returned," announced Lady Grayson placidly.

Clarence entered the room and threw himself into a chair.

"Did you not get anything?" asked his mother.

"We each got a brace of partridge," answered Clarence grumpily.

"Then why are you looking so cross?" asked Lady Grayson.

"Because these curst poachers are like to kill me," snapped her son.

Phoebe bit her lip and shot a terrified look at her sister, who shook her head slightly, bidding her to remain calm and guard her tongue.

"What happened?" asked Lady Grayson.

"Oh, nothing much," said Clarence. "Someone fired carelessly. Took my hat clean off my head. Ruined my hat, curse 'em."

"But Jarvis was with you," protested Phoebe, as if Jarvis's very presence should have acted as a talisman.

"Of course he was with me," said Clarence. "But he wasn't walking next to me all the time. When I catch the person who is doing this," he fumed.

"Oh, Clarence, please do not go out shooting anymore until after we are married," begged Phoebe. "I just know if you do not stop wandering around like this something terrible is going to happen to you."

"Nonsense," said Clarence.

"It is not nonsense," said Phoebe. "Caroline—" she began. Her sister cleared her throat and gave Phoebe a warning look. "Agrees with me," Phoebe finished lamely. "Please say you will not take any more of these needless chances. I should hate for you to get killed and miss our wedding."

"I should hate that, too," said Clarence.

"Well, then. You must promise me," said Phoebe, "not to do this any more."

As they were talking, Caroline turned to Jarvis, who had come in and sat down next to her. "I thought you were going to keep an eye on him," she whispered.

"I tried," he answered in an undervoice. "But I

could not stay with him every moment. That would have looked so suspicious even Clarence would have figured out what I was about. Besides, I am beginning to think that, after all, the only danger in the woods is poachers. One actually sent a bullet my direction."

"Good heavens!" gasped Caroline.

"What is it?"

"This game grows more dangerous every day," she whispered.

"I am afraid I do not understand what you are talking about," said Jarvis.

"Damien was not at luncheon, and no one has seen him all afternoon," said Caroline in a low voice.

"Oh, you do not think he has designs on *me*," Jarvis said.

Caroline shrugged and looked out the window. What she saw made her grasp Jarvis's arm. He looked, too, and saw what had so upset her. A lone man emerged from the woods. He was wearing sturdy boots, a heavy coat, and carried a gun. He strolled back across the lawns, and as he came closer to the house his face was easily recognizable. "Damien," breathed Jarvis.

15

Shortly after Clarence and Jarvis had joined the ladies, Damien made his appearance. "Good," sighed his mother. "Now I may be easy. I have both my boys home safe."

Damien bent to kiss her cheek. "Were we in danger?" he asked.

"If you were out in the woods this afternoon you were," replied Lady Grayson. "Poachers again."

"No!" exclaimed Damien in surprise.

"Where were you this afternoon, by the way?" asked Caroline.

"I felt the need of some exercise, so I went for a walk," said Damien.

"Well, I am glad you are home safe," said Lady Grayson. "I suppose you are all famished. Shall I ring for tea?"

Caroline observed Damien at tea and later that evening at dinner. Other than his intense dislike for Jarvis, Damien betrayed little of his thoughts or feelings. What sort of hard-hearted man could take jealous joy in plotting his brother's death and yet still manage to appear so fond of that brother? What a diabolical mind he had. Now he will most likely pretend to have given up on his attempts to murder his brother, she thought. And just when we have relaxed our vigil he will strike again. But how? Where? Clarence had promised Phoebe he would stay out of the woods, so there would be no more opportunity for imaginery poachers to shoot at him. What scheme would Damien concoct next?

The following morning Isobelle paid a morning call. "Papa sends his regards, especially to you, Lady Caroline," she said. "You have made a conquest. My father is quite taken with you."

"He is a very sweet, courtly gentleman," said Caroline diplomatically.

"I shall, of course, have to tell him your kind words," said Isobelle. "For he quite pumps me regarding everything you say each time I return from visiting."

"If he is smitten I am surprised he has not come with you," said Phoebe.

"Oh, he would like to have. But his gout has been acting up so terribly lately I am afraid he has been quite laid up."

"The poor man," sympathized Lady Grayson.

"Do tell him we are sorry to hear he is feeling unwell, and we hope he may be able to come to the ball," lied Caroline.

"Oh, yes," said Lady Grayson. "It would be most unfortunate if he could not come."

"I can make no promises on his behalf," said Isobelle. "He has been eating too much rich food again. You know how he loves it. And he has already begged a rich dessert for tonight from Cook."

Lady Harborough shook her head. "Men are such children," she said. "And not at all sensible. Phoebe has only just gotten Clarence to promise to stay out of the woods until after they are married. Why he went out after the first shooting is a mystery to me."

"Shooting?" said Isobelle sharply. "What is this? Has someone been shooting at Clarence?"

"Yes," said Lady Grayson. "I am surprised you had not heard of it, for it has happened more than once. Only yesterday he and Jarvis were out hunting partridge and someone nearly shot him by accident."

Isobelle's face turned pale, and she lifted her cup to her lips with a shaking hand.

So, thought Caroline, she does not know how dangerous her little game has become. Perhaps now she will stop it.

"I should be going," Isobelle said suddenly.

"But, my dear, you have only just gotten here," protested Lady Grayson.

"Yes, I know," Isobelle replied distractedly. "But I really should not have left poor Papa alone. It makes him terribly melancholy to be left alone when he is not feeling well." She set down her teacup and stood up. "I am so sorry to rush off," she apologized.

"Let me ring for Smythe and have him send to the stables for your—" Lady Grayson began.

"No, no," Isobelle interrupted her. "I shall have no problems fetching my dogcart. I am sure they have not even unharnessed my horse yet. Thank you for the tea. I shall see you all at the ball," she concluded and hurried from the drawing room, leaving the other ladies to stare after her.

"How very odd," said Lady Grayson finally. "I have never seen Isobelle so distracted. I do believe the news of Clarence's brush with danger upset her." She shook her head. "Poor thing. She is very fond of Clarence. She has been, you know," she said to Lady Harborough. "Ever since Damien left."

Ever since Damien left, thought Caroline. And shortly before his family knew of his return, the ghost of Grayson Hall had begun to walk again. Whose idea had it been, she wondered, Damien's or Isobelle's? Now that Damien had returned was he once again the great love of Isobelle's life? The thought that, together, Damien and Isobelle had planned to do away with Clarence and enjoy his title and fortune had occasionally crossed Caroline's mind. But now she knew this was not a possibility. A look of surprise could be feigned, but not even the famous Sarah Siddons herself could make the blood drain from her face. Isobelle's shock had been very real.

In sudden need of a shawl, Caroline excused herself and hurried to the porch room. She pulled aside the curtain and looked down below onto the front courtyard. There was Damien, helping Isobelle into her dogcart. Isobelle smiled down at him, and Caroline frowned. Had he already charmed her into going along with his evil scheme? Had he promised her a future as the new Lady Grayson with himself as her husband? Caroline let the curtain fall and sighed.

Instead of fetching her shawl, she took her cloak and gloves and, tying on her bonnet, headed to the maze where she could think in peace. After quarter of an hour she had worn a path in front of the little stone bench, but had found no answer to the many questions crowding her mind. What would Damien do next? Would Isobelle still want to play ghost now that she had a chance to play a different game for bigger stakes? And how was she, Caroline, ever going to prove any of her suspicions?

"I see the beautiful Lady Caroline is no more afraid of the cold than she is of ghosts."

Caroline jumped and glared at Damien, who smiled broadly at her. "I am not a hothouse plant," she snapped.

"No. I suspect you are a much wilder variety," said Damien. "I admire a woman of action and spirit."

"I did not come out here for your admiration, sir," said Caroline tartly.

Damien chuckled. "I am sure you did not." He was silent a moment. "How did we ever get off on such a wrong foot?" he asked finally.

Caroline made no reply.

"Oh, yes. I believe it had something to do with calling your sister a fortune hunter."

Still no reply.

"Is there more?" asked Damien. Still he received no answer. "Let me see. What else can I have done? I believe I might have insinuated that your sister is not particularly brilliant."

Caroline's face reddened, and her eyes took on a dangerous glint. She turned to leave.

"Wait," he said. "I am sorry. Best we overlook that. It was churlish of me to point out something which has most likely been obvious to you for years." Caroline stiffened. "Just," Damien continued quickly, "as it would be most unnecessary for you to point out that my brother's mental powers are not exactly, er, gargantuan. But Clarence has a big heart. And he is not an idiot. And neither is your sister. She is, in fact, a sweet, pretty little thing, and she will do very nicely for Clarence."

"And what does that mean?" demanded Caroline. "Your brother is not exceptionally bright and my sister is stupid, so—"

"No, no," Damien interrupted her. "Please do not take offense. In truth I meant none. Your sister is a sweet girl. Clarence is a good-hearted fellow. They will deal famously."

Caroline studied Damien for a moment, then understanding dawned in her eyes. "Oh, very clever. Try to win me over by complimenting my sister and pretending concern for your brother. What a . . ." Caroline cast about in her mind for a word vile enough to hurl at her clever antagonist. "Brute," she finished.

"What! What have I said now?" protested Damien.

"Oh, come now," said Caroline irritably. "Do you think I am so very stupid? Do you really think you can get away with this?"

"With what?" demanded Damien. "You have already held me responsible for the reappearance of our family ghost. What new infamy do you wish to lay at my door?"

As if he did not know! Caroline gave him no answer, and he glared at her. "Does this insanity run in your family? If it does, I may change my mind and put a stop to this marriage."

"Do not think that you can! Do not think your evil mind can concoct any scheme which I cannot unravel," said Caroline, her temper making her reckless. "And when Phoebe marries your brother I'll see to it they turn you out of this house."

Damien was breathing hard now, and with his nostrils distended and his eyes wide open in rage he reminded Caroline of some dark, wild stallion. "You may not be mad, but you are confused. Be careful, my merry widow. I'll not have you meddling in things you do not understand."

"I understand much more than you think," said Caroline threateningly.

"You understand nothing!" roared Damien, and in spite of her intention to face the villain, Caroline took an instinctive step backwards. Damien looked for all the world as though he would strike her, and she swallowed hard. They stood for a moment, their eyes locked, then he spun around and stalked out of the garden.

Caroline watched him go, her breath coming in gasps, as though she had been running. She looked around for something to kick and, finding nothing substantial, kicked at a pebble in the gravel path and sent small stones flying. She resumed her pacing with a fury, muttering epithets and wishing every imaginable curse on the second Grayson son.

"Lady Caroline," called a now-familiar voice from beyond the hedge.

"I am here," she called, trying to compose herself.

Jarvis was not fooled. "Here now, what is this?" he asked.

Caroline resumed her pacing. "I have just had words with your cousin, the wicked, black-hearted, odious villain."

"I had supposed as much," said Jarvis. "I saw him leave the maze in a rage and wondered if perhaps . . ." Jarvis ground to an embarrassed halt and cleared his throat. "I thought perhaps you might wish for the company of someone with a sympathetic ear."

Caroline sighed and sank onto the bench. "What a vile, beastly man he is," she said.

Jarvis sat down next to her but said nothing.

"He knows I have found him out," she continued. "That is why he was so angry. I have quite thrown a rub in his way. Mayhap he will now leave Clarence alone," she concluded, trying to convince herself as much as Jarvis.

"You had best be careful," he cautioned. "You may have put yourself in danger. Why not let me handle this from here on?"

Caroline shook her head determinedly. "He does not know with whom he is dealing. But I shall show him." She sat silent a moment.

"What are you thinking?" asked Jarvis.

"I am trying to think like our enemy," she said. "This is all rather like a chess game, is it not? First he moves. Then I move. If I move here, will he move there? If I make this move, will he be trapped?" She

225

tapped her chin thoughtfully. "I must have a move to cripple him, especially as he now has Isobelle eating out of his hand."

A slow smile began to grow on her face, and Jarvis smiled as well. "And have you decided on your next move?" he asked.

Caroline beamed with satisfaction on her companion. "I have found the move which will put him in check." She turned to Jarvis. "Would you care to help me?" she asked.

"I would be honored," he replied enthusiastically.

"Good. Do you think you can procure a hammer and nails and some boards for me?

Jarvis looked puzzled, but assured Caroline that he could.

"Excellent. Meet me early tomorrow morning in the great hall at, shall we say, seven? That should be early enough."

"It certainly should," said Jarvis in horror.

Caroline laughed. "I am so very glad you came along. I feel much better."

"And I am glad I came along, too," he said. "Only think what an adventure I would have missed if I had not. But I do wish I knew what it is we will be doing tomorrow."

"You shall have to wait and see," said Caroline playfully.

Jarvis sighed. "I cannot drag the secret from you?" he asked.

Caroline smiled. "Not with a million wild horses," she said, rising.

Jarvis rose, too, and offered her his arm. "Very well, then," he said. "I shall try to possess my soul in patience and wait for tomorrow to be dazzled and amazed. And now, may I escort you back to the house before going in search of the things you need?"

226

Caroline smiled up at him. "You most certainly may," she said, "and thank you." Jarvis looked at her questioningly. "For all your help. I don't know how I should have gone on if you had not been a member of this very peculiar group," she said.

"I have enjoyed it," he said. "And, I must admit, that is due mostly to the presence of a most lovely and charming guest." Caroline blushed, and he patted her hand and led her from the maze.

That evening in Grayson Hall was anything but convivial. The gentlemen did not linger long over their wine, joining the ladies almost directly after they had left. Damien had entered the room like a storm cloud, bringing a gray, oppressive atmosphere with him. Clarence, normally jovial, seemed puzzled and subdued. Jarvis, while polite as usual, seemed to be talking in hushed tones. Even Phoebe, picking up on the tension in the room, became timid and quiet.

"Why do you not all sing for us?" suggested Lady Grayson brightly. Caroline forced a smile and pronounced herself willing to oblige, although she knew under the circumstances it would be torture.

The very one who had created the tension saved them by pronouncing himself not at all in voice. He picked up a book from a nearby table and began to thumb through it.

The other four members of the younger generation settled for a game of cards while the two older women seemed content merely to chat and gossip about mutual friends.

For Caroline the evening seemed barely even able to crawl by. She looked up once from her cards to see Jarvis regarding her. He smiled encouragingly, and she smiled back and tried to concentrate on the game. Smythe finally appeared with the tea tray, and it seemed to Caroline as though most of the members of their house party breathed a sigh of relief at his entrance.

Not once during the evening had Damien spoken to her, and Caroline told herself she was glad. Why she should feel as if she were being punished when it was he who was the villain, she did not know. She was glad to finally make her escape and shut herself in her bedroom where she did not have to see him. Unfortunately, he seemed to have followed her there, for she could not get him out of her thoughts, even when he was no longer in sight. "Horrid man," she muttered, ringing for Sibby. "I shall show you." And the more she thought about how shocked Damien would be when his ghostly helper came calling and could not escape, the happier she became. By the time Sibby had unpinned her curls and helped her into her nightgown, Caroline was feeling every bit as good as she had earlier that day when her clever idea first came to her. She fell asleep with a smile on her face and awoke the next morning with the same smile securely in place.

Jarvis was as good as his word and met her the next morning in his shirt sleeves, carrying a bucket containing a hammer and some nails, and several boards tucked under his arm. "Oh, splendid!" she said, shutting the door of the great hall after him. "You have got them."

"Of course, in spite of the fact that this is an hour at which no civilized man would arise except to fight a duel. You did not think I would fail you, did you?"

"Considering the fact that, as you have just said, it is a most uncivilized hour, it did occur to me that your bed might be a stronger lure than my little adventure."

"Never," insisted Jarvis. "Lead on."

"That is, of course, precisely why I chose this time," said Caroline, crossing the room to the hearth.

"Because this is an hour when no civilized human being would choose to be up." She set down the candelabrum she carried and pushed against the stone, causing it to swing open.

"I begin to see for what purpose you desired the boards," said Jarvis, appreciation lighting his eyes.

Caroline took up her light. "It is clever, is it not?" she said with a smile.

"Most," agreed Jarvis as he ducked and followed her into the secret passageway.

They emerged once again half an hour later with their ears still ringing. "I do believe I should hate to be a troll," remarked Jarvis, wriggling a finger in his ear.

"Yes, it was quite deafening down there," agreed Caroline. "How is your thumb?"

Jarvis examined his purple thumbnail. "I must admit it still hurts," he said. "But the wound is not mortal. Do you fancy an early breakfast?"

"I am feeling quite famished," said Caroline.

"I, too," said Jarvis. He held up the bucket. "Let me return my tools to Jem, and then I shall see if Cook fancies finding us something to nibble on while we are waiting for the rest of the house to stir."

Caroline and her fellow conspirator enjoyed a leisurely and very quiet breakfast, attended only by Smythe, who came and went silently, adding new dishes to the sideboard as Cook prepared them. "I must say," said Jarvis, "it is rather pleasant to be up before everyone else."

"Do not tell me you have never been awake this early before," laughed Caroline.

"As a child, perhaps. But not since I grew into a rational adult."

"Surely you have fought a duel or two?" prompted Caroline.

"My dear woman, I value my skin much too highly

to make a habit of calling fellows out."

"And no one has ever called you out?"

"I live in perfect harmony with my fellow creatures," stated Jarvis. "Let me ammend that. I live in perfect harmony with all my fellow creatures save one. And he can hardly call me out as we are related."

"I am surprised he has let a small thing such as that stop him," said Caroline. "Whatever could have caused such an intense dislike to spring up between you?" she mused.

Jarvis shrugged. "Who can say? It has been there since we were boys. Most likely it started with some boyish prank and grew from mutual irritation to intense dislike."

"What a pity," said Caroline. "We always got on so well with our cousins. I can remember many happy family gatherings at Ethelwaite."

"I can remember many gatherings here at Grayson Hall," said Jarvis. "Yet, I think there has always been an undercurrent." Caroline looked questioningly at him, and he shrugged. "I suppose the Woolcocks have always felt the Graysons had received more than they deserved—both in lands and title. However, with privilege comes responsibility, and I must admit I should not particularly cherish the role of head of this family. After all, who would want to have to deal with malcontents such as my cousin or hangers-on such as myself."

"Are you a hanger-on?" asked Caroline, amused.

"I have been here visiting since before you came. Surely that must qualify me to be a hanger-on," he replied.

"Oh, pooh," she said, laughing. "I think I have been handed a bag of moonshine."

"No. I assure you. I am a most worthless fellow," said Jarvis with a smile.

Caroline laughed and assured him he was not, while he continued to insist he was, and so they continued until Lady Grayson joined them.

"My, but you are both up early this morning," she said.

"We thought it would be a novel experience to see the morning from a robin's view," replied Jarvis. "How did you sleep, Aunt?"

"Quite well, I thank you," said Lady Grayson. "Although I must say it took me a good while to fall asleep. With the ball nearly upon us I have much to think about."

"You have only to ask and I will be delighted to help in any way," offered Caroline. Even as she spoke her mind was sent running far from thoughts of the mere mechanics of the ball. Only a very few days left before Phoebe was presented to friends and neighbors alike as the future Lady Grayson. And then, as far as their enemies knew, only two months until they would be married. Damien would be most anxious to have his brother dead before he could produce an heir. And how he would relish being rid of him before the ball. She felt sure he would make his next deadly move before then. Well, she would be ready for him. She hoped.

Clouds had been steadily collecting while Caroline and Jarvis breakfasted. Now it had begun to drizzle, and looking out the window, Caroline realized she was cold and excused herself to go fetch her shawl. She met Damien in the corridor on her way to her bedchamber. He was no longer scowling. In fact, he looked almost penitent. Not possible, she thought, and with the slightest of smiles and a nod would have walked past him, but his hand on her arm stopped her. "Wait, please," he said.

He sounded almost humble. So he should sound

after his churlish behavior the day before. She gave him her chilliest look.

"I deserve such treatment," he admitted. "I am sorry I lost my temper with you yesterday. Please forgive me. I am a brute."

She would like to have said, "You certainly are," but breeding and good manners won the day. "Let us consider the incident forgotten," she said stiffly. She couldn't help adding, "And if there is anything I said which you did not deserve, please accept my apologies."

Damien grinned. "That was indeed a most interesting apology," he said.

"If you do not care for it," replied Caroline, "I am sorry. But it is all the apology I am prepared to give you."

Damien sighed. "You are still angry with me," he informed her.

Angry with him? The man was indeed a master of understatement. She detested and distrusted him.

"Ah well," he sighed. "One day, soon perhaps, this lowly second son will become worthy of your high esteem."

Did he really think the possession of his brother's lands and title would make him a man worthy of esteem? "When you have a title?" asked Caroline coldly.

"Is a title so important to you, then?"

"Is it so important to you?" she countered, and before he could say anything more she left him and shut herself in her room.

He stood staring after her a moment, an angry look on his face. But before long a smile had replaced it. With a shake of his head and a chuckle, he headed down the stairs in search of his breakfast.

16

Three days remained before the Allhallows Eve ball at Grayson Hall. Clarence had stayed out of the woods as he promised and had encountered no more close brushes with death. And things had at last quieted down. Grayson Hall's ghost had been strangely antisocial. "Most likely she is waiting til Alhallows Eve," Sibby told her mistress.

"That would indeed be dramatic," admitted Caroline. "I shall be much surprised if something does not happen, for there is a lull in this household, the type which can only precede a storm."

Caroline and Damien had settled into a state of truce, each being extremely polite to the other. Once he had even made her laugh. She had, of course, not allowed that to dull her senses, and she congratulated herself on her vigilance. Every night she had been checking on Phoebe and had, on more than one occasion, crept into the corridor to make sure any small noise she happened to hear was not a ghostly masquerader. She was, admittedly, becoming a little tired. "You could use a nap this afternoon," suggested Sibby.

Caroline sighed. "I suppose I could," she admitted. "Ah, well. I have a feeling this will soon be over. I hope you are still watching Rose."

"Yes," said Sibby. "But she has been good enough."

"Keep your eyes open, for someone has been serving as a messenger between Grayson Hall and Hallowstone House," said Caroline.

"More than one servant has served as messenger between the two houses," Sibby observed. "But who knows who took what to who or if the messenger ever knew if the note they took was harmless or not."

Sibby pinned the last curl in place and Caroline stood up. "I think I shall run along and see how Phoebe slept."

Phoebe was still finishing her toilette. "And how are you this morning, dearest?" asked her sister, settling herself comfortably in a chair.

"I did not sleep a wink last night," sighed Phoebe.

"Did you hear noises, see anything?" asked Caroline excitedly.

"No. I merely could not sleep."

"Excitement over the ball, perhaps?" suggested Caroline.

Phoebe nodded. "It will be such fun," she said. "You never did tell me what your costume is. Who are you going as?"

"I am going to be the Maid of Orléans."

"Joan of Arc?" said Phoebe. "But she is French."

"She is also a saint. I felt it appropriate for an All-hallows Eve ball to come as a saint."

"But how shall you dress?"

"I have a cream-colored gown which I have bordered with fagots and gold satin. I had thought of tying some fagots to my back as well, but I am afraid that would prove most uncomfortable, so I will carry a sword instead."

234

"Good heavens! I hope you may not stab someone with it," said Phoebe.

I hope I may not have to, thought Caroline. "And what shall you be?" she asked. "You have not yet shown me your costume."

"Is that not funny? We have been in such a bother over the ghost since you came, all thought of the ball has quite gone out of my head until now," said Phoebe. "I am going to wear my gown which Mademoiselle Franchot made especially for me. Look." Phoebe ran to the wardrobe and pulled out a dainty white gown trimmed with rosettes and white ribbons. She turned the gown around, and Caroline saw two tiny gossamer wings protruding from the back.

"Oh, how clever! However did she do that?" exclaimed Caroline.

"Rose has offered to braid some gold ribbon in my hair for a halo," continued Phoebe. "Was not that kind of her?"

The once-traitorous Rose blushed guiltily, and Caroline murmured, "How very kind. So tell me," she continued, after giving Rose a look to remind her she was still on probation. "Does Clarence make his appearance dressed as a devil?"

Phoebe shook her head. "He refused. He said he wanted a more interesting costume."

"What will he be?"

"He is going as John the Baptist."

"After he was beheaded, I presume," said Caroline.

"I don't know how he will see to dance with his head tucked down inside his costume, but he has assured me he will have no problem. Jarvis is going to be a devil."

"No doubt we shall have many of those," said Caroline. "I wonder what Damien plans to be."

"I think he is coming as a devil also."

"Accurate, if not original," murmured Caroline. "And what of Mama and Lady Grayson?" she asked.

"Mama is merely wearing a mask and calling it a costume," said Phoebe scornfully. "But Mother Grayson is coming as the ghost."

"The ghost," repeated Caroline. "Grayson Hall's very own ghost?"

Phoebe nodded unenthusiastically. "She found an Elizabethan gown in an old trunk, and she is sure the ghost will feel honored to be represented at the ball."

Caroline smiled. "Your future mother-in-law is a dear. Every maligned ghost should have such a champion."

Rose had finished with Phoebe's hair. Phoebe examined her handiwork and pronounced herself pleased, and the sisters went down to breakfast. The gray drizzle from two days before had turned to a persistent rain which lurked outside, waiting to turn back all who ventured out. Clarence, being a man who loved the outdoors, was getting restless. "Curst rain," he muttered. "What is a man to do when he can't even poke his head out of doors without being near drowned? I have half a mind to ride even though it is raining."

"I have no desire to drag you back after you have taken a jump in the mud and broken your horse's leg and yours," said Damien. "Why don't you give our cousin a lesson in billiards? Now that I think of it, you could both use the practice." He smiled at his brother. "Last time we played I believe I beat you both."

"You have the devil's own luck," replied Clarence.

"'Tis you who make my luck," said Damien with a smile. "You cannot pick up a cue stick without leaving me something when you are through."

Clarence laughed and hauled Jarvis off to play billiards.

"Why does no one play shovelboard in that room?" asked Caroline.

Damien looked at her in surprise. "I suppose it is because no one knows how to play shovelboard," he said.

"You have a shovelboard parlor. Have you no desire to learn?" she asked.

"No. For then where would we play billiards?"

Caroline shook her head at him.

"There is something I would like to learn, however," he said. "And you and Phoebe could both be of great assistance to me."

"What is that?" asked Phoebe, eager to be of help.

"I danced little enough in India. I fear I am rather rusty."

"Oh, we would be delighted to help you," cried Phoebe, jumping up. "Would we not, Caro?"

Caroline was not delighted to help, but Lady Grayson thought it an excellent idea and shooed them off to the drawing room with her blessing.

"There is no room," objected Caroline.

"Oh, that is easily fixed," said Damien, and he began moving chairs against the wall.

"Caro can help you, and I will play the pianoforte," offered Phoebe. "I do not play as well as you, Caro, but I am sure I can play well enough to keep time. If you do not mind the mistakes," she added.

Caroline felt rather like the victim of conspiracy. "What would you like to work on first?" she asked with more politeness than enthusiasm.

Damien looked down at her and smiled, and her heart began to flutter erratically. She knew what he would say even before he said it. "Let us try the waltz," he said.

"Very well," she said, trying not to let his intense look mesmerize her. "You have, as you may remember, three steps. One, two, three. One, two, three," she demonstrated.

"One, two, three. One, two, three," he repeated humbly and mimicked her steps.

"Very good," she said. She looked at him suspiciously. "I thought you said you had not danced much in India."

"I did not say I had not danced at all," he said. "I merely said I was rusty. Besides, it is easy to imitate your steps like this. It is quite another thing to do these steps while trying to guide you across the room. Let us try that and see how I do."

"Very well," said Caroline. "Play slowly, Phoebe, until I tell you to speed up." She placed her hand on Damien's shoulder, and he took her extended one in his. Slowly, dramatically, he circled her waist with his arm, sending a tingle through her body. Beast, she thought. He is doing this on purpose.

She looked up at him accusingly. His smile widened, and she was strongly tempted to slap him. "Are you ready?" she asked.

"The waltz is a wonderful dance for becoming better acquainted, wouldn't you agree?" he asked. "How can two people remain enemies after they have waltzed together?"

"May I remind you that you are not yet waltzing?" Caroline pointed out. "I will count three, and then we will begin. One, two, three. One . . . Ouch!"

"Beg pardon," said Damien.

"You have started on the wrong foot," said Caroline impatiently.

"Many times," said Damien, looking at her meaningfully. "I am sorry. Are you hurt?"

"No. I shall be fine," she said politely. "Let us try

again. "One, two, three. One, two, three."

This time Damien got started on the right foot. With gentle pressure he moved Caroline about the room. "Oh, excellent!" she exclaimed. "Let us try it a little faster, Phoebe. Phoebe began to play faster, and Damien picked up his pace, twirling Caroline around the room. Neither heeded the sour notes coming from the pianoforte, nor did they miss a step when Phoebe lost her place and stumbled to a stop. They waltzed in silence, Caroline's eyes closed, her lips parted in a smile, Damien looking down at her as if he would very much like to kiss her. "Goodness!" exclaimed Phoebe under her breath.

Damien twirled Caroline to a stop. They stood for a moment, almost close enough to kiss, she looking up at him and he smiling down at her. "I do believe this is the first time you have looked at me without irritation, anger, or cynicism," he murmured. "What a delightful experience it is."

Caroline took a step backwards and blinked as if trying to wake up. Whatever was she thinking of, fraternizing with the enemy this way? "Yes, well, I believe you have quite mastered the waltz," she said. "What shall we try next?"

"A country dance?" suggested Phoebe.

"Very well," said Caroline unenthusiastically.

The next twenty minutes she spent showing Damien the steps of her favorite country dance. "I think you are ready to try it now with music," she said at last.

Phoebe launched into a song, playing with more spirit than accuracy, and Damien and Caroline began their dance. Caught up in the movements of the dance, they did not hear Clarence and Jarvis enter the room until Caroline happened to look up. She stopped suddenly, feeling at once guilty and embar-

239

rassed at being caught enjoying Damien's company.

Jarvis's lips spread in a cynical smile, and his cocked eyebrow made Caroline blush. "A dancing lesson? How charming. I'll wager our dear boy needed it."

"He is a very fast learner," said Phoebe.

"I am sure he is," agreed Jarvis.

Suddenly Caroline felt the need to retreat to the safety of her room. "If you will all excuse me," she said lightly. "I think I shall go take a little rest."

Jarvis never said anything to Caroline about her perfidy. Of course, he didn't have to. She was well aware of the magnitude of her sin. She tried to console herself with the idea that her new friendly relations with the enemy would give her an advantage. He would be bound to trust her now. He would get sloppy. He would get caught because she would still be ever vigilant. Yes, she surely had Damien at a disadvantage now. Caroline sighed in disgust. Who was she fooling? She was the one who had been put at a disadvantage. When had he managed to worm his way into her affections so successfully?

Caroline laid on her bed but got no rest. Rest was impossible. She could not turn off her mind. And, for all her feverish mental activity, she was no closer to a solution to her problems than she had been when she first lay down. I must simply not allow myself any feelings of kindness toward him, she told herself. I must keep in mind at all times who and what he is.

And with that grave determination she went down to tea. On entering the room, she placed herself next to Jarvis and visited determinedly with him, ignoring his cousin.

Damien did not appear to be ruffled by her defection, happily drinking his tea, munching on tiny sandwiches, and listening to the others talk.

240

"I do believe everything is in readiness for our guests," Lady Grayson was saying to Lady Harborough. "Lady Elizabeth is very particular about where she sleeps. She must be completely removed from any possible household noise, so I have put her at the farthest end of the house. And I have put Paddy near you, my dear. Naturally, I had to put Lady Anne across the hall."

"Of course," agreed Lady Harborough.

"Why is that?" asked Phoebe innocently.

The two older women exchanged knowing looks, but Phoebe received no direct answer to her questions. Affairs of the heart were something in which to indulge and about which to gossip only after one was married. Girls who had not yet entered that land of privilege were to be kept as ignorant and innocent as possible. Lady Harborough merely said, "She is there because it is the most convenient room in which to place her."

"Oh," said Phoebe, slightly perplexed.

Damien simply smiled.

"Lady Anne's husband does not accompany her?" asked Lady Harborough.

"The old curmudgeon. When, in their many years together have you ever known him to accompany her anywhere?"

"Ah, well," continued Lady Grayson on a happier note, "She has always been able to make the best of things."

Caroline had been half listening to Jarvis, half listening to the mothers. Now she was listening to neither as her mind dealt with this new problem. More mayhem and confusion. It would make her task of protecting Phoebe and Clarence all the more difficult. She smiled at Jarvis and worried. Boarding up the secret passageway would stop the ghost, but how

241

was she to keep Clarence safe?

"And I hear the Prince of Wales is considering abdicating and going to live in America," Jarvis was saying. "Do you think the climate will suit him?"

"I beg your pardon," stammered Caroline.

"So you should," he said in a low voice. "You have not been attending to a single word I have been saying."

"I believe it would do me good to stir myself a little," said Caroline. "I should not have had that second piece of seed cake. Would you care to visit your ancient relations in the long gallery?"

"I should be delighted," said Jarvis.

Caroline feared when they excused themselves that Damien would invite himself along as well. However, he showed no inclination to stir, and the two left the room alone.

"I am worried," said Caroline when they had reached their destination. "With extra people in the house, however will we be able to keep an eye on Clarence?"

Jarvis took her hand. "Have a little faith in me, dear lady. Have I yet left him alone?"

Caroline had to admit Jarvis had been most conscientious in watching his cousin, always offering to bear him company wherever he wanted to go. "But what about nighttime?" she said. "How can we be sure his brother will not sneak in and murder Clarence in his bed?"

"That worry has always been with us," Jarvis reminded her.

"Yes, but—"

"I really think you have nothing to fear," insisted Jarvis. "My cousin has been keeping his door locked lately."

"He has? However do you know that?"

A slight flush tinged Jarvis's face. "Worried about just such an eventuality as you described, I must admit I tried it one night. It was locked."

"Well, that is one less thing we must worry about," said Caroline, relieved.

By mutual consent they strolled along the gallery, admiring the portraits. "I suppose you think my theories all rather far-fetched, and you are doing this merely to humor me," Caroline ventured.

"I must admit, I found it all a little hard to believe," replied Jarvis. "That blow to the head went a long way toward convincing me that if something terrible happens to Clarence we will know at whose door to lay the blame. Of course," he continued, seeing the fresh worry on Caroline's face, "we shall make sure nothing does happen."

When Caroline left her room to go to dinner that evening she found herself, for some unexplainable reason, drawn to the long gallery. She stood, looking at the portrait of the family scapegoat. "Look at all the trouble you have caused," she told the first Lady Grayson with a sigh.

Before she could get much further in her conversation with the ghostly nuisance, the uneasy feeling that she was being watched settled on Caroline, and she turned to see Damien strolling down the corridor. Here was the last person she wanted to see alone. "I was hoping to catch you without your shadow," he said with a smile.

"I find your cousin to be a most likeable man," she told him stiffly.

"He has that talent," Damien observed.

"But then, so do you," said Caroline, remembering how he had wormed his way into her good graces

243

only that afternoon.

"So it would seem anyone can be likeable. If they choose."

Whatever was he getting at? "It would seem so," she agreed.

"Did you like me for a little while today?" he asked suddenly.

Caroline knew not how to answer this bold attack. She stammered and stuttered. Finally, all she could manage was an incensed, "Really!"

"Have I told you yet how very much I admire you?" he asked.

Caroline looked at him in amazement.

"I suppose enemies are not allowed even the luxury of admiring one another," he said. "This afternoon I almost hoped we would no longer be enemies."

"I do not know what you are talking about," said Caroline, concentrating on Lady Grayson's portrait.

Damien grabbd her arm. Why must he always do that? "You know exactly what I am talking about, Caroline," he said sternly. Then, in softer tones he added, "And I think you care for this silly war in which we are engaged no more than I."

"If you have tired of this war I suggest you leave the field," she said coldly.

"I cannot do that," he answered and let go her arm.

"Neither can I," she said.

There was no more to say. They left the long gallery and went downstairs and into the dining room in silence. Caroline suddenly found herself without an appetite.

She found it difficult to concentrate that evening when pressed into service at the pianoforte while her fellow houseguests and their host sang, and was relieved when Smythe finally made his appearance with the silver salver, for it heralded her imminent escape.

Sibby tried her best to cheer her mistress as she helped her undress by making encouraging noises. But as Sibby had no helpful new information to impart, Caroline refused to be cheered. She went to bed but did not sleep. Finally, she decided to forage in the library for a properly dry and dull tome that would send her to sleep.

Although there was no one in the library, the candles were still lit, indicating recent occupancy and, most likely, the upcoming presence of either another avid reader or a fellow insomniac, neither of whom Caroline wished to encounter in her wrapper and slippers. Best be quick. She tiptoed to the nearest shelf and snatched a book.

She turned to leave, but angry voices just outside the door stopped her in her tracks. Oh heavens! Here she was about to witness a nasty quarrel, and in her wrapper, too. Embarrassment and fear, as well as a healthy curiosity drove her behind the heavy velvet drapes by the window.

She had barely hidden herself when the voices entered the room. The heavy curtain still swayed slightly, and she prayed the two antagonists would not see it. It would have been awkward to meet them before. But at least then she had been standing in the open and with a book in her hand. She still held the book in her hand, but now she was skulking behind the draperies. What possible excuse could she give?

Fortunately the two men were much too busy to notice the slightly moving drapes, or the two pink slippers peeking out from under them. "Why do you not save us both a great deal of trouble and find some pressing social obligation to carry you away?" suggested Damien.

"Oh, you would like that, wouldn't you, cousin?"

"I can play this game as long as you can," said Damien. "And I can certainly outwait you."

Jarvis made a sound of disgust.

"Such a look," said Damien. "I am a barbarian, aren't I, to bring such delicate things out into the open."

Caroline could hear the sneer in Jarvis's voice. "Barbarian is too kind a word for what you have always been, dear cousin."

"And what is the word for what you are?" replied Damien. Caroline could hear the clink of glass on glass and the gentle sloshing of liquid. "I would offer you some," continued Damien, "but I would rather drink with the devil himself."

The library door slammed shut, and Caroline bit her lip. Why, oh why had she done such a foolish thing? Now she was trapped indeed. How long would she have to wait before Damien drank himself to sleep, or at least into enough of a stupor that she could escape undetected. And what if he should discover her before that happy event could take place? The dust of the curtain danced to the edge of her nose and tickled it. She crept an arm up and clamped her fingers tightly on her nose. The book in her hand began to feel heavier with each passing second.

Again, she heard liquid tumbling into a glass. Damien sighed. He fell into a chair opposite the curtain and sat staring into the dying fire. After a moment he rose and put another log on, and at the sound of this Caroline's heart fell. It would appear her enemy meant to remain here for some time.

And he did. At regular intervals Caroline could

hear him refilling his glass. She wondered what he was drinking and how much more the man would need to render him unconscious. She moved slightly and clutched her book in both hands. Her legs ached, and she longed to sit down, but she remained as she was, trying occasionally to shift her weight from one foot to the other.

Her patience was finally rewarded. Something sounding suspiciously like a snore drifted behind the curtain. Hopefully, she listened. There it was again. A snore. Definitely a snore. She peered out from behind the draperies. Damien was slumped in his chair. An empty glass and decanter sat on the table next to him. Overjoyed, she came out from behind the curtain. Unfortunately, in the process she dropped the book. It fell to the floor with a telltale thud, and Caroline's heart jumped.

Damien jumped, too. "Wha . . ." He looked around stupidly and blinked. "What's this?" he said. "Do I have a caller?" He pushed himself out of his chair and weaved his way over to her.

Caroline bent and retrieved the book. "I could not sleep. I was just looking for something to read," she said nervously.

Damien looked disappointed. "Oh. You did not come to see me?"

"I most certainly did not," snapped Caroline, suddenly wondering why she was standing about making excuses to a drunk. "You are hardly in any condition to be seeing anyone," she informed him.

"You think I am foxed?"

"I will bid you good night," said Caroline, attempting to brush past him.

"No. Do not leave," he said, barring her way. "You have barely even said hello."

"I most sincerely hope you are not about to

attempt to force your attentions on me," said Caroline sternly.

"Do you? Do you *sincerely* hope that? Or do you merely insincerely hope it?" he countered. "There is a difference, you know. I would be willing to wager that, in spite of your stern look, your hope is of the insincere variety." He took a step forward, arms outstretched to encircle her waist.

But Caroline was faster. Mercilessly, she brought her book soundly down on his head. He staggered back with a yelp, and she ran past him. She turned in the doorway and said, "I sincerely hope that may give you something to think about. Good night!"

17

Damien was not at breakfast the next morning, and Caroline hoped he was suffering greatly from the headache he so richly deserved. She encountered him later that morning on her way to the winter parlor, and he looked at her with knitted brows, as though he was trying to remember something.

Caroline was not about to help him remember anything. She bid him a pleasant good morning and asked in feigned concern how he had acquired the bump on his forehead.

"You do not know?" he asked her.

"I? How ever should I know. It was not there when last I saw you," she replied.

Damien shook his head. "You have hit me so many times since I first met you that now you are even invading my dreams to do so."

Caroline feigned innocence. "I beg your pardon?" she asked.

Damien shook his head. "Never mind," he said, and continued on his way, leaving a wickedly grinning Caroline behind.

Early that afternoon Lord Paddington (Paddy to his dear old friends), his sister Lady Elizabeth, and

Lady Anne Bates arrived at Grayson Hall. After the groom of the chambers had directed them and their servants to their sleeping quarters and all three had had a chance to freshen up, they joined the family for tea. "Paddy, dear, it is so wonderful to have you here under our roof again after all this time," said Lady Grayson.

Lord Paddington was a middle-aged man who was nearly as wide as he was tall. Brown eyes and a snub nose made him look like an oversized stuffed toy escaped from a nursery. Deep wrinkles at his eyes proclaimed him a man of sanguine temperament. "It has been some time," he agreed. "Last time we were all here, old Clarence was alive. Was that not so, Elizabeth?"

Lady Elizabeth had the same brown eyes as her brother, but there the resemblance ended. She was as thin as he was plump. Her nose was pinched and her expression sour. Caroline wondered if that sour expression was why Lady Elizabeth had never married, or if she had acquired it upon realizing she was doomed to spinsterhood. She spoke and her words were as spare as her frame. "That is true, brother," she said.

"He is sadly missed," said Lady Grayson. "But Clarence is doing most admirably well at filling his shoes."

"Glad to hear it," said Lord Paddington, giving Clarence an approving look. Damien entered the room, and Lord Paddington stared in surprise. "And who is this? By Jove, it cannot be."

"Oh, but it is," said Lady Grayson, enjoying her old friend's surprise.

"But you told me the boy was dead, Evangeline," huffed his lordship. "Dashed good to see the young puppy alive and well, ain't it, Lizzy?"

"He was not dead after all," said Lady Grayson, stating the obvious. "Is that not amazing?"

"Most amazing," agreed Lord Paddington, greeting Damien. "How very good to see you are still among us, young fellow. And so you have returned to your family. Giving your brother a hand with estate matters?"

"He needs little enough," replied Damien politely.

"But who is this?" said the pretty woman who had been sitting next to Lord Paddington. Caroline remembered Lady Anne Bates, the reigning beauty of an earlier generation. She had married a wealthy peer thirty years her senior, who had tired quickly of her and left her to her own devices. Her husband was now an invalid, and she had been carrying on with Lord Paddington for the last two years. She was still a fine-looking woman, in spite of the encroaching wrinkles and slightly sagging skin. There were few gray hairs among the beautiful dark curls, a stroke of fortune which aided her in presenting an illusion of youth. Her eyes were still a lovely, deep blue. And those eyes were trained with frank interest now on Jarvis.

"Why, this is our cousin, Mr. Jarvis Woolcock," said Lady Grayson. "You have not met him before?"

"I am sure I would remember if I had," said Lady Anne, smiling invitingly at him.

Jarvis, always polite, smiled back warmly, and the company settled in to enjoy their tea.

The new arrivals seemed to pump new vigor into the others and conversation was lively. Lady Grayson had not seen her friends since the London season had ended and there was much to be discussed—the latest abuse of poor Princess Charlotte, the newest fashions, who was cuckolding whom. Lady Elizabeth's pinched nose became even more pinched as the conversation continued. It was obvious she disapproved

251

of the type of behavior in which her brother and Lady Anne were engaged.

"We have had our share of excitement right here at the Hall," said Lady Grayson. "You will never believe this, but after all these years the ghost has begun to walk again."

"No!" declared Lord Paddington, amazed. "Have you seen it?"

"We have all seen it," answered Lady Harborough. "And the horrid thing seems to have taken a marked dislike to my poor Phoebe."

"How many times have you seen it?" asked Lady Anne.

The ladies looked at each other, trying to remember. "Well," said Lady Grayson, "There was the time Phoebe and her mama saw it."

"I saw it in the corridor," said Lady Harborough.

"And once I saw it in my bedroom," put in Phoebe.

"What did the ghost look like?" Lady Anne wanted to know.

"Very pale," said Phoebe, "with dark hair. And she was dressed all in white. She was most terrifying. I am glad we have not seen her for awhile. I hope she is gone."

"But where would she go, child?" laughed Lady Anne. "After all, this is her home."

"You mean to say you think she will never leave?" Phoebe asked, and the blood drained from her face.

This had gone far enough. "She will be gone," said Caroline firmly. "And quite soon."

"How very determined you sound," teased Lady Anne.

"I am determined that nothing and no one will mar my sister's future happiness," said Caroline, looking at Damien.

"I should like another cup of tea, Mother," he said calmly.

At dinner Caroline found herself seated between Damien and Lady Elizabeth and wondered silently what she had ever done to deserve such torture. Beyond offering her sympathies to Caroline on the loss of her husband (an event which had happened two years ago), Lady Elizabeth had little to say. And Damien was excruciatingly polite, venturing no more controversial or interesting comments than, "Does the veal seem rather tough to you?" and "I am quite fond of peas and new potatoes."

Caroline was sure he was behaving so merely to be provoking. If that was the case he was succeeding admirably. She looked with a jealous eye down the table to where Jarvis was being especially witty and urbane. She listened to Lady Anne's tinkling laugh and ground her new potatoes between her teeth. She did not care, she told herself, that Damien was showing no more conversation than the potatoes on his plate, that Jarvis and Lady Anne were having more fun than anyone else at the table. She certainly did not care that Damien was talking very little. She didn't care to talk with him. Not at all. But if she were to be trapped next to him, he could at least have the manners to entertain her. She strained her ears to hear what Jarvis was saying. "So then the chevalier said, 'But my dear, who would have expected a mole in such a place to be artificial?'"

Lady Anne tapped his arm with her fan. "How naughty you are," she said playfully.

"I?" Jarvis protested, all innocence. "But it was not I who told the story. It was the chevalier. And how can he be blamed when the entire incident was really the lady's fault?"

Caroline smiled, then, feeling Lady Elizabeth frowning next to her, coughed and took a sip of her wine.

"My cousin is very entertaining," commented

Damien. "Would you like me to entertain you with a ribald story? I have several."

"I am sure you do," said Caroline coldly. Then, before he could say more, she turned with determination to Lady Elizabeth and engaged her in conversation.

Caroline pumped the older woman ruthlessly on every subject she could possibly think of, from roses to religion, and she finally found a subject on which Lady Elizabeth could hold forth indefinitely—the morals of the day. Caroline had innocently asked her what she thought of the new Paris fashions, and Lady Elizabeth told her in no uncertain terms. "Young girls today have no shame. Dampening their skirts in such a vulgar manner. They might as well wear nothing. What their mamas can be thinking of to allow them to behave so! But then, their mamas have no more sense than the daughters, engaging in all manner of immoral, lascivious behavior." She looked disapprovingly down the table at Lady Anne, and Caroline knew why their hostess had put Lady Elizabeth in a bedchamber as far as possible from her brother and his amoureuse.

To Caroline's relief, dinner finally ended, and the ladies left the gentlemen to their own devices. Once in the drawing room, Lady Anne seated herself by Caroline. "I am sure you do not remember me, my dear, but I remember your mama introducing us when you first had your come-out. You were such a pretty thing. And I must say, in spite of the hardship you have suffered, you are as beautiful as ever. Your mama tells me you are about to embark upon some remodeling . . ."

It was hard not to like Lady Anne. She was flighty and vain, but she seemed kindhearted and more than willing to be friendly. She seemed especially willing to be friendly with Jarvis, Caroline noticed, when the men finally joined them.

Lord Paddington appeared to feel what was sauce for the goose was sauce for the gander, for he smiled wolfishly at Caroline and took the seat next to her which Lady Anne had vacated. "I knew your papa, my dear," he said, as though that must endear him to her. "Who would have thought old Harborough could have produced such a beautiful daughter."

"I believe I have my mama's looks," said Caroline.

Lord Paddington looked at Lady Harborough, as if searching for the resemblance, and nodded. "Your mother was a beauty in her day," he admitted. "But I don't think she was quite the beauty her daughter has turned out to be." He forced his smiling face into serious lines. "It is most tragic to see a woman widowed so young. You must be very lonely."

"Rarely," said Caroline dampeningly.

"And so many confusing things to attend to. Estate matters . . ."

"I have someone most competent to attend to matters of estate business," said Caroline. "Of course, I do miss Harold," she continued. "And no man could ever take his place. Did you know my husband?" she asked suddenly.

"Er, no. I am afraid I had not more than a nodding acquaintance with the young man."

"He was a fine, wonderful man," said Caroline, embroidering on her image of the loyal widow whose life was buried with her dead husband.

"I am sure he was," said Lord Paddington earnestly. "Such a brave child." He took her hand in his pudgy one and patted it. "If you should ever need anything, I hope you will not hesitate to call on me. Your father and I were great friends."

How quickly his lordship's relationship with her

father had progressed. In just a few moments he had gone from not knowing her father to being great friends with him. "You are very kind," Caroline murmured, trying to withdraw her hand.

Lord Paddington gave her a leer thinly disguised as a fatherly smile, and she smiled back weakly.

"Perhaps Lady Caroline would favor us with a song," suggested Damien.

She should have given him a grateful look, but one could hardly afford to show gratitude to the enemy. She did agree readily to sing, however, and Lord Paddington let go of her hand with reluctance. She played the socially acceptable number of songs, then sat down (as far from Lord Paddington as she could), and allowed Lady Anne to entertain them. Lady Anne was happy to oblige and offered to continue playing if the group would care to sing. Fortunately, Lord Paddington was nearly as fond of music as he was of pretty women, and, temporarily distracted, he left Caroline alone.

The evening passed pleasantly enough, and Caroline found herself almost regretting the appearance of the tea tray. But appear it did, and soon it was time to retire. The houseguests made their way to their respective bedchambers to undress and sleep.

Caroline, however, remained dressed and awake in hers. Sibby was now used to these unusual proceedings and bore her mistress company, sitting in the chair opposite Caroline's. Caroline was busy with her own thoughts, so Sibby sat waiting and ready to listen if her mistress cared to speak. "I don't like it," Caroline said finally.

"What?" asked Sibby.

"The fact that nothing has happened. Our villains know there is little time left to them. Why do they not act?"

"Do you think they are now waiting until after the ball? After all, they can hardly do anything while the house is full of guests. If truth be told," Sibby continued, "I would be willing to wager they will wait now until everyone, including us, is gone. If they want to do his lordship in they will probably even wait until Lady Phoebe has gone and there is no one to see."

Caroline sighed despondently. "You are probably right. I have failed," she concluded miserably.

Sibby opened her mouth to speak, then shut it. After all, what could she say? It looked very much as if her mistress was right.

The two women continued to sit by the fire. Sibby's eyelids began to droop and finally fluttered shut. Her head fell on her chest, and she began to snore gently.

"Poor Sibby," said Caroline softly. "Your mistress is indeed a trial to you." She got up and stretched. Why was she not sleepy? She had gotten little enough sleep the last few nights. Restless, she took a turn about the room. That did little to relieve her, so she opened the door and crept out into the gallery, thinking to go down to the library and read.

She looked down the dark corridor and gave a start. A figure clad in white was hovering near one of the doors farther down the hall. I have you now, thought Caroline gleefully and rushed down the hall.

Her prey looked up and gave a startled shriek and tore off down the hall with Caroline in hot pursuit. The ghost hesitated a moment, as if confused, then opened a door and disappeared inside.

Caroline knew she had her now, for the creature would never have time to get inside whatever hidey-hole lurked in that room. Like a dog following a scent, she charged mercilessly after her victim. She threw open the door and stopped short.

Caroline's ghost had not made for some priest's hole, but had thrown herself into the arms of none other than Lord Paddington, who was struggling valiantly to simultaneously quiet her and untangle them both from the bedclothes and the bed curtain, which she had ripped and brought down on them. "Oh!" she cried at the sight of Caroline.

"Why, bless me!" declared his lordship. "'Tis no ghost, my dear, It is Lady Caroline."

Lady Anne sat up. "Lady Anne?" Caroline asked, blinking. She felt a deep blush warm her face. "I am so terribly sorry," she apologized. "You see, I thought you were the ghost."

"You thought I?" began Lady Anne. "Oh, but that is famous." Lady Anne began to laugh. "I thought *you* were the ghost," she said. "You scared me half to death."

"But what were you doing out in the hall, my dear?" Lord Paddington asked his lady love. "I had thought you were fagged to death and were going straight to bed."

Lady Anne gave him a look which clearly said, "Must you ask? I changed my mind and came looking for you."

"Oh," he said as understanding dawned.

"If you will excuse me," said Caroline, embarrassed. "I think I will retire for the night." She backed out the door, and a hand on her shoulder caused her to jump and scream. "Oh, Mr. Woolcock. How you startled me," she gasped.

Lord Paddington and Lady Anne were at the door in an instant. "Are you all right, my dear?" asked Lord Paddington, eyeing Jarvis suspiciously.

"I am fine," said Caroline. "Mr. Woolcock merely startled me."

"I heard a cry," said Jarvis.

Right outside your bedroom door, thought Caroline with sudden insight. So that was what Lady Anne was doing in the hall.

"It was nothing," said Caroline. "Merely Lady Anne and I each mistaking the other for an apparition. Oh my," she said, as a familiar dark figure came toward them. "It would appear we have awoken the entire household."

Damien nodded to the others. "Did someone see our ghost?" he asked.

"No," said Caroline, blushing at her stupidity. "It was all a mistake." Again she apologized to Lord Paddington and Lady Anne and turned back toward her bedchamber. She heard Jarvis's voice drift down the corridor as she made her way back. It was not hard to identify the footsteps behind her.

"And what, pray," said a deep voice, "brought you out for a stroll this lovely night? Were you looking for me?"

Caroline ignored him and kept walking.

"Perhaps you were looking for Paddington," Damien continued.

Caroline whirled around and glared at him. "I suppose you find this all highly amusing," she said accusingly.

Damien wiped the smile from his face and tried to look contrite. "Er, no. I only find it . . . mildly amusing." No longer able to keep a straight face he burst out laughing.

The absurdity of the entire thing hit her, and Caroline began to giggle in spite of herself.

Damien smiled. "I do so enjoy laughing with you. It is such a rare experience."

This sobered Caroline instantly. Rare! It should not be happening at all. Whatever was she thinking of? "I will bid you good night," she said and stalked to her room. Damien did not follow her, and the fact that this bothered her made her even angrier than she had already been.

She entered the room and slammed the door shut behind her, making Sibby wake with a start. "What is it?" she gasped, jumping up. "Was it the ghost?"

"No. Merely Lady Anne feeling amorous," Caroline replied. She stopped for a moment to examine herself in her looking glass. "I could not sleep, so I decided to have a look around," Caroline explained. "And who should I see tiptoeing about the corridor but Lady Anne. In the dark I mistook her for Isobelle and, naturally, gave chase." At the thought of her ridiculous escapade Caroline began to laugh. "Oh, Sibby, it was most ridiculous," she said. "I pursued her right into Lord Paddington's bedchamber."

Sibby's mouth dropped and her eyes bulged. "No!" she breathed. A smile blossomed on her face and grew wide as Caroline continued.

"There she was," said Caroline. "She hadn't bothered to even part the bed curtains. They were torn and falling down around her and his lordship. And she was squealing like a stuck pig. And his lordship, oh, he was a sight. If her ladyship sounded like a pig, his lordship looked rather like one. I believe our Prince Regent is not the only one who has had to resort to wearing a corset, for I dare say his lordship looked even larger in his nightshirt than he did in his clothes." Caroline slipped off her dainty kid slippers. "Ah, goodness. What a night. Let us get in our beds as quickly as possible."

Sibby began to unbutton her mistress's gown. "If you were having such an enjoyable evening, why then the thundercloud face and the slamming door when you came in just now?"

Caroline's face took on an exasperated expression. "We woke half the household. Mr. Woolcock was up."

"And Mr. Damien Grayson, the one you so despise," added Sibby with sudden insight. "And what did he think when he found you with Lord Paddington and Lady Anne?"

"Nothing at all, for it was made perfectly clear what had happened. Anyway, I do not care a fig what he thinks."

"Is that why you looked in the looking glass when you came in just now?" asked Sibby innocently.

Caroline frowned. "That will be quite enough," she said.

Sibby smiled. "Yes, my lady," she murmured.

18

Caroline encountered Lord Paddington on her way down to breakfast the next morning, and she suspected it wasn't a chance meeting. She was sure he had been waiting for her. "How did you sleep last night, dear girl?" he asked. "I hope you did not have any more encounters with ghosts."

Caroline smiled politely and replied that she had not.

"And what, I wonder," he said playfully, "were you doing wandering these halls so late at night? Were you lonely? Looking for someone, perhaps?"

The poor old rogue. Caroline almost hated to repulse him and hurt his feelings. "I truly was not looking for anyone save Grayson Hall's troublesome ghost," she said. "But if I had been looking for someone to protect me, I would have most certainly turned to you."

His lordship beamed at this simple flattery, and Caroline could have sworn he threw out his chest. Of course, his chest and stomach were already thrown so far out it was hard to be sure. "I would not want to see such a beautiful young woman frightened to death. If you should hear or see anything, or if you are the least bit frightened, you have only to tap on my door," he said.

Caroline wondered what he thought would possess her to run the gloomy corridors of Grayson Hall in the dark if she were afraid, but she smiled and thanked him politely.

Breakfast was not quite so lively as dinner, for Lady Anne was still in bed. "My poor, dear Annie," said his lordship, heaping his plate with eggs and several thick slices of ham. "After her terrifying night it is no wonder she is still abed."

"What's this?" demanded Clarence. "Another adventure and I have missed it?"

"If you could call my pursuing your guest down the corridor adventure," said Caroline, glad Damien was not present to mock her.

"But why were you chasing Lady Anne?" wondered Clarence. "Was it a game?"

"She thought Lady Anne was the ghost," explained Jarvis.

"Caro," said Clarence. "Lady Anne don't look like a ghost."

At this point the subject of discussion herself entered the dining room. "If there is a ghost in these parts that does look like her I should love to be haunted," Jarvis declared and was rewarded with a smile.

"Shameless flatterer," said Caroline as she and Jarvis rambled about the maze later that day.

Jarvis chuckled.

"You nearly were, you know," said Caroline.

"What?"

"Haunted by Lady Anne."

"Oh?"

Caroline smiled mischievously. "It was your door she was hovering near when I surprised her last night."

"Does that make you jealous?" asked Jarvis suddenly.

Did it? Actually, no. It should have. Mr. Jarvis Woolcock was certainly nice looking enough, with his brown, curling locks and that charming smile. What a perverse creature she was. Why could she not be wildly attracted to this man who was such enjoyable company? "Should it make me jealous?" she countered.

"I was hoping it might," he said. "But I fear you have lost your heart in enemy territory."

Caroline knew exactly what Jarvis meant, and she denied it hotly. "I would never be so foolish as to jeopardize my sister's safety and happiness."

Jarvis gave her a quizzical look and then sighed in mock hopelessness. "Ah well, if my cousin does not steal you from under my nose, Lord Paddington is bound to win you."

Caroline laughed. "Fie on you."

"Come, now. Admit it. You are falling under his spell," teased Jarvis.

Caroline made a face. "I think of the two of us, you are faring much better," she said.

"Lady Anne is indeed a beautiful woman," admitted Jarvis.

"I hear her husband is unwell," said Caroline, all innocence.

"You are a minx," said her companion.

They came to the heart of the maze and sat on the stone bench. "It is a fine day," said Jarvis, gazing about him. Caroline did not answer, and he turned to see her deep in thought. "What troubles you?" he asked.

"Hmm?" asked Caroline.

"What troubles you on such a fine day? The sun is out. And we have not seen the ghost for some while."

"Yes. And do you not find that odd?" asked Caroline.

Jarvis looked as if he did not. "Why should that strike you as odd? Perhaps you have discouraged our ghost from haunting your sister. It could even be possible that my cousin has decided against doing away with his brother."

"It could be that he has seen we will not be frightened away and has abandoned that plan," said Caroline. "But do you honestly believe he has abandoned his idea of being rid of Clarence?" she asked.

Jarvis rubbed his chin thoughtfully. "I suppose not," he admitted at last.

Caroline sighed. "Neither do I. Oh, I suppose he may wait 'til the ball is over and all the guests have left. But it seems to me he would do well to arrange a fatal accident now, while there are so many people around. It is difficult to keep track of everyone's coming and going when a gathering is in progress. I am, in fact, surprised he has not yet succeeded." Jarvis sat next to her, frowning at the laurel hedge and chewing his lip. "Where is your cousin, by the way?" she asked.

"Damien? He has gone out shooting."

Caroline relaxed. "Thank God Phoebe made Clarence promise not to go out. At least we do not have to worry about him this morning."

"Yes," agreed Jarvis. "That is one less worry. Perhaps I shall pay a call on our fair neighbor this afternoon," he said suddenly. "Mayhap I can discover what she is up to at least."

"How will you do that?" asked Caroline.

Jarvis shrugged. "I am not yet sure, but I will think of something. Perhaps I shall mention the ghost and see what response I get. If our dear Isobelle predicts she will walk again soon, then we shall know to be on the qui vive."

"Excellent idea," said Caroline.

"Lady Caroline," called a voice from somewhere outside the hedge.

"Duty calls," teased Jarvis.

Caroline laid a silencing hand on his arm, and they sat with their breaths held, listening as Lord Paddington entered the maze, calling her name at intervals. Finally, all was silent. "Thank you," Caroline breathed. She smiled at Jarvis and said archly, "I should offer to help you in similar circumstances, but I strongly suspect you would not care for such help."

"You wound me," said Jarvis.

Caroline laughed, and they left the maze and ambled back to the house in companionable silence.

They had barely gained the house when Lord Paddington found them. "Ah, Lady Caroline. There you are," he said jovially. "I have been looking for you."

"Have you?" asked Caroline, all innocence.

"Are you just now come into the house?"

Useless to deny it. There she stood with her cloak and bonnet. "Why, yes," she said. "Were you looking for me outside?"

"Yes. I was out in the garden. I called your name, in fact. I wonder you did not hear me."

"That is most peculiar," agreed Caroline. Then, fearing his lordship would press her further about her whereabouts, she asked, "Was there something particular you wished to see me about?"

"Oh, no. Nothing in particular. I had thought you might fancy a bit of exercise," said his lordship. "But

I am sure you do not want to go out in that chill air again. Perhaps a stroll in the long gallery before luncheon. Would you care to accompany me?"

"I am sure we should like that very much," said Caroline, including Jarvis.

Lord Paddington gave Jarvis a look which plainly told him he was not welcome and, with a bow and a mischievous smile, Jarvis retreated and left the field to his lordship.

Caroline looked helplessly after him as his lordship led her away. "I imagine you would like to be rid of your cloak and bonnet. I shall be happy to escort you to your room," his lordship offered.

If Sibby had not been in the room, Caroline suspected his lordship would have been as happy to stay there and engage in a cozy tête-à-tête. His lordship definitely had rakish tendencies, and Caroline couldn't help but wonder what he had been like in his prime. How was she going to be able to protect Phoebe and Clarence with Lord Paddington clinging to her like a limpet? With great difficulty she moved him from her bedchamber and off in the direction of the long gallery.

"Do you know the stories behind all these portraits?" Lord Paddington asked as they entered the long gallery.

"I have learned a good many of them," said Caroline.

His lordship pointed to a dark, dashing-looking man in Tudor costume. "Ah, there was one," he said. "Rather looks like our young Damien, don't he?"

Caroline looked at the dark eyes and the sneer disguised as a smile and thought it reminded her very much of Damien.

"Of course," his lordship was saying, "Damien is a much nicer fellow than this Grayson ever was. This

267

one was a bit of a rogue. Family legend has it he took his bride by force."

"Did she kill herself?" asked Caroline, thinking of similar dark legends she had heard as a girl.

His lordship looked at her as if she was crazy. "Heavens, no. Whyever would the girl want to do that?"

Caroline blushed and shrugged. "I always thought that was rather the thing to do if one was taken against one's will."

"Don't you believe it," said his lordship. "I had it from old Clarence himself. The girl was perfectly happy. Yes, he does remind me of Damien," continued his lordship. "Of course, as I said, Damien is not such a rakehell. Nice lad, really. A bit of a temper as a boy, but there ain't a mean bone in his body."

Caroline was sorely tempted to set his lordship straight about the son of his old friend. But what was the sense? Damien's true character would be revealed soon enough.

"The boy reminds me of myself when I was younger," said his lordship. "Of course, there's still fire in the old hearth," he said and winked at Caroline.

Caroline smiled weakly. "I am sure there is," she said. However did one fend off an old rogue without hurting his feelings? Caroline decided to try bringing up a subject which she suspected excited Lord Paddington even more than beautiful women. "I wonder if luncheon is ready yet," she said. "I am suddenly quite famished."

"Now that you mention it," said Lord Paddington, "so am I. Let us go see what Evangeline's cook has concocted for our midday repast."

Caroline was saved from sitting next to Lord Paddington by the presence of Lady Anne. "Wherever have you been, you naughty boy?" she scolded, linking arms with him. "I have been looking for you this last half-hour. Evangeline had her cook prepare a syllabub for you, and we are having some lovely cutlets."

"Really!" exclaimed his lordship. He instantly lost interest in Caroline and went with Lady Anne into the dining room, where she placed him at her side. Caroline noticed with a smile that she commanded Jarvis to sit at her other side.

Jarvis did not seem to mind in the least. Ah well, was there a gentleman among the members of the ton who did not enjoy an occasional dalliance with a married woman?

Damien had returned with nothing to show for his morning's shooting. "There was little enough sport this morning," he told his brother as they ate. "You missed nothing by staying in."

Clarence was a man born to activity, and Caroline was sure by the expression on his face he would have loved a good tromp in the woods whether he had gotten anything or not.

Phoebe obviously deduced the same thing. "I am sorry I made you promise not to go out," she said.

"Ah well," he said with forced heartiness. "We had a ripping game of piquet."

"What do you say to a ripping game of billiards?" said Damien, setting down his napkin.

"By Jove, that sounds like a good idea!" exclaimed Clarence.

Damien smiled at Lord Paddington. "Your lordship?"

"Don't mind if I do," he said amiably. "I'll wager I can still teach you young scamps a thing or two. Do you join us, young Woolcock?"

"I am afraid I must decline," said Jarvis. "I have an afternoon call to make."

"Going to see Belle, eh?" said Clarence sapiently. Jarvis acknowledged this with a nod of the head. Lord Paddington was all ears. "Belle? Who is Belle?"

"Miss Isobelle Payne is our neighbor," said Damien. "I believe you have met her before."

"Ah, yes. That pretty little thing with the dark hair and big eyes. Used to run tame around here. I believe I should like to make the young lady's acquaintance."

"You shall have opportunity to meet her tomorrow," said Lady Grayson. "She and Sir John will be coming to dinner before the ball."

"Splendid!" declared his lordship. "You be sure and seat her betwixt Annie and myself. Well, boys. Shall we have that game now? Excellent luncheon, Evangeline. My compliments to your cook."

The men left in search of entertainment, and the ladies lingered over their meal, discussing the upcoming ball, reviewing the guests who would be coming for just the evening and the ones yet to come who would be staying at Grayson Hall. Caroline did some mental tallying as Lady Grayson rattled off names. "And then there are Lord and Lady Croft, Baroness Avonleigh and her son (such a dear boy), my dear Elizabeth is coming from Idlewilde with the marquess. I had so hoped they would be able to come earlier, for I know you have not seen her this age and more . . ." All toll her ladyship had named off twenty more people. However was she going to keep track of Phoebe and Clarence in that mob? wondered Caroline.

"That would explain why I had not seen Mr. Woolcock at any of the ton parties," Lady Anne was saying.

At the mention of Jarvis, Caroline dragged her wandering mind back from the future and tried to pick up the lost threads of conversation.

"Of course," continued Lady Anne, "Hector was in such poor health last season I made it to few parties, but I certainly would have remembered Mr. Woolcock if I had seen him."

"He is a dear boy," agreed Lady Grayson. She shook her head sadly. "The Woolcocks have been quite run off their legs for years. I was amazed when Jarvis returned from the Continent and announced his intention of settling in England. Not that one cannot live in this country frugally, you understand. But I cannot imagine Jarvis doing so."

"Perhaps he has made money on the change," suggested Lady Anne. "He certainly appears to be a clever enough young man. And so charming."

Lady Grayson gave her old friend a sly look, but as Lady Elizabeth was present, said nothing.

Of course, there was no need. It could not be anything but obvious to all that Jarvis had caught Lady Anne's eye. It appeared whatever his fortunes had been at one time they had now changed for the better. He had acquired money, or must at least have the promise of it in the future, and now he had caught the eye of a lady who would most likely soon be a very wealthy widow. Caroline found herself mildly jealous, but as she was only mildly so, she decided she should be a good sport and allow Jarvis the freedom to switch his allegiance from herself to Lady Anne. Poor Lord Paddington, she thought. He was about to lose his long-held position as Lady Anne's favorite cicisbeo. Caroline remembered his interest in the beautiful Miss Payne and decided with a smile that Lord Paddington was in no need of her sympathies.

The ladies repaired to the winter parlor and spent a

cozy afternoon gossiping and sewing. They were going down to tea when they encountered a very shaken Jarvis on the stairs. "Whatever has happened?" asked Caroline. "You look as if you have seen a ghost."

"Oh, did you see the ghost?" put in Phoebe. "But how could you? It is broad daylight."

"I have not seen a ghost," he replied. "I have not seen anything. Or anyone. Which is all rather unsettling as someone has just shot at me."

"Shot at you!" echoed the ladies. "Oh, you poor, dear boy," said Lady Anne.

"Who shot at you?" asked Caroline.

"Poachers?" suggested Lady Grayson.

"Poachers, my eye!" declared Jarvis. "More likely someone wanting to do me harm."

"But why would someone want to do you harm?" asked Damien innocently, when everyone was finally gathered for tea and Jarvis's story gone over again.

Jarvis regarded him coolly. "I wonder where you were this afternoon," he said slowly.

"Tsk tsk," replied Damien. "You know where I was. I was playing billiards with Clarence and his lordship."

"Jarvis, this is no time to be making small talk with your cousin," scolded Lady Grayson. She turned to her eldest. "What are you going to do about this?"

Clarence looked completely perplexed.

"I suggest," said his brother, calmly helping himself to a cucumber sandwich, "that for the moment, you do nothing."

"Nothing!" exclaimed Jarvis and Lady Grayson in unison.

"Really, dearest," said Damien. "What can he do that he has not already done? Our tenants have all

272

been made aware of the fact that we have a poacher in these parts. And a sizeable reward has been offered. There is little more we can do at present."

"You could go out and search for the fellow," suggested Lady Anne.

"Wouldn't find anything," said Lord Paddington. "The fellow is most likely long gone by now. Damien is quite right. It sounds like you have done all you can until you actually catch the culprit in the act of shooting something."

Or someone, thought Caroline.

Jarvis did not look at all pleased by such cold-blooded logic, but he said nothing.

He managed a word with Caroline before dinner. "Who can have done this to you?" she asked him.

"Most likely none other than the very one who took those shots at Clarence."

Caroline bit her lip. "But he was here, playing at billiards with Clarence and Lord Paddington," she said.

"So he says," replied Jarvis. "Would you care to wager that he did not remain with them the entire afternoon?"

Caroline sighed. "Oh, dear," she said. "It would appear I have placed you in danger."

"I shall be fine," said Jarvis. "But I must caution you. Take care. Keep your suspicions to yourself. Do not question my cousin about his activities this afternoon or say anything to alert him as to your suspicions."

"As to that, I am already afraid he is well aware of my suspicions by now," said Caroline.

"Nonetheless, I would caution you to say nothing more," said Jarvis. "The man is dangerous and to be avoided at all costs."

"Not an easy thing to do when we are all staying in

the same house," said Caroline. "And what of Miss Payne? What did you learn from her this afternoon?"

"What?" asked Jarvis, shaken out of a melancholy reverie.

"Miss Payne. What did you learn from her? About the ghost's future activities," prompted Caroline.

"Oh, yes. Nothing, really. It was a most fruitless trip."

"Lady Anne missed you, I believe," said Caroline lightly.

A slow smile grew on Jarvis's face. "And is she the only one who missed me?" he asked.

"I am sure we all missed you," replied Caroline modestly.

Before he could say more Lord Paddington found them, ending their conversation.

By dinner Jarvis had recovered from his brush with death enough to be his charming self again. Caroline watched as he flirted with Lady Anne. "I think you have been replaced in my cousin's affections," murmured Damien, taking a seat next to her.

Caroline was not about to discuss Jarvis with Damien. "Lady Anne is a charming lady," she replied.

"Lady Anne is insatiable," replied Damien bluntly. "She will be putting poor old Paddington out to pasture soon. And then he will be very lonely." He looked soulfully at Caroline, who shifted uneasily in her chair.

"Really," she said. "You are the rudest man."

"Yes, but I am honest. And that is more than my charming cousin can say."

Honest! Caroline was about to deliver a stern reproof, but Damien moved away from her before she could and engaged Phoebe in conversation. It was

274

just as well, she thought. Most likely, he had been baiting her. She watched him contemplatively. If he decided she suspected too much what would be her fate? She could hardly be shot by poachers. A fall downstairs, perhaps? Caroline shuddered and wished fervently that Clarence had been an only child. A delicate rattling sound brought her attention to her teacup. She was alarmed to see that her hands were shaking. Things had to be getting out of hand, indeed, if merely speaking with Damien was upsetting her this way.

"I do not in the least like the turn things have taken," she told Sibby later.

Sibby stopped unpinning her mistress's hair. "If you ask me, things took a turn for the worse the minute Lady Phoebe came here. How could they get any worse?"

Caroline sighed. "I wish I had not urged Phoebe to stay. She is in danger. Clarence is in danger. Now even poor Mr. Woolcock is in danger. And I have no idea what may happen next. Why, oh, why did I ever discourage Mama from breaking the engagement?"

"You could still talk to her," Sibby suggested.

"The ball is tomorrow night," Caroline reminded her.

"I am not saying we must all leave before the ball," said Sibby. "But you could have her ladyship talk to Lady Grayson and ask her not to mention the engagement. Perhaps the guests will forget why they have come."

"I doubt any of the guests have forgotten why they were invited," said Caroline. "But I am going to insist that Mama call off this engagement and that we all leave the day after the ball."

"But what of his lordship?" asked Sibby softly.

"His lordship will have to fend for himself," said Caroline firmly. "After all, I have my sister's safety to consider."

"Not wishing to sound disrespectful," ventured Sibby. "But can his lordship fend for himself?"

"He will just have to."

"And what about you?"

"What about me?" demanded Caroline.

Sibby became very busy brushing Caroline's hair. "Oh, nothing," she said.

"All right. Out with it," commanded Caroline.

"Is there no one here you will miss?"

"Mr. Woolcock and I are merely friends," said Caroline primly.

"I didn't mean Mr. Woolcock," said Sibby.

"Then whom did you mean?" asked Caroline.

"You know," prodded Sibby.

"Sibby!" exclaimed Caroline in shocked accents. "Do you think I am quite mad?"

"I don't think his lordship's brother could be all those things you say he is," said Sibby defensively. "Only last week Effie had the toothache, and Mr. Grayson gave her the money to have it drawn and the day off to boot."

"How very generous of him to be giving his brother's staff the day off," said Caroline sarcastically. "What has all this to do with me?" she finished irritably.

"Nothing," said Sibby in the wounded accents of one whose advise would be scorned. "I would just hate to see you make a mistake."

"My only mistake would be to remain under this roof any longer," said Caroline. "Things have come to such a pass that if I can but keep Phoebe and Clarence alive until after the ball I shall feel I have accomplished something." She got up and began to pace. "I only wish I knew what our ghost and her accomplice plan to do next. I am going to go down and check the secret passageway," she announced suddenly.

"Whatever for?" objected Sibby. "You told me yourself you and Mr. Woolcock boarded it up."

"I merely want to reassure myself that it is still in that condition," said Caroline, drawing on her wrapper.

"Oh, here," said Sibby in exasperated tones. "That will not nearly be warm enough." She grabbed a shawl, draping it around her mistress's shoulders. "Do you want me to come with you?" she asked.

"No," said Caroline, picking up her candle. "I shall be fine."

She crept from her room. This time she did not encounter Lady Anne in the corridor, and Caroline wondered idly in whose bed she was that night. Was it her own or had she gone visiting?

The house was still, and Caroline met no one en route to the great hall, a circumstance which, oddly, brought her no comfort. She pushed open the stone door to the secret passageway and, shielding her candle from the draft, entered the tomblike darkness. She shivered as she crept along and wished she had worn her cloak. In fact, she began to wish she had not come. What a silly idea this had been, to be sure. Yet she crept on, driven by stubbornness.

As she approached the end of the passage she noticed a small light tickling the darkness ahead. She stopped and a feeling of sheer terror grabbed her suddenly by the heart as she realized hers was not the only candle in that black passageway. A voice she knew only too well called, "Lady Caroline, I presume?"

19

Caroline stood frozen, unable to speak. She watched with wide and frightened eyes as the spot of light became a pool illuminating a tall dark figure. Have you come to clandestinely admire your handiwork?" asked Damien. "That is your handiwork, is it not?"

In spite of her pounding heart and sweating palms, Caroline felt a thrill of triumph. In their battle of wits this had been a thrust he had obviously not expected.

"I had wondered why our ghost had been so unsocial," Damien said.

"So now you know," said Caroline. "Why are you here?" she asked suspiciously.

Damien sighed. "I suppose you think I have been down here ripping the boards from the entrance with my bare hands."

That was exactly what she thought, but she said nothing.

"Come," he commanded and headed back in the direction from which he had been walking. Reluctantly, Caroline followed him. They came to the end of the passage, and Damien held his candle high so

Caroline could inspect the doorway. The boards were still in place. "I am sorry to have interrupted you," she said politely.

"It is in my best interest to leave that entrance boarded," he said.

Caroline looked doubtfully at him. The quivering candlelight made his face look ghostly. The cold crept up her arms and made her shiver. "Here," said Damien. He handed her his candle and took off his jacket and draped it gently over her shoulders. For a moment he stood tantalizingly close, his hands on her shoulders. She felt his lips touch her hair. "It is a pity you cannot bring yourself to think of me as something other than a villain," he said.

It was indeed a pity, thought Caroline. His breath came in warm puffs, caressing her hair.

"We might find we could actually enjoy each other's company," he said. Caroline made no reply. "Shall we go back?" he suggested in resigned tones.

She handed him his candle, and they made their way silently back down the passageway. Caroline stopped halfway, listening intently. "What was that?" she whispered.

"What was what?"

"I could have sworn I heard someone calling me just now," she said.

"The ghost of Grayson Hall?" he teased.

"My lady," came a faint voice from the end of the passageway.

"That is Sibby," said Caroline. She picked up her pace and hurried to the entrance. She emerged to find Sibby waiting for her, panic on her face. "Sibby, what is it?"

"His lordship," replied Sibby in an urgent voice. "He has fallen downstairs."

Before the words were barely out of Sibby's mouth,

Damien had dashed past her and out of the room. Caroline followed as quickly as she could, trying to hold up the skirts of her nightgown and wrapper and keep the jacket around her shoulders from falling off as well.

Damien paused at the top of the stairs, perplexed. "Not those," called Sibby. "The back stairs."

"What the devil . . . ?" Damien muttered and ran to the end of the corridor and disappeared down the stairs.

Caroline was now winded and forced to follow at a slower pace. Panting, she approached the stairs and the distinctive sounds of moaning reached her ears. "Thank God," she breathed. "He is alive at least."

She reached the head of the stairs and saw Jarvis, already kneeling next to the fallen Clarence. Damien rushed to his brother's side, and Jarvis stood up. "I don't believe anything is broken," Jarvis said, eyeing his cousin, who lay sprawled across the first landing. He had struggled to his elbows and was attempting to rub his head.

"What happened?" asked Damien.

"I fell," replied his brother.

"I can see that, you dunderhead," snapped his brother. "How did you fall, and what the devil were you doing on the back stairs?"

"I heard a voice outside my door. Thought it was Phoebe at first. Thought maybe she'd had a nightmare and seen the ghost."

"What did the voice say?" asked Damien.

"It said," Clarence raised his voice into a high falsetto and crooned, "'Clarence, Clarence.' So I went out into the corridor. Saw a light from the stairs and saw something white along the bannister. Thought it was the ghost."

All eyes turned to the bannister. There lay a white

gossamer peignoir. The ghost. "It called you by name?" asked Jarvis.

"How touching," murmured Damien. "What happened next?"

"I ran after it. Tripped over something on the stair. Fell."

Jarvis walked partway up the stairs and picked up a shiny black boot.

"Now, how did that get there?" wondered Clarence.

"More to the point, whose is it?" asked Jarvis. "Have you been leaving your boots on the stair, old man?" he teased.

"That ain't mine," said Clarence.

"No. It isn't. Yours are by Hoby, as are mine. This is of inferior workmanship, possibly by . . ."

"A very good bootmaker in Delhi," interrupted Damien, snatching the boot from him.

"I say, Dam," said Clarence, struggling to his feet. "That is not one of your funnier pranks. I could bloody well have broken my neck."

Caroline and Jarvis exchanged looks, and a dark flush stole across Damien's face. "I apologize, old fellow. Here. Can you walk?"

Clarence rubbed his neck and his back. "Yes. I am none the worse for wear. Only a little banged up."

"Then I suggest we go to bed," said Damien, heading up the stairs. "Thank God nothing is broken. It would be most inconvenient if you were unable to dance tomorrow night."

It was probably most inconvenient that he had not broken anything, thought Caroline. Thank God Jarvis had come along. Otherwise, Damien could easily have escorted her back to her bedroom then gone on to finish off his stunned brother. "It is a good thing Mr. Woolcock found his lordship," Sibby was saying. "For I would not have known what to do.

And his lordship was looking that stunned, too. I thought sure he had broken something.''

"I am surprised he did not wake the entire household," said Caroline. "Falling down those stairs he must have certainly made a great deal of noise.''

"Well," said Sibby thoughtfully. "Now that I think of it he didn't, really. He just let out this short cry and tumbled down the stairs. If I hadn't already poked my head out into the hall looking for you, I doubt I would have heard him.''

"Hmm. I am surprised Mr. Woolcock heard him.''

Sibby nodded. "I am, too. In fact, I don't know where he came from. I just looked up, and he was there like a guardian angel, appearing suddenly.''

"It is most fortunate for Clarence that you and Mr. Woolcock found him. I shudder to think what might have happened to him elsewise." Caroline sighed. "What a household.''

Caroline tumbled into bed exhausted. But for a long time her mind refused to give her body the peace it needed. She lay in her bed and stewed over her sister's fate. However, even an active mind such as Lady Caroline's must occasionally pause in its wanderings, and when hers eventually did, her tired body took advantage of it and pulled her into sleep.

She awoke the next morning feeling anything but refreshed and wondered how many tense days and sleepless nights the human body could withstand before it collapsed. Sibby looked at her mistress's smudged eyes and said accusingly, "You did not sleep. A fine sight you will be tonight at the ball.''

"I shall have on a mask. No one will see my face," replied Caroline.

"It is a pity you cannot wear the mask all day," said Sibby heartlessly.

Caroline smiled and shook her head. "This must

be why I keep you, dear Sibby. I can always count on you to keep me humble." Caroline peered into her looking glass. "It is a pitiful sight," she admitted. "What shall I wear today?"

"Best wear your green morning gown," advised Sibby. "That color always brings your face alive, and heaven knows it could use some life this morning."

Once dressed and with her rich auburn curls tied up in a green ribbon, Caroline had to admit she looked much better. The rich green of her muslin gown did much to minimize the dark circles under her eyes. A little Bloom of Ninon also helped. So did a hearty breakfast, and by midmorning Caroline was feeling ready to face the arduous task which lay ahead of her.

Lady Grayson, normally an early riser, had been up even earlier that day, making sure all was in readiness for her guests. But Lady Harborough was never up before eleven. Caroline found her still in the hands of her hairdresser. "Good morning, my girl," she called cheerily to her daughter.

Caroline kissed her mama on the cheek. "You are in fine fettle this morning, dearest," she said.

"And why should I not be?" replied her ladyship. "My brilliant daughter has frightened away the ghost which was making our lives so miserable."

"Mama, we cannot be sure of that. In fact—"

"We have not seen the thing for days," interrupted her mother. "I am sure it is quite gone. Phoebe may now safely marry Clarence. And, unless I am very much mistaken, you may receive a proposal or two yourself before our visit is over. I always say, there is nothing like a gathering for finding a husband. It is really almost as good as a London season."

This speech so threw Caroline she completely forgot why she had come to see her mother in the first place. "Proposals? Whatever can you mean?"

"You sly puss," scolded Lady Harborough. "Which will you have, Mr. Woolcock or Lord Paddington?"

"Neither," declared Caroline. "Mama, of whatever are you thinking?"

"Why, your happiness, of course," said Lady Harborough. "You are far too young a woman to remain a widow, shut up in that musty old ruin of Harold's, moldering away. You need to be married, setting up your nursery."

"With Lord Paddington?" Caroline began to laugh. "Oh, Mama, be serious, do. Lore Paddington is old enough to be your husband. And old enough to be my father. Whatever would I want with a fat old toad like Paddington?"

Caroline's mother looked almost insulted. "I'll have you know, young lady, that in his day Lord Paddington was a fine figure of a man."

"Well, his day is long past," her daughter answered with asperity. "You highly disapproved of Sir John dangling after me, yet I see little difference between him and Lord Paddington."

"Sir John is much older," said her mama. "And he is not an earl," she finished, revealing the real reason for her disapproval.

"They are both too old," said Caroline firmly.

"Lord Paddington is very rich," said Lady Harborough.

"Mama, if I am ever to remarry, please allow me to marry someone nearer my age. I have already had a husband several years older than myself."

"All right, then," agreed Lady Harborough reasonably. "Let us talk of Mr. Woolcock. He seems very interested."

"Oh, Mama, is it not enough that you have gotten Phoebe off?" asked Caroline in exasperation. Then, remembering why she had come, she said, "Which reminds me. If Harris is done with you I should like a few words with you alone."

Lady Harborough dismissed her hairdresser with a wave of her hand and waited for her daughter to speak.

"It is about Phoebe I have come," said Caroline. "Mama, I have been very wrong."

"Wrong!" her mother interrupted. "Why, child, you have been absolutely inspired. All that talk of moving Phoebe's engagement up. It has obviously scared off our ghost."

"Mama, our troubles are still very much with us. I am afraid there is much I have not told you. Phoebe and Clarence are both in danger. Only last night Clarence took a fall down the stairs which could have been fatal."

"Good heavens!" exclaimed Lady Harborough. "He did not sprain an ankle, I hope. Will he be able to dance?"

"Mama!"

"Caroline. You are making much of little."

Caroline could hardly believe her ears. This from a woman who suffered palpitations at the slightest thing? "Mama, this is serious," she said. "I fear I cannot keep Clarence safe, and if he lives to marry Phoebe, she will be in grave danger. We must leave Grayson Hall. You must call off the engagement."

"Call off the engagement!" Lady Harborough looked at her daughter in amazement. "Have you taken leave of your senses? I vow I do not understand you at all, child. It was you who insisted I *not* call off this engagement."

"I am aware of that," said Caroline.

"Then I do not understand why you wish me to do so now," said Lady Harborough, exasperated.

Caroline ground her teeth. "I have just told you, Mama."

"Well, pray do not tell me again. It is quite enough to give me a megrim. Now, do let us talk of something more pleasant, my love. Mr. Woolcock seems to be most particular in his attentions. What do you mean to tell him if he declares himself?"

"Mama, let us not talk of Mr. Woolcock. I wish to talk of Phoebe."

"I do not," said Lady Harborough with finality. "I have quite made up my mind. We stay." And with that royal decree Lady Harborough rose and left the room, leaving her daughter to follow fuming behind.

Caroline did not return to the dining room with her mother. She fetched her bonnet and cloak and headed out into the chill autumn air where she was sure she would be able to pace in peace. Why must Mama be so perverse? Caroline kicked at the gravel on the path with the toe of her slipper, sending tiny stones in all directions. "Oh, however will I be able to keep watch over them with the house full of strangers?" she wailed. The ball itself loomed in front of her like a nightmare. Although this occasion was a far cry from the fashionable crushes one attended in town at the height of the season, it was shaping up to be a very well attended affair. Grayson Hall would be full of guests, and the inn at Upper Swanley would be packed with revelers as well who would be turning up at the hall to add to the confusion. "Not to mention those just coming for the evening," Caroline muttered unhappily. How would she ever keep an eye on Clarence and Phoebe with nearly a hundred people swirling about them? "Impossible," she sighed. So whatever was she going to do? There was only one thing she could do. She hurried inside in search of Clarence.

She finally tracked him down in the library, her gentle tap on the door awakening him from his slumbers. "Caro," he said. "I was just . . . Estate business, you know."

"Poor Clarence," she said sympathetically. "Is it so very boring?"

Clarence nodded sheepishly. "But I manage all right. I have Rutherstone to advise me. Good man, Rutherstone. Loves this place nearly as much as m' brother and I."

"Your brother is very fond of this estate," Caroline observed.

Clarence nodded. "Grew up here. It's his home."

"Yes. But as the eldest son it belongs to you," Caroline pointed out.

Clarence shrugged and nodded. Simple, generous soul that he was, it would never occur to him that someone might not be content with things as they were. His door was always open to the other members of his family. How could he ever understand that, although it was open it was still his door, and that made the fact it was open even more galling. How could she explain to him that of what he thought so little someone else coveted enough for which to kill? One might have as easily explained to Esau the value of his birthright. Caroline scratched her head.

"Is something the matter?" asked Clarence.

Caroline chewed her lip and took a turn about the room. "Clarence," she said. "I am sure you have noticed that people often change over the years. Difficult circumstances may make an old man bitter, or may turn a childhood friend—or brother—into, well, someone different." Clarence smiled and nodded, and Caroline took hope. "When we are children there are many things we do not trouble ourselves about, but we grow older and sometimes feel, per-

287

haps, a sister—or brother—has been favored." Clarence nodded again. "Now, I am sure your brother was very different as a boy."

"Dam? Oh, no. He has not changed at all," said Clarence.

"Yes, but I feel perhaps he may resent your good fortune," Caroline began.

"Oh. I see what you are getting at," said Clarence. "Yes, you are right. I think he does."

Now we are getting somewhere, thought Caroline. She smiled at Clarence as a teacher would smile at a student who was beginning to finally grasp a difficult lesson. "And he may be jealous to the point of wanting to, er, do something about it. Which is why I want you to promise me that you will not go off alone with your brother."

"Me?" said Clarence, perplexed. "You mean Phoebe, don't you?"

"Yes, her also. But it is you who is in danger."

Clarence scratched his head. "Danger? Oh, yes. In danger of losing Phoebe to Damien. No. Really, Caro. Damien might wish he had met her first, but he would never steal her away from me."

Caroline ran a hand across her forehead. Clarence was not clever enough to understand hints and innuendos. "Clarence. I want you to promise me you will go nowhere alone with your brother from now until the ball is over," she said sternly.

Now Clarence looked truly perplexed. "I don't understand," he said.

'I know you do not," said Caroline. "But the truth is—"

There was a tap on the door, and Damien himself entered the room. "Damien, old fellow, we were just now talking about you," said Clarence.

A guilty flush stole across Caroline's face, and

Damien gave her a knowing look. "Do tell," he said. "Mama is in urgent need of you. She says our guests will be arriving any moment, and she wants you on hand to help with the greetings and introductions."

Clarence rose and excused himself.

Caroline could have screamed from frustration, but she was not about to let Damien see her vexation. She smiled sweetly at him and followed Clarence out of the room. Damien fell into step with her, and it was all she could do to keep from grinding her teeth. The last thing she wanted was a tête-à-tête with him.

"You look as though you did not sleep well," he said. "Is the strain of watching me beginning to take its toll?"

Caroline gave him her frostiest look. "If you will excuse me, I must find my sister," she said.

"Oh, no," groaned Damien. "Never tell me you now go to enlist your sister's aid."

"Have no fear," Caroline replied. "I intend to tell you nothing."

Damien shrugged as if to say it would not affect his plans whatever she decided.

She left him and went in search of Phoebe. If the dishonorable Damien Grayson thought to become the next earl of Alverstoke he thought wrongly. They would all stand together against him, and he would be powerless to harm Clarence.

Phoebe was not in the winter parlor where Caroline had last seen her. Instead, Caroline found Lady Anne enjoying a comfortable chat with her mama. "Your sister has gone to her room, I believe," said Lady Anne. "To try on her costume for the ball."

"Why are you looking for your sister?" asked Lady Harborough suspiciously.

"Oh, no reason in particular," said Caroline innocently.

"Caroline," said her mother sternly. "I sincerely hope you are not planning to speak with her regarding a certain matter we discussed this morning. That subject is quite closed."

"Yes, Mama," replied Caroline meekly. "I am aware of that, and that is not why I wish to speak with her." Caroline wished Lady Anne a speedy good morning, then beat a hasty retreat before her mother could question her more thoroughly. It was really not the same thing she had discussed with Mama that morning, Caroline reasoned. After all, that had centered around calling off the wedding. This had to do with protecting Clarence. Of course, if Phoebe happened to suggest calling off the engagement to protect Clarence that would not be Caroline's fault.

Caroline reached her sister's room only to discover Phoebe had come and gone. "She went to help her lordship greet the guests," said Rose.

"But there are no guests yet," protested Caroline. Rose gave her no answer, and Caroline hurried downstairs in hopes of yet catching a few moments alone with Phoebe.

She was again foiled when she was waylaid by Lord Paddington. "I hope you will honor me with a dance tonight, my dear," he said.

"Of course. I should be delighted," she lied.

Lord Paddington beamed in satisfaction. "A waltz?" he suggested.

The waltz was a favorite dance of rakes and lovers alike. And rightly so, for it was a tantalizingly sensuous dance. The thought of Lord Paddington's pudgy hand on her waist was anything but tantalizing, but Caroline had not the heart to refuse him. "I shall look forward to that," she said, and excusing herself, hurried on.

She was next stopped by Smythe. "I was about to

deliver these, my lady," he said. "It has just come for you from Hallowstone House."

"Thank you, Smythe," said Caroline.

"What is this?" asked Jarvis, sauntering up to her.

"Goodness! You startled me," said Caroline. "I declare there are people coming out of the woodwork at me this morning."

"Wait 'til the afternoon. There will not be a corner in the house where you may go without bumping into someone," Jarvis said. "What is this?" he asked, looking at the hothouse orchids Caroline held in her hand. "Something from an admirer?"

Caroline opened the accompanying card and, in spite of her pressing concerns, couldn't help smiling. "They are from Sir John," she said. "How sweet."

"You do seem to be getting a collection of elderly admirers," teased Jarvis. "Perhaps I should hurry and declare myself before one of them swoops you from under my nose."

Caroline giggled. "There is no danger of that," she assured him. "So you may take your time. I do begin to wonder, though, how I am ever going to keep an eye on Phoebe and Clarence tonight when it looks as if I am going to be busy dodging Lord Paddington and Sir John the entire evening."

"I shall help you," said Jarvis consolingly.

Caroline gave him a gratified smile. "Thank you. It makes me much easier in my mind, I assure you, knowing you will be helping me. And now I fear I must find Phoebe. I intend to tell her all the things which have developed these last few days and instruct her to keep a careful eye on Clarence as well. Under no circumstances should she allow him to be alone with his brother."

Jarvis laid a hand on Caroline's arm. "You do not really think Damien will do anything tonight of all nights, do you? How would he ever get an opportunity?"

"With all the confusion of a ball? What better chance to lure his brother away and do him in unnoticed. And, now that I think of it, do you have a pistol?"

"Yes," said Jarvis slowly.

"Well, you had best take care to have it safely locked away tonight. The way Damien feels toward you it should not surprise me in the least if he were to use it on his brother and make you the villain in this dangerous game."

"Good heavens!" exclaimed Jarvis. "You cannot mean that."

"Oh, but I do," said Caroline. "Please be careful. I have an awful feeling about this night."

"Do not worry yourself," said Jarvis, patting her arm. "I have everything well in hand."

ars, do you: How would he ever forgive any?

With all the confusion of a ball. What better nance to lure his brother away . . . ng in ow the . . .

20

Don't worry, Jarvis had said. But it was impossible not to worry. And Caroline's worries increased as the houseguests began to arrive, and she found herself unable to get Phoebe alone. Jarvis had promised to help her, she reminded herself. But she would have felt better if she could be sure Jarvis truly shared her concern. She strongly suspected he had pledged his help only to humor her, and she couldn't help wondering how diligent a guardian he would be with Lady Anne at the ball to distract him.

By luncheon there were four new faces at table. Caroline drew Phoebe aside as they rose to leave the dining room, whispering, "I must talk to you."

"Lord and Lady Carew have arrived, your ladyship," Smythe announced.

"Oh, Phoebe, my dear," declared Lady Grayson, taking Phoebe's arm and leading her toward the door. "You will adore Lady Carew. She is the sweetest creature."

Caroline sighed. She turned her head and caught sight of Damien wearing an amused smile. I would wager he loved to pull the wings off flies when he was a child, she thought. Well, he shall not see this fly squirm. She gave him her most charming smile. "I hope you are planning to ask me for a dance tonight," she said.

"Are you sure you will not be too busy to spare me one?" he asked.

"I am sure I do not know what you mean," said Caroline huffily.

"I am sure you know exactly what I mean," countered Damien.

Caroline's expression turned frosty, and he chuckled. "I think we waltz exceedingly well together. If I promise not to tease you anymore will you give me a waltz?"

Caroline nodded, still unsmiling. "I should be happy to," she said graciously. And deep down inside she knew she would be happy to waltz with Damien, traitorous creature that she was. Why, oh, why couldn't Lord Paddington look like Damien Grayson. Or, better yet, why couldn't Damien be harmless, like Lord Paddington?

Shortly after luncheon Caroline escaped to her bedchamber in the hopes of getting a nap before tea. But, once again, her mind would give her no rest. She lay upon her bed and tossed. "I should speak with Phoebe," she told herself. "Perhaps at tea I shall have an opportunity." With that idea Caroline consoled herself.

There were more new faces at tea time, and by the time Caroline had freed herself from an especially loquacious dowager her sister had left the room to dress for dinner.

I shall surely have no trouble prying Rose away from her for a few moments, thought Caroline, hurrying upstairs. She found Phoebe in her bedchamber, but she was not alone. Not only was Rose in attendance, but Lady Harborough was there as well. "Mama!" declared Caroline. "What are you doing here?"

"I am visiting with your sister, as you can plainly see," said Lady Harborough. "I am glad you are come, Caro. Mr. Woolcock tells me you have received a posy from Sir John."

Caroline knew where this conversation was leading. "Oh, goodness, where is my head? I quite forgot I promised Lady Grayson to check on the flower arrangement for the dinner table." With that she beat a hasty retreat back to her own bedchamber.

Now she was more frustrated than ever. One should be able to see one's sister alone if one desired. Shouldn't one? However was she going to be able to warn Phoebe? Her eyes fell on the dainty escritoire sitting in the corner. She sat down, dipped her quill in the inkstand and began to write.

Clarence is in grave danger. Do not leave him alone for an instant this evening. If you must be away from him, deliver him to me on any pretext of which you can think. Do not allow him to be alone, however. Follow these instructions carefully. Your future happiness and Clarence's very life could depend on it. Caroline read her note with satisfaction and signed it. It would be hard to harm either Clarence or Phoebe if they were both together. And it should make them easier to watch as well. She dusted the parchment paper, folded it, and rang for Sibby. "I want you to take this to Phoebe when you are done with me," she instructed.

Sibby nodded and put the note in her pocket. Then the two women began the serious work of turning Caroline from the glamorous Lady Caroline into the saintly Joan of Arc. She was put in a simple gown of sarcenet which had been trimmed at the bottom with gold satin cut to resemble flames. Her arms and shoulders were loosely wrapped with gold cord and her hair tied simply, several luxurious locks allowed to fall to her neck in ringlets. She smiled at her reflection when they were finished. "I look positively saintly," she said.

"You look lovely," said Sibby. "But you do not look saintly."

"How should you know? You have never met a saint," laughed Caroline.

"True," admitted Sibby, "I have not. But if I did I am sure she would not look half so elegant."

Caroline did look elegant. Her gown hung in soft folds and clung alluringly to her. The diamonds in her ears and at her throat glistened. And she supposed if she had really wanted to look like Joan of Arc she should have used plain rope from the stable instead of the expensive gold cord looped tantalizingly across her breasts. "Well," she said at last. "I want to look like a saint, but I do not want to look like a dowd."

"You will turn every head," Sibby predicted.

"Just so I turn Lord Paddington's head. That is all Mama cares," said Caroline in disgust.

"Lord Paddington!" exclaimed Sibby.

"Lord Paddington appears to be losing interest in Lady Anne. Or perhaps it is the other way around. At any rate, Mama feels we should suit, and I shall spend half the night dodging him, I am sure. I will be glad to return to Wembly where I am safe from amorous old men."

"I thought Mr. Woolcock was partial to you," said Sibby.

"He has neither title nor fortune to recommend him. Mama has only the faintest interest in him now," said Caroline.

"There is talk in the servants hall he expects to come into money."

Caroline shrugged. "Who knows? Whatever his circumstances, I am sure he would have to inherit a title as well as a fortune to make Mama as partial to him as she now is to Lord Paddington."

"Lord Paddington is so old," said Sibby, making a face.

"Yes, but Mama does not see him as old, for he is very near her own age. And then there is Sir John. I can count myself fortunate he is only a knight, else Mama would have him in the running as well."

Sibby giggled. "That is worse than Lord Paddington," she said. "I hear Sir John has the gout."

"I can think of something else he has which is far worse than the gout and effectively removes him from the lists," said Caroline.

"What is that?"

"Isobelle." The two women smiled. "Now," said Caroline. "Hand me my sword." Sibby handed Caroline the rusty old broadsword she had borrowed for the occasion. "Now I look more like the Maid of Orléans," she said. "And one never knows. This may come in handy."

"That thing is so dull you could not even pierce a piece of parchment with it," observed Sibby.

"It will serve well enough if I need to hit someone over the head," said Caroline. "Now, off with you. Deliver that note to Phoebe for me and keep your fingers crossed that this night will go well. And beware of goblins."

Sibby giggled. "Oh, we are well prepared belowstairs, my lady. We have our jack-o'-lantern carved and sitting on the back step of the kitchen."

"Good," replied Caroline. "And I hope all the jack-o'-lanterns Lady Grayson has had carved for the great hall will keep the goblins away from Clarence tonight."

Her note safely dispatched to Phoebe, Caroline

went downstairs to dinner feeling relieved that she had made yet another wise move in the battle of wits in which she was engaged. Just let Damien try and lure his brother away now!

The drawing room was crowded with bodies. A headless Clarence, clad in what suspiciously looked like a lengthened dressing gown, loomed above the other guests. Under his gown Caroline could glimpse breeches, and his feet were clad in a pair of very elegant shoes. She went to him and tapped him on the arm. "John the Baptist, I presume," she said.

An eye peered at her through a crack in his pinned-up robe. "Caro!" he exclaimed in muffled accents. "You look dashing. Who are you?"

Caroline raised her sword. It was heavy and awkward to lift, and its ascent was a wobbly one. Clarence ducked. "Can you not guess?" she prompted.

A hand reached inside the top of the dressing gown as Clarence scratched his head. "I give up. Tell me."

"I am Joan of Arc. See? Here are the flames."

"Now that you have told me I can see it," said Clarence.

"And where is your head?" asked Caroline, pointing to the empty platter in Clarence's hand.

"Wanted to rig up something," Clarence admitted. "But Phoebe and Mama both made such a to-do about it I gave up the idea. Do you think people will know who I am?"

"I am sure they will have no trouble guessing," said Caroline, looking around at the other guests. There were a fair number of angels and ghosts and two devils thus far. The slim one she knew to be Jarvis in spite of the ugly mask which covered his head, for he had told her his costume earlier. It was not hard to guess the identity of the short pudgy one, either, even before he turned his head. Lord Paddington smiled at Caroline and hurried across the room to greet her. "You look positively lovely, my dear girl," he said, grabbing her hand and raising it to his lips. "I never saw a more beautiful angel."

"I am not an angel," protested Caroline.

Lord Paddington chuckled. "Are you not? That is good news indeed," he said.

"Lord Paddington," scolded Caroline archly. "For shame. That is not what I meant and well you know it. I am Joan of Arc. Can you not tell? Look. Here is my sword. Here are the flames and the rope."

"Oh, yes, yes. I know that. I was only funning," said his lordship. "You look exquisite."

"And you look . . ." she said, pausing. What did he look? *Ridiculous* would be the best word. He was clad entirely in red and had managed to secure two fat red satin horns on his head. The plump, merry face smiling under those horns looked as evil as a baby's. "You look," she began again and was saved from having to lie outrageously to Lord Paddington by the appearance of Lady Anne, clad incongruously as an angel. "Lady Anne!" exclaimed Caroline in enthusiastic tones. "How charming you look."

Lady Anne turned round so they could see her gossamer wings. "Did not my dressmaker do a beautiful job?" she asked.

"You look charming, as always," said Lord Paddington, taking her hand and raising it to his lips.

"Thank you," said Lady Anne. "That is a devilish fine outfit you have on," she said to Lord Paddington, who laughed appreciatively at her pun. She smiled on them, her eyes ranging the room. Her smile widened as a devil with a grotesque mask approached them. "Hello, dear boy," she said.

"Hello," replied a deep voice.

"Why, it is not Mr. Woolcock at all," laughed Lady Anne. "It is quite another dear boy. Is that you, Mr. Grayson?"

Damien bowed.

"My heavens, but we are quite besieged with devils," said Lady Anne. "However will we tell them all apart?"

Caroline was wondering the same thing. By how many more would the demon population increase? In their costumes she had trouble telling the difference between Jarvis and Damien, whom she knew. How she would tell them from the other guests she had no idea. She bit her lip.

"Are you worried about something?" asked Damien.

"Why should I be worried?" she countered.

Dinner was announced and the guests began to file into the dining room. "Oh, I just thought the sight of so many similarly clad guests might cause you consternation," replied Damien. "How very difficult it will be to keep track of who is who." He lowered his voice. "And what better chance to do away with someone than under cover of the confusion of a masked ball?" Caroline's mouth dropped. Damien smiled and offered her his arm. "May I take you in to dinner? I believe we are seated next to each other," he said.

"And who arranged that?" asked Caroline.

"My mother, of course," he replied. "After I spoke to her. I know you will want to watch me carefully to make sure I do not poison my brother."

"If you were not so odious I would venture to say you are a very amusing man," said Caroline coldly.

Damien looked pleased. "Would you?" he asked eagerly.

Caroline made no reply. She hardly knew what to say to this beastly and perplexing man.

They took their places around a table set with the finest of Sèvres china. Crystal goblets winked in the candlelight and fine silver gleamed. Delicious smells floated out to the guests from behind screens where servants applied finishing touches to the food. Damien turned and smiled at Caroline. His eyes looked black in the soft glow of the candlelight, and he looked dangerously sinister. And attractive. He smiled and Caroline felt a flop inside her chest. "Did I tell you yet how incredibly beautiful you look tonight?" he murmured.

Unable to speak, Caroline shook her head.

"I suppose you hope to pass for the Maid of Orléans," he said. "But you look much too beautiful to be Joan of Arc. You look more like Psyche. You certainly are as untrusting," he added. Caroline opened her mouth to give him a hot retort, but he ignored her and continued talking. "And what do you intend to do with that sword at your feet? I hope you do not plan on hitting me with it. That thing would leave a nasty scar."

At that moment the dowager on his right claimed Damien's attention and Caroline was left to her own thoughts. She looked across the table at Lady Anne and Jarvis. It would appear that Damien was not the only one who had requested special seating arrangements. Jarvis had obviously said something amusing. Her ladyship laughed and rapped him with her fan. He glanced at Caroline and smiled helplessly. In return she gave him a look of urgent pleading which she hoped he would interpret correctly and know that she needed to speak with him.

Dinner seemed to drag on for an eternity. Caroline made small talk with her neighbor and tried to ignore Damien, who was being uncharacteristically polite. He understood she was doing some work restoring Wembly Manor. Who was her architect?

Excellent soup, was it not? Caroline tried to keep in mind that this was the enemy and made her answers as short as possible. If he thought to throw her off guard by being so friendly he was very much mistaken.

After dinner the houseguests scattered. Those who had not brought their masks down before dinner went to fetch them and admire themselves one last time in their looking glasses. Some drifted back to the drawing room for a cozy gossip before the festivities. Most, however, made their way to the great hall to admire the jack-o'-lanterns and harvest decorations.

Damien finally excused himself and removed his unwanted presence from Caroline to go greet the first arrivals for the ball. Caroline took advantage of his absence by grabbing the devil with the grotesque mask who was sauntering by her and saying, "I am glad you have found me. I was not sure you understood the look I gave you earlier."

"I thought you were looking at me," said a muffled voice. "But then, I was sure I hoped too much. Where shall we meet, lovely creature?"

"Jarvis?" asked Caroline doubtfully.

"No. Charles. At your service," said the devil with a bow.

"Oh, dear, you are not the right one," said Caroline fretfully. "I am so sorry. I quite mistook you for someone else."

"I am sorry, too," said the devil. "Perhaps," he began.

Caroline felt a tap on her shoulder and jumped nervously. She turned to see yet another devil at her elbow. "Is it you?" she asked doubtfully.

"Yes, it is I," said Jarvis.

"Thank heaven," said Caroline. She took his arm and pulled him off to a deserted corner of the room.

"I nearly confided in the wrong man. This is all dreadfully confusing."

Jarvis's jeering mask smiled at her, but his tones were properly regretful. "Yes, it is," he said. "And it could become more so."

They both scanned the rapidly filling room. Although they had nothing to do with Allhallows Eve, various figures from Greek mythology were present. Caroline was sure several darkly clad gentlemen with fearsome masks represented Hades. The ladies decked out in hothouse flowers most likely were Persephone, she concluded. Then there was the expected assortment of ghosts and angels, and enough devils to tempt all of Upper Swanley. Some of the costumes were makeshift. Some were very elaborate and looked expensive. Many fell somewhere between the two extremes and looked much alike, such as Jarvis and Damien's and the man Caroline had mistakenly spoken to a moment before. She sighed. "Well, at least we have only one John the Baptist thus far. That is fortunate. Which is why I wanted to see you."

"I saw the look you cast me," said Jarvis in low tones. "It quite alarmed me. What's toward?"

"Damien means to strike tonight," announced Caroline.

"How do you know?"

"He as much as told me so," said Caroline.

"He did, did he?" said Jarvis slowly. "What did he say exactly?"

Caroline frowned in concentration. "He said it would be very difficult to keep track of who is who. And then he said, 'What better chance to do away with someone than under cover of a masked ball?'"

"He is very sure of himself," said Jarvis thoughtfully. "But we shall see who laughs last." He patted

Caroline's arm. "Never fear. Everything will come out all right." He looked across the room at Clarence.

Caroline followed his gaze and smiled in relief, confident that all would be well.

Isobelle and her papa entered the room. "Well," said Jarvis cheerfully. "All the players in the farce are now here." He waved at them and they made their way across the floor to where he and Caroline stood.

Sir John took Caroline's hand and bowed over it. "Thank you for the flowers," she said. "They are lovely."

"You are more than welcome, my dear," said Sir John.

"It is nice to see you out and looking so well, sir," said Jarvis.

Sir John was in full evening dress. And although it was the dress of another generation, complete with powdered wig, it did not appear in the least outmoded in the strange company of goblins and saints. "I am feeling well," he said. "My foot troubles me some, but I hope to dance at least once this evening." He turned to Caroline. "If you will honor me."

"I should be delighted," said Caroline kindly.

"And what, pray, are you?" Jarvis was asking Isobelle.

"I am the goddess Diana, huntress and protector of women," she informed him.

"A very fetching costume," he said, taking in her simple white gown, the gold bracelet on her upper arm, the bow and the quiver of arrows.

Caroline wondered at Jarvis's mocking tones. It was not like him to tease so. She wondered, too, at the icy stare the unmasked Isobelle gave him. If he had been courting Isobelle, as Clarence and Damien had both suggested on different occasions, something

304

had certainly gone awry. Caroline remembered his last visit to the beautiful Miss Payne. He had gone to pry information about the ghost out of her. Had he betrayed his suspicions? Had they had words? The ghost had not walked since he visited Isobelle. Perhaps he had told her she had been found out and threatened her with exposure.

As Caroline mulled this over, a devil approached her and a familiar low voice said, "Lady Caroline, I believe you promised me a waltz."

Startled out of her reverie, Caroline looked up to see Damien holding out his hand. Automatically, she put hers in his and went with him, then wondered why she had. "The musicians are just now tuning up. How do you know they are going to play a waltz?" she asked him.

"Because I have requested it," answered Damien simply.

The Honorable Mr. Damien Grayson seemed to already consider himself Lord of the Manor. "And do you always get your way?" she asked, irritated.

"Does any human creature?" he replied. "I got my way little enough in my younger years. And I doubt it hurt me to have my will thwarted. But I must admit, I have grown into a very determined man. And there are some things which a man must reach out and take."

"Such as?" prompted Caroline.

"Such as this dance. With you." As if on cue, the music began. Clarence, as host, led Phoebe out onto the floor and began the dance. Damien's arm encircled Caroline's waist, and he drew her to him. "Let us for this one dance forget we are enemies and enjoy being together." Caroline stiffened. "You are thinking that is impossible," he said. "But it is not. Forget about everyone else for just this one moment,

Caroline. Forget about everyone except yourself and me. Imagine that we are the only two people on the dance floor, that we have met for the first time, under favorable circumstances, with no misunderstandings, no worries, no other people to come between us."

His words were almost hypnotic. The room glowed with the soft light from hundreds of candles and softened their surroundings to watercolor texture. The strings played sweetly. Caroline tried not to relax, tried hard not to enjoy the warm feeling of a strong arm about her, tried not to exult in the way they glided across the floor as one. "You are so beautiful, so vibrant," he crooned, and she tried not to let his words woo her into an attitude of surrender. She tried, but she failed. In a moment of weakness, she closed her eyes and gave herself completely to the joy of the moment. She had loved Harold, but never in her life had she felt like this.

The music stopped. Damien took his arm from her waist, and the spell was broken. Whatever was she thinking of? She glared at him, and he burst into laughter. "You should listen to your heart," he said softly.

"My head is much more reliable," she retorted.

He merely smiled and bowed. Then he left her. She stood for a moment, watching him wistfully. If only they had met before he had run off to India, before he had returned such a hard and bitter man.

A pudgy hand on her arm drew her back to the present. "Perhaps I may claim this dance and hope for a waltz as well," said Lord Paddington. Caroline went with his lordship but kept an eagle eye on Damien as they took their places for a set of lively country dances.

It was no easy task to keep track of Damien among

the milling costumes at the edge of the floor. Once he stood visiting with two other devils, and she was sure he had done it to confuse her. For a moment her fellow dancers blocked him from her view, but she caught sight of him again, leaving the other two.

Halfway through the dance Lord Paddington became winded so she considerately felt faint, and they left the floor. She made sure he placed her in a seat near the doorway where she could see the comings and goings of everyone before dispatching him for punch.

If she had thought to get a moment's peace by ridding herself of Lord Paddington, she was much mistaken. He had no sooner left than Sir John was bowing over her, requesting a dance. She declined but bid him sit next to her, which he did and began talking to her about the glory of bygone days. She smiled, nodded, and half-listened, her eyes scanning the room, trying to keep track of the movements of Damien and Clarence.

Lord Paddington joined them, and Caroline felt she would go mad as her two elderly suitors vied for her attention, distracting her so she could barely concentrate. An angel with a lovely face and blond curls came into view. "I think one of my wings has come undone," complained Phoebe. "Can you look at it, Caro?"

"Phoebe! Where is Clarence?" Caroline demanded.

"I do not know," said Phoebe. "He left me to dance with Lady Elinore and I have not seen him since. Of course, I have been busy dancing with—"

"Never mind that," interrupted her sister. "Why have you not kept Clarence in sight? Did you not get my note?"

"What note?" asked Phoebe, puzzled.

"I gave Sibby a note for you before we went down

to dinner. Do you mean to tell me you never received it?" asked Caroline, fear giving her voice a sharp edge.

Phoebe's eyes widened in answering panic, and she shook her head mutely.

Lord Paddington and Sir John were listening avidly, and Caroline collected herself with great effort. "That silly maid of mine," she said lightly. "She has no memory at all. Well, love. Let us go see if we cannot mend that broken wing of yours." Excusing herself, Caroline took Phoebe's arm and drew her toward the doorway, but instead of leaving she paused, her eyes searching the room. "Tell the footman to fetch Sibby to you and find out who intercepted my note for you," she instructed. Not that it much mattered now. Any information they could get from Sibby would, most likely, come too late. But the task would give Phoebe something to do and keep her from getting underfoot.

Phoebe obediently rushed off. Caroline continued to search the room. No one could have gone out this door or she would have seen them.

Her eye fell on the French doors at the other end of the room. She saw Isobelle slip out the door. Caroline bit her lip. Where Isobelle was Damien was sure to be as well. Caroline began to make her way along the edge of the dance floor. Where was Jarvis? She could surely use his help right now. Caroline made her way past the clumps of visiting guests, smiling and nodding, but never allowing herself to be stopped. She was halfway to the door when she caught a glimpse through the throng of bodies of a figure in red slipping out onto the balcony. Damien! Where was Jarvis? Well, there was no time to search for him now. Caroline remembered the broadsword in her hand and knew what she must do.

21

Caroline raised her sword and gently prodded the plump behind of a dowager blocking her way. The woman yelped and jumped and glared at her. And moved. "Excuse me. I am so sorry," Caroline said humbly and hurried by. She whacked a man in the shin, and he too gave her a less-than-friendly look. But, as with her first victim, he moved out of her way, and Caroline continued to hurry across the room, whacking a path through the many human obstacles before her. Out of the corner of her eye she caught sight of a devil making his way toward her. She caught his hand and hissed, "Where have you been? I have been looking for you."

"Where are you going?" he asked.

"To the garden. Hurry!"

Caroline and the devil made their way to the French doors, leaving a string of angry people behind them. They slipped out the door onto the terrace and dashed down the stairs to the garden. "I say," called Caroline's companion as she hurried ahead of him down the gravel path which led to the maze. "Do you think we might find some place a little less chilly to be alone?"

Caroline stopped dead in her tracks. "You are not Jarvis," she said accusingly.

"I never said I was," said the devil. "I'm Charles."

"You again!" Caroline looked at him in disgust. "You will just have to go back," she said.

"Go back!" he exclaimed, pulling off his mask. "But we have just gotten here. I should hate to come out here into the cold without receiving even so much as one kiss. And look, there is a bench," he said, taking her arm.

Caroline attempted to snatch her arm away. "Let go, please," she commanded him. "I do not have time to stand here talking with you."

"Then let us not stand," suggested the young man, smiling. "Let us sit." He pulled her onto the bench. "And let us not talk."

Caroline struggled in vain with her suitor. She would have cheerfully struck him with her broadsword, but it dropped in the struggle. "Let me go," she shrieked in frustration.

"Let her go," said the now-familiar deep voice. "And leave. You are not wanted here."

"And who are you to be ordering me about?" demanded the young man, jumping up.

"I am a man with a nasty temper, one who has never failed to kill his opponent in a duel. And I am your host."

The devil picked up his mask and stormed off, and Caroline rose to face her enemy. Manners demanded she thank him for helping her rid herself of her unwanted suitor. Yet one did not normally thank a villain one had surprised in the act of committing a horrible crime. And speaking of crimes, where was Clarence—already dead in the bushes?

"What are you doing here?" demanded Damien. Before she could answer, however, he was already moving away. "Never mind telling me. Go back to the house," he hissed over his shoulder.

"I am not letting you out of my sight," she hissed back. She picked up her sword and followed him.

"I said go back," he spat at her. "Leave!"

"Oh, you would like that, would you not?" she replied, trotting along after him. "Go back and let you murder your brother in peace. Well, you shan't be able to now. It will be you who leaves. For good."

They were about to enter the maze when he stopped for a moment to listen.

"That is far enough," said Caroline, poking her broadsword into his back. "We are going back to the house, and you are going to make a full confession to your mother."

Whether or not Damien would have done as he was told will never be known, for at that moment they heard the anguished cry of a man in pain. "Clarence!" Damien called, and dashed for the heart of the maze, Caroline stumbling along behind.

They stopped short at the sight of Jarvis, lying on the ground, an arrow in his shoulder, Isobelle standing over him. "She shot me," he moaned, holding a hand to his bleeding wound.

"He was going to kill Clarence," said Isobelle.

The cause of all this trouble was standing, a headless goliath, turning from his cousin to his brother, obviously confused. "I had a note from Belle to meet her here. Said it was important—life or death."

"It was death," said Damien. "Yours. And that note wasn't from Belle."

"I have had enough of your insinuations," cried Jarvis. "Do you see me with a gun?"

The moonlight gave a poor light for searching a dark shrubbery. Nevertheless, Damien went without hesitation to a spot in the hedge directly behind the stone bench and pulled out a pistol. "Mine," he said.

"You have hidden it there and hoped to blame me

for this," accused Jarvis, struggling to his feet. "I need a surgeon," he moaned.

"We shall be happy to send for one," said Damien calmly. "You may recover tonight at the Hall then be on your way in the morning."

Caroline was thoroughly confused. Who was villain? Who was victim? "That gun—" she began.

"I knew things must come to a head soon," Damien said to her. "Jarvis had to commit his murder while I was here to blame and you were here to witness it. I bribed Jarvis's man to keep me aware of his movements." Jarvis's mouth fell open at this. "Oh, do not think too badly of the fellow," Damien told him with a smile. "It was a most handsome bribe. He has always longed to have a little inn of his own, and I have promised to help him achieve that goal." Damien again turned to his brother. "Jarvis's valet did not mind being party to a little skulduggery, but I believe he drew the line at murder. It was not hard to recruit his help. He saw my dear cousin headed alone to the maze this afternoon and came and got me. I took Smythe along as a witness, and we searched the maze and found my gun conveniently hidden near the bench."

"It is a lie!" exclaimed Jarvis hotly.

Isobelle looked at him in disgust. "You wicked, horrid man," she scolded. "Clarence, I had no idea he meant to murder you. I . . ." She hung her head. "I asked him to help me get rid of Phoebe. Jarvis had discovered the secret passageway and suggested I pretend to be the ghost of Grayson Hall. If Phoebe thought the house was haunted she would become scared and break the engagement."

"And Clarence would marry you," finished Damien. "Fie on you, Izzy. And I always thought it was me you loved. Did you want to be Lady Grayson so very badly?" he asked gently.

"I never wanted to kill Clarence," Isobelle said earnestly. "Honestly, Damien. I had no idea what a double game this," she paused to glare at Jarvis, "monster was playing. But when I came to call and learned someone had been taking shots at Clarence in the woods, I began to suspect he had played me false. He came to call, and I asked him outright what he was up to. He told me to keep quiet and I would yet be Lady Grayson, only I should be married to someone much more interesting than Clarence." Isobelle finished her speech and cast a scornful look at Jarvis.

Caroline looked at him with equal contempt. "And to think I thought he was courting me," she muttered.

"So I sent Jem off to take a shot at him," continued Isobelle. "I thought it would scare him out of doing this wicked thing. But I came tonight prepared to protect Clarence."

"I am going to bleed to death," announced Jarvis in stoical tones.

"Much anyone cares," said Damien. "Come along then. Let us see if we can get you into the house without anyone seeing us. Help me, old fellow," he said to Clarence. Clarence scooped up his cousin effortlessly and bore him off, disappearing behind the hedge of the maze. Damien smiled and shook his head. "It does come in handy to have a Samson in the family," he said. "Take him up the back stairs," he called after Clarence. He turned to the two women. "If you ladies would be so good as to return to the ball and act as if nothing has happened we may yet get through this night without scandal," he said, and disappeared between the hedges.

Caroline began to follow him. "Lady Caroline." Isobelle's voice implored her to stop. She did and remained with her back turned to Isobelle. "I never meant any real harm against your sister," said Isobelle. "Truly."

"No lasting harm came of this. You are more fortunate than you deserve," said Caroline coldly.

"Lady Caroline," called a male voice. "Oh, Lady Caroline."

Caroline muttered something very unladylike and called back to Lord Paddington.

"I say, I cannot find you," he complained.

"We are here at the heart of the maze," called Caroline.

"But where is that?" demanded his lordship. "Oh, curse it all. This path leads nowhere."

"Stay where you are," called Caroline. "Miss Payne will come and fetch you." She turned to her companion. "Your penance shall be to find his lordship and fetch him back to the ball. Play your cards well and you can still marry an earl." And we can be rid of you, she thought, slipping out of the maze.

As she ran down the gravel path she could hear Lord Paddington calling for help and giggled. That takes care of one suitor, she thought.

She returned to the great hall to find the ball continuing as though nothing had happened. The only person not having a wonderful time appeared to be the guest of honor. Phoebe was dancing with a gangly youth, a solemn expression on her face, her eyes searching the room. The dance ended, and she left her partner and made her way to the edge of the room, still searching. She finally spied her sister and hurried to her, a worried look on her face. "Oh, Caro," she said. "I have talked to Sibby and she said she encountered Jarvis on her way to my bedchamber. He offered to give me any message she might have, and she gave him your note. But I never received it. What does it all mean? And where is Clarence?"

"Never fear, love. It means your troubles are at an

314

end, and Clarence is quite safe. He will be joining us soon."

Clarence returned in half an hour, and Damien followed another thirty minutes later. Caroline had been captured by Sir John, who sat patting her hand and telling her what a sweet young lady she was. "You remind me of my dear Isobelle," he was saying when Damien appeared at her side.

"There are certain similarities," said Damien.

Caroline looked insulted at this. "And what might those be?" she asked as he led her away.

"Why, you are both very beautiful, very clever, very determined ladies," he replied. Caroline blushed. "And right now I hope you are as determined to dance this waltz with me as I am to dance it with you," he continued.

He held out a hand to her and, with a thudding heart, she gave him hers. "Another waltz. Did you request it?"

He merely smiled. "Now," he said in a voice that made her heart thump even more wildly. "We will forget we were ever enemies. And you will give me that stubborn heart of yours before the night is over, Caroline." Before she could reply, he swept her onto the floor and twirled her ruthlessly around until she was dizzy and clinging to him. Before the music had ended he had danced her out of the room, and she found herself in his arms, leaning against a wall. Without asking her permission he kissed her, and that left her almost more dizzy than their dance. He smiled down at her and, taking her hand, led her off. "There is a cozy fire lit in the library," he said. "We have much to discuss. I do not care to wait another two hours to do so." He led her into the library and settled her next to him on the sofa.

"I hardly know what to say," she murmured. "You seemed such a villain. Why did you not tell me you suspected Jarvis."

"Would you have believed me?" he asked.

"No," admitted Caroline. "I suppose I would not. In fact, now that I think of it, you did try to tell me on more than one occasion."

"By the time we met you had already fallen under the spell of my cousin's charm," said Damien. "And, of course, I was the obvious choice for such villainy. I am sure Jarvis told you all about me early on—the second son who resented his brother's good fortune. What Jarvis most likely forgot to mention was that my resentment was not directed toward my brother. It was my father with whom I quarreled most often."

"But Grayson Hall, the family fortune—"

"I love my family home," said Damien. "But not nearly so much as I care for my brother. And as for fortune, I have made my own. I intend to purchase or restore," here he looked meaningfully at Caroline, "my own estate. Of course, no one knew that, not even Jarvis. And if Jarvis could murder Clarence and blame it on me he would be rid of both of us. He is next in line for the title, you know."

"I should have known," said Caroline ruefully.

"I suspect he had planned to be rid of me long before this," Damien continued.

"What do you mean?"

"I am sure that near-fatal attack on me while I was yet in India was no accident of fate. And who, pray, notified my family of my death?"

"Why, they heard it from Jarvis!" exclaimed Caroline. She sighed. "Such evil behind that charming facade. And to think I confided in him, trusted him. He knew my every move before I even made it. I thought I was in a battle of wits with you when my enemy was by my side all along." She shook her head in disgust. "No wonder the ghost knew when to appear and when to remain hidden. The very night before you came we lost her. I'll wager she was hiding in his room. Poor, foolish Isobelle. What a double game Jarvis was playing."

"Yes," agreed Damien. "I am sure my cousin would have been delighted to see our ghost frighten away your family so he could kill Clarence with few witnesses and few questions. Of course, then I showed up and he had the perfect scapegoat. As for Isobelle, waste no pity on her. She has received exactly what she deserves. Nothing."

"I would not be so sure of that," said Caroline, thinking of poor Lord Paddington. She smiled shyly at Damien. "I am so sorry I mistrusted you," she said.

"I suppose I can hardly blame you," he replied. "My rude behavior when first we met must have made me look a terrible villain."

"I suppose I can hardly blame you for being suspicious of us. You did not know our family, and you were suspicious of any and all. And with good reason."

"And do not forget," Damien reminded her, "you had just attacked me with that curst parasol."

"You do have a temper," observed Caroline.

"I am a passionate man," murmured Damien. "As well you will find out."

Caroline blushed and said, "You can hardly blame me for being equally suspicious of you. Looking back, I see how truly clever Jarvis was. He planted seeds of mistrust in my mind early on. And in light of his remarks your behavior often looked very suspicious. Drugging your cousin that night," she chided.

"That was an error in judgment," he admitted. "But I enjoyed it immensely."

"It is no wonder I thought you had been up to some mischief the night I found you snoring in the great hall and Jarvis lying on the floor . . ."

"With a self-inflicted wound," put in Damien. "In fact, I would be willing to wager that decanter was shattered on the floor, not my cousin's head. He had his revenge that night, slipping sleeping potion in my brandy."

"And you were so foxed you never noticed," scolded Caroline. "A fine help you were. And then there was Clarence's fall down the back stairs," she continued. "By then Isobelle had resigned her post as the Grayson Hall ghost so Jarvis did his own haunting, calling to Clarence and luring him to the stairs with that flimsy peignoir. I wonder whose that was," she said thoughtfully.

"Caroline. Dearest. This is all most intriguing, but I find I would rather not waste any more time puzzling out this mystery," said Damien.

"But is that not why we came here?" protested Caroline.

"It is not why *I* came here," he replied. "I told you before, I am a passionate man. And I am not one who likes waiting for what I want. God knows I waited long enough to return home." He paused, suddenly at a loss for words, and Caroline felt her pulse quicken. "Caroline," he began again. "You once said you rather liked it on the shelf. But I fear I cannot allow you to remain there. Not when I want you so badly for myself. I am going to take you down. I have no title—"

"Mama will not like that," put in Caroline.

"But I have the fortune. Would you not like some help in restoring Wembly Manor?"

Caroline watched the flames dancing on the hearth. "Did I tell you Mama once wished me to encourage Jarvis?"

Damien raised his eyes heavenward.

"Poor Lady Anne," she continued. "What will she do now for a cicisbeo? Lord Paddington is getting ready to abandon her for a younger woman, and you

318

have allowed Isobelle to shoot Jarvis, who was to be his replacement."

"She may have that insolent young pup who was accosting you in the garden," said Damien shortly.

Caroline continued to stare into the fire. "And then there was Sir John—"

"Caroline! If you do not answer me this instant I vow I shall strangle you," declared Damien.

"You are a passionate man," said Caroline archly. "Can you think of no better way to display your passions than with the threat of violence?"

"Yes, I can," he said softly, and pressed his lips against her neck. "Caroline," he whispered.

"Do you think we shall suit one another?" Caroline asked conversationally.

"I shall have you whether we suit or not," he informed her.

"Then I best grant you permission to take me off the shelf," she said.

Damien's only reply was to venture a kiss farther down her neck, and Caroline half-closed her eyes, enjoying the delicious feeling. Suddenly something white fluttered into her field of vision, and she jumped and let out a squeal.

Damien looked up in irritation. "What the devil—"

"Phoebe," gasped Caroline, putting a hand to her heart. "For a moment I thought there truly was a ghost at Grayson Hall."

"I am sorry to interrupt you," said Phoebe, blushing. "But Clarence and I have been looking everywhere for you two. He wants to announce our wedding date."

"Tell him you have found us and that he may announce another wedding as well," said Damien.

"Whose is that?"

"Us, silly," laughed Caroline.

"Oh! I am so happy! Clarence will be, too," declared Phoebe, clapping her hands. "I must go find him this instant," she said and disappeared.

"Yes, an excellent idea," said Damien, about to resume where he left off.

Caroline pushed him away. "I should have thought that little interruption would have effectively cooled your ardor, my passionate man," she said.

Damien brought her hand to his lips. "Nothing will ever cool that," he said. "But I suppose we had best leave this pleasant pastime until later. Elsewise we'll have both Clarence and Phoebe back pestering us."

They stepped out into the corridor and walked arm in arm back toward the great hall. "All the Graysons are about to live happily ever after. I think your ghost may rest easy now," said Caroline.

Damien looked at her reproachfully. "My ghost? Please do not give me any share in my mother's fancies. He patted her hand. "If we do have the ghost of Lady Grayson in residence, I am sure she is grateful to you for exposing Isobelle and restoring some dignity to her reputation. I am sure she does not like to be thought of as an evil apparition bent on terrorizing future Lady Graysons."

A sudden draft ruffled the skirt of Caroline's gown, and she heard the faint sound of laughter.

Damien heard it, too. "I wonder if Lady Anne has already found a replacement for Jarvis," he said.

Caroline cocked her head, listening. She heard nothing, and the air was now still. "I wonder," she said with a smile.